# THE ISLAND BRIEF

*A romance*

## PIPPA McCATHIE

THE BOOK FOLKS

First published by The Book Folks

London, 2021



Mass market paperback edition, 2024

ISBN  978-1-80462-300-8

www.thebookfolks.com

*This book is dedicated to Arlette.*

CHILD IN A LYCHEE TREE

By Douglas Beaumont

She's hidden away in the lychee tree,
grubby knees bunched under chin,
tanned half native,
straddling one branch and two cultures.

Up there she can see for miles
over the sea to cold English cousins,
sickly skin under Fair Isle jumpers,
pale fingers pointing,
at her dark-skinned strange ways.

Right up close
dogs in the sun-baked yard, bark,
scrawny chickens scratch.
Eggs are found later under the manioc
for cook to curry for supper.

Nanny calls from below,
lips smiling, sari slipping,
"There you are, my bad girl!
Too many lychees give you nightmares."

That night I dream she's leaving.

# PART I

# PROLOGUE

*September 1992*

The engines roared, gathering power, then the plane began to surge down the runway. Abi felt her body pushed back into the seat, a cruel hand holding her there. She crouched nearer to the window, as far away from her father as she could get. He sat between her and her brother. They'd asked if they could sit together, but he'd refused.

"You sit there. Charlie, you here. Do as you're told," he snapped.

One day she'd make Carl pay. It pleased her to refer to her father as Carl, a small private defiance.

They were airborne now. Down below she could see swaying sugar cane and scattered buildings dotted along the coast. The amazing turquoise shimmer of the lagoon was soon replaced by the dark volcanic rock of the mountains. The plane banked more steeply, then gained height, leaving the island behind. Abi twisted round, desperately trying to keep her home in sight, but it was no good, clouds began to drift past the window, thickened and engulfed them. Mauritius was gone.

She sat back. There was a pain in her throat, and in her palms where her nails dug in, but she refused to cry. She gave a quick glance sideways. Her father's eyes were closed. As carefully as she could she leant forward to look at Charlie. He was hunched in his seat, arms wrapped across his body.

"Are you okay?" she mouthed. He bit his lower lip and nodded, but there were tears in his eyes.

Carl stirred. Quickly, Abi sat back. Once he had settled, she inched her hand slowly into the pocket in her skirt and grasped the small, familiar leather box. In her mind's eye she could see it – brown with a gold pattern tooled around the edge. She imagined pressing the button on the side, knowing the lid would spring open to reveal a delicate gold filigree brooch in the shape of a hibiscus flower, studded with seed pearls. She clung to the box, the one connection she had left with her mother, Nanny Vimala, Uncle Douglas, and everyone. Carl must never know that she had it in her possession.

Carefully she leant forward and pulled out the writing folder Uncle Douglas had given her just a few days ago. The leather pouch was smooth with handling.

"My father gave it to me," he'd said. "You must have it. It will remind you to write to us. Letters only take five or six days from London to Mauritius, no time at all."

Slowly she slid open the zip round the edge, opened it up. On one side there was a strap into which you could slip a pad of paper, on the other were slots for stamps and envelopes, and in the middle was a loop to hold a pen or pencil. In this first letter she'd tell them every detail of what had happened since they'd left the house early that morning. It seemed like weeks ago, it was only hours.

Turning her body towards the window, hiding what she was doing from her father, she crouched down and began to write.

# CHAPTER 1

*October 2018*

It was a cold Friday morning, and the black cab was crawling along past Dalston market. Abigail Kendall glanced out of the window at the market stalls crowded along the road. The colours and smells, bright materials, piles of fruit, spices and herbs, all triggered memories. It was one of the reasons she avoided places like this. On this day of all days, best to look straight ahead, ignore it all.

But it was too late. She saw the woman first out of the corner of her eye, small and plump, smooth skin a rich brown and wearing a bright blue sari trimmed with gold. Abi couldn't stop herself swinging round to get a better look. The hair was achingly familiar too, an inky black plait falling down her back. Abi nearly shouted to the driver to stop.

"What's that, love?" He glanced at her in his rear-view mirror.

"Nothing. I didn't say anything." She took a deep breath, tried to control the hammering in her chest. "How much longer will it take?"

"Fifteen, twenty minutes."

Obviously the woman wasn't Nanny Vimala. She'd be nearly eighty now. Stupid. Charlie would say she needed counselling. What nonsense. It was just that, coming on top of the lawyer's letter and all the memories that had raked up, she was ready to see the past around every corner. Abi ran a hand through her hair, then wished she hadn't as she had to gather it up again and force it back into the tortoiseshell clip.

She must try to calm down before her meeting. The last thing she wanted was for this lawyer to realise how nervous she was. She put up a hand to the brooch pinned to her jacket, running her fingers over the delicate filigree and pearls. It gave her courage to feel it nestled there.

* * *

"Mr Amrakash?" The hotel receptionist looked up as Raj Amrakash crossed the foyer from the breakfast room. "Your guest is waiting for you in the Kensington Lounge on the first floor. It will be quiet at this time of the morning, so you won't be disturbed."

"Thank you."

Raj made his way to the lift. As the doors whispered shut, he straightened his tie then ran a hand over his dark hair, did one jacket button up, then unbuttoned it again. He frowned at his reflection in the mirrored walls. There was absolutely no need for all this fidgeting. He was meeting a client to go through the terms of a bequest, that was all. He was an experienced lawyer; it wasn't as if he didn't know what he was doing. Cambridge, the Middle Temple, ten years in the family practice in Mauritius – all that had prepared him well for most eventualities.

But it wasn't that simple. There was too much history. These were his thoughts as he arrived at the door of the lounge. He took a deep breath, opened it and went in.

Standing looking out of one of the windows was a tall woman. The last time he'd seen her she'd been a gangly teenager dressed in shorts and a blue polo shirt. Now she was wearing dark trousers and a long jacket in jewel colours. Her hair, the colour of honey, was tied in a clip, but strands were escaping. She turned as he entered, and he saw the delicate freckles across her cheeks, the straight nose, and the unexpectedly dark eyelashes. He had to admit the teenager had turned into a beautiful woman.

She thrust out a hand and said, "Mr Amrakash? I'm Abigail Kendall." Her voice was deep and her tone brisk.

"I know," he said as he shook her hand briefly, then indicated one of the groups of chairs. "Shall we sit?"

He put his briefcase on the table in front of him, felt her eyes on him as he did so. He made no immediate attempt to open the case, just sat and studied her as she settled herself.

She seemed outwardly relaxed, but he noticed her hands were clasped hard together in her lap, causing the skin to tighten white over the knuckles. He rather enjoyed the thought that she was nervous, then he realised he hadn't offered her a drink. Damn.

"Can I get you some coffee?"

Abi glanced at a table in the corner which contained a coffee machine, cups and bottles of water. "Just water, thank you."

He got up and poured himself a coffee, brought it back to the table with her water and a glass. As he bent to place them on the table, some of the coffee slopped into the saucer. She said nothing but he was sure she noticed his clumsiness.

"Shall we begin?" he asked, sounding more hesitant than he intended.

"Fine by me," she said. "I feel like one of those characters in a book, about to hear something to my advantage."

He noticed the fair skin flush immediately after she'd said it. She's embarrassed herself, he thought with satisfaction. He took a document from his briefcase, unwound the red string that kept it closed, and took some papers from it.

"Let me give you a little background. My father, Prem Amrakash, was Douglas Beaumont's advocate, solicitor you would say, and also his friend. When my father died last year, I took over Douglas's affairs. As I'm sure you know, Douglas died a month ago."

"Actually," Abi interrupted, "I didn't, not until I got your letter, then I spoke to my brother and he told me about it. We haven't heard anything from Uncle Douglas for years. He stopped writing in the early nineties."

Raj frowned. If this was so, why on earth had Douglas made this bequest?

"Are you sure about that?"

"Of course, I am," she said sharply.

Annoyed by her tone, Raj took his time looking through the papers in front of him, then selected a document and handed it to her.

"I have a copy of his will here. Perhaps it would be better if you read the relevant part." He pointed to a section marked along the margin with highlighter pen. "That's the paragraph, there."

Except for a rustle of paper, silence had descended on the room. He could hear the distant rumble of traffic outside, and a murmur of voices in the corridor. When she looked up, he was surprised to see anger in her fine grey eyes.

"Why would he do this?" she demanded.

"I'm not sure. Your uncle drew up a will years ago on the advice of my father, and that one seemed quite straightforward. I had no idea that he'd made an amendment to that will until I visited Monique three weeks ago. That's his widow—"

"I know who she is."

"Yes, of course," he said coolly. "If I had known that he had been thinking about making these changes, I might have tried to persuade him not to. His main legatee, his son Antoine, is considering selling Belle Etoile, and this rather complicates matters."

She homed in on only one part of what he'd said. "You would have tried to change his mind about this update to the will?"

"I might have," Raj said, his voice even more chilly. "I think this could be" – he searched for the right word – "problematic. Unfortunately, it is perfectly legal."

"And in spite of these doubts, you came all the way to London to tell me this?" She waved the bit of paper and it crackled in her hand.

Raj could feel the anger building inside him. The trouble was it wasn't far from the truth, but he didn't want her to think it was his only reason for being here. There'd been an invitation to a retirement party for his pupil master at his old chambers. But, if he was entirely honest with himself, he probably wouldn't have come if there hadn't been the incentive of meeting this woman he remembered with such mixed feelings.

"As I told you in my letter, I was going to be in London anyway and I thought it was an opportunity to talk to you about Douglas's bequest." He sounded as if he was making excuses and, feeling irritated with himself, added, "It is, after all, an unusual one."

"It certainly is." She rose from her chair and strode over to the window, stood for a moment with one hand gripping the curtain. When she came back, she didn't sit down again.

"How long are you going to be in London?" she asked.

He frowned. "Until next Wednesday."

"Can I take this copy with me?"

"Yes, but–"

She picked up her bag and pushed the papers into it.

"I'm sorry. I've got an urgent meeting." She glanced at her watch then back at him. "Have you a card with your details?"

Raj rose from his chair and searched his pockets, feeling a fool when he couldn't find a business card.

"I'm afraid I haven't got any cards with me. I can give you my mobile number, I think you've got my e-mail."

Abi took out her phone and tapped in the information he dictated.

"I'm sorry to have to rush."

He didn't believe her excuses.

"I'll phone you, later, tomorrow perhaps."

Without another word she hurried across the room and a moment later the door snapped shut behind her.

What on earth had got into the woman? And what the hell was he going to do now? For the rest of the day he couldn't get Abigail Kendall out of his mind.

* * *

As she had told Raj, it was only two days earlier that she and Charlie had spoken about Uncle Douglas's death.

"I got your message," Charlie had said. "I knew Uncle Douglas had died, but what's this about a will?"

Abi hadn't answered his question but asked one of her own. "Why didn't you tell me that he'd died?"

There was a pause. "I didn't think you'd want to know."

"Course I would!"

"And what would you have said if I'd told you?" asked her brother. "Probably that you weren't interested."

She couldn't think of a response to this.

"I'll go and find the letter."

Abi had rummaged through the piles of magazines and paperwork on a table in the bay window of her living room.

"Here it is," she had said, scanning down the page of expensive paper. "This lawyer, or rather, advocate as he calls himself, says he's going to be in London for a week from the fifteenth – that's tomorrow. He wants me to meet him, but I'm going to tell him I can't, not with the boss on sick leave."

"What's happened to Lawrence?"

"Didn't I tell you? He was knocked off his bike last week."

"Nasty. That must be making a lot of extra work for you."

"I'd rather be busy," Abi said. "Now listen to what the lawyer says. 'My practice has charge of Douglas Beaumont's estate and I am his executor. I have been asked to inform you that he has left you a legacy. As the terms are a little unusual, I would like to meet to discuss this', and he gives details of where he's staying and his e-mail."

"You must go."

"Oh no, Charlie."

"For God's sake, Abi, you have to."

Abi knew he was right.

"I suppose," she said. "What on earth do you think the legacy is?"

"I've no idea. Look, Abi, I thought this might–"

"And why should Uncle Douglas leave me anything?" Even after all this time she could feel her throat tightening. "He deserted us."

"No, he didn't," Charlie said wearily. "He just stopped writing. There could have been any number of reasons."

"Like what?" Abi snapped.

She heard Charlie sigh. "Just meet up with Raj Amrakash and make sure you phone me as soon as you can afterwards. I want to know what all this is about, even if you don't."

"His name's rather familiar," Abi said, "but maybe that's because it's Mauritian sounding. Does it mean anything to you?"

"Yes, it does." Charlie sounded exasperated. "He used to come to Uncle Douglas's. He was good at football. I don't think you liked him."

"What makes you say that?"

There was a pause, then eventually Charlie said, "He was probably one of the younger kids you were made to look after on those picnics. Don't you remember how cross that used to make you?"

Abi gave a rueful smile. "I do." But the smile soon faded. "Okay, I'll go. Give my love to Beth and the kids."

"Abi, I ought to tell you–"

"Not now, love, it'll have to wait. Justin will be home in a minute."

Abi had stood for a moment after she ended the call, unable to keep the memories at bay, but the sound of the front door opening brought her back to the present with a jolt. Justin. Quickly she'd tucked the letter under a magazine on the table.

* * *

In his study in Cambridge Charlie lent his elbows on his desk, steepled his fingers and stared out the window, then pushed himself up from his chair and went in search of his wife. He found her in the garden busy digging up bindweed, her brown hands covered in earth.

Beth looked up as he approached. "Hallo darling," she said, shades of her South African accent still noticeable after all these years.

"I just spoke to Abi."

"Oh yes?"

Charlie told her what Abi had said.

"She's going to phone and tell us about it once she's met up with Amrakash. I think I've persuaded her to go to the meeting, which is an achievement."

"Did you tell her about the e-mail?"

"I tried to."

"Charlie!"

"I know." He grimaced. "But the very mention of anything Mauritian and she flares up."

"True, but you'll have to come clean some time."

"I suppose. I wish to God she wasn't still so angry with Douglas, and Nanny Vimala for that matter. It was so long ago, but as far as she's concerned it could have been yesterday."

Beth lent on her spade and looked at him.

"Don't you feel a bit let down by them too? After all, the letters stopped so suddenly."

"I know, but I'm sure there was a perfectly good reason."

"Like what?"

He didn't answer immediately. He'd been eleven years old in 1992 when they'd left Mauritius, Abi three years older. It had all been very frightening – their mother dead, their father a cold, unpredictable bully, and all that was safe and familiar left behind. He'd clung to Abi as his anchor, and she'd shielded him from so much. Strange now how their roles seemed to have been reversed.

The day they arrived in this strange, cold country their father called home, they'd moved in with Cousin Rose, a bird of a woman with pale eyes and a permanently anxious expression. While Abi was sent to school down the road in Beckenham, he'd started as a weekly boarder at Dulwich College, and their father had left the country once again.

"The thing is," he said to Beth, "I have this niggling memory. I can't pin down when it was, maybe the first time Carl came on leave from Malawi. Rose had a big larder, it was a great place for hide and seek, lots of boxes you could duck behind. I was crouched behind one when the door opened. I thought it was Abi, but it wasn't, it was Rose fetching something. I could hear Carl's voice in the kitchen demanding to know how many there had been. I didn't hear what Rose said. She had this breathy little voice, and it was always more whispery when he was around. But the thing that sticks in my mind is what he said. 'No contact, do you understand? Destroy everything with a Mauritian stamp.' The thing is, when we first got back from Mauritius it wasn't a case of e-mails, Rose had no computer. It was letters, every week, from Uncle Douglas and Nanny Vimala, and from Monique. Abi used to write reams back, and I wrote off and on. Then they suddenly stopped, and I'm sure it was just before Carl went back to Africa."

"Have you ever mentioned this to Abi?"

"No."

"Why not?"

"I'm not sure," he said slowly. "For ages I pushed it out of my mind, and anyway, she's always reacted so badly to any mention of Mauritius. But now there's this inheritance from Uncle Douglas – okay, you don't have to say it, I'm a coward."

Beth put a muddy hand up to his cheek. "No, love, you just don't like hurting people."

"But this business has brought it all back to the surface, whether I like it or not."

"For you as well as Abi?"

"Yes. But it's okay for me, I've got you and the boys. All Abi has is her job."

"And Justin."

Charlie snorted. "He's worse than useless."

# CHAPTER 2

Feeling hemmed in by the jostling crowds hurrying down the steps into the tube station, Abi wished she'd got another taxi.

What had got into her walking out like that? She'd behaved like a prize idiot. But she'd had to escape, get away from those arrogant eyes and that cold voice, and the accent that tapped into so much of her childhood. How dare he suggest she wasn't a fit person? Unwise? She'd show him unwise. But now she was swinging from anger back to embarrassment. She'd have to phone and apologise for being so rude. And there were so many questions to ask. For a start, what on earth was she expected to do with an acre of land, five thousand miles away in Mauritius, with a summer house on it?

That summer house – she remembered it so clearly.

It had been on a lower level than the main house, nearer the cliffs, reached by a flight of shallow steps made of slabs of stone winding down through a thick stand of bamboo, until the ground flattened out to a grassy space called the *arpen bas*. And there in the middle was a folly built by some ancestor of Uncle Douglas's.

It was octagonal, built up three or four feet off the ground, its base of stone, the single room made of cast iron and wood. The roof was pagoda shaped, rising to a peak where a weathervane had once stood, blown away in some long-ago cyclone. To the north and north-west it faced the landward sides, where the main house of Belle Etoile was hidden behind mature bamboos. These ended at the boundary wall to the west and, to the east, at a stony slope which was cut off by the cliff top. To the south the windows faced the downward slope of grass ending in a sheer drop to dark volcanic rocks, white coral sand and wild, white tipped waves thundering up the shore.

Stone steps took you up to the verandah that encircled the building, protected by wrought iron railings, and the windows and door had sturdy shutters which were put up when bad weather threatened. Abi remembered how inside the sun shone through the cracks once the shutters had been slotted into place, causing bright, dancing lines of dust to crisscross the room.

She was so taken up in the past, she nearly missed her stop, but managed to squeeze out as the doors began to close at Angel tube station. By the time Abi walked through the door of the Commonwealth Arts Foundation, she'd resolved to push the meeting with Raj to the back of her mind. Uncle Douglas's will and all that it entailed would have to wait.

Abi always felt a sense of pleasure coming into this office. It felt more like home, at times, than her flat, given Justin and his tantrums. But she didn't want to think about him either. Concentrate on her friends here, that's what she needed to do. As Abi walked through the main office, Benson Rudd who looked after all their finances stopped her to ask when they could meet up to go through some financial statements.

"Give me a minute to have a look at the post, Ben, and I'll get back to you."

"No problem," Ben said, comforting Abi with his broad smile and the warmth of his Jamaican accent.

Evelyn Albani, their flamboyant publicity officer, waved a sheaf of colourful paper above her head. "The drafts of those leaflets have just arrived, shall I put them on your desk?"

"Thanks, Evelyn. I'll have a look soon as I can."

Rangi Karaka, who had joined them recently from their New Zealand office, told her he needed to speak to her about an application for funds for a new school in Soweto; and Darren Shuttleworth, who looked after anything that didn't come within anyone else's remit, grinned and promised to find something he needed her for as soon as possible.

"Don't you bloody dare," she told him.

The only one who didn't pull her weight was Mina Patel, Lawrence's young PA, who was supposedly helping Abi out while he was away. In truth she was more of a hindrance than a help.

"I think I've got some messages for you," she told Abi, rummaging around on her untidy desk. "The meeting with the man from the Foreign and Commonwealth office, he says he can't make it at 10.00 on Monday, it'll have to be 9.00. Lawrence phoned to ask how things are, I told him it was, like, seriously busy with him not here! And that report, you know, the children one?"

"Child Action?" Abi asked.

"Yea, that'll be delayed because they're waiting for some figures from Uganda."

"Okay. Have you changed the new FCO meeting in my diary?"

"Er, no. I didn't know you'd want me to do that."

"Never mind, I'll do it myself," Abi said, exasperated by the girl. "And, Mina, if you speak to Lawrence again tell him everything's fine. I don't want him worrying, understand?"

"Cool," Mina said, shrugging.

Abi sighed and sat down at her desk, changed the diary entry, then pulled the incoming mail basket towards her.

The third letter she looked at had her sitting up in her chair, staring aghast at the piece of expensive paper in her hand. She thrust her chair back and strode out to the main office. Rangi and Evelyn looked up as she came in, Mina did not.

"When did this come in?" Abi slapped the letter down on the girl's desk.

Mina looked up, dark eyes wide. "Oh yes, sorry. I found that in the Director's in-tray. The date stamp's a bit blurry. It looks like it came in a while ago."

"You mean it wasn't in today's post?" Abi picked the letter up, tried to decipher the date stamp. It looked like September, that'd make it at least two weeks ago.

"No. I just put it with today's post so that you'd find it."

"You should have told me about it as soon as I came in," Abi said. "And Lawrence hasn't replied yet?"

"Look, I'm sorry," Mina said sulkily. "I can't be expected to remember everything. It's been, like, chaotic, with Lawrence away and everything."

"I realise that. We've all been very pressured, but you should have brought this to my attention, Mina. We can't afford this kind of slip up."

Without waiting for any further excuses, Abi went back to her desk. This was the last letter Abi would have wanted to miss. And today of all days. She looked up sharply as her office door opened again, but it was only Evelyn with the leaflets. One look at Abi, and she closed the door behind her.

"So, what's Mina done now?" she asked, perching on the edge of Abi's desk.

Abi looked up at her friend. Wearily she showed her the letter. "And she doesn't seem to understand that these things matter. Damn it, I saw the man this morning, and that was a bloody disaster too."

"Oh. How come?"

"I won't bore you with the gory details."

"I'm not bored." She transferred to a chair opposite Abi's desk. "It was that Mauritian lawyer you were meeting, wasn't it? Why was it a disaster?"

"Evi, I haven't got time now. I promise I'll tell you all about it at some point. Let's just leave it that I made a complete fool of myself, and now this letter – it's from him. I have to do something about it, and quick."

She grimaced at her friend then ran a hand down her face. Evelyn came around the desk and gave her shoulders a hug.

"Phone him. Go on, the direct approach is best."

"You always say that. What would I do without you?"

"God knows," said Evelyn, throwing her hands up. "Do it. I'll go and see if I can talk some sense into Mina."

"Thanks, Evi. You're a gem."

Abi rummaged in her pocket for her mobile and scrolled down to the number she wanted, but it went straight to voicemail. Damn. She left a brief message then decided she'd phone the hotel. No luck there either, she was told he was unavailable. She left another message and said it was urgent.

Abi sat back. What a hellish coincidence. Surely, there had to be some connection. But there was no way of knowing until he phoned back.

* * *

At the end of her extraordinary day, Abi had hoped for a peaceful evening, but it had been anything but.

Arms wrapped tight round her body, she stood tense in the middle of the living room, waiting to hear Justin's car start up and roar away. Only then did she let out a shuddering breath. Slowly the hammering of her heart slowed, then her shoe crunched on shards from the glass Justin had thrown at her.

"Shit, shit, shit!"

These rows were getting more frequent and they always brought back memories of her father, savage grey eyes and thin lips despising her. She got out the dustpan and brush and began to clean up the mess of glass and red wine. In amongst it she found Justin's front door key, he'd thrown that across the room as well. She hung it on the hook by the fridge and, just as she finished wiping the floor, her mobile rang. Her heart started to hammer again, but it was Evelyn's name she saw on the screen.

"Evi, thank God it's you."

"What's up?"

"I think we've just had our final row. Justin's moving out."

"About time too. Are you all right?"

"I'm fine," Abi lied.

"Do you want me to come round? Mum's here so the kids won't be on their own."

Abi smiled a little, thinking of Evelyn's two girls, her god-daughters.

"No, no, you must spend as much time with your mum as possible while she's over from Malta, it's not as if she visits that often. I'm fine, don't worry."

"So long as you're sure. You could always change the locks this time."

Abi gave a shaky laugh. "No need, he said he's never coming back." She ran a shaking hand through her hair and changed the subject. "You said you wanted to hear about this morning's meeting."

But the ringing of the landline interrupted her.

"Damn. I'd better get that. How about lunch tomorrow?"

"Sorry, I can't. I'm driving Mum home. Go, I'll speak to you on Monday."

Abi dashed to the living room and grabbed up the phone, deeply relieved when she heard Charlie's voice. She told him about Justin storming off.

"I can't say I'm sorry, Abi. Do you think he'll come back?"

"God knows, Charlie. I don't want to talk about it anymore."

She was relieved when he didn't argue.

"I wanted to know how it went with the Mauritian lawyer," he said.

"Oh Lord, it seems like ages ago now. That's what got Justin going. He found the letter and went off on one, thought I was fixing up a date. How stupid is that? And you won't believe what happened when I got back to the office. Of course, it could just be a ghastly coincidence, or the bloody man is playing games."

"You're rambling, Abi. Which bloody man? What coincidence?"

"Sorry, I'm so knackered." She didn't answer his questions, just asked one of her own. "What time is it?"

"Nearly half six."

"Charlie, can I come up for the weekend?"

"Of course, come now."

"That'd be great."

"Beth's making one of her lasagne. I'm sure it'll keep until you get here. The twins have got some gig or other, so it'll just be the three of us."

"Thank you, darling. I'll be there soon as I can."

# CHAPTER 3

Abi glanced at the speedometer and realised it was about to creep past eighty-five. She slowed until it was hovering round the seventy mark. The drive from her flat in Woodford Green to her brother's house in Cambridge was so familiar that she'd been on automatic pilot. Just ahead was the sign for the Trumpington park and ride – not long now.

Fifteen minutes later she was pulling into the driveway of the familiar semi-detached house with its tatty old fence and garden full of shrubs. She made her way round the side of the house to the kitchen door. As she put up her hand to open it, the door flew open and she was nearly knocked off her feet by two large, gangling eighteen-year-old boys. Their identical faces lit up when they saw her, and she was enveloped in a communal hug.

"Hi Abi!"

"Good to see you."

"Got to go."

"Hallo Mattie, Pip," she said, laughing. In spite of her height, she still had to look up at the twins. "Where are you off to in such a hurry?"

"A gig."

"At the Guildhall."

"See you later."

"Must dash."

The double act was always the same. She smiled as she watched them run down the path, jump on their bikes and pedal off.

Abi closed the door behind her and put her bag down by the kitchen table just as Beth walked into the room.

"Hallo sweetheart," she said, reaching up to hug Abi. "You've just missed the boys."

"Not quite. I nearly got flattened by them as I came in. I can never get used to how enormous they are."

"Ach, I know," Beth said. "It's all from your side of the family. I sometimes think I'm as wide as I'm tall."

"Nonsense," said Abi. "Anyway, Charlie likes you cuddly."

"Charlie certainly does," he said, coming into the room at that moment and putting an arm round his wife. He leaned over to kiss his sister. "Now, what's all this about?" he asked.

"Give her a chance to get her breath, man," Beth said. "Open the wine while I put the supper in the oven."

Usually when she arrived at her brother's house, the tension would slip away, but not this time, there were too many dark doors threatening to burst open.

As Charlie poured wine for them all, he gave her a nervous glance. She knew that look. He'd done something he thought she'd be angry about.

"What's up?" she asked.

"There's something I need to tell you."

"You're worrying me, Charlie."

Beth smiled from one to the other. "Tell her, darling. Get it over with."

"It's because of me you got that letter from Raj," he said in a rush. "He e-mailed me, mid-August I think it was. He did his law degree at St Jude's; did you know that?" Abi shook her head and he went on quickly. "Anyway, he gets the alumni mag and he saw an article about me getting the archaeology professorship, recognised the name, and thought I'd be able to help him find you."

"And you just sent my address off without even asking me?"

"I was going to tell you—"

"Tell, not ask! Like when?"

"Look," Charlie said, picking at his thumb, something he always did when he was stressed. "I'd just taken on the new job and I was so busy I hardly knew which way I was facing. This e-mail came through and I thought it was probably something to do with your work, so I just replied. You're so weird about Mauritius, I never know how you're going to react."

"Are you surprised, Charlie, after what I went through?"

There was a loaded silence, then Charlie said quietly, "I was there too, Abi, remember?"

All the anger went out of Abi and was replaced by a wave of guilt at her selfishness.

"I'm sorry, love. I know." She put out a hand to touch his. "I know I didn't protect you as I should have."

"Abi, you're my sister not my mother, anyway, you did."

"Okay. Let's not go there." Abi took a deep breath and blinked back tears, then called herself a wimp. "So," she said briskly, "he got my address from you. At least that clears up one mystery."

Beth, leaning against the work surface, had been watching them, but now she went to the fridge, got out lettuce, cucumber, watercress, and began to prepare a salad.

"I'm glad I didn't end up having to hold the coats," Beth said.

Abi squeezed her arm and smiled at her.

"You're very good at letting us yell and then picking up the pieces."

Charlie grinned at his sister, relief in every line of his body. "Okay, I'm not waiting any longer. What's all this about?"

Abi looked at them and wondered where on earth to start.

"I had the meeting with Raj Amrakash this morning." She took out the clip that held her curls in check, stretched back and ran her hand through her hair, then went on when she saw their expectant faces. "His father used to be Uncle Douglas's lawyer and Raj took over when his father died."

"And this legacy he mentioned in his letter, what is it?"

Abi took a deep breath. "It's that flat piece of land in the corner of the grounds at Belle Etoile, beyond the bamboos."

"The *arpen bas*."

"That's it, plus the summer house, and its contents, whatever that means."

"Good Lord," Charlie said. "Do you remember we used to call it *nous lacaze?*"

"I'd forgotten that."

"Is that Creole?" asked Beth.

"Yes. It means, our house, our home."

"In his will, Uncle Douglas says he wants me to go to Mauritius and inspect my inheritance, take possession of the afore-mentioned contents, etc, which, so far as I can remember, are a few Lloyd Loom chairs, tennis racquets, buckets and spades, and not much else. And this bequest wasn't in his original will, this was added later as an amendment to an updated version that wasn't discovered until a few weeks ago."

Charlie looked at her across the table, eyes wide. "What on earth did he do that for?"

"I've no idea," Abi said. "You know, it's strange, that summer house is one of the few things that's really clear in my mind. You usually remember much more than I do. Why is that? After all, you're younger than me."

"I don't know. You're getting on a bit, of course."

Abi smiled. His teasing was meant to help, but she knew it would take far more than that.

"And who inherits the rest?" Charlie asked.

"Monique and Antoine, I suppose."

"The estate is pretty big, I'd say about seven acres, together with the house and the out-buildings. A valuable piece of real estate."

"I know."

"Didn't you ask who else was involved?" Charlie said.

"Well, the meeting ended rather abruptly."

"Abi! What did you do?"

"Nothing."

"Come on!"

"Give her a chance to explain," Beth told him.

Arms crossed, his long body leaning back in his chair, Charlie stared across the table at his sister. Abi felt that old sinking feeling of having been put to the test and come up wanting.

"Look, he was so bloody arrogant, standing there looking like a cross between that Pakistani cricketer and Hugh Jackman."

"Who?" Charlie said, totally confused.

"He's an actor, darling," his wife told him, "and if that is what this Raj looks like, I certainly want to meet him!"

"No, you don't," Abi said firmly. "It was obvious he didn't like me, you know, that extreme politeness bordering on insult. I'm afraid I got a bit stroppy, and then I made my excuses, said I had an urgent meeting and left." She held up her hands, responding to the expression on her brother's face. "Okay, I admit it, I over-reacted."

"Over-reacted? I should say so!"

"I just had to get out of there, Charlie. That accent, God, it brought back so much. You don't know what it was like. And work's getting out of hand with Lawrie away, Mina's being a pain, and we're understaffed at the best of times. Fitting the meeting in this morning just added to it all, which made his attitude even more annoying. He even admitted that if he'd known about this new will before Douglas died, he would have tried to get him to change his mind. Can you believe that?"

"Yes, I can."

Abi glared at him across the table and Beth glanced sideways, frowning.

"Quite apart from the complications of it all, have you still not realised who he is?" Charlie asked.

"What do you mean? He's Prem Amrakash's son. I remember his father, and Raj looks a bit like him, that tall patrician look. Didn't you say he was one of the kids that used to come on Uncle Douglas and Monique's picnics?"

"Yes, we met him several times at Belle Etoile, but there was one occasion which may explain his attitude, well, partly. You've got a long memory for some of the shit that happened to you, maybe he has too. I remember playing with him on the beach below the house, with Nanny V and Zabette, you know, Douglas's cook. Raj ran into the water after a piece of material he–" Charlie stopped, silenced by the expression on his sister's face, then added, "Not one of your best moments, I suppose."

Unable to avoid the memory, Abi had to admit Charlie was right.

*June 1989*

Abi didn't want to play with the boys. They were so young and silly. She was eleven and three quarters, for goodness sake. Sitting on the beach towel next to Nanny Vimala and Zabette, she chewed at the end of her plait, picked up a piece of coral and threw it in Charlie's direction, picked up another and held up her hand to do it again.

"Do not throw things at your brother, Abigail," Nanny V scolded.

Abi dropped the piece of coral and scowled.

"Go and play. Look, Raj and Charlie have found some lovely shells. Go look."

Abi knew that tone of voice. It would be pointless to argue. Resentful, but obedient, she wandered down to the water's edge.

"Abi!" Charlie waved at her. "We've found a sea urchin shell. Look."

"It's not a whole one," she said dismissively.

Charlie's face fell, but he said defiantly, "Doesn't matter. I like it. So does Raj, don't you?" Charlie dug the other boy in the ribs and he obligingly agreed.

The look Raj gave Abi was cool and rather wary. She was used to bossing Charlie around, being a whole three years older, but this boy was different. She didn't think it'd be as easy to get him to do as she said. The thought annoyed her.

"We're going to build a sandcastle," she stated.

"I don't want to," Charlie said. "I want to look for more shells."

"You can do that later."

"I too would like to look for shells," Raj said quietly.

"Looking for shells is boring," Abi said firmly. "Go and get the buckets and spades from Nanny, Charlie."

Her brother shrugged and trudged up the beach. Raj stared back at Abi for a moment then thrust his hands into the pockets of his shorts and stomped off towards the edge of the sea where waves rushed hungrily up the sand.

It was always so much rougher here because of the break in the reef. She'd heard Nanny V talking to Zabette about witches, saying it was nonsense to think they had anything to do with this wild coast. But Abi did wonder sometimes when they stayed with Uncle Douglas and she heard the wind whistling round the house, the sea roaring down below, and saw sea birds swooping and squawking along the black rocks.

Raj was nearly at the water's edge. "Don't go any further," she shouted. "It's dangerous." But he took no notice of her, so she began to walk down to fetch him back. As she did so she saw him take something out of his pocket. A piece of bright gold material flickered in his hand. Quickly she darted forward and grabbed it from him.

"What's this?"

He ran at her, crying out in rage as he jumped and snatched at her prize, but she held it above her head, taunting.

"I'll give it back if you tell me what it is!"

"Give it to me!"

"Tell me."

"It's mine," he sobbed. "Give it to me!"

Slowly Abi let her hand fall, feeling ashamed of herself. She held it out to him. "Okay, no need to get cross. There it is."

The gold scrap fluttered and, as Raj lunged to grab it from her, the wind snatched it away. Aghast Abi watched as it dipped and dived, a glittering, featherlike creature. A moment later it swooped out over the waves, then sank into the water a few feet from the shore.

Raj screamed, ran to the sea, and started to wade out.

"Nanny! Nanny V!" shouted Abi, panicking now as she dithered on the edge of the waves. They'd been warned so many times. Don't go in the water. The current can carry you away.

Nanny V got to him first, in the water up to her knees, her sari swirling around her. She grabbed Raj up and brought him back and all the while he screamed at her, stretching out his arms towards the sea then pummelling her with his fists.

"*Mo nata! Mo nata!*"

"*Doucement, doucement,*" Nanny crooned in Creole.

"What's he so upset about?" Abi asked, frightened at his reaction, aware that she'd behaved very badly.

"Abigail!"

She could tell that Nanny V was very angry. And so was Raj. He turned a furious, tear stained face on Abi. The look in his eyes made her take a step back.

"I hate you!" he shouted and sank down on to the sand, sobbing. "I hate you!"

# CHAPTER 4

*October 2018*

"It was that piece of material, wasn't it," Abi said quietly.

"Yup. Don't you remember, Nanny told us afterwards it was a piece of one of his mother's saris. She'd only been dead a few months. It meant a hell of a lot to him."

"I'd forgotten all about it."

"Perhaps you didn't want to remember."

"Probably." Abi grimaced in self-disgust. "As you say, not one of my best moments."

"What happened?" asked Beth, tapping absent-mindedly at Charlie's hand to stop him picking at his thumb.

Reluctantly Abi told her, then said to her brother, "And you think that's why he behaved like he did this morning? Surely not."

Beth answered this. "I don't know. These things can really stick in the mind. I had a soft toy, a monkey, when I was a kid. My grandmother, Gogo, gave him to me when I was about two years old. When we left Cape Town he got left behind, but I still think about Harold the Monkey, it still gets to me." Beth got up and bustled around, getting the lasagna out of the oven and fetching plates and cutlery.

"Perhaps," Charlie said quietly, "it's a bit like you and Mum's filigree brooch. Look at what lengths you went to keep that from Carl."

Abi thought of that taxi journey to Raj's hotel, the feel of the brooch pinned to her blouse. This, more than anything, helped her to understand.

"I'll have to apologise when I see him again," she said.

"Good God, no. Someone as proud as that, he'd hate to be reminded of it."

Charlie refilled their glasses and Beth began to serve the food. The fragrant aromas of minced meat, herbs and cheese sauce floated up into the air and Abi was surprised to find she was hungry.

"When are you going to see him again?" he asked.

"I don't know. It's a bit difficult, what with work and everything."

"The everything being Justin?" Charlie asked shrewdly.

"Partly. I turned my phone off halfway here because he kept texting. When I turn it on again there'll probably be a pile more. I'm going to ignore them."

"Good for you," said Charlie. "So, this is finally it between you two?"

"Definitely. He'll give up soon. Forget about him. As to Raj, I've left a message on his mobile and at his hotel for him to ring me, but he hasn't yet."

"Well no, not if your phone is turned off."

Abi grinned. "True."

"Leave it for now. Let's go back to when you met him this morning," Charlie said. "You said something about a coincidence?"

"It was when I got back to the office, that's when the next bombshell dropped." Abi scooped up a forkful of lasagna. "This is what I mean about him playing games. There was a letter addressed to the Director of the CAF and signed by Raj."

"Another letter?" asked Charlie.

"Not to me, to Lawrence. It got overlooked when he had his accident. Raj had signed it but it was on behalf of him and three others."

"And what was it about?" Charlie asked.

"Apparently, before he died, Uncle Douglas was talking about turning Belle Etoile into an educational resource for islanders and visitors. They want to convert part of the house into a gallery about him and other writers and artists who've been influenced by Mauritius, you know, like Mark Twain and that bloke who wrote *Paul et Virginie*. They also want somewhere to run writers' holidays, things like that. This group Raj is part of is trying to raise funds for the project, and Belle Etoile would be perfect since it's been in Uncle Douglas's family for so long. His father may have been English, but I'm sure Mauritians think of him as one of them. He must have taught quite a few of the people who're now pretty influential. After all, the Royal College is the Mauritian Eton or Harrow, isn't it?"

"I suppose. He taught there for years."

"Anyway, their Ministry of Arts and Culture have said they'll put up half the money, and the rest has to be raised by other means, hence their request to the Foundation for a grant."

"But why do you think that means Raj was playing games?" Charlie asked.

"He's Douglas's executor, and he's also one of the people behind this idea. He must have known I'd see the application."

"But you said it wasn't addressed to you."

"I suppose not," Abi admitted. "But still—"

"Abi, you're not thinking straight." Charlie sounded exasperated. "Why should Raj make any connection between you and the Foundation?"

"He might have Googled me," Abi said weakly.

Charlie gave her a straight look but didn't comment.

She pushed the food left on her plate back and forth with her fork, fighting against the fact she knew Charlie was right. Neither he nor Beth said anything, just waited for her response, but she couldn't think of a thing to say. In the end it was Charlie who broke the silence and Abi wasn't expecting the question he asked.

"What about Monique and Antoine? In the obituary I read it said Douglas was survived by his wife and son. She can't be that old, she was much younger than him. I wonder if she's still at Belle Etoile."

"Raj didn't say."

"I wonder what Antoine thinks of all this. Was there any mention of them in the letter to the Foundation?"

"No, there wasn't," Abi said, frowning. "That's a bit odd, isn't it?"

* * *

Raj had enjoyed the party well enough, meeting up with old colleagues, hearing about their work, their marriages, children, and in some cases their divorces. And he'd answered plenty of questions about his private life, yes, he'd married, no, he was a widower now, yes, he'd taken over his father's practice, and so it went on. But all the time, in the back of his mind, had been that morning's meeting with Abigail Kendall. And now, back in his hotel room with nothing to distract him, he could no longer keep it safely tucked away. He glanced at the piece of paper the receptionist had handed him as he came in. It just said Miss Kendall had phoned. Why hadn't she phoned him on his mobile? But then he remembered he'd left it charging when he went out. He'd have to get back to her soon. He only had four days left before he flew home, and this business about the will was much better sorted out face to face. He picked up his phone, maybe she'd left something on his voicemail. Yes, there was a cryptic message from Abi just asking him to contact her.

He opened his laptop to check his e-mails. The first one that came up was from Antoine Beaumont:

> *Hi Raj,*
> *Did you get anywhere with the Kendall woman? I think I should contact her myself. Can I have her details? I need to know what's going on. When will you be back?*
> *Regards,*
> *Antoine*

No way, thought Raj. The last thing he wanted was Antoine by-passing him to get to Abi. The Kendall woman? Surely Antoine had known her well as a child. Douglas was Abi's mother's cousin, in Mauritian terms a close relationship. Antoine should have more respect. But he seemed to have little respect for anybody, not even his own mother. You only had to look at his behaviour after Douglas's funeral.

*September 2018*

Raj watched Antoine as he made his way across the crowded sitting room at Belle Etoile. His expensive, dark grey suit hit just the right note. That was something Antoine always got right, his clothes. He stopped to speak to several people as he threaded his way through the room, accepting condolences, listening to comments about the funeral service, but he didn't linger with any of the guests. Soon he arrived at Raj's side and grasped his arm.

"Can I have a word?" he asked and, without waiting for a response, almost pushed Raj out through the French doors on to the back verandah.

No one else had ventured out. It had been a wild day, and now rain threatened. Raj could hear the crash of the sea on the rocks and the warm wind rushing through the *filao* trees, like voices whispering secrets.

"About *Maman*." Antoine's tone was abrupt. "I'm very worried about her. She's beginning to get… confused. You can see how it is with her."

"She's upset. It's only natural."

"I know that. So am I, for God's sake."

Raj wondered how true that was, then told himself not to be uncharitable.

"It's more than that," Antoine went on. "Sometimes I don't think she even knows what day it is."

"But she's barely sixty," Raj protested.

His scornful tone must have got through to Antoine. "Poor darling," he added quickly. "This year has been hard for her."

"So, what are you suggesting?"

Antoine passed a hand over his mouth and glanced at Raj. His pale eyes narrowed. Raj had always found those eyes disconcerting. The tanned face, only a little paler than Monique's, and the dark hair just didn't seem to fit with those water blue eyes.

Antoine crossed his arms and leant on the wooden rail of the verandah, while Raj leant against one of the supporting pillars and waited.

"She needs someone to take care of her," Antoine said at last. "For a start, I don't like her living here on her own, it's too isolated, and who knows when she might wander out and fall or something? Those cliffs are dangerous, you know."

"She's got her friends."

"But it's not the same, is it? They're just staff. How do I know they're not going to take advantage of her state of mind?"

What on earth was Antoine on about? They were far more like family than staff. Zabette, the cook who doubled as housekeeper and companion, Tushti, an ancient maid who did very little nowadays, but Monique refused to part with her, and an equally ancient gardener, known as *Tonton* Gabriel, who came in three days a week, often with a hoard of grandchildren in tow. They'd all been at Belle Etoile for as long as Raj could remember.

"I think that's highly unlikely," Raj said coldly. "But if you're that worried, why don't you move back in?"

He knew Antoine wouldn't do that. Belle Etoile was too isolated for him. His modern flat up in Moka was much nearer to all his business interests and his glamorous set of friends.

"No, no. I need to be near my work and my contacts." He lit one of the thin cigars he always smoked, having to cup his hands close against the wind to do so. "And there's another problem. I don't think she can cope with the money side of things. I'm thinking it would be best if I had power of attorney, so that I can look after all that for her. And it'll make things easier when I sell the place."

"Sell it?"

"Yes. That's what I– what we both want. *Maman* has life enjoyment of the house, but she'd be much happier in a smaller place, or even in a home where there are plenty of people to look after her. She'd much prefer that."

"I find that hard to believe," Raj replied. He couldn't keep the contempt out of his voice.

Raj knew how much Monique loved Belle Etoile and he was sure she wouldn't want to leave all her memories of Douglas behind. The idea of putting her in a home went against everything he'd been brought up to believe in. It was the responsibility of the younger generation to look after the elderly.

"She hasn't said that exactly." Antoine drew deeply on his cigar then blew out two neat circles of smoke. Immediately they were whipped to shreds by the wind. "I don't think she knows what she wants, and the dementia is only going to get worse."

"Dementia? Nonsense. I think you're exaggerating."

"No, I'm not," he snapped. "Look Raj, I need the control. I've had a very good offer and I don't want–"

"From whom?" Raj's voice was sharp.

"I can't say any more at the moment." Antoine's chin came up and his gaze slid away.

"And what about Douglas's wishes. You know his plans for an arts centre. I'm sure he talked to you about it."

But then perhaps he hadn't. It had been on the tip of his tongue to tell Antoine about the group he'd put together, and his contact with the Arts and Culture Ministry. Then he realised it had never occurred to him to do so and ask Antoine if he'd like to be part of all this. An approach to Douglas's son should have been an obvious step, but no, it wasn't.

Raj was very glad he'd kept it all to himself when Antoine said, his voice scornful, "Dear Papa, ever the romantic." Then he seemed to realise that sounding dismissive of his father, today of all days, might be inappropriate. "Not a practical project, I'm afraid. And it wouldn't be in *Maman's* best interests. I want to do what's best for her, and for that I need more control."

"And once you have that control you will be free to sell the place to the highest bidder." Raj didn't bother to hide his anger.

"Well, if that's going to be your attitude, maybe I'll just have to find another lawyer."

"That's up to you. But Douglas made me his executor, I'm afraid you can't change that, and it means I have some say in the matter."

"And whose idea was that, I'd like to know?" Antoine was no longer bothering to hide his feelings. "Yours?"

"Don't be stupid," Raj snapped. "I took over from my father, and–"

This was no good, he must control his anger. Falling out with Antoine wouldn't help the project or Monique. Raj was very fond of her. Years ago she had been Douglas's housekeeper and there'd been many who'd criticised him for marrying her, but Raj's father had never been one of them. "She's a truly good woman," he'd told his son once, "and she's made Douglas a happy man. A pity the son doesn't seem to take after her."

Raj needed time to think, and time to talk to Monique, assess what her state of mind really was.

"It's quite common to appoint your lawyer as executor," he said. "He probably thought you'd have quite enough to do looking after your mother. I'll think about what you've said, and I'll talk to Monique."

"You don't need to."

"I think I do."

# CHAPTER 5

*September 2018*

Two days later Raj had driven to Belle Etoile once again. It was a sunny September day and he always enjoyed the drive down the A9 through *Nouvelle France, La Flora, Britannia* to *Riviere des Anguilles* and on along the coast. The names were almost like an outline of Mauritian history and geography: France and Britain, flowers and rivers.

Arriving at the familiar wrought iron gates, he pulled up the rusting catch and pushed them open. The right one swung back easily enough, the left one, slightly low on its hinges, had to be pushed harder as it scraped against the sandy gravel of the drive. He made a mental note to get someone in to sort them out before they got worse.

He drove slowly up the winding driveway between tall palm trees that stood like elegant guardsmen either side. Here and there were allamanda bushes with their yellow trumpet flowers and, as always, the wind whispered through the *filao* trees which surrounded the property. He could smell their piney scent, along with the sea and sand in the salty air. The rough, wide bladed grass below the palms was brown in patches, but as soon as it rained the grass would change colour almost overnight.

The drive opened up into a circle, the moss-encrusted fountain at its centre dormant now. In days gone by there'd been a complex pumping system using sea water to feed the fountain, but that was long gone. Over to the left, partly hidden by shrubs, was a two-storey annexe with garages below and an outside staircase to the rooms above.

The wooden house itself was one of the few in the French colonial style left on the island. Beautiful as they were, they were expensive to maintain and had been replaced everywhere by tougher concrete which stood up better to the humidity and to cyclones. This old house, being so near the sea and the wild south coast, was battered more than most by the weather.

Four sets of French doors lined up along the back of the verandah, leading into cool, wooden floored rooms where antique brass fans moved the air around. There were three dormer windows in the grey tiled roof above, and at either end of the verandah was a room with a single window in each, like the eyes on a hammer head shark, Raj always thought. The paint on the wooden boards was peeling and the decorative frieze on the ridge of the roof had some gaps and needed repair, but it was still an elegant, graceful home. How could Antoine ever consider selling it? But then, given the expense of repairs, perhaps he was right. He could sell it to a rich incomer, or to one of the Chinese property developers that seemed to be popping up all over the island. Everything in Raj rebelled at the idea, leaving him feeling depressed and frustrated.

Raj parked the car on the drive by a shallow semi-circle of steps, like a lolling tongue spread to scoop you in. *Tonton* Gabriel was leaning on a spade supervising two of his grandchildren as they weeded some flower beds. Raj waved, and the old man called a greeting. As Raj mounted the steps a small, slight figure in a colourful overall came out to greet him.

"*Bonzour* Zabette," he said, smiling at her as he shook her hand. "How is madame today?"

The old cook's lips trembled a little as she waggled a hand from side to side. "*Li bien triste*," she said. "Very sad. She sits in her *salon*, looks at the sea and says little."

Raj said nothing, he couldn't. He gave the old woman's shoulder an awkward pat and went in through one of the French doors, across the room which, a couple of days ago, had been crowded with the guests at the wake, to a small room at the back of the house where he found Monique sitting in a cushioned wicker chair by the window, brown hands resting on the arms. She didn't turn as Raj entered the room. Her short greying curls clustered round her bent head and her narrow shoulders were hunched as if they carried a heavy weight. Only when he came up beside her did she look up and Raj saw there were shadows under her eyes like dark bruises.

Raj bent to kiss her on each soft cheek, but she hardly seemed to register the greeting, until a small hand came out to grasp his arm.

"My dear boy, how good to see you," she said. "Does Douglas know you're here?" Then a look of confusion came into her face and her eyes filled with unshed tears. "No, of course not."

It was one of those occasions when the heart is suddenly wrenched by a grief usually kept under control. He wondered how on earth he should respond. In the end he avoided the question.

"How are you feeling?" he asked as he sat down in an armchair opposite her.

"I am very tired." For a while neither spoke, then she looked straight at him and it was as if the woman he knew had returned. "There was something Douglas wished me to give you. His will."

"Don't worry. I have it."

"No, no, you haven't." She frowned, thin fingers plucking at the neck of her blouse.

"I have, Monique. It's in the safe in my office."

She became more agitated, twisting her fingers together. "But I never posted it. I didn't do as he asked. And then he became so ill, and I forgot."

Raj leant forward and took one of her hands in both of his.

"I have the will. He left Belle Etoile to Antoine, but you have life enjoyment. While you live here it cannot be sold without your express permission. Douglas left you more than enough money to continue just as before. Would you like me to bring the papers and go through them with you?"

"No, no. This is not what I mean. It's the summer house. He said she should have it." She pulled her hand away and began to drum her fingers on the arm of the chair. He noticed her eyes travel to a portrait on the wall beside the window, a small pastel of a girl of about nine, her gold hair tied back with a blue ribbon, her grey eyes surrounded by dark lashes. "You have to tell Abigail about the summer house."

The name and the portrait had given him a jolt. For a moment he couldn't think how to respond, then he'd asked, "Tell her what?"

"That is what is in the will. If Douglas was here, he would have explained." Her fingers grasped his sleeve. "You must look in his studio," she insisted urgently, "in the camphor chest. She must be told, she must."

"I'll look. Don't worry," Raj said, worried by her agitation.

"You must do it now, Raj. In the chest, underneath the tray."

The pleading in her eyes was intense.

"All right. I'll go now," he said.

Monique sighed deeply and leant her head against the back of the chair. "You're a good boy. Douglas always said so."

Douglas's studio was in a single storied extension at the back of the house, a large airy room with windows on two sides, facing the cliffs rather than the activities of the house. Here, in a chaos of paint, turpentine and other paraphernalia Douglas had painted portraits and magnificent landscapes, and at a small table in the corner he had written poetry, always with a fountain pen, in his long, sloping script.

The familiar smell of the room hit Raj as he pushed open the door, but there all familiarity ended. Now it was painfully tidy, easels and canvasses stacked neatly against the wall, with no sign of the tubes of paint, brushes, palettes and rags that had always surrounded Douglas while he worked. Raj closed the door behind him and felt his throat constrict as he saw the paint-streaked khaki overall hanging there. It looked so forlorn without Douglas's wiry body to fill it. The only thing that seemed to have been left unchanged was the elaborately carved Chinese chest which stood in one corner of the room.

Raj went over and bent to look at the brass padlock. The clasp wasn't closed, so he slipped it from the hook and lifted the lid. The warm smell of camphor flowed up at him. The chest was stacked with photograph albums and sketch books, and the tray which Monique had mentioned covered one third of the top, balanced on ridges that ran its length so that it could be pushed smoothly from side to side. It was empty. Raj lifted it out. Underneath were more albums and boxes of ancient colour slides. He was about to replace the tray when he realised something was taped to the bottom. He flipped the tray over and, stuck with sticky tape, was a large envelope. It was addressed, in Douglas's distinctive hand, to Raj at his office. Raj pulled away the tape, opened the envelope and took out several sheets of paper. The first was a letter.

*June 2018*
*My dear Raj,*
*I am attaching a new will and wish you to keep it safe. I am also enclosing some other information which should give you an idea of why I have done this. Your secretary tells me you are in Reunion and there's no signal for that infernal invention, the mobile phone. Please come to Belle Etoile as soon as you get back. I*

*need to see you as a matter of urgency, but I'd rather
discuss this matter in private.
I look forward to seeing you next week so that we can
go through this in detail.
My best regards,
Douglas*

Quickly he'd read through the rest of the envelope's contents and, for some time afterwards sat perched on the edge of the chest, mind racing. Monique hadn't been entirely right. He was sure Douglas had only left him part of the explanation.

# CHAPTER 6

*October 2018*

The sea roared around the black rocks, throwing up white mountains of spray that fell like sharp needles. Abi stood locked to the gritty sand, unable to move. Her mother was standing on a rock. Deep sea surrounded her. Abi could see her mother's golden hair being blown about by the shrieking wind, her dress flapping against her body. As she watched, the sea crawled up until it curled round, round the slight body like a shroud. Slowly her mother's body disappeared below curling water. The last thing Abi saw was her mother's hand, waving. The last thing she heard was her own voice screaming for her mother to come back.

Someone was calling her name. There was a hand grasping her shoulder, shaking her.

"Abi, Abi! Wake up."

"Wha-at?" In the light from the open doorway, she blinked and stared up into Mattie's anxious face. His twin stood looking over his shoulder.

"Mattie, Pip – I was dreaming."

"It must have been a nasty one," Mattie said.

"We heard you calling out," added Pip.

Abi shivered, not only because of the cold. "What time is it?"

"Half one," Mattie said.

"We just got in. You okay now?" Pip asked.

"Yes, I'm fine," she lied. "Go to bed. Sorry I disturbed you."

"That's cool."

"No worries."

After the door had closed behind them, Abi sat up. She shivered, bunched her knees up against her body and wrapped the duvet tightly around her. She'd not had the dream for ages, had hoped it would never return, but here it was again. This familiar room gave her no comfort now. All she felt was utter desolation.

There was no point in trying to get back to sleep yet. She reached out for the book she'd brought with her, but couldn't concentrate and found herself re-running the events of the last twenty-four hours over in her mind. So much had been thrown open and there was no way to put it all back in the box.

She was sure of only one thing, she had to see Raj again before he went back home. First thing in the morning, she would contact him and find out what his plans were. But before calling him she'd need to read through the will and the letter to the Foundation, get them straight in her mind.

Feeling slightly better, Abi turned off the light and burrowed down under the duvet, but it was a long time before she slept again.

* * *

Charlie and Beth didn't try to dissuade her from leaving early the next morning and she was grateful for their understanding.

"You've got to get it sorted," Charlie said.

Abi's phone buzzed. She glanced down at it. Justin's name showed on the screen. "Oh no!" she said.

"What's up?" asked Beth.

"It's Justin."

"Ignore him," said her brother.

"Easier said than done," Abi muttered.

"Concentrate on sorting Douglas's will. And give Raj my regards, I'd really like to meet up with him again some time."

Abi grimaced at him. "I wish I was more like you," she said, wrapping her arms round her brother. "You're always so nice."

"It's the burden you have to bear, having a saint for a brother."

Abi's phone rang again. Justin. She turned it off and looked at Charlie, who made no comment. As she gave a last glance in her rear-view mirror, he was standing in the driveway, hand raised, looking anxious.

Back at the flat, she parked in her usual spot. She made her way up the path just in time to catch her downstairs neighbour coming out, wheeling her ancient bicycle, the basket on the front full of books.

"Hallo Maisie, off to the library again?"

Maisie Broderick smiled. "As always. That's my Saturday morning routine."

"How do you get through so many books each week?"

"It's what comes of being a lady of leisure, darlin'. When you're knocking eighty, you'll be the same."

Abi grinned at her as she noticed the lurid cover of the book on top of the pile.

"Going to get some more of those thrillers you like so much?"

"Definitely. My granddaughter, Sarah, the one what's in the police, she says they're a load of rubbish, but I love 'em."

"Enjoy yourself," Abi said, smiling and lifting a hand to wave as her friend got on her bike and started off. Maisie waved back, wobbled dangerously, then disappeared around the corner.

The first thing Abi did when she got in was check her answerphone. There were six messages, but none of them was from Raj. Stupid, how could they be? She hadn't given him her landline number. Five, however, were from Justin.

"Abi, darling, I'm so sorry. I didn't mean what I said. It's just that I love you so much. Phone me, please. Abi. What the fuck is going on? No, I'm sorry, I didn't mean that. I love you…"

Her finger hesitated over the delete button. She thought of Charlie and deleted all of them.

Sitting down on her soft, ancient sofa, she put her briefcase down on the coffee table, opened it up, rummaged through and took out Douglas's will. Once she'd read it through again, she'd feel ready to talk to Raj. She hadn't concentrated on it in that hotel lounge with Raj watching her like some handsome bird of prey. That's what he looked like, with that straight nose and slightly hooded eyes.

Now she read on:

> *…It is my wish that she should travel to Mauritius herself to claim this inheritance in the knowledge that her absence and my loss of contact with her has been a great grief to me.*

She closed her eyes tight, pressed her fingers against the lids. After taking a deep steadying breath, then another, she opened them to see, there at the bottom of the next page, the familiar scrawl of Uncle Douglas's signature.

Abi put a hand up to her mouth. "Oh shit," she said and swallowed hard, squeezing her eyes shut against the urge to cry, then gave herself a shake, sniffed, blew her nose, and picked up the letter to the Foundation.

*Before his death Douglas Beaumont expressed a wish that the house and part of the grounds of Belle Etoile, his home on the South coast of Mauritius, should be converted into an educational resource for the benefit of the Mauritian people, particularly children, and for the wider world.*

*As a teacher, artist and poet, education was very dear to his heart, and his influence on young Mauritian artists and writers has been profound. This influence has extended beyond these shores, for instance three South African universities have added his works to courses on African and Indian Ocean literature, and his poetry has long been studied at the Sorbonne and at several British universities.*

*We would wish his legacy to live on and we have, therefore, set up a trust to raise funds for two projects, and our Ministry of Arts and Culture have promised they will match what we raise.*

*The first project is to launch a series of writing holidays affording people the opportunity to visit this unique island and gain inspiration from its beauty and cultural diversity. The second is to convert part of the house into an arts centre to celebrate and commemorate the life of this talented man, and of the many other artists and writers who have had contact with and been influenced by our beautiful island. We would be most grateful if you could consider contributing to the funding of these two projects.*

*I will be visiting London between the 14th and 22nd of October and would very much like to meet you in order to outline our plans in more detail.*

The person described in this letter wasn't the man she'd known. Obviously, she'd been aware of Douglas's work, particularly his painting because he'd painted a portrait of her when she was nine or ten years old. Where was it now? She had no idea. And there'd been another of her and Charlie together, which her brother had in his study at home. But to her he'd just been her darling godfather, Uncle Douglas, who'd taught and given her so much. He'd been far more of a father to her than her own had ever been, then he'd disappeared out of her life almost overnight.

"Part of me feels so guilty," she told Evelyn when she phoned her later that evening.

"Guilty? What for?"

"Well, my job's all about education, in the Commonwealth, art, literature, the lot, and yet here's this man who was an actual member of my family and I knew so little about his artistic achievements."

"But why would you have known? It's not the sort of thing you pick up as a child."

Abi wasn't willing to let herself off so lightly.

"But he painted me and Charlie, and I was so familiar with his studio at Belle Etoile, although it was out of bounds when he was working."

"If it was out of bounds, then no wonder you didn't know much about his work."

"I suppose." Abi pulled her laptop towards her. "I've been doing some research. If you Google him tons of references come up. The one I've just read is a copy of the obituary in the *Mauritius News*, that's a newspaper that caters for Mauritian ex-pats. Charlie mentioned that he'd read it."

"After all these years of avoiding your past, you now seem to be making up for lost time."

"Well," Abi shrugged, "in the circumstances, I thought I'd better do some research."

"And what's wrong with that?"

"It's just that I feel I'm going against my – oh, it's so difficult."

"Going against what you've trained yourself to think all these years?" Abi didn't answer and Evelyn changed tack. "How exactly are you related to him?"

"His mother was Mauritian, her family owned Belle Etoile, and his father was half English, half French. They moved to England from France in the thirties, because the war was brewing. His father was my mother's uncle, that makes him Mummy's first cousin, doesn't it? He went to live in Mauritius in his early twenties, I've just found that out in a Wikipedia entry. He got a job teaching art and English. The same article said his style, in painting that is, was influenced by Van Gogh and Gauguin, although I remember some of his work being much more delicate – at least, the one he did of me and Charlie was. And they say his paintings now fetch four and five figure sums, particularly in South Africa and France."

"Sounds impressive."

Abi hardly noticed the interruption.

"Apart from his painting, he had several poetry collections published. Apparently, he's considered to be one of the most influential twentieth century literary figures in the Southern hemisphere, quite apart from being a very talented artist."

"And this chap was your godfather?" Evelyn asked.

"Yes." Abi gave a rueful little laugh but, a moment later, felt tears come to her eyes. "And he's dead."

"Oh sweetheart, don't upset yourself," Evelyn said softly. "So often I've wanted to talk to you about it all, now I can. I think it's great the barriers are finally coming down. Do you the world of good."

"I suppose. Thanks for listening, Evi. What would I do without you?"

"Heaven knows. Now get some rest, you sound as if you need it."

But as soon as she put down the phone, Abi took up Raj's letter again, read it through once more, then reached out her hand for her mobile and scrolled down to Raj's number. Voicemail again, so she left a short message. She'd just have to be patient, but that wasn't something she was good at.

# CHAPTER 7

It was nearly half past one and Abi had left two more messages on Raj's voicemail, but he still hadn't come back to her. Damn the man. Why couldn't he phone? Something to eat, that'd be a distraction. She went along the hallway to the kitchen and opened the fridge door but it was virtually empty. She really must get some food in. In the end she opened a tin of baked beans, heated them through and stood in the kitchen while she ate them. She was just bending to put the bowl in the dishwasher when the phone rang. Swearing as she hit her shin on its open door, she hopped into the living room and grabbed the receiver.

"Hallo?" Abi said, rubbing at her bruised leg.

"Miss Kendall. Raj Amrakash, I got your messages."

"Good – ow!"

"Are you all right?"

"Fine, fine." She hobbled to a chair. "I'm sorry to have left so many messages, it must feel like I'm nagging."

"Not at all," he said coolly.

"Well, I… er… it's just that with you going home in a few days' time, I was wondering, would it be possible for us to meet?"

Her hesitancy annoyed her. What was it about this man that had her behaving like a gauche teenager? She tried to sound more efficient, and more friendly.

"Look, I must apologise for rushing off the other day. You must think me a real idiot. I've read through the will again, and then there's your letter to the Foundation, I need—"

"My what?"

"Your letter, to the Commonwealth Arts Foundation."

"But how did you know about that?"

Hell. It was a reasonable question. With a sinking feeling Abi explained.

"I— I work for the CAF. I'm Assistant Director. Your letter was addressed to my boss, Lawrence March, but he had an accident two weeks ago, so I'm in charge until he gets back, which won't be for a couple of weeks yet." Stop gabbling, she told herself.

"I'm sorry to hear that."

"A weird coincidence, but there you are," she said.

"Indeed," she heard him say. She had a horrid feeling he was laughing at her and tried to sound more business-like.

"Perhaps we could meet to discuss both Uncle Douglas's will and the funding. Not today, of course, but have you any time tomorrow morning?"

"I'm afraid not. I'm going to Cardiff to see my niece, she's a junior doctor at the Royal Infirmary. Could I suggest dinner this evening?"

For a moment Abi didn't know how to respond, but before she could say anything, Raj went on.

"I have a friend from home who runs a restaurant called The Taste of Mauritius. I was planning to eat there this evening. It's in Islington, just around the corner from the tube station."

That was only a stone's throw from her office. Abi wondered how she'd never noticed it before.

"Could we meet there at, say, eight o'clock?" asked Raj.

Part of her wanted to say no, but she couldn't think of a good reason to do so.

"That'll be great," she said before she could change her mind. "Tell me exactly where it is."

* * *

The aromas of food that greeted Abi as she opened the door of the restaurant were like a slap in the face. She wanted to turn and run. What was it about the sense of smell that can take you back so vividly?

The long, narrow room was brightly lit and extremely crowded. There was a highly polished wooden floor, and the coral-coloured walls were covered in photographs and paintings of the island, from beaches of white sand and black rocks to colourful Hindu temples. To the right of the door was a bar and at one end of it was a large platter filled with fruit, a pineapple, a hand of small bananas and a bunch of dark pink lychees. It wasn't as if she hadn't seen all these and more on supermarket shelves in London, yet in this context it seemed different. She stood in the doorway, stunned by the waves of memory.

A small, smiling man, very dark skinned with gleaming white teeth, bounced up to her.

"Ah, Miss Kendall, welcome, welcome. I am Navin Naidoo."

As he held out a hand and shook hers firmly, she wondered how he knew who she was.

"Raj is waiting for you," he said and waved a hand towards the back of the room. "Please do follow me."

Abi had no choice but to do as he asked.

Raj was sitting at a table for two, in a corner at the back of the room. He rose as they approached and the glow from a wall light made his eyes glitter and his white, open necked shirt stand out against his dark skin.

"Please do sit," Navin said as he pulled out her chair. "Can I get you something to drink? Raj has a Phoenix beer, the best in the world and brewed in Mauritius. Would you like to try?"

His friendly boasting was hard to resist. She nodded and smiled her assent and he bustled off to fetch her drink.

"Anything from home is the best in the world as far as Navin is concerned," Raj said, looking slightly apologetic.

There was an awkward silence. Abi moved a knife half centimetre to the left, shook out the napkin and put it on her lap, moved the knife back again. When she looked up, Raj was watching her with a slightly mocking smile.

"I think—" he said.

"I must—" said Abi.

"After you," he said.

"I must apologise for disappearing off so quickly on Friday."

"You've already done so."

"Yes, I know, but I should explain."

"There's no need." His tone was cool.

"But I want to." Abi was beginning to feel irritated with this polite fencing. She paused then surprised herself by saying, "Charlie remembered you."

"Your brother? I remember him too. He was good at cricket."

"He said you were good at football."

"I always liked Charlie."

For a second her mind hovered round the incident on the beach at Belle Etoile, should she say something? Then she remembered what Charlie had said. Best not.

"I did my law degree at St Jude's," Raj said. "Another coincidence. It was after I saw an article about Charlie in *The Judaean* that I e-mailed him asking for your address."

"He told me." Abi didn't say that he'd only done so the day before.

"I really enjoyed my time there. Cambridge is a beautiful city."

"Charlie would agree with you. He and his wife, Beth, love it. She's South African and they have twin boys, they're eighteen now. Do you have any children?"

"No. My wife was unable – she had cancer, she died four years ago."

"I'm so sorry." Abi could have kicked herself. "That was clumsy of me."

"Don't worry. You weren't to know. And believe me, you English ask far fewer questions than Mauritians do."

Abi was relieved when Navin bustled up, poured her beer, and gave them the menus.

"Have you tried Mauritian food before?" Navin asked Abi.

"Yes," she said. "I was born in Mauritius."

"Aah!" He threw his hands up in delight. "*Ou coz Creole?* You speak Creole?"

"I used to, but we left when I was fourteen. I'm afraid I'm rather rusty."

"When you go back, it will return, like that." He clicked his fingers. "When will you be visiting our beautiful island?"

"I don't know. It's very expensive to go all that way." Abi gave a nervous smile, unable to think of any other reason that would satisfy him.

"But you must save your money and go. The UK is very good, very fine, but Mauritius, that is paradise. Did you know it is known as the Star of the Indian Ocean? But you must know this, you are Mauritian yourself."

"Well, not quite."

"Certainly, you are. You were born there, that is all that is needed."

"Come on, Nav, give the tourist talk a rest," Raj said in English, grinning at his friend. "What are your specials? Have you any butter fish?"

His friend's face fell, mouth turned down at the corners like a clown.

"*Mo desolée*. If you'd given me more warning, I'd have tried to find some. I know how much you like it. But we do have some heart of palm, and *dhal puri* with *curri poulet*, that is chicken curry," he said to Abi. "We also have some very good, braised venison, unfortunately not Mauritian, but of course, Scottish is good too. I will leave you to look at the menus. Take your time. I'll return in a moment."

Once he'd gone Abi asked, "How do you know Navin?"

"His mother was my parents' cook. We grew up together, like brothers."

"You're lucky to still be friends."

"Why wouldn't we be?"

"My nanny's daughter used to be my best friend. We lost touch."

She hadn't thought about Janisha for years.

*November 1991*

Charlie and Abi sat in the rockery with Nanny V's eldest daughter, Janisha, for company. Charlie was forever digging, scraping away at the hard, cracked earth in the dry season and scooping up the red cloying clay in the rainy months. He had a collection of treasures in his room, pieces of broken china, a box full of bent spoons and forks, another of bits of shells and coral.

She and Janisha weren't really interested in digging and although she felt that, at thirteen, she was too old for playing in the mud, it was at least something to do. With careful fingers they moulded the clay into different shapes, birds and fish, and lined them up neatly in the sun to dry. Legs and hands streaked with drying mud the colour of cinnamon, they sat back to admire their handiwork.

Charlie thrust out a hand towards the drying shapes. "I wonder what it tastes like," he said.

"No, no." Janisha laughed, tapping at his hand. "Not for eating. Just look."

Abi frowned at him. "Don't be stupid, you can't eat mud."

"Why not? Have you ever tried?"

"No, course not. You just can't."

"You're so bossy," her brother complained. "It's an experiment. Archaeologists are scientists and scientists do experiments."

"Charlie, you can't," Abi wailed, knowing she'd be blamed if he did so. She searched around for something to distract him. "If you're hungry I'll pick a guava for you."

Janisha looked up, clicking her tongue just like Nanny did. "Abi! Your *maman* will be angry if he eats one without washing."

Abi shrugged. "It's better than mud. Anyway, your little brother eats them like that, and they don't do him any harm."

"Yes – but–"

"Abigail? Abigail! Come here immediately!"

It was one of those moments you always remember, clear as a photograph – a click, and there it is forever. The heat, the smell of mud, the scent from the frangipani under whose shade they were crouched. She'd realised since that this was the moment when the structure and comforts of her life began to crumble and dissolve, never to be the same again. But at that moment how could she have known?

Her father's harsh voice called again across the parched garden.

"Abigail?"

She looked up. There he was, standing half hidden behind the purple bougainvillaea that climbed up the side of the verandah, his hand shading his eyes as he gazed out across the parched garden. Any minute he'd come down the steps and see them. And he'd be even more angry if he saw they were playing with Janisha. Abi couldn't understand why he objected, but she knew from bitter experience that he did.

There was a moment's silent communication between the two girls, Janisha questioning, Abi agreeing, and a moment later her friend ran off round the side of the house, the only sound the slap-slap of her sandals. Abi envied her, wished she could escape too. Instead, she grabbed Charlie's hand.

"Come on," she said, and began to drag him back to the house, ignoring his protests.

As her father caught sight of them, a look of distaste came into his face, but all he said was, "I want to talk to you in my study."

Abi's heart sank. That ominous phrase usually meant she'd done something unforgivable. She went quickly through her behaviour of the last few days, but nothing stood out as a possible cause for this summons.

"Take your brother to Nanny, get yourself cleaned up, then come straight back, understand?"

She did as she was told, followed by a silent Charlie. He too had sensed something was wrong. Abi wondered where their mother was, hoped she wasn't in trouble too.

Quickly she washed all the visible parts of herself under the tap outside the back door, the water warm from the sun-bathed pipes. Inside she could hear Charlie fussing and the familiar murmur of Nanny's voice as she calmed him with a mixture of Creole and English.

"*Shoo, shoo*, little one, there is *gateaux coco* for tea."

Abi wished she could stay in the kitchen and share the sugary coconut cakes rather than obeying her father.

"Nanny," she said as she came back into the kitchen, "what does Father want?"

Nanny's dark eyes didn't meet hers. "Go now, Abi. He waits for you."

Abi felt a lurch of fear. Nanny's eyes were full of tears as she lifted a corner of her sari to her face with a henna spotted hand.

"Go, go," she said, her voice shaking as she pushed Abi toward the door.

With dragging feet Abi made her way through the deserted dining-room. With every step fear mounted inside her. When she pushed open the door of her father's study, the first thing she heard was the swishing of the two brass ceiling fans, and then the click, click of his nails as he drummed his fingers on the arms of the wicker chair on which he sat.

"Sit down."

Her father's voice sounded even colder than usual. He didn't meet her eyes but got up and began to pace about the room, hands clasped behind his back. Abi wondered again where her mother was but didn't dare ask. He cleared his throat and, if Abi hadn't known it was impossible, she would have thought he was nervous.

"Your mother has had… an accident," he said.

"What kind of accident?" Abi asked, feeling as if someone had just poured iced water through her body.

# CHAPTER 8

*October 2018*

There was a faraway look on Abi's face as if her mind had disappeared down some unexpected avenue. Raj waited for her to speak. The silence dragged out.

"You seem to have lost touch with most of the people you knew in Mauritius," he said. Immediately after the words were out, he regretted them. It sounded as if he was criticising her.

There was a flash of anger in her eyes.

"It's more like they lost touch with Charlie and me, not the other way round."

Raj didn't know what to say in response to this, so he tried another tack.

"Do you have the copy of the will I gave you?"

She bent to the bag she'd placed by her feet, a colourful affair of bright tapestry and beads. "Yes, they're in here." She lifted the bag, took the papers out, and gave him a direct look. "You indicated on Friday that you didn't approve of its terms."

"I know, I'm sorry but–"

"I didn't realise until this morning that he says he wants me to claim my inheritance in person. What's that about?"

At that moment Navin returned. "So, you have made your choices?"

Raj was relieved to be given time to think and scanned the menu. Abi did the same. They made their choices and both asked for another Phoenix beer.

While all this was going on, Raj's mind was racing. He wished he could remember more about Abi's family. It would give him a better idea of where she was coming from. Of course, there was Charlie. Then there'd been her mother, slim and quiet, her hair as pale as champagne, and her father, a powerful man with dark sleeked-back hair. Raj remembered being frightened of him. He also remembered a Nanny, plump, smiling, a long black plait down her back, but he couldn't recall her name.

Once Navin had gone, Raj knew he couldn't sit silent any longer. He was reluctant to say anything that he couldn't back up with solid facts, but he had to admit she deserved an explanation.

"I think he deeply regretted the loss of contact. He says in the will that it was… how did he put it?"

"…has been a great grief to me," she quoted, without glancing at the papers she'd placed on the table.

"Although he didn't often refer to it, I got the impression he couldn't understand how it had happened."

Abi shrugged. "He stopped writing," she said, her voice flat.

"Are you sure? I mean, did you change your address or something?"

"No. When we got back to the UK we moved in with my father's cousin, Rose. The letters stopped about six months after we got back to England. We lived with her for nearly ten years at the same address."

"And your father, was he living with you?"

He could see her face harden.

"No, he got a job in Malawi, manager of a sugar factory, same as he'd been doing in Mauritius. He used to appear unexpectedly every few months but never stayed for long. He died there a year before Rose moved away."

Her tone didn't encourage further questions on the subject. A waiter arrived with their first course, then Abi picked up the conversation once more.

"Why do you think Douglas left me the summer house and the *arpen bas*?" But she didn't wait for an answer to her questions. "Charlie said Douglas was survived by his wife and son. Antoine must be in his late thirties, and Monique not even sixty yet. I shouldn't imagine they're pleased about all this."

"I don't think that's so in Monique's case," Raj said carefully, picking up his fork and spearing a piece of palm heart. "She was the one who made sure I was aware of the new will."

"I just don't understand," Abi said. "Perhaps it would be a good idea if you told me what you think. Yes, I know you don't approve of the legacy, but what do you think is behind it?"

Raj shrugged. "I can't give you facts. Douglas never spoke to me about his reasons. He did write and ask to see me, but the letter never got to me. I was on a climbing holiday in Reunion, and by the time I got back he'd had the first stroke. He could no longer speak and was paralysed down one side. This was at the end of May. I'm afraid Monique hasn't been able to help much either, she's a bit – how do you say – out of it, some of the time perfectly lucid, but at other times she talks as if Douglas is still alive. I don't know if this is permanent or if it's just part of the grieving process, but Antoine seems to think she's suffering from the beginnings of dementia."

"How awful. I always loved *Tante* Monique, she was so gentle. I didn't really have much contact with Antoine, he was five years younger than me, but he and Charlie used to play together. Monique adored him."

"She's his mother."

"I know, but there was an intensity to it," Abi shrugged. "Maybe I was seeing more than was there, teenagers do."

"No, you're right, I've seen it myself."

"I didn't like him much. He was a bit sulky." A look of embarrassment came into her face and he watched as her pale skin grew pink. "I'm sorry, I expect he's a friend of yours. He's probably changed a lot."

"Not really. I'm not that close to him."

Raj searched for a diplomatic way of saying what was in his mind.

"We don't move in the same circles. He trained as an accountant and now he's into import and export, that kind of thing, and we have completely different interests and friends."

Their plates were cleared and Navin bustled up to check on them, supervised the arrival of their main course, then bustled off again. Raj was glad the restaurant was so busy. Much as he liked to see his friend, he needed to concentrate and not be distracted by Navin's chatter.

"As to Douglas's reasons, apart from the fact he cared about you–"

She gave him a look full of doubt, opened her mouth to speak, but he didn't wait for her to interrupt.

"Apart from that, I think he was trying to put an obstacle in the way of Antoine's ambitions. Douglas probably guessed his son would want to sell. Antoine leads an expensive life and doesn't seem to care much about

Belle Etoile, and his father would have known that. Antoine can challenge this new will, but it looks watertight to me and, under Mauritian inheritance law, because you're now part owner of Belle Etoile, the property can't be sold without your agreement."

Abi's eyes widened. "He was just using me to keep control of his son?"

Raj could see that she was angry and, if he was entirely fair, she could hardly be blamed for it.

"That's not the way I'd put it."

"But it's the case, isn't it?"

"I think it's a side effect, if you like, of what would have been Douglas's wishes anyway, which were to show you that he cared about you."

For a while they ate in silence, Abi lost in thought, Raj glancing up at her from time to time, waiting for her to ask more questions. At last she did.

"So why didn't he put all this in the original will?"

"Perhaps he hadn't realised until recently the extent of Antoine's debts, which I'm pretty certain are considerable," Raj said. "I'm glad he made the new will. It gives us some control over what Antoine does, and it helps Monique. You wouldn't want her to be forced to move out of her home, would you?"

"Of course not."

She sounded quite offended at the idea. That was all to the good. Raj was aware the British didn't have quite the same attitude to elderly relatives as Mauritians. For all he knew she may approve of Antoine's intentions, but this reaction indicated otherwise.

"Antoine is talking of putting her in a home, but that's ridiculous at her age. Quite apart from anything else, I'm certain she'd hate it, and Douglas would have too. This gives us some time to make sure her interests are taken care of, and to raise funds for this project. If we end up being able to offer Antoine the same sort of money he would get from, say, a property developer, or one of the big hotel companies, then that solves our problem."

"You mean your problem."

Raj was irritated. Had she no idea how lucky she was? Never mind the summer house, what was so bad about owning an acre of land on a beautiful island? But there was no point in allowing his irritation to show, he needed her on his side for the time being. He decided to get away from the subject of the will and try talking about the application to the Foundation.

"I had no idea you worked at the Commonwealth Arts Foundation," he said.

"Why would you?" She sounded dismissive, then gave him an apologetic smile. "Sorry, that sounded rude. I've worked in that sort of area since I left university, a combination of education, the arts and charity stuff. I've been at the CAF for six years. This acting director business will only go on as long as Lawrence is away, probably for another two weeks."

"I'm sorry to hear it."

"You said that before, but I'm afraid you're stuck with me."

He looked up exasperated, then saw that she was smiling. He smiled back, feeling the atmosphere relax a little.

"I meant about your boss's accident. I don't know yet if the fact you're in charge is a good thing. It depends on whether or not you agree to contribute to our project."

"I'm afraid that's not just up to me." She sounded much more confident now they were talking about her work. "I'll have to put it to the Board, and before I do that, I need to know more about it. If you put a detailed proposal together, I'll certainly take it to them. Can you give me a brief outline of who's involved and what you have in mind?"

Raj leant forward, elbows on the table, hands clasped. This was much safer ground.

"Towards the end of last year Douglas was talking about using Belle Etoile for some educational purpose. He wasn't specific at the time, but he did mention residential writing and painting courses for youngsters from the island, and maybe further afield. He asked me if I'd do some research into fundraising and mentioned a couple of people he thought would like to be involved. It was all very vague, Douglas wasn't the most practical of men, but the idea really appealed to me. I spoke to three friends, one is a junior minister in the Ministry of Arts and Culture, one is head of the English department at the Royal College, where Douglas used to teach, and the other is a chap who owns a couple of art galleries. The latter two, like me, were taught by Douglas at school, and Devina Edouard, the minister, is equally enthusiastic. The four of us, with Douglas's permission, formed a sort of ad hoc Belle Etoile arts committee. I also put in an application for listed building status, but nothing's come of that yet, these things take an age, but if we get it, it'll help. There you have it, that's as far as we've got."

The waiter came to clear their plates, handed them dessert menus, took their order and then Raj went on.

"When Douglas had the stroke, everything ground to a halt and we decided there wasn't much more we could do until his condition improved. In spite of his age, he was pretty tough, and the doctors seemed to think he might recover. Sadly that never happened. He had a second stroke in August and that was that. It wasn't until after he died that my friends and I met up again and decided what we wanted to do, hence the letter to the Foundation."

"And what does Antoine think of all this?"

He didn't feel he could let her think Antoine was all for it, but he wanted to get her on side before revealing all the obstacles.

"He's not convinced. To be honest, I've hardly said anything to him yet. But I'm hoping we can talk him round, particularly if we get sufficient funding."

"Are you and your friends thinking in terms of putting any money into the project yourselves?"

"Probably. As I said in my letter, the government will match, rupee for rupee, what we can raise by other means. We need to be able to compete with any other offer Antoine – and you, of course – might get."

Her head jerked up and she stared at him. This, he thought, is the first time she's really taken in that she has some control over what happens to Belle Etoile. He wondered if this was an advantage or not.

By the time they left the restaurant, after a polite argument about who should pay the bill, which Raj won, he was sure he'd got Abi's interest, at least in her capacity as acting director of the Foundation, but she wasn't giving much away.

As they stood on the pavement trying to attract the attention of a taxi, he asked her, "So when are you going to come and have a look at your inheritance?"

She turned her head away from him and he waited.

"I'll think about it."

"Don't leave it too long. We can't move on with our project until the matter of the will is resolved."

"I realise that." Her tone was cool.

"I'd be grateful for any brochures or other information from the Foundation that you feel would be helpful to us."

"I'll put some stuff together first thing Monday morning."

"It would be good if we could meet again, perhaps discuss when you could visit. My flight home doesn't leave until half past eight Wednesday evening."

"I'm not going to be able to make any concrete decisions that quickly," she protested. "For a start I couldn't possibly take any holiday at the moment, not with Lawrence away."

"I understand. But perhaps, if you need to check out the project, as opposed to your inheritance, the CAF could pay your fare."

He knew he was pushing his luck a bit, but felt it was worth it. She laughed a little.

"You're a persistent man."

"So I'm told," he said. "Would you be able to drop the paperwork at my hotel? Or should I fetch it from your office?"

"I'll get it to you somehow. I'll phone."

Raj took a card from his coat pocket, gave it to her.

"I remembered this time. That has all my details on it, mobile, e-mail, etc. I look forward to hearing from you."

A taxi drew up and she held out her hand, shook his, her manner formal now, and rather awkward.

"Thank you for your introduction to Navin's restaurant. I certainly enjoyed the food."

But not the company? he thought.

"It was my pleasure," he said as he closed the door of the taxi, but she pushed down the window just before it drew away.

"By the way," she said, and he wondered what was coming. "I'm really sorry about that business on the beach, with the piece of your mother's sari."

Raj had no chance to respond. As he watched the black cab weave its way into the traffic, he stood on the pavement frowning after it. So, she did remember. How very embarrassing. He was still standing on the pavement long after the tail lights of the cab had disappeared into the traffic.

* * *

Abi sat in the taxi, her face still hot with embarrassment. What had possessed her to blurt that out at the last minute?

She'd enjoyed the evening far more than she'd expected to. All these years she'd kept the door firmly closed on memories of Mauritius, but since yesterday morning everything had changed. There was no way she'd be able to go back into her shell now. Perhaps if she faced the past, she'd be a whole person again. Where had that thought come from? Stupid pseudo psychology, she told herself. She was a whole person, a rounded, experienced woman. But that hadn't stopped her putting her foot in it. She felt the heat returning to her cheeks as she thought again about that last rush of honesty and groaned.

"Problem, love?" the driver asked.

"No," she said, "just a difficult evening."

She was relieved when he didn't try to continue the conversation.

Allowing herself to think about the past was like probing a wound to see if it hurt. Best to concentrate on the immediate problems, like the conflict of interest between her personal inheritance and the request for funding. Had Raj thought of that? Surely, as a lawyer, it would have occurred to him.

Abi came to as the taxi turned into the end of her road.

"Cheer up, love," the driver said, grinning at her as she handed over the money, "worse things happen at sea."

She smiled back. "Probably," she said and walked up the short path to her front door.

It was as she was putting the key in the lock that someone came up behind her and put a hand on her shoulder.

"You're all dolled up. Been out with the new boyfriend."

"Christ Almighty, Justin!" Abi protested, her heart hammering. "You scared the shit out of me. What the hell are you doing here?"

"Didn't you get my messages? Come on, Abi, I wanted to see you. We can sort this out."

"You said you were moving in with your sister and never coming back," Abi said wearily.

"I was angry. Come on, sweetheart," he said, coaxing. "You know I didn't mean it. Let me in."

"Go away, Justin. I'm knackered, all I want to do is go to bed."

"With your new man?" He sneered, thrusting his face closer to hers. She could smell alcohol on his breath.

"Don't be bloody stupid. If you want to talk, phone me tomorrow." She was trying to edge through the door, ready to close it on him, but his foot was in the way.

"What for? Just so I can get your voicemail? Have you even seen my e-mails? I had to phone your brother, and he wasn't exactly helpful, just said he didn't know where you were, which I didn't believe. Look, all I want to do now is fetch the rest of my stuff," he said, sounding a bit more reasonable, "then I promise I'll leave you in peace."

Perhaps it would be easier if she let him in. He could pick up the few odds and ends he'd left and then she'd be rid of him.

"Okay. You can fetch your things, but be quick, I'm tired."

He followed her meekly up to the flat and she stood aside to let him in.

"Do you mind if I get a drink?" Justin asked.

"Well–"

"Just tap water, Abi. I'm thirsty."

She shrugged. "Go ahead. Your stuff's in those carrier bags on the kitchen table."

But when he came back to join her by the front door, he hadn't got the bags with him.

He smiled. "Come on, darling. I'm sorry for being such an arse. Let me stay." He put his arm round her, tried to kiss her, gripping her to him so hard she could barely breathe.

Abi pushed hard at his chest, given strength by a mixture of fear and anger.

"Get off me!" she shouted, deeply regretting that she'd let him in.

He careered backwards, slipped on a rug and fell on his back. For a moment he lay still, and Abi went towards him, horrified at what had happened, but he jumped up.

No longer smiling, he grabbed at her wrist and his nails dug into her skin.

"I'm not going anywhere until you tell me where you've been. Who've you been with? That Mauritian wanker? Had a good time with your new fucking boyfriend?"

Abi was really frightened now. It was her father all over again. All those years ago she'd known his moods couldn't be controlled, not by her mother or by her, and the cold panic she felt now was the same as she'd felt then.

"Justin. Let me go." She took a shuddering breath. "Look, we can talk, but not now. It's nearly midnight. Please leave."

She managed to wriggle her wrist out of his grasp, get to the door and open it. Her heart was beating so hard in her chest, she felt she might suffocate. He stood there, swaying slightly, then stumbled to the door. She flinched as he passed her.

"I'm not letting this go. I'll see you tomorrow."

He went out into the hallway and Abi slammed the door and put up the chain. She lent her forehead against it and listened to him stumbling down the stairs, then the front door slammed. Only then did she move. Shaking with relief, she poured herself a large whisky, gulped at it and spluttered as the fire hit her throat. Tomorrow she'd take the bags round to his sister's. After that he'd have no reason to return.

Once in bed she lay curled on her side, eyes tight shut, but sleep wouldn't come. A kaleidoscope of images danced around in her mind; Raj's dark eyes mocking her, Navin grinning, Justin raging. As she finally slid into sleep, Justin's face morphed into her father's.

# CHAPTER 9



*November 1988*

Hilary heard a tentative knock. She called, "Come in," and was relieved when Abi appeared round the door, her face shiny clean, her nightdress only just reaching her knees. The child is growing so fast, she thought, I must ask Nanny Vimala to buy her a new nightie.

"Hallo, darling," she said as she turned back to the dressing table and went on carefully applying her make-up. She frowned into the mirror. No make-up could hide the dark shadows under her eyes. With hands that shook slightly, she smoothed down the skirt of her dress – yellow chiffon, the colour of allamanda flowers. When she'd bought it, the colour had flattered her, but now her skin was pasty, and she wasn't sure it did her any favours. But no choice, Carl had told her to wear it.

"Nanny V said to come and say goodnight," Abi said.

"Is it that time already?" Hilary said. "Oh goodness, I must get on."

Abi stood and watched as she pulled out a drawer and took a jewellery box from it. For a second Hilary hesitated, fingers hovering over the red leather box. She glanced at her daughter, but she didn't really see her as she set the box aside and took out a smaller one. It was newer, brown leather with a tooled gold pattern round the edge and a small gold button on one side. Hilary pressed it and the top flew open. Inside was a brooch, gold filigree studded with seed pearls.

"That's lovely, Mummy," Abi said, putting out a finger to touch it. "Is it new?"

"Yes." Hilary smiled.

"It's very pretty."

"It is, isn't it?"

Hardly realising what she was doing, Hilary pinned the brooch to her dress. She leant back slightly, studying the effect in the mirror, caressed the smoothness of the pearls. A moment later she looked round, once more becoming aware of Abi's presence.

"Sorry darling, did you want something?"

Abi opened her mouth to reply, then shut it again as the door was pushed open. Carl strode into the room. In spite of the humid heat, he was wearing a suit and tie. He looked uncomfortably hot and it was obvious he was in a foul mood. Hilary clenched her hand over the brooch where it rested in the folds of chiffon.

"Damn it, woman. Aren't you ready yet?"

She felt the blood drain from her face and turned back to the dressing table, lifted a hairbrush, her hand trembling even more now.

"I'm sorry, Carl. Abi darling, off you go."

She presented a powdered cheek to be kissed. Dutifully Abi leant forward and kissed her mother, then turned to her father.

"I like Mummy's new brooch. It's beautiful," the innocent voice said.

In spite of the heat, Hilary felt a chill deep inside. She couldn't bring herself to look at her husband.

"Quickly, Abi darling," Hilary urged. "Go to Nanny."

Carl came up behind her and gripped her shoulder, his fingers digging into it through the thin material of her dress. He forced her round to face him.

"Where did you get that brooch?"

"This?" she said, trying desperately to sound calm, but her throat had closed up and the word came out in a strangled gasp.

"Yes, this." Then he appeared to notice the child standing there, gazing at him. "Abigail. Do as your mother says."

Still Abi hesitated and Hilary watched as she made her way to the door, feet dragging. "Mummy?" she said, her eyes full of tears, but Hilary blew her a kiss and gave a little wave.

She felt a flood of relief as the door clipped shut behind her daughter. The feeling didn't last long.

"Perhaps you would now explain where you acquired this trash." He flicked a hard finger at the brooch, causing the pin to dig into her flesh.

"D-Douglas gave it to me." She forced herself to straighten her back and look him in the eye. For a moment she thought she had failed to convince him, but then he glanced at his watch.

"Christ woman, it's six o'clock. If you're not down in five minutes to greet the guests, I'll make sure you remember never to be late again."

*October 2018*

The following morning, after a night full of menacing dreams, Abi did her best to relax, but each time the phone rang she thought it would be Justin. One call was from Charlie to tell her he'd had a call from him. Abi said not to worry, she'd dealt with it. She couldn't face telling her brother about last night's encounter. Instead, she told him all about the dinner with Raj.

She went out for a long walk to try and calm herself, but when she got back to her flat the answerphone was flashing. Reluctantly she pressed the button. It was Justin.

"It's me, Abi. Darling, I'm so sorry about last night. You know I love you. I'll bring a takeaway round this evening. We can talk. If I don't hear from you, I'll take that as a yes."

What on earth had made him think she wanted to talk to him? And what time did he mean this evening? It was already half past five. Abi felt a wave of panic. She picked up the phone and punched in his number. He answered almost immediately.

"You got my message?" Justin said, his voice sounding as if nothing had changed between them. "What shall I bring, Chinese or Indian?"

"Neither," Abi said. "I don't want to see you."

"Come on, Abi, don't be silly."

"I'm not being silly." She realised she was shouting and lowered her voice. "It's over. Don't come round."

"Please, Abi. We need to talk."

"No, we don't." She tried to put as much conviction into her voice as she could. "I do not want to see you."

"Going out with your new boyfriend then? Bit of a slapper, aren't you, out of my bed and into his."

"Oh, for Christ's sake, don't be so infantile, anyway it's my bed isn't it?"

She knew immediately it was the wrong thing to have said. If he'd shouted it would have been less shocking, but the stream of foul abuse this generated was poured out in a quiet, sibilant voice Abi hardly recognised.

"I'm not listening to this," she said after a few frozen moments. "Goodbye Justin." She slammed the phone down and stood there shaking, not sure whether it was with anger, fear or disgust. It was probably all three.

She spent the rest of the evening tensed up, waiting for the phone or the doorbell to ring. Neither did. At eleven she dragged herself to bed, pulled the duvet right up over her ears, and prayed that he'd leave her alone.

* * *

At ten to eight on Monday morning Abi let herself into the office. She felt safer there. In the clear light of day last night's events didn't seem quite so threatening, but she still felt unsettled and deeply resentful that Justin should make her feel unsafe in her own home.

Rangi was already in the office.

"You're an early bird," he said, looking up from his computer screen.

"An early start makes me feel virtuous," Abi said.

"You look tired. Don't over-do it."

Abi smiled at him. "I won't."

When Mina arrived over an hour later, they went through the diary together. The next two days were chock-a-block, and Abi couldn't work out how she would be able to meet up with Raj again. She pushed the problem to the back of her mind.

By the middle of the morning, having had two project meetings and made, or received, a dozen calls and answered several e-mails, her desk phone rang yet again.

"Personal call, Abi," Mina said and put it straight through.

"It's me, Abi," Justin said. "Please, please, don't put the phone down."

Her stomach lurched. "I'm busy. Go away."

"Please darling, we've meant so much to each other. You can't do this."

"Yes, I can, Justin." She slammed the handset back in its rest, feeling sick. Ignore him, she told herself, he'll give up in the end.

Reluctant though she was to talk to Mina about her personal life, she had to warn her not to put Justin through if he called again. Feeling a fool, she went into the outer office.

"That call I just had—"

Mina looked up and grinned knowingly.

"Your lovely man. He's got such a gorgeous voice."

Abi gritted her teeth. "He's no longer my lovely man. We've split up."

"Aaah," Mina said, eyes alight with curiosity. "But you've been together for two years." It was obvious that, in Mina's book, this was quite an achievement.

"These things happen."

"You must be feeling awful."

"I'm fine. Just don't put him through if he phones, okay?"

"Okay, okay," she shrugged and flashed Abi a resentful look.

"Did you get out those brochures I asked for?" she asked.

"No. I'll get them now."

"You do that," Abi said, hanging on to her patience by a thread. "And don't forget the sample financial statements and proposal letter. Leave them on my desk. I'll pick them up after the meeting at the Sri Lankan High Commission."

Evelyn had wandered over while they'd been talking, her manner casual but her eyes sharp. She followed Abi back to her office and closed the door.

"That was Justin again, wasn't it?"

"Yes."

"He's getting a bit out of hand, isn't he?"

Abi waved a dismissive hand. "Nah, I can deal with it, don't worry."

"But I do, love. Won't you let me–"

Abi cut her off. "Evi, it's okay. I'll deal with it, but I haven't got time to think about it now."

She picked up her jacket and put it on, smoothed her hands down the emerald green material. Justin had told her she was too old to wear such bright colours.

Evelyn shrugged. "Okay, but you take care."

Abi gave her friend a quick hug. "Course I will. See you later."

* * *

Because of delays on the tube, she arrived in Hyde Park Gardens with barely a minute to go. She hoped this presentation wouldn't take too long. She still had to get back to the office to check the information for Raj, then get it couriered round to his hotel. When had he said his flight was? Eight o'clock on Wednesday evening. She'd much rather have handed it over herself and had the chance to go through the ins and outs of applying for funding. Directly she got back to the office she'd phone him.

When Abi got back at six o'clock, Mina had already left, but there was a large envelope on Abi's desk and, when she checked through the contents, all the papers she'd asked for were there. She gave a sigh of relief and punched in Raj's number. It rang and rang. Sighing, she was just about to cut off the call when he picked up.

"It's Abigail Kendall."

"I know." She could hear that he was smiling. "That's what it said on my screen."

"Of course. Er, thank you again for a lovely meal last night."

"*Pas d'quoi, mo plaizir.*"

It was the first time he'd spoken to her in Creole and he sounded as if it really had been a pleasure. Abi wished he didn't make her feel so unsure of herself. She tapped a finger on the envelope in front of her, tried to sound efficient.

"I have that information for you. I could have it sent round to your hotel first thing tomorrow."

"That would be kind, although I would like to discuss it with you personally. Could you give me a few minutes tomorrow?"

She flipped through her diary, ran her finger down the page. There was a reception at a client's office pencilled in for late afternoon. She'd get Mina to phone and make her excuses.

"I've got a space at half past five?"

"I can do that."

"Do you know where we are?"

"Give me the address, I can find you."

She gave him the details, said goodbye and disconnected. The office was quiet now. She picked up her bag, locked up and made her way to the tube station, trying not to glance behind her as she walked. It was ridiculous to be so on edge. But would Justin keep phoning this evening? She'd leave the answerphone on, maybe even switch her phone off, although she hated to do so.

It was half past seven when Abi let herself into the flat. She dumped her laptop, briefcase and handbag on the chair by the front door, went into the kitchen and poured herself a glass of wine, then wandered into the living room to her desk and glanced at the answerphone, sipping at her drink as she did so. The green flashing number told her there were three messages. She ignored them and turned to fetch her laptop. For a second what she saw didn't register. A moment later she felt as if all the air had been punched out of her.

Sitting in the corner of the room, in her favourite armchair, was Justin. He smiled.

"Hallo darling, I've been waiting for ages," he said.

Abi could feel her heart hammering at her ribs as he pushed himself up from the chair and came towards her. A smile curled his lips, nothing like the three-cornered smile that had charmed her so when they first met. This had no humour in it, just triumphant satisfaction. For the second time in a matter of days, Justin reminded her of her father.

She managed to say, "How did you get in?" but she hardly recognised the voice as her own.

"With my key."

"But you threw it– I put it–" she turned to go to the kitchen, but he shot out a hand and grabbed her arm with hard fingers.

"I took it off the hook last night. After all, I wouldn't want to be without it, would I?"

"How dare you?" Abi shouted. She tried to pull away from him. It was no use.

"How dare I?" Justin voice was quiet and more frightening for that. "Of course, I dare. This is my home. You know that."

Anger rose inside her, pushing some of the fear aside.

"I know nothing of the sort. This is my home. Mine. You walked out, remember? I don't want you here."

"Oh, come on, Abi darling." His voice was caressing now. The lightning change was familiar. He'd always had an ability to slide from mood to mood in seconds. "You know you don't mean that." His fingers still gripped her arm, cutting off the blood flow, making her hand throb. She must stand up to him, give no sign of the pain. He dragged her across the room towards the sofa.

"Come on," he said, "let's sit down and talk."

"Justin." She was relieved that her voice sounded more normal now. "I've said all I want to say. Please go."

Taking no notice, he forced her down until she was sitting on the very edge of the sofa. He sat down beside her and gripped her other arm as well. His face was so close to hers that she could feel his breath on her face.

"You know we love each other," he said.

All Abi could manage was a shake of the head.

"Silly girl. You're just tired, it's all that extra work with Lawrence skiving off, and then that idiot Mauritian bothering you. But don't worry, I'm back now and everything's going to be alright."

Abi couldn't believe what she was hearing. He seemed to have completely lost touch with reality. She'd been such a fool. All that charm, the sudden phone calls to tell her he loved her, the dancing attendance. At first it had seemed romantic. Now she saw what a prison he'd built around her. He'd never been interested in her job, always sulked when they went out with her friends, even more so if she'd wanted to go anywhere without him. Charlie had been right all along.

Thinking about her brother was a mistake. He wasn't here to help her. She had to deal with this on her own. She clenched her teeth together and waited.

"I know we've had our rows, but deep down, you know we're meant to be together." He smiled ruefully. "My sister says I should put my foot down."

Abi couldn't help saying, "But she loathes me."

"Nonsense. She just wants the best for me, and I know the best for me is to be with you. You'll see, she'll come round."

But I don't want her to, a silent voice screamed inside Abi's mind. She wondered if this could be a way out.

"You're right, she does want the best for you." Keep your voice calm and steady, she thought, that's the trick. His grip on her arms relaxed a little. Please God let this work. "But she doesn't really think I am, best for you I mean. You know she's always said you should have someone who's willing to look after you, not have a career. I'm not like that. Don't you think–"

"No, no. I can't let my life be ruled by my sister, can I?" He laughed. The sound made her feel sick.

"But Justin, she knows you so well. She may see things more clearly than you."

That was a mistake. Anger flared in his eyes. With horrifying suddenness, he pushed her violently away. She fell to the floor, knocking a vase off the coffee table. Before she could recover herself, he was crouching over her, his face contorted.

"This is all because of that fucking Mauritian isn't it? You bitch. You, filthy slag."

With horrifying speed, he swung his hand up and hit her across the face. Pain exploded and Abi heard herself scream. She scrabbled backwards, but it was no good. The table was in the way. His fist came down, but she managed to flinch away. The blow hit her arm. She reached out a hand, found the vase and managed to fling it in his face. It hit him in the eye then crashed and shattered on the floor.

There was so much noise. Shouting. Banging. It was a few seconds before Abi realised some of it was coming from outside the room.

"Abi! Abi! Open the door." That was Maisie's voice.

"Open up in there! This is the police."

A look of incredulous shock came into Justin's face as he stood over her. There was a trickle of blood running down his cheek, and he still had an arm raised, ready to strike again. Abi had no idea where she found the strength, but she did. She leapt up and pushed him aside. The next moment she was in the hall and flinging open the front door.

Maisie stood there with a young woman beside her. Abi recognised her, it was Maisie's granddaughter. She strode past them and into the room as Abi collapsed, sobbing, into Maisie's arms.

# CHAPTER 10

Several minutes had passed since Justin had left. Abi sat on the sofa holding a packet of frozen peas wrapped in a towel to her cheek. Beside her sat Maisie, her hands round a mug of tea, and opposite was Maisie's granddaughter, Sarah.

Looking up at her now, Abi found it difficult to believe how impressive she'd been. Like her grandmother she was small, her face deceptively soft and gentle. But when Abi had opened the door Sarah had summed up the situation in no time and taken charge.

Maisie, her arm round Abi, had followed. "You're okay now, darlin', the cavalry's arrived," she'd said, grinning.

"Do you want to tell me what's been going on?" Sarah had asked quietly.

Justin was in the doorway of the sitting room, a sickly smile on his face. "So sorry," he said, "bit of an accident with a vase. Fell off the table. I'm sorry if we—"

Abi had felt white hot rage surge up inside her.

"You, lying bastard! Shut up, Justin! And get out!" Her voice was shaking so much she could hardly get the words out. "Now!"

"Hang on a minute," Sarah had said, holding up a hand.

"I beg your pardon," Justin said, grappling for his last shreds of dignity. "What the hell has it got to do with you?"

"I'm a police officer. Sergeant Sarah Broderick. Now, would you like to tell me what's been going on?" It was obvious she wasn't going to give up without an answer.

"Sarah," Abi pleaded. "I just want him to go."

"Are you sure?"

"Yes. Please."

"Okay, but I'll take your details first, sir, just in case Miss Kendall changes her mind."

"You must be joking!"

"Far from it." There was ice in her calm voice. She took a small notebook from her pocket, slipped a pencil from a slot on the side, and waited. Abi could hardly believe it when Justin gave his name, number and his sister's address.

"Thank you," Sarah said calmly. "I'll be round to have a word with you tomorrow. Now perhaps you would do as Miss Kendall asks."

Without a glance back, he strode to the door, pulled it open and slammed it behind him. The noise reverberated through the flat.

"Good riddance. I never liked him," Maisie said briskly. "Too bloody charming by half."

"Gran!"

"Well, no point in pretending. Reminded me of your grandfather, Sarah. It took me thirteen years to get rid of him, and another five to convince myself it wasn't all my fault. You're better off without him, Abi."

"I know you're right. I just don't know how I could have been so stupid?" A lump rose hard in her throat, but she refused to start crying again.

"We women, we're too forgiving, that's our trouble." Maisie patted her knee.

"Are you sure you don't want to press charges?" Sarah asked gently.

"Absolutely."

"You do realise I could go ahead anyway?"

"Please don't. I just want to forget all about it."

"Has he been violent before?" Maisie asked.

"Not physically. We used to quarrel, you've probably heard us, Maisie, and he's always been a bit possessive, and volatile, but nothing like this."

Abi felt a sudden wave of panic. Had Justin still got that key?

"What's up?" Sarah asked.

"I think he still has a key." She tried to dismiss her fears with a smile. "But I'm sure he won't come back."

Sarah seemed to disagree. "I'd get your locks changed, sooner rather than later. Just to be on the safe side. I've got a pal who's a locksmith. Do you want me to give him a ring now?"

"Isn't it a bit late?"

"Don't worry about that. He owes me a favour."

"Go on, love," Maisie said. "Take it from me, you'll feel much safer. Anyway, I don't want to have to dash up here with a poker, ready to clock him one, every time I hear anything out the ordinary."

Abi gave her a shaky grin, then winced as her bruised cheek reacted. This reminder persuaded her to accept Sarah's offer.

By half past ten the locksmith had been and gone. Abi reassured them that she would be all right, so Maisie and her granddaughter left.

Abi remembered all the work she'd been intending to do this evening, but there was no way she was going to start on that now. She'd have to make another early start tomorrow. At least, if she set off for work an hour or more earlier than usual, there'd be less chance of Justin hanging around to catch her as she left. She pushed this idea away. He'd been warned now, so she needn't worry.

Exhausted and empty, she climbed into bed, feeling comforted by the thought of the shiny new lock on her front door.

* * *

Early next morning Abi stood again in front of the mirror. A bruise had spread across the side of her face and her eye was puffy. However carefully she applied her make-up, she couldn't hide it. She pulled open her dressing table drawer and dropped in the tubes of foundation and other bits and pieces she'd been experimenting with. As she did so, she noticed a familiar battered leather box, the gold pattern round the edge wearing away now. She picked it up and took out the filigree brooch, pinning it to the neck of her jumper. It gave her courage.

Early as it was, there were plenty of people around when she left the house and she discovered she felt safer in a crowd. But that didn't stop her glancing behind her as she walked to the station. When she finally arrived safe at the door of her office, she felt heady with relief, but it was followed swiftly by resentment. This was no way to live. Surely after last night he'd leave her alone. But her attempt to reassure herself failed. The only thing to do was to concentrate hard on work and try to forget about Justin.

Abi was relieved that Evelyn wasn't yet in, she wasn't ready to answer the inevitable questions. Rangi greeted her in his usual easy-going way, then frowned but said nothing further. Benson and Darren both looked up, but Rangi gave a tiny shake of his head and they too tactfully said nothing. But when Mina sailed in at half past nine, she gave Abi no doubt at all that the bruise showed, loud and clear.

"Oh… My… God!" she exclaimed. "What on earth happened to you?"

"I fell over," Abi lied, ready for this. "Silly. Slipped in the shower."

"You poor thing. At least it wasn't a domestic, what with Justin having moved out."

"Yes," Abi said, trying to smile, "at least it wasn't that."

She sat down at her desk, but moments later, when Evelyn arrived, she heard Mina telling her all about it. Sighing, she looked up as Evelyn came in and closed the door behind her.

"Oh, my dear, that doesn't look very nice," she said as she came over to get a closer look. "Do you want to tell me about it?"

Abi gave her a weary smile. "Not really. Okay, I didn't fall over in the shower."

"It was Justin?"

"Yes. I hadn't realised he'd taken his key back and when I got home last night he was there. And before you ask, I got the police. Maisie's granddaughter, Sarah, is a police sergeant. She was visiting and they heard the fracas. She got rid of him for me. She was pretty impressive."

"Horrid for you. Do you think that's the end of it?"

"How the hell do I know!"

"Sorry, silly question. Look, do you want to come and stay with me and the girls for a bit? They'd love it if you did."

"It's very kind of you, Evi, but Sarah got the lock changed last night so he won't be able to get in again. I'd rather stay at home, to be honest."

"Fine," Evi said and gave her a quick hug, "but just shout if you change your mind. I'll stop nagging. Get down to work, that'll help."

Abi gave her a wan smile, determined to take her advice. But instead she sat at her desk going over and over what had happened. It was quite some time before she managed to get any work done. A call from Lawrence mid-morning cheered her up.

"The doctor says I'm making good progress," he told her. "I should be able to get back to the office by the end of next week. How are things going?"

"Sue told me I mustn't bother you with work."

He laughed. "My dear wife is over-protective, and I'm sure she's fed up with having me under her feet. She says she's a freelance journalist not a freelance nurse, although that doesn't stop her waiting on me hand and foot. I think she'd be delighted if I found something to occupy me, so, what's been happening?"

Abi brought him up to date on all the different projects and finished by telling him about Raj's letter, although she didn't mention the delay between its arrival and her seeing it.

"That sounds interesting. You say you've met him?"

"Yes, I had dinner with him."

"Oh? What did Justin think of that?"

Abi's stomach lurched. "You might as well know," she said, "we've split up."

For a moment there was silence, then Lawrence, forever tactful, asked, "Whose idea was that?"

"Mine. His moods were just getting out of hand, and then last night–" Abi found she couldn't go on.

"What happened last night?"

"Oh, it just came to a head." Quickly she changed the subject. "Anyway, about this Mauritian project, Raj is coming around to the office later so that I can give him the usual package. I think this one might have legs, Lawrence, but it's a bit complicated."

"I suppose it would be for you, what with your mixed feelings about the place."

"And that's not all."

"What do you mean?"

Abi heard Sue's voice in the background, and Lawrence calling, "Won't be a minute, darling."

"We'll go through it all when you get back to the office," Abi said. "If I talk to you any more about work now, Sue will kill me."

His rich chuckle came down the line. "Okay, we'll speak later in the week, and Abi, chin up love, you've done the right thing. Justin was never good enough for you."

"You sound like my brother."

She disconnected and sat for a while, resting her chin on her clasped hands. Charlie would certainly agree with Lawrence, and so would Beth. Should she phone and tell them what had happened? No. Not now. She dragged her thoughts away from it all and picked up the phone as it rang again.

*  *  *

Raj found the offices of the CAF quite easily. Black painted railings guarded the basement and there were steps up to the front door in a pillared porch. It was a handsome building, not unlike the one in which he'd shared a flat all those years ago as a young law graduate. He was shown into Abi's office by a girl who eyed him curiously as she ushered him in. Abi rose to greet him.

"Thanks, Mina."

"Can I get coffee? Tea?" Mina showed signs of wanting to linger.

"I'll look after that," Abi told her. "You can get off now."

"She's very keen," he said as the door closed behind her.

Abi gave a tight smile. "That's one way of putting it." She walked over to a couple of armchairs set by a small table. "Shall we sit here, it's more comfortable. I'll get the coffee. How do you like it?"

"Black, no sugar please."

"I won't be long."

Raj had been taken aback by the sight of the bruising on Abi's cheek. He had little doubt where it had come from, he'd represented enough abused women to know the signs. He was surprised at how angry he felt on her behalf.

Abi came back with a cafetiere in one hand and two mugs in the other. The aroma of coffee spread through the room.

Discussing the project and the possibility of funding was easy enough. By a quarter past six they'd been through all the information Abi had put together and were sitting back with their second mug of coffee.

"It seems our plans match up well with the kind of project you've tackled in the past," Raj said.

"They do. I'll run this past Lawrence and the Board as soon as possible. He says he should be back in the office next week, so we shouldn't have to keep you waiting long for a decision."

Abi leant forward to put her mug down on the table and Raj noticed her wince and she put a hand up to her arm. There must be more than just the bruises on her cheek, he thought, but he didn't comment.

"Do you ever get to visit the projects you're funding?" he asked.

"Sometimes, and occasionally I have to give a paper at some conference or other. The last project I visited was helping women in Uganda to start up small businesses. They were so imaginative, and their energy was amazing." She relaxed as she spoke, and her eyes filled of enthusiasm. "We do quite a lot of work trying to empower women. It's always such a buzz when you see the positive results."

"But I should imagine it's an up-hill struggle sometimes. I've done some work with women's groups at home, trying to get across to them what their rights are under the law. Our government has been pretty pro-active in that area, particularly over violence in the home, but there's still a long way to go."

With a sinking feeling, he realised what he'd said. He wished he could take the words back. Their eyes met as a flush rose up her cheeks.

"I'm sorry," he said, not sure how to go on. "I also do a lot of matrimonial work– I recognise– I'm sorry," he said again.

"That's okay." Her tone contradicted the words. "I threw him out last night. It won't happen again."

Raj wanted to advise her on how to deal with the situation, which was ridiculous. Just because they'd known each other as children gave him no right to interfere now. He hoped she was right when she said it wouldn't happen again. In his experience these things were never that simple.

# CHAPTER 11

That evening when Abi arrived home, Maisie called to her as she was making her way up the front steps.

"I've been waiting for you, sweetheart," she said. "Hang on a sec." She ducked back into her flat and returned a moment later half hidden behind an enormous bunch of flowers. "These were delivered earlier."

"Who on earth are they from?"

"Don't know. There's a card," Maisie said, her eyes alight with curiosity.

From its nest inside the bouquet, Abi took out a small envelope. Frowning, she opened it up and took out the card. It made her feel sick. There was a message written inside, in familiar writing:

*Sorry, sorry, sorry, I love you, Justin*

Maisie took the card from her shaking fingers and read it. "Men!" she said, putting an awful lot of feeling into one small word. "Don't you take any notice, love."

"I'm not going to," Abi said, glad that her voice was steady. She thrust the flowers at Maisie. "You have them."

"I'll do better than that," said Maisie decisively. "I'm going to see my friend in hospital this evening. I'll take them to her."

Abi tried to smile. "Great idea."

"You know you can get my Sarah in whenever you need to. She's based at the station in Cobbett Street." Maisie patted Abi on the arm. "Forget about the stupid prat."

"I intend to." But as she let herself in, she knew forgetting about Justin wasn't going to be easy.

As was her usual habit, the first thing she did was check the answerphone. There was only one message. Abi put out a hesitant finger, drew it back, then told herself not to be stupid, it could be important. Before she could change her mind, she pressed the play button. Justin's voice said, "Abi, I'm not going to—" She pressed delete before she heard any more.

Deeply thankful that she had plenty to do that evening, she opened her laptop. It told her there were twelve e-mails. Six of them were from Justin.

* * *

Abi waited on the crowded platform at the tube station on Wednesday morning. As the doors of the train slid shut, she turned and thought she saw a familiar figure running down the stairs towards the platform. She craned round, trying to see over the heads of the crowd, but he was no longer there. She told herself not to be so silly.

But then she found the small blue envelope in her post. The address was typed and normally she would have slit it open without a thought, but not this time. Heart beating hard, she pulled out a card with an innocuous painting of cornflowers on it. Inside was written:



During the rest of the day Abi had several more e-mails from him and half a dozen texts. She deleted them all. By the time she got home at half past seven she felt drained and exhausted. She made herself an omelette and sat flicking through television channels. Nothing appealed, but she left it on, the murmuring noise was companionable. She poured a second glass of wine. In spite of feeling wide eyed with exhaustion, she knew she wouldn't be able to sleep for hours yet.

When her mobile rang, she snatched it up and looked at the screen. It wasn't Justin, but she didn't recognise the number.

"Hallo?"

"Hi, Abi? It's Raj."

She was surprised at how pleased she was to hear his voice. "I thought you were leaving this evening."

"I am, but the flight's delayed. I'm sitting here in departures, bored to tears, so I thought I'd phone and see if you've decided when to come to Mauritius."

Her heart sank. "I'm not sure."

"Not sure when or not sure if?" he asked.

"Both, either." She felt a little resentful, but then she heard him chuckle and told herself not to be so touchy. "Sorry, I'm not making a lot of sense. It'd be such a hell of a big step, going back."

"Won't it be easier if you look on it as a business trip? I know my colleagues would be keen to meet you. And, like that Ugandan project, it'd make it easier for you to advise your Board and make decisions, if you've visited the site and talked to the people."

"I know the site, as you call it, and some of the people."

Raj paused. "But still, it would be best from the point of view of the whole project. Just a flight there and back, maybe—"

"I'd have to justify the expense though."

"Well, when did you last have a holiday?" Again, there was a pause. "Look, I realise there are a lot of unresolved issues, but perhaps going back would help."

"You sound like a therapist," she complained.

"I get the impression I'm not being paid a compliment. But I do think it would be a good thing. You might be able to find out why Douglas stopped writing."

"How? Who'd tell me?"

"Monique perhaps", he said, then went on without waiting for her to respond. "I had another look at the will. You know what Douglas says, about how losing contact was a great grief to him? Doesn't that make you think a little?"

"I suppose." Abi wondered why it seemed so much easier to talk to him on the phone. Maybe because those dark eyes weren't studying her every move and change of expression. "If it wasn't intentional, what reason could there be?"

"Have you talked to your brother about it?"

"Not really. We don't talk much about Mauritius. I suppose we're protecting each other. Our life there, well, the last couple of years, was a nightmare." What she said next came out with no warning at all. "Did you know that our mother committed suicide?" The words felt strange in her mouth. She'd never said them out loud before.

There was another silence at the other end, but longer this time.

"I knew she died. I didn't know it was suicide. I'm sorry. I should have known."

"Why would you?" Her tone was harsh. "You were a child at the time."

"But still – I understand better now why you're so reluctant."

"It's not just that."

"Maybe not, but it's enough, isn't it."

"We seem to have changed sides in this discussion."

She heard a deep chuckle. "We do. Ah," he said, and his tone had changed. "They're calling my flight. I suppose I'd better go. It's been good talking to you."

"Thanks for calling, Raj." She knew she was thanking him for more than just that. "I'll let you know as soon as I decide what to do."

"There was one other thing, although perhaps I shouldn't say it."

"Go on," Abi said, wondering what was coming next.

"Well," he sounded unsure of himself. "That chap–"

"The one that hit me," she said, helping him out.

"Yes, it might be a good idea to be five thousand miles away for a while."

"You may have a point. Have a good flight."

"Thanks. Oh, and by the way, I've sent–" But at that moment the call was cut off.

* * *

The e-mails and texts from Justin continued through Thursday, and gradually they became more threatening. Abi deleted them all. Thank God she'd thought to unplug her answerphone.

When she arrived home on Thursday evening, yet another enormous bouquet had been taken in by Maisie. Abi told her to keep them and, feeling reluctant to be on her own, invited Maisie in for a drink. She opened a can of Guinness, Maisie's favourite, and poured herself a glass of wine, and they sat down at the kitchen table.

"It's so weird. He hasn't actually faced me, just sends endless e-mails, texts and bunches of flowers. What is he trying to do?"

"Wear you down, seems like. Speak to Sarah, dear." Her diminutive neighbour was firm. "She knows how to deal with this sort of thing, used to be on the Domestic Violence Unit."

"But what can she do? He's not hurt me, well, only that once."

"Come on, darlin'! Isn't that enough?" Maisie leant her arms on the table and gazed earnestly at Abi. "Look, I don't want to frighten you, love, but I don't think it'll end with these stupid flowers and that. Like I said the other night, I speak from experience. It's not on."

Deep down Abi knew Maisie was right, and Evelyn had said the same thing. Why should it surprise her? She thought back to her childhood, hovering on the sidelines of her parents' relationship and wondering, at the time, why her mother didn't stand up for herself. Now she was beginning to understand.

"I suppose I could ask Sarah to have another word with him," Abi said slowly.

"That's the ticket. You do that."

Abi sighed. "Yes. I'll think about it."

Maisie opened her mouth to say something else, then seemed to change her mind. She drained her drink and got up.

"I must get going, my bingo night tonight." At the door she reached up and gave Abi a hug. "Chin up, love. You talk to my Sarah."

"I will," Abi said, but then she remembered she'd shredded Justin's note and deleted his e-mails and texts. What evidence had she to give Sarah? No, she wouldn't phone tonight. All she wanted to do now was forget about Justin and everything associated with him.

But a call from her brother made that impossible.

"I've just had Justin on the phone again," he told her. "Are you two back together again?"

"Christ no!"

"He seems to think you are?"

"What the hell do you mean?"

"It was all a bit odd," Charlie said. "He asked after Beth and the boys, went on about my new appointment. It's the first time he's ever shown an interest in the family or my job. Then he said you'd had a bit of a row. So, I said I knew about that, which seemed to take him aback. He waffled on about that sort of thing happening with most couples, and said it had all blown over, then asked if I'd spoken to you lately, and did I know where you were this evening."

Abi didn't respond. She felt guilty that she hadn't phoned Charlie to explain what had been happening since they saw each other last.

"I have to say I was a tad blunt," Charlie went on. "I said that if everything was fine between you, how come he didn't know where you were, and he said something about you not realising how much he loved you. What's going on, Abi?"

"He's being a bit of a pain, Charlie. Don't worry about it."

"Don't give me that. Has he been violent?"

Abi couldn't think what to say.

"He asked me to tell you that you were meant for each other and that he'd never give up. Then he put the phone down."

"Oh God," Abi said, feeling sick again. She couldn't bear to tell Charlie that Justin had hit her. It would make him so angry, and it seemed like an admission of weakness. Yet she desperately wanted to confide in him. She took a deep breath.

"He won't accept we're finished, keeps e-mailing, texting, sending flowers and stuff. I'll deal with it. It's just annoying, that's all."

"Are you sure that's all?"

"Yea, don't worry, I'll deal with it," Abi repeated, doing her best to sound confident and unperturbed. It was after she'd ended the call that she realised she'd told him nothing about the dinner with Raj or the meeting they'd had in her office, or the phone call from the airport.

# CHAPTER 12

Abi's mobile rang at six the next morning, dragging her from sleep. She answered it without thinking.

"It's me."

Instantly she was wide awake, her heart beating painfully in her chest.

"Don't put the phone down," Justin said. "I'm outside. By your front gate. Let me come up."

"Go away, Justin! Just fuck off!" Abi shouted.

"I'm not leaving until you agree to see me."

"In your dreams," Abi said. She cut off the call and threw the phone across the room, then jumped out of bed, grabbed it up and switched it off. But she couldn't leave it off for long, she used it for work as well as everything else. What the hell was she going to do? At half past eight she had a meeting she couldn't miss.

Abi wrapped her dressing gown round her like woolly armour. She put her hand up to the light switch in the living room, then snatched it back. Justin would see it go on. In the gloom she crept across to the window and tried to create a tiny gap between the window frame and the curtain, just enough to be able to see out. It was still dark outside, except for the pool of light created by a streetlamp. A solitary walker with a dog on a lead came briefly into view then disappeared. The only other sign of life was a familiar figure standing leaning against the fence by the gate. As she stood there, he looked round. Abi stumbled back, her fingers pressed to her mouth. She had no idea if he'd seen her, but she wasn't going to take the risk of looking again.

She groped her way back across the living room to the kitchen. He wouldn't be able to see the light in here. She switched it on, filled the kettle, got out a mug, put in a tea bag and took the milk from the fridge. The ordinary routine was calming.

What to do now? Go out and confront him? The thought made her stomach churn. But she had to get to work, and to do so she had to get past Justin. Hands clasped round the warmth of the mug, she stood looking out of the kitchen window at the small, narrow garden which Maisie tended so carefully. Down the bottom was a fence with a gate in it. Of course! She'd ask Maisie if she could go through her flat and out to the short alleyway which would take her to the end of the road.

The disadvantage to this plan was that she'd have to wake Maisie. But then, if she didn't, and Maisie found out, she'd be really annoyed, wouldn't she? Abi made up her mind. She'd make it up to Maisie, get her some of those Belgian chocolates she liked so much.

Half an hour later, with Maisie urging her to phone Sarah as soon as she got to the office, Abi stepped out of the back gate and made her way to the main road. She hurried to the station and, as she got there, a train was pulling in. Dizzy with relief, she watched out of the window and only relaxed when the platform ended and the tunnel began.

Abi was out of the office all morning, going from one meeting to another. When she finally got back at three o'clock, she found a large jiffy envelope on her desk. It was addressed in a sloping scrawl she didn't recognise and marked 'Personal'. Oh no, thought Abi. It wasn't Justin's handwriting, but he could have got someone else to address it. Heart beating hard, she opened the envelope and shook out the contents.

A book thumped down in front of her and a note fell out with it. She turned the book over to look at the title: *Island in Watercolour – Mauritian impressions painted by Mariam Su Yen with text by Suzanne Bhayat.*

Abi opened it and began to turn the pages. The paper reminded her of the cream vellum that Uncle Douglas had used for watercolours, and the illustrations, from delicate line drawings to double paged colour-filled paintings, depicted every aspect of island life. The font they'd used was like handwriting, which added to the impression that the book was a labour of love. It was beautiful, and it tugged at Abi's heart.

She picked up the accompanying note. At the top was the logo of the Garden Hotel, and below was a short paragraph in the same sloping scrawl:

> *Dear Abi,*
> *I found this in Waterstones at Piccadilly Circus and*
> *thought you might enjoy it. A small incentive to come*
> *and see the real thing.*
> *Regards,*
> *Raj Amrakash*

It was such a relief that it wasn't from Justin. She was touched by the thoughtfulness of the gift.

When Mina came in a few minutes later, Abi was still leafing through the book. She looked up and her heart sank. Mina was holding an enormous bunch of red roses.

"These were delivered for you," Mina grinned.

"Throw them out, or you can have them if you like."

"Don't you even want to know who they're from?"

"I know already. Just do as I ask Mina."

"Okay. You're the boss." At the door her curiosity got the better of her. "Are they from Justin then?"

"Mina!"

Mina scuttled away, closing the door with a decided snap.

Abi rummaged in her bag for Sarah's card and punched in the number.

*November 1988*

Hilary had often wondered how the summer house had survived, exposed as it was in the middle of the *arpen bas*, paint peeling and tacky with salt. She ran the last couple of yards and went quickly up the steps, opened the door and slipped inside. As she did so she felt the protectiveness of the sturdy building wrap around her.

There were cushioned window seats and, stacked by the door, were several deck chairs. She noticed they'd recently been re-canvassed. On the floor was a collection of croquet mallets and the paraphernalia of other outdoor games. A dilapidated sofa, covered in a faded cotton throw, stood opposite the door, and in the middle of the room was a square table, surrounded by four folding chairs. On it was a polished wooden box with a brass hook and eye to keep it closed. It contained packs of cards, dominoes, marbles and other games. A smell of weathered wood, salt and damp canvas filled the room.

Douglas had promised to tell Tony where she was as soon as he arrived. She glanced at her watch. Half past four. Curled up on one of the window seats she waited, her body tense, but she couldn't keep still for long and got up to pace back and forth across the creaking floorboards.

Carl was on his way to the airport. Very soon he'd be in Johannesburg. He wouldn't be back for a whole glorious week.

When Tony finally arrived, she heard him before she saw him. For a terrifying second, she convinced herself the footsteps were Carl's. Movement and breath suspended, she waited, but as Tony appeared in the doorway, life flowed back through her. She ran to him, flung her arms round his body and felt his own clasp her hard against him. For a minute neither spoke, then gently he pushed her back. As he did so the sleeve of her dress slipped a little from her shoulder revealing a deep purple bruise. His eyes darkened with anger.

"He's hit you again."

She pulled her dress straight to cover the bruise. "It's nothing."

"Nothing?" he exclaimed, and she flinched. "What was it this time?"

She hadn't intended to tell him, but found it just came out.

"It was the brooch you gave me. Abi saw it and pointed it out to Carl." His frown made her jump to her daughter's defence. "How was she to know? She thought he'd given it to me. I told him it was from Douglas, but I don't think he believed me. Thank God there was enough doubt for him not to take it away, he's wary of Douglas. I know he'll back me up, but I hate having to ask my poor cousin to lie for me."

He led her over to one of the window seats, pulled her down beside him, his usually kind eyes bleak.

"Let me speak to Carl. I'll deal with the bastard."

"No, no, you mustn't. Please, Tony, promise me you won't."

Reluctantly he agreed, but she wasn't at all sure she'd convinced him. He pulled her to him, kissed her gently, stroked her hair.

"My poor darling. I want to take you away from him. Have you thought any more about coming to Durban?"

"Yes – no – how can we? What about the children?"

"We can take them with us, and Nanny Vimala if you wish."

"It's not possible. He'll take them back and then I'll never see them again." She put a hand up to his cheek and there were tears in her eyes. "What are we going to do?"

# CHAPTER 13



*October 2018*

At half past nine on Saturday evening Abi's doorbell rang. Heart beating hard, she made her way into the hall and only opened the door once she'd checked the chain was up. Sarah Broderick stood there, smiling.

Feeling lightheaded with relief, Abi unlatched the chain and opened the door.

"Come in. I'm so glad it's you."

"I'm sorry to call so late," Sarah said as she stepped inside, "but I thought you'd want me to report back sooner rather than later."

"That's fine." Strange the innocuous phrases we use, Abi thought, it wasn't really fine at all, she didn't want to hear anything about Justin, but she knew she had to. "Did you manage to speak to him?"

"I did. I spoke to him last night, but I'm afraid he's not willing to acknowledge his behaviour is unacceptable, let alone against the law." Before Abi could protest, she went on. "But that's not unusual. Has he contacted you since you rang me yesterday?"

"No, thank God."

"I must warn you it doesn't mean he won't. I told him you didn't want any contact and warned him if you made an official complaint, we would act on it."

Abi gripped her hands together in her lap. "What did he say?"

"Initially he insisted it was none of my business." Sarah smiled. "I reminded him I was here the other night, and I told him your phone call made it my business. At that point he changed tack and said you'd misunderstood, all he wanted was for the two of you to get back to normal, as he called it."

"Normal!" Anger rose up inside Abi. "What's normal about all the e-mails and texts, and standing outside my front gate at some God forsaken hour of the morning? And what's bloody normal about this?" She pulled her sleeve up and showed Sarah the bruise on her arm.

"You don't have to tell me, Abi," Sarah said calmly.

Abi slumped back in her armchair. "Sorry, it's just getting to me."

"Which is hardly surprising," Sarah reassured her. "And just because he's not willing to accept responsibility just yet doesn't mean that he won't in the end. These things take time."

Theoretically Abi understood what she was saying, but she still felt that it was somehow her fault. She'd made the decision to become involved with Justin in the first place. Was this a repeating pattern, like mother, like daughter? No! That was such a bloody cliché.

"Abi, listen to me." Sarah leant forward and touched her arm gently. "You are not responsible for Justin's behaviour. No one has the right to force their attention on you, no one has the right to hit you, and no one has the right to force you to have contact with them." She ticked these points off on her fingers. "Let me give you a few tips on how to deal with him."

By the time Sarah had gone through a list of things she could do, she felt more in control. One thing she suggested was that Abi change her mobile number and, in the end, Abi agreed. But what Sarah said next seemed to go off at a tangent.

"Are you due any holiday?"

"Yes, but there's no way I could take any at the moment, my boss is off work for at least another week."

"Pity. If you weren't around for a while, it might help."

"I suppose."

"I've jotted down a couple of websites that might be useful to you." She put a piece of paper down on the coffee table, next to the book that Raj had sent.

"What a lovely book," she said. "Where is that?"

"Mauritius. A friend gave it to me."

Sarah opened the first few pages. "Beautiful drawings. I went there on holiday once, I loved it. Do you know it?"

"I was born there."

"Were you? How lovely. If you still have family there maybe you should visit," she said brightly, then she got up. "I must get going. Don't forget, ring me any time if you need to."

* * *

Raj arrived back in Mauritius early on Thursday morning. As he stood waiting for his luggage to appear on the carousel, he turned on his mobile and several texts came up. One was from his sister, Narinda, another was from Abi asking how his journey had been and giving him her new mobile number, and another was from Antoine. He tapped out responses to Abi and his sister and ignored Antoine, but as he came out into the airport car park his mobile rang. The screen told him it was Antoine again. Raj sighed and responded.

"*Bonzour*, Antoine."

"At last! I've been trying to get hold of you for days." There were never any preliminaries with Antoine.

"I'd gathered that. You knew I was going away. I just this minute got back."

"Good. Can we meet later today, say lunch time?"

"No Antoine."

"Why not? It's important."

"At the moment the only things on my mind are a shower and a change of clothes."

"But this is urgent."

"So is my shower. Look, I'll meet up with you early next week and bring you up to date."

"That's no good. These people are– I need to see you today." Antoine's voice crackled with urgency.

"No way," Raj snapped. "It's half past eight in the morning and I've just come off a fifteen-hour flight. I'm not–"

"Look Raj, this is important."

Raj hung on to his patience with difficulty.

"Antoine, I'm going home, and nothing is going to stop me. As it is, I've a meeting at four this afternoon I can't avoid, and tomorrow I'm in court all day. I'll do my best to phone tomorrow evening."

He cut off the call. As he got into a taxi, his phone rang once more. Antoine again. He ignored it.

* * *

As Raj came out of the Curepipe district court late on Friday afternoon, after a day of complicated negotiations over the ownership of a fleet of fishing boats, the last thing he wanted to do was talk to Antoine. Raj's rather spartan flat, where he'd lived since his wife, Parmita, had died, was within walking distance of his chambers. His sister had thrown up her hands in horror when he'd moved there. She'd hoped he'd marry again within a couple of years, and probably pictured his house full of nieces and nephews, but he'd only wanted to escape.

Back in his office on Saturday, after speaking to the other members of the Belle Etoile committee, he put together the draft proposal Abi had asked for and e-mailed it off to her. He'd managed to put off speaking to Antoine, and when he got a text from him asking for Abi's contact details, Raj ignored it.

An hour later he was driving along the coast road at Pointe d'Esny, past rambling purple and pink bougainvillaea. He passed a few tourists making their lazy way back to their hotels, a cyclist with faggots of wood strapped to his cross bar wobbling along precariously, and a pair of sari clad women with bundles of laundry balanced on their heads, each with one arm up to steady the load. Raj smiled, breathed in the sea air, and he sighed with pleasure.

His sister, Narinda, had invited him to have dinner with her and her husband, Vijay, that evening, and he was looking forward to relaxing with them, and telling them about his visit to their daughter, Shirin, in Cardiff. Since Shirin was a doctor, like both her parents, they would want to know all about the work she was doing.

By the time he was settled on Narinda's verandah, a cold beer in his hand, the evening spectacle had begun. Colour was splashed across the sky – grey blue, indigo, scarlet, orange and gold, and, in the middle, the red half circle of the sun was slowly creeping down below the horizon. Raj watched it, as he had so many times before.

A few strides away the sea murmured up and down the beach and reflected back the vivid colours. The patches of black rock gave the impression they'd been tumbled into the water by some giant hand, while the breeze whispered through the *filao* trees that edged the sand. Raj glanced across at Narinda.

"This is perfect. Who'd want to live anywhere else?"

"Talking of living somewhere else, tell me all about your visit to Shirin."

"I'll do that when Vijay arrives, no point in repeating it all."

"Raji!"

"You'll just have to wait," Raj said, grinning at her. He looked back at the sunset. "Did Papa ever tell you that if you stayed very quiet and listened hard, you'd hear the sun whisper goodnight as it finally disappeared."

She returned the smile. "Yes. He was full of stories like that."

"I spent night after night listening. Sometimes I was sure I heard a ghostly voice at the very last moment." His smile faded. "I miss him so much. I really need to pick his brains about the past."

"About work?"

"Sort of," he said, then added, "I met up with Abigail Kendall when I was in the UK, about Douglas's legacy."

Narinda's eyes widened. "I see. Is that why you need Papa's input?"

"Yes. What I'll have to do is go through all those papers of his in my office."

"I'm sure Georgette will help you with that," Narinda said.

"True. She's the best office manager ever."

"And you could ask her grandmother as well. She was Papa's secretary for over fifteen years."

"Good idea. I hadn't thought of talking to Marie."

"Tell me, what's Abi like now?"

Raj put his glass down, got up and wandered over to lean on the wooden railings, his back to his sister.

"She's stunning to look at, tall, and still with that incredible golden hair and dark eyelashes, strange combination. She's certainly got style, wears rather spectacular clothes. But as to what I thought of her personality-wise, the first meeting we had was a disaster. She came to the hotel, was abrupt and rather rude, and when I told her about the legacy it completely threw her, and she walked out."

"What extraordinary behaviour!"

"I certainly hadn't been looking forward to meeting her again."

"But all that was years ago, Raji," Narinda interrupted him. "She was a child then, and her home life was completely dysfunctional."

"There speaks the therapist."

"Darling, she had a terrible time. I remember hearing Papa and Mami talk about it. She had a monster for a father and a mouse for a mother."

"But she did have Douglas."

"There is that, but it was much more difficult for her than it was for her brother, I got the impression she spent a lot of time protecting him from the worst of it all."

"I didn't realise you saw that much of them," Raj said, turning to look at her.

"I saw enough, and that was about the time I was getting interested in psychology. I suppose I was taking more notice than I would otherwise have done."

"You've always been very observant."

"So have you."

"I suppose."

The brief tropical dusk was nearly over, the sunset rapidly fading. Narinda rose and turned on two lamps. Almost immediately they attracted moths of many sizes, small as an ant, large as a thumb.

"Did you see any more of her while you were there?" she asked, coming to stand by Raj.

"Yes, we had dinner at Navin's restaurant."

Narinda grinned. "How is that old reprobate?"

"Just the same. He sent his regards. Anyway, that meeting with Abi was much easier than the first one." He thought of saying something about Abi's apology as she left the restaurant but decided he'd rather not. "The amazing thing is that she works for the Commonwealth Arts Foundation. They're the people we've applied to for funding for the Belle Etoile project, and she's their deputy director, which complicates things. It puts her on both sides of the fence, so to speak."

"So, she has some influence over whether you get the funding you've applied for, but she'll also have a say in whether or not Belle Etoile is sold to the highest bidder?"

"Yes." He grinned ruefully down at her. "Interesting, isn't it?"

"Does Antoine know all this?"

"Not yet. I've rather avoided him since I got back."

"You're going to have to tackle him soon."

"I know, but it won't do him any harm to stew for a bit."

Narinda didn't comment. "Did you persuade her to come and look over her inheritance?" she asked.

"I tried. I sent her a copy of that book of Mariam's as an incentive. The trouble is there's something else that might complicate matters." He grimaced, wondering if he should say what was in his mind, then took the plunge. "I'm pretty sure she's in an abusive relationship. I've seen the signs too often to mistake it, Nari, so have you."

"Poor woman," she sighed. "Of course, the psychology of it is pretty textbook."

"That's what I thought. I wonder what Douglas would have said?"

Before Narinda had the chance to respond, Raj's mobile rang. He took it from his pocket and looked at the screen. "It's Antoine again," he said.

"Get it over with, answer it."

He grinned at her. "You always were one to tackle problems head on."

"Well, it's only fair on him. I'll go and see how the dinner is coming on. Andiana insisted on doing your favourite *rougaille poisson salée*, and she's made pineapple cake with chocolate sauce."

"She's worth her weight in gold, that cook of yours."

"Vijay would agree with you. I hope he'll be home soon, but he had to go and see a patient who's going through chemo. Go on, phone Antoine, then you can relax and tell us all about Shirin."

*February 1985*

The heat was oppressive, carrying the cloying scent of frangipani in through the window. The brass ceiling fan whispered round, round, but had little effect on the sluggish air. Douglas Beaumont could hear laughter in the garden. Antoine's two-year-old voice calling; Zabette, the cook, answering him.

He looked up from the book on his lap. It was pointless trying to read, he couldn't concentrate. On the bed his wife's slight body lay under a thin sheet. Her head turned back and forth on the pillow and her eyelids flickered, half opening. "*Non... non...* my baby..." It was more of a moan than coherent words.

"Monique?" He rose and bent over her, smoothed her hair back from her forehead. He was sure the fever was higher. The doctor had said it might get worse before it got better. Would she be better off in hospital? But she'd made him promise not to take her there. A nurse would be arriving to keep an eye overnight. No, she was best at home. He squeezed out a towel in the bowl of water on her bedside table, gently wiped her face with it.

"Monique? It's Douglas. Can you hear me?"

There was no reply. Her eyes were open now, gazing up at his face, but there was no recognition in them. The fingers that had been plucking at the sheet, grabbed his wrist.

"He made me promise, he made me," she whispered.

"Who? Made you promise what?"

"He said... he said he would take Antoine."

Douglas's heart constricted at the thought. "Who?"

She didn't answer. Her eyelids flickered and closed, her breath coming quick and short. Once again, he soaked the towel, wiped her neck and shoulders, then straightened the sheet, feeling the embroidered edge under his fingers. Hilary had worked on them for weeks, putting in every minute stitch to create the lacy edging. She'd given them to Douglas and Monique as a wedding present.

Wearily he walked over to the window and pushed the shutter aside. Antoine was running about the garden on his fat little legs, trailing a toy truck on a string. Zabette sat on the steps watching him. Douglas watched Antoine, smiled a little. He looked so like his mother, dark black curls, coffee skin slightly paler than hers, eyes as large and long lashed, although pale blue rather than Monique's bitter chocolate colour. He was growing so fast. What would happen if Monique didn't survive this awful fever?

Monique began to moan again. He bent over her. "I'm here, *chérie*."

"Douglas?" She seemed to recognise him this time. "Don't let him… my baby… don't let…" She continued to speak, so low that he had to bend close to hear what she said. What she told him chilled him to the bone.


# CHAPTER 14


*February 1985*


There was a light knock on Prem Amrakash's office door. His tiny dynamo of a secretary, Marie Pillay, came in.

"Monsieur Beaumont is here to see you, sir." She was obviously surprised by the unexpected visitor. So was Prem.

"Show him in, and bring tea, please."

She ushered in a tall, balding man. His tanned face was creased with laughter lines and his dark eyebrows almost met above his nose.

"Prem, *mon vieux*, how are you?"

"This is a pleasant surprise, Douglas." Prem came around the desk, shook hands then laid a hand on his friend's shoulder. "What brings you to Port Louis? You always say you hate the heat and noise in town."

"I do. But I wanted to see you, and since I had to come and pick up some paints and canvasses from Delamare's, I thought I'd drop in."

He sat down in a chair opposite Prem's desk. The smile had disappeared and Prem noticed that Douglas looked unusually strained.

"I hear that Monique has been unwell. How is she now?"

"Much better."

"What was wrong?"

"Some kind of fever which turned into pneumonia, but Dr Dupré is sure she's on the mend now. She's tough, my Monique."

"I wish I could say the same of my wife," Prem said sadly.

"Is Ashvina still not well?"

"I'm afraid so."

They were interrupted by Marie who came in with the tea, placed the tray on the desk before him, and disappeared discreetly back to her own office. Prem poured the hot, vanilla scented liquid and passed a cup to Douglas.

"So, what can I do for you?" he asked.

Douglas sipped at his tea. "I have a favour to ask." He sounded troubled.

"Tell me."

"It's the boy. A while ago you mentioned there's a simple form of adoption."

"That's correct, heard by a judge in chambers, very straightforward."

"Can you arrange it?"

"Absolutely," Prem said.

"For his own... security." The slight hesitation was not lost on Prem. "It's what we want."

"But why now? When I spoke to you before, not long after you told me he wasn't your son, you said it didn't matter, that you felt as if he was. What has changed?"

"When the fever was at its worst, Monique was delirious." Douglas took a deep breath, rubbed a hand across his eyes. "She told me who the father is."

Prem's eyes widened. "Ah. Can you tell me?"

Douglas did so, his voice hardening as he spoke the name.

"It wasn't rape, she was willing, but at that age – *bon Dieu*, she was barely fifteen – he must have pressurised her. He can be charming when he wants, and she says she thought he loved her, but she knows different now."

There was a shocked silence. "I see. There've been rumours he has an eye for young girls," said Prem. "I understand now why you wish to put things on a more official footing. I'll make the arrangements."

"Thank you, Prem. We're in your debt." He smiled. Some of the strain seemed to have slipped from his shoulders. "Now tell me, how are your two. Young Raj must be – what? Nearly six now?"

"Yes. I have a recent photo of them here, let me show you." He opened a drawer in his desk, took out a photograph. His eyes glowed with pride as he passed it across the desk.

Douglas looked at the picture of a little boy, dark curls clustered round his serious face, the large, deep brown eyes staring out at the camera. He was holding the hand of a girl who looked to be about thirteen, slim and dark haired as the boy. Douglas smiled.

"A handsome child. And Narinda is growing into a beauty. I'd like to paint the two of them together, would you let me?"

Prem smiled. "I would be delighted, but Narinda might not agree. She's always complaining about having to look after her brother. It takes her away from her studies, she says."

"Her studies? She's still determined to be a doctor?"

"A psychologist, she says. A modern young woman."

"And how do you feel about that?" Douglas asked, looking at Prem with a quirk of his eyebrows.

"Ashvina talks constantly of a suitable husband, she's more of a traditionalist than me, but I too would like to see her settled. Perhaps she can do both. We will see."

Douglas pushed himself up from his chair. "I must get on. Give my regards to your family. And let me know when I can do that portrait."

Prem saw his friend out then went back to his desk. For some time he sat gazing ahead of him, deep in thought.

*October 2018*

Frowning, Raj put his mobile back in his pocket. After all Antoine's efforts to contact Raj, the expected lengthy complaints about where he'd been and why he hadn't returned calls hadn't happened. It'd been obvious he wasn't alone, but Raj couldn't identify the background noises, and after a couple of minutes Antoine had ended the call. Raj was puzzled and a little disturbed.

As he walked across the tiled floor of Narinda's sitting room, he glanced at the double portrait which had pride of place on the wall. A thirteen-year-old girl sitting on a rush mat, arm straight by her side as she leant on her hand, a slight smile on her face. A small boy, some eight years younger, cross-legged in front of her, unsmiling. It was a very good likeness, the light touch of the pastels perfect for the subject. Both were looking straight at the artist and, in the background, was sketched the outline of the *Chaîne de Moka* mountain range. The only thing Raj could remember about sitting for the portrait was that Douglas had bribed them to keep still with unlimited amounts of home-made lemonade, and *makatias* – small, sweet bread rolls with a coconut filling. He smiled, remembering.

He went into the kitchen attracted by the smell of the rich tomato and garlic sauce of the salt fish *rougaille* and the gentle scent of basmati rice. But he wasn't allowed to hang around and savour it. After greeting him and asking him accusingly why he was so thin and when he was going to get married again, the old cook shooed him out of the room, saying she must concentrate on her work, so he went back to join his sister on the verandah.

"Did you speak with Antoine?"

"Yes, but he didn't seem that keen to talk. I think he must have been at some do or other."

"Ah well, you've done your bit. While you were on the phone I went and had a look for these," she said, handing him two photographs. One was of three children, two boys of about the same age and a blonde girl a little older. They were on a beach, unaware of the camera as they concentrated on building a sandcastle, buckets and spades scattered around them.

"That's Charlie, obviously that's you, and the girl is Abigail. And this one was taken the same day. We were at Flic-en-Flac, a picnic with Douglas and Monique."

In this one the children were lined up in order of height, side on to the camera. First was Abi, then Raj, Charlie next, all smiling over their shoulders at the photographer, and at the end, scowling and grumpy, was Antoine.

"Where on earth did you find them?"

"In my photo drawer. I took them. I was so proud of that camera. It was the first one I'd ever owned. I could probably find more photos if you like."

"Abi hasn't changed much. Can I borrow these?" He caught Narinda's smile, tried not to respond to it, but found his lips twitching. "It's just that I'd like to scan them in and send them to her."

"By all means. Do you remember it at all?"

Raj put the photographs in his shirt pocket. "Vaguely. I seem to remember I quite liked her then, it wasn't until later—"

"And now?" Narinda was giving him a knowing look which he tried to ignore.

"She's a totally different person, not so much in her looks, but in herself. Nearly thirty years, it's a long time. Strangely enough I feel she's more vulnerable now."

"She was vulnerable then, but you were a kid, why would you have noticed?"

"I suppose." Narinda was waiting for him to go on. He shifted in his seat, knowing she wouldn't give up the subject easily. "I've never met anyone quite like her. There's so much going on under the surface. It's as if you're dealing with several different people."

"We're all a bit like that, aren't we? One persona for family, one for work, one for social occasions."

"Perhaps, but because of knowing her before, and the fact my contact recently has been on two fronts, I've seen more facets of her than I would otherwise. She interests me, that's all, Narinda."

"And I think you'd like to get to know her better."

"That's not going to happen. She's five thousand miles away."

"Okay, but there are other women." She smiled, eyebrows raised, then was serious again. "I know you get cross if I interfere, Raji, but it's been a long time now."

"What has?"

"Don't be obtuse. Since Parmita died."

He frowned. "What's that got to do with it? You think I'm still grieving for her?"

"Not exactly, no. I think you're feeling guilty because you're *not* grieving for her, you never really have in the conventional sense, and it's the guilt that makes you keep away from women. You bury yourself in your work, you've got hardly any social life, other than your football and your card games, and that Japanese hap thingy."

"Hapkido."

"But Raj, what are you trying to prove?"

That was the best and the worst of Narinda, she never bothered to pretend, and she often knew how he was feeling before he'd worked it out for himself. He wanted to deny what she'd said, but that wasn't possible, because she was right, about his wife at any rate.

"Raji, when you got back from England all those years ago," his sister went on, "still unmarried, needing a wife for the sake of your career if nothing else, and Parmita was the first suggestion Papa and Mami made, I think you convinced yourself it'd work, because it was less trouble to give in than not."

"For God's sake, I'm not that much of a pushover."

"Okay, but you hadn't had an enormous amount of experience of women."

"How do you know?" Raj protested.

"I'm not saying you had no girlfriends, but you must admit you were a bit of a workaholic, particularly when you were busy establishing yourself. Marrying Parmita, who was sweet, biddable, pretty, why not? If you'd had children it might have been different, but once she got ill there was no question of that." She paused, then put a warm hand on his knee. "All I'm saying is to let her rest now. No more guilt, eh? And no more living like a monk."

Raj felt he had to defend himself. "But I'm not one of those men who can just waltz in and sleep with somebody, say 'thank you so much' and waltz out again." He looked across at his sister and decided to try to explain what was in his mind. "Marriage to Parmita taught me that if sex is based on nothing much more than the need to procreate, then it's a pretty empty business. That, I suppose, has added to what you've called guilt, because I feel it was just as unfair on her as it was on me."

"Unfair in what way? That you were made to marry?" she asked gently.

"No, because we weren't, were we? I mean unfair because there was no real love in it."

"That's a very western way of looking at things."

"Maybe, but it's how I feel."

"And now there's Abi—"

"Don't be ridiculous," Raj snapped. "Since we were kids, I've met the woman three times, talked to her on the phone, exchanged a few e-mails, and that's it. Don't start reading things into this that just aren't there."

His sister's eyes glinted as she looked at him, a half-smile on her face. He could feel irritation rising, then a door slammed inside the house and they heard footsteps approaching across the tiled floor.

"Ah, here's Vijay," Raj said, deeply relieved at the interruption. "I'll tell you all about my lunch with Shirin now he's back."

It wasn't until they were sitting down to their meal that Raj got around to the subject of Antoine and Belle Etoile once more.

"I think you should try to speak to him again," Narinda said, "sooner rather than later."

"It's up to him now."

"But Raji—"

"I'll try again tomorrow," Raj said, exasperated.

"Has she been nagging you?" Vijay asked.

"Non-stop."

"Terrible isn't it. You can see how living with this woman wears me away to nothing." He indicated his generously proportioned form and grimaced like a mask of tragedy. "I'm a hero, I tell you, a hero to put up with it."

"I feel for you," Raj said, grinning.

"What's going on with Antoine?" Vijay asked.

"He's in a panic, but I'm not entirely sure why. He keeps saying he needs to give the people he's involved with an immediate decision on Belle Etoile, but when I press him, he won't go into details. I've promised to meet up with him early next week, so I hope I'll find out more then. He wants to speak to Abigail Kendall himself, but I've been stalling on that. I really don't want him to bother her yet, but I can't put it off much longer. After all, in normal circumstances they'd probably have made contact directly the will came to light."

"Why don't you want him to speak to her?" Narinda asked.

Raj didn't reply immediately. He wasn't entirely sure what the answer was. He was certain Abi would be very angry if he handed over her e-mail address or, worse, her phone number without permission, but why hadn't he asked her? Partly because of what she'd said about Antoine when they had dinner – that she didn't like him much and found him sulky and rather difficult – but there was more to it than that. Since he'd seen her bruised cheek and sensed the tension in her, he felt protective towards her. It seemed to him that Abi already had quite enough to deal with without having Antoine on her back. On the other hand, she was a grown woman, successful, assertive, at least in her work. Why shouldn't he leave her to fight her own battles? He glanced at Narinda, saw the bright curiosity in her eyes. He'd have to be careful how he answered her question.

"She wasn't exactly complimentary about Antoine," he said, "and as Douglas's executor I want to keep control of what goes on. I'd rather they both went through me for now."

"I think that's a wise decision," said Vijay, coming to his rescue once again. "Let's hope you can keep that control."

"In the end though," Narinda said, "they'll have to make contact, won't they?"

"Yes," Raj admitted, "but for now it puts a useful obstacle in his way. When I saw him at Douglas's wake, it was clear he wanted to sell up as soon as possible. And something else rang alarm bells – he was trying to convince me that Monique's incapable of looking after herself. He said she'd be better off in some home or other."

"What?" Vijay sounded as shocked as Narinda looked. "This is not the action of a good Mauritian son."

"You're damn right, it isn't," Raj said, "but then, a good Mauritian son Antoine is not. And I'm sure he exaggerated Monique's mental condition. She really didn't seem that bad when I saw her. Actually, Nari, could you go and visit her? I'd be grateful for your opinion."

"By all means. I've only seen her a few times since Douglas died. She was a little confused, but that's quite natural in the circumstances. I'll go this week."

"*Merci, ma soeur.* I don't think Antoine is going to let up and I'd like to be able to tell him his worries – let's be kind and call them that – about his mother are unfounded." He frowned. "The problem is I can see it from his point of view as well."

"Tell me the exact terms of the will," Vijay said.

Raj went quickly through the details. "Under our inheritance law it means his hands are tied when it comes to selling up as both legatees have to approve whatever is done in the future. I was doubtful about the wisdom of it at first, but I've changed my mind. At least it slows Antoine down a bit. All that is further complicated by Douglas's wish to create an arts centre. But Antoine just brushes that aside. And now we have the further complication of Abi working for an organisation to whom we've applied for funds."

"An interesting situation," Vijay said.

"Interesting! It's a nightmare."

Vijay helped himself to more rice and *rougaille*, added a generous portion of lime *achard* and some chillies pickled in dry sherry. Once this was done, he looked up at Raj.

"I might be able to give you a little of the low down on Antoine's associates."

"Would you?" Raj said eagerly. "How come?"

"I probably shouldn't tell you this since the information comes through a patient, but still," Vijay said, and added, "keep it to yourself."

"Certainly," Raj promised.

"The people he's involved with are from Johannesburg, but I think the parent company is based in Dubai. Their main business is in property, worldwide, mainly hotels. That's legitimate, but it's rumoured they also have connections with arms dealing, particularly into Somalia and the Congo, nothing definite, but the authorities are keeping them under surveillance. It's people like that who could seriously damage our finance industry if they get a foothold here."

"An Arab syndicate. Great! That's all we need. Do you think Antoine's aware of all this?"

"I don't know, but if I've heard the rumours, surely he must have too."

"Antoine's never been that particular about the circles he mixes in," said Narinda. "He just likes the good life. I gather he spends a lot of time at that new casino at Pereybere."

"Of course," Raj said, slapping his hand down on the table. "That's where he was when I spoke to him on the phone. I could hear that kind of activity in the background. But he's never done anything criminal, has he? The deal they're offering him over Belle Etoile could be above board."

"It could," said Vijay, but it was obvious he had his doubts. "Antoine can be ruthless, Raj, in the way that a cornered animal is, and unscrupulous. Remember that." He changed the subject. "Do you think Abigail will come and have a look at her inheritance?"

"She's going to have to at some point."

"Let's hope he behaves himself when she does."

"Don't worry, he can be very charming when he chooses to be," Narinda said, with a sideways glance at her brother.

"That," said Vijay, with a knowing look, "is exactly what I meant."

The thought of Abi being taken in by Antoine made Raj cringe. That'd be great, wouldn't it, after her recent experience. If she did decide to make the trip, he'd have to keep an eye on things.

When he got home, he was still thinking about Abi, wondering what she'd thought of the book he'd sent her. At half past midnight, as he was getting ready for bed, he found out. His mobile buzzed, it was a text from Abi.

*Thanks so much for the book. Gorgeous drawings. I'll think about what u said, Abi*

He hoped she didn't leave it too long. Tomorrow he'd e-mail her copies of those photos. Keeping contact was a good idea on so many different levels, and that was one way of doing so.

# CHAPTER 15

After a frantically busy Monday morning, Abi managed to take a quick mid-afternoon break. As she leant back in her chair, she couldn't stop herself thinking back to the night before. She'd had to endure a phone call from Justin's sister.

"He says he's going to end it all. Will you be satisfied when my poor brother is dead?"

Abi had slammed the phone down. Thank heavens the stupid woman didn't have her new mobile number.

But now she couldn't stop herself going over the conversation. What if Justin did try to kill himself? She'd be responsible. She slumped forward, put her head in her hands and twisted her fingers in her hair, pulling at it hard. This couldn't go on. She had to talk to someone. But who? And what on earth could she do? Justin would no more listen to her than he had to Sarah Broderick. Sitting there, Abi felt very lonely indeed.

There was a sound of raised voices and laughter in the outer office and when she opened the door, she was delighted to come face to face with Lawrence. The first thing she noticed was that he was no longer on crutches, although he was leaning on a sturdy walking stick. He hugged her with his free arm and gave her a kiss, his beard scratching at her cheek.

"The boredom finally got to me," he said, "so I persuaded Sue to drop me off while she does an interview with some B-list starlet for an article she's writing. I've been told I have an hour and no more. I hope you don't mind."

"Mind? Oh, Lawrence, it's so great to see you!" Abi tucked her arm through his and led him into the room. "Come and sit down. You're looking good. How's the leg?"

"Much better. I only have to use this" – he gave the walking stick a shake – "for a little while, and then it's a bit more physio and I'll be back to normal."

Abi stood back, expecting him to sit behind his desk, but he took one of the other chairs. He grinned at her.

"No, no, you're still the boss for now, Sue's orders."

"I'll get Mina to bring some coffee," Abi said.

"She's bringing it. I just asked her. So," he went on, "how's it all going?"

"Fine," Abi said breezily, "but I can't wait for you to get back."

"I got the e-mail you forwarded from Raj Amrakash. His proposal is an efficient piece of work. It would be good if we could help him. What do you think?"

"It's up to you and the rest of the board."

"Not entirely. Your local experience could carry a lot of weight."

Abi grimaced. "I wouldn't say I had much experience of Mauritius as it is now. I expect it's changed beyond all recognition. And anyway, Lawrie, it's difficult for me."

"In what way?"

"I find it so hard to detach myself from my own feelings about the place."

"That's not surprising, you were born there. Tell me, what exactly are your feelings about Mauritius? I know they're mixed, but you've never gone into any detail."

"It's hard to describe," she said. "It's all so tied up with my mother's death, and my uncle – well, cousin really – deserting us. Charlie says I shouldn't describe it that way, but even he can't get away from the fact Uncle Douglas stopped writing, with no explanation at all. Then there was my father, he always made life difficult for us. We were never consulted about staying or leaving after Mum died, just told that in a month's time we were off 'home', as he called it. Neither of us argued. We were both still in shock after Mum's death." She threw up her hands as if to brush it all away. "Let's talk about something else."

But it seemed Lawrence wasn't done with the subject. "Does all that mean you'd never go back?"

"I really don't think I could face it."

"Pity, because I think the Belle Etoile project has potential, but it would mean one of us going to have a shufti."

"What?" Abi stared at him in consternation. "It costs a fortune to get there!"

"I know what it costs. I've been doing some research on the net. Then of course there'll be the cost of somewhere to stay, but with your local connections–"

"Oh no, Lawrence. No way," said Abi, shaking her head vigorously. "I haven't got any connections left."

"Yes, you have." He was grinning at her provocatively. "You've got this Amrakash chap."

"How did you know I used to know him?"

Lawrence's eyes widened. "I didn't, but that's even better. Perhaps you could stay with him and his family."

"You are a horrible man," Abi said slowly and with deep feeling. "There is no way in the world I'd go and stay with him."

"Why? If he's an old friend–"

"He absolutely is not."

"Oh? That sounds pretty definite. Tell me about it."

What could she say? When we were kids, I was really shitty to him. I'm sure he doesn't like me. But that wouldn't be entirely true. By the third meeting they'd had, his attitude had changed, and hers too. And then there'd been that business about the bruise on her face, the understanding in his eyes, his phone call from the airport, the e-mail she'd received this morning with those two photos attached. She remembered that day, it had been a happy one. But then there were all the other memories, so much she didn't want to face, times she hated to think about.

Before she had the chance to put any of these thoughts into words, there was a knock on the door and Mina came in. She was holding an enormous bouquet of flowers, and there was a knowing smirk on her face.

* * *

Raj stood at the window of his office watching the comings and goings at his old school across the road. When he'd decided to move to the highlands from his father's old office in Port Louis, where most of the legal practices had their chambers, he'd been pleased this suite of offices had been available. The austere, stolid building of the Royal College, with its surrounding wrought iron railings, and the war memorial of two soldiers holding up a laurel wreath, was so much part of his life. It gave him a sense of security. But he doubted Antoine would have the same feelings about it. He'd been bullied because his father was a member of staff and teased because of his mother's lowly background. Raj remembered feeling sorry for the younger boy and trying to intervene a couple of times, but Antoine had shown no gratitude and Raj had soon decided he was just making things worse.

He glanced at his watch. It was just after half past three. Antoine was late as usual. At ten to four Georgette Pillay came into the room.

"Antoine Beaumont's here, and he has someone with him."

Raj could tell she wasn't impressed.

"Do you know who it is?"

"Antoine didn't bother to introduce him. He sounds South African."

"What's wrong with him?"

Georgette wrinkled her nose. "I don't know. You'll have to decide for yourself."

Raj grinned. "Can you show them in, then bring coffee? I'd rather you did it. I want to keep this as confidential as possible."

"Okay, just this once."

A moment later Antoine strode in, a determined smile on his face. He held out his hand to shake Raj's, then indicated the man with him.

"This is my associate, Pieter Brandt. We're in business together."

Brandt was a stocky man, deeply tanned with crisply curling brown hair and sharp eyes. His smile was wide, and he oozed confidence.

"A pleasure to meet you," he said as he gave Raj a firm handshake. "I'm sure we can do business together."

Raj thought this a little presumptuous. He noticed Antoine flash a nervous look, tinged with resentment, at the other man.

"A nice little place you've got here," Brandt said, looking around. Hands in his pockets, he crossed to the window and glanced out, then turned and came back. "Aren't most of you lawyers based in Port Louis?"

"Quite a few, yes."

"But I suppose, if most of your work is small town stuff, you're better off up here. So, shall we get down to it then?"

Raj had been planning to hold the meeting around the small boardroom table at one end of his office, but now he changed his mind. He'd rather sit at his desk, get it across to this South African that he, Raj, was in charge.

He indicated that they should take a seat in the chairs opposite. "Please sit. My colleague is making coffee." He steepled his fingers below his chin and waited.

"I'm glad you've finally been able to fit us into your busy schedule," Antoine said, then smiled as if it occurred to him that sarcasm wouldn't help. "You're an elusive man, Raj."

"Sorry about that," Raj said coolly. "I've been busy trying to catch up since I got back from the UK. But now you're here, what can I do for you?"

Antoine sat forward in his chair. "How about telling me what's going on for a start. What's happening with the Kendall woman?"

Before Raj could respond, a light knock on the door preceded Georgette with the coffee tray. As she bent to place the tray on the desk, Pieter Brandt leant back in his chair and watched her, running his eyes down her legs and back up with a smirk on his face. Raj had known Georgette all his life and she was like another sister to him. Brandt's behaviour annoyed him intensely.

"Thank you, Georgette," he said. "I'll sort this out."

The icy glance she directed at Brandt showed Raj she was aware of the man's scrutiny. Brandt watched her leave the room, only turning back when she closed the door behind her with a decided snap.

"A very pretty girl," Brandt said.

Raj could happily have punched the man's smooth, tanned face, but instead he ignored the remark and concentrated on pouring coffee and handing out cups. He sat back down and smiled as coolly as he could.

"I've no wish to be rude," he said, turning deliberately to Antoine, "but these matters are confidential."

Antoine waved a dismissive hand. "I've got no secrets from Pieter. He knows all about Papa's will and everything."

"I'm still not entirely comfortable discussing your affairs in front of a stranger. Perhaps you could explain the nature of your business relationship, and then we can go from there. I'm sure you understand," he said, glancing at Brandt.

For a moment Raj thought Antoine was going to protest, but his friend put out a restraining hand and looked at Raj, his eyes calculating. He glanced at Antoine and said, "Shall I?"

"Oh, go ahead," Antoine said sulkily, sitting back in his chair and folding his arms.

"My principals are in the hotel and tourism business," Brandt said. "We're looking for a site to set up an exclusive resort, I'm talking really exclusive here. The clients we would be catering for would be very wealthy and influential: international businessmen, top-flight celebrities, members of various royal families; they'd expect absolute privacy."

It was obvious Pieter Brandt thought Raj should be impressed. He wasn't. Mauritians were used to the world's rich thinking they could buy privacy on the island, whatever their behaviour, but it wasn't a concept he'd ever bought into.

"Antoine says his father's place will be the perfect site, tucked away, slightly off the beaten track, it would definitely fit the bill. You'll understand that we need to get things finalised as soon as possible, so Antoine's inability to give us his hundred per cent support is causing serious problems."

"It's not that I'm not with you all the way. It's Abigail Kendall," Antoine said as he flashed Raj a resentful look, "and Raj here, who're putting barriers in the way."

"I'm aware of that," Pieter said, then turned back to Raj. "With such a fantastic opportunity on your doorstep, you wouldn't want my associates to look elsewhere, would you? To the Maldives or the Seychelles? They've set their heart on Mauritius, and particularly on Belle Etoile, and I'm afraid they're not going to take no for an answer. They're the sort of people who're used to getting their own way." He smiled and added, "Of course, if it took off, it would provide employment for the locals, which has to be a good thing, and we could certainly make it worth your while too. Does that clarify things for you?"

His patronising tone was irritating, and his veiled attempt at bribery, clumsy.

"Well no," Raj said, "it doesn't really. But I'm sure everything will come clear in due course, once I've done some in-depth research." He watched the man's face as he said this. The only reaction was a slight narrowing of his eyes.

There were so many unanswered questions. Why was there such urgency to it all? Why was Antoine scared of his companion? But when he thought back to what Vijay had told him on Saturday evening, that became easier to understand. This man was nothing like Raj had imagined. He'd expected someone smoother, less crude in his arrogance, but perhaps Brandt was just one of the monkeys. God only knew who the organ grinder was. And Antoine may have told Brandt the bare terms of Douglas's will, but had he said anything about his father's wishes? Raj had a shrewd idea that wouldn't have been mentioned.

"And your principals are?"

"They're based in Johannesburg. A reputable, international company, I assure you."

Raj waited for him to fill in the details, but he didn't. He was about to push for more information when Antoine said, "Isn't that good enough for you?" He began to chew at the edge of his thumb as he scowled across at Raj.

"Not really," Raj said.

Much as he would have preferred to deal with Antoine on his own, he decided to give a little ground and see what would come up.

"Ms Kendall hasn't made a decision yet. We met up several times while I was in London, talked about the will, and I told her we would need a decision as soon as possible. She promised to think about it. That's how we left it."

"For Christ's sake," Antoine exclaimed, "is that all you can say?"

"At the moment, yes," Raj said calmly.

"But that's just not good enough."

"Given the terms of your father's will, it's all I can offer. As I've already pointed out, as his executor I have a duty to make sure his wishes are considered."

"How much would it take to buy her out?" Brandt asked.

"I don't think it's a matter of money," Raj said, hoping he was right.

"Then what?" asked Antoine.

"Your father was her godfather. As a child she cared a great deal about him, and about your mother. As you know, Antoine," he said, giving him a direct look, "this is a good deal more complex than a simple inheritance. Quite apart from anything else, there's the potential for heritage status and there are the arts centre plans."

"Are you referring to Douglas Beaumont's romantic scheme to turn the property into some kind of museum?"

It was obvious Brandt thought he'd caught Raj out. Raj ignored the question and looked at Antoine.

"Am I to understand," Raj said, his tone icy, "that you've discussed your father's wishes with your associates?"

Brandt's hands tightened on the arms of his chair, but he gave no other indication he'd noticed the snub.

"Of course, I have." Antoine was on the defensive. "I've been completely up front with them. They agree with me that it's totally impractical and very unlikely to get off the ground."

"What on earth makes you think that? I've done quite a lot of research into its feasibility, and I have several friends who are eager to come on board. Apart from that, Arts and Culture are interested in doing all they can. What's more, Abigail Kendall has expressed her approval of the plans."

Pieter Brandt intervened again. "Perhaps we could make a contribution to this project but locate it elsewhere. I've heard of an extremely desirable site in–"

"I don't think so," Raj interrupted, giving him a chilly smile. "The point of siting it at Belle Etoile is that it was Douglas Beaumont's family home. It seems to me that says it all."

"I would have said it was for me to talk of what my father wanted," Antoine snapped.

"Go ahead," Raj said. "You know it as well as I do. And you know he'd wish for your mother to go on living there for as long as possible. That's no problem for us."

"This is ridiculous," Antoine said, choosing to ignore what Raj had just said. "I'm going to contact Abigail direct. She can't be allowed to stand in our way, after all, she's had no contact since they left, has she?"

"No, but that doesn't make any difference to the terms of the will. Under the law you must get her agreement if you want to sell, and I don't think there's any likelihood she'll make a decision until she's been back to the island."

"Ah! So, she's planning to come?"

"Yes, I believe so," Raj said, very much hoping that he was right. Raj decided to hand Antoine a lifeline. "Let me sound her out again and I'll get back to you."

It was Pieter Brandt who responded. "Is that all you're willing to do?"

"At the moment, yes. And I must repeat," Raj said, and once again he addressed his remarks to Antoine, "as your father's executor it's my duty to do my best to see Belle Etoile turned into the educational resource centre he wished it to become. Quite apart from that, I want this to happen, Antoine. It'd be the best use of the property and it'd be good for the island."

Brandt was no longer trying to conceal his contempt. The gloves were off.

"It's obvious that working in this small, rather backward community, you're not used to the ways of international business. That's a pity. I think you'll find you're making a big mistake." Abruptly he rose. "Antoine here is learning fast. I'd listen to him if I were you. Come on, we've done all we can," he said to Antoine.

It was obvious to Raj that Antoine was torn. He glanced nervously between the two of them then pushed himself up from his chair. As they got to the door Brandt turned back to Raj.

"I'm sure I can speak for Antoine when I say we're not going to give up on our plans. Understand that we expect movement on this, and soon."

Raj thought it sounded very much like a threat directed at them both.

"I understand you very well, Brandt," he said, not bothering to keep the contempt out of his voice. "I shall be keeping in contact with Antoine. Good day."

Immediately after they left, Georgette appeared in the doorway. The look on her face spoke volumes. Raj grinned at her. "You obviously weren't very impressed with Antoine's friend?"

"Why on earth is Antoine involved with such a man?" she exclaimed. "I was very tempted to pour coffee all over his head."

"I'm very glad you didn't," Raj said, laughing. "I think he's the type who'd sue."

"Why on earth is Antoine involved with such a man?"

"I don't know," Raj said, serious now. "There's obviously the money, but I'm not sure what direction it's going in, to or from Antoine. Brandt was very cagey about his principals, as he called them. I didn't really press him hard enough on that."

As she loaded the coffee cups on to a tray she said, sounding worried, "Do you think Antoine's out of his depth?"

"Probably. Would you mind if he was?"

"Not directly, but I was fond of Monsieur Beaumont, and so was *Grandmère*. She certainly wouldn't want Madame Beaumont to be hurt by Antoine's activities."

"That's one of the things that worries me too," Raj said.

*  *  *

It wasn't the last Raj saw of Antoine that day. Leaving his office a few minutes later, he was stopped by a hand grabbing his shoulder as he came out on to the busy pavement. It was Antoine.

"Can I have a word?"

"Fine, if you want to walk with me to my car. Where's your South African friend?"

"He had a meeting."

Antoine seemed unsure of how to say what was on his mind. Raj waited patiently for him to go on as they wove their way through the crowds and across the road, Antoine with his head down and hands thrust into his pockets. Raj had to grab his arm to stop him walking out in front of a brightly painted, over-loaded bus. Still without speaking, they made their way past the imposing entrance of the church of St. Thérèse, with its high steeple above.

As they did so Antoine suddenly burst out, "I need a decision on this, Raj."

"You made that quite clear."

"It's ridiculous to think that hare-brained scheme of Papa's could ever work."

"Nonsense. Like I said, I've got great hopes for it."

"But it's just not going to happen," Antoine insisted.

"Why not?"

"Because I've given… assurances."

"What assurances?"

"That's confidential."

Exasperated, Raj stopped. Antoine did too, glancing sideways at him then away again.

"Look, you said you wanted a word, I'm listening," Raj said, exasperated. "If you're not going to be up front with me about your dealings with these people, I can't help you. I've explained what the situation is with Abigail Kendall. I've tried to make it clear what I feel I can and can't do as your father's executor. I'd also like you to know I don't take kindly to being threatened, and you can pass that on to your unpleasant friend. As far as I'm concerned, there's not really any more to be said."

"You don't understand!" Antoine snarled at him.

"No, I don't. Explain it to me."

For a moment, standing there in the middle of the noise, dust and traffic fumes, Raj thought Antoine was going to tell him what was on his mind. But the moment passed. With a muttered curse, Antoine turned and strode away through the crowds. Raj was about to go after him, but what was the point? He wondered if he should contact Abi and tell her about his worries. No, better not. He'd wait and see if he got a response to the e-mail and the photos. But he hoped she'd make a decision soon.

As he watched Antoine disappear out of sight, Raj felt more worried than he had at any time since Douglas had died.

# CHAPTER 16

"Bloody hell, not again!" Abi exclaimed at sight of the enormous cellophane wrapped bunch of flowers.

Lawrence, who had turned to see the cause of the exclamation, saw Mina in the doorway, her face wiped clean of any smile. He turned back to Abi.

"What's the problem?" he asked. "Flowers are good, aren't they?"

"Not in this case," Abi muttered.

"Well, what do you want me to do with them?" Mina asked peevishly. "I certainly wouldn't complain if my boyfriend kept sending me lovely bouquets."

"He's not my boyfriend!" Abi shouted, jumping up so suddenly that her chair crashed back.

Lawrence took charge. He limped over to Mina and took the flowers from her, then shooed her out the door. He came back across the room, placed the bouquet on Abi's desk, took the card from its depths and handed it to her.

"I should check who the sender is if I were you," he said reasonably.

"You can open it. I already know. They're from Justin." Abi sat back down and dropped her head into her hands. "Go ahead. Take a look."

Lawrence did as she suggested and read out what was on the card. "'Don't do this to me. I'll get you back in the end'. What's going on, Abi? You told me the two of you had split up, and I must say I was pleased to hear it. Is he pestering you?"

"You could say that."

"Come on, love, tell me about it."

Abi looked at her friend. She'd been longing to have someone to confide in. She poured it all out, finishing up with what Sarah had told her about her interview with Justin.

"And then," Abi finished wearily, "I had his bloody sister on the phone last night telling me he was going to kill himself."

"Not him."

"What?"

"Definitely not his style, I'd say."

"Do you really think so?"

"Yes," Lawrence said decisively. "My poor girl. You've had a hell of a time, and you've had to cope with me being off work as well. Talk about lousy timing. I'll definitely have to come back sooner rather than later."

Abi could feel tears threatening. "No way. Work's fine, it's kept me sane. It's stupid to be so undermined by it all. I wish I could just ignore him."

"That's not the way it goes, though. This kind of harassment would get anyone down. Do remember, love, it's him choosing to behave like an arse, you haven't made him."

"That's what Sarah Broderick said, but still—"

Lawrence interrupted her again. "There's no 'but still'. She's right. Do not start blaming yourself, understand?"

"In theory I know you're right, but emotionally – it's so hard to accept the Justin I thought I loved is the same man that's doing all these ridiculous things."

"I think ridiculous is far too kind a word to use."

"Perhaps."

"You need to get right away from it all," Lawrence said. "When did you last take a holiday?"

She couldn't remember. There'd been the odd couple of days here and there, a long weekend in Guernsey for a friend's wedding, a short break in Amsterdam with Charlie, Beth and the boys.

"Not for quite a while I suppose. But I'm not a great one for long trips away. And I'm not that keen on being on my own. Still, once you get back and things are running smoothly again, I might think about it."

"You do that," Lawrence said. Abi's eyes met his. She knew that look. He was up to something.

"What have you got in mind?" she asked, suspicious now.

"Oh, nothing in particular. Ah, here's Sue," he said as they both heard voices in the outer office.

Lawrence's wife pushed open the door, all bustle, and bright, smiling eyes. "Hi Abi, is he being a nuisance?"

"Not at all."

"There's no way to keep him away from work completely. If you hadn't been sending him regular e-mails, he'd have been fit to be tied. But I'm going to carry him off now. I'm parked on a yellow line, Lawrie."

Lawrence gave Abi a hug, urged her to phone at any time if she wanted to talk, and assured her he'd be back at work early the following week. Abi felt much better for having talked to him and arrived home that evening feeling better than she had in days.

But it didn't last. That night she had the dream again, the beach, the woman, the wind and the sea, and the terror, all the same.

*January 1990*

Drinks parties. Hilary had always hated them. The brash noise of empty chatter and laughter getting louder and louder as they knocked back their wine, beer and gin. Women in bright dresses or saris, jewellery glittering. Men sweating in lounge suits and ties, so unsuitable in the heat of a Mauritian evening. And Carl watching her, hawk eyed.

She stood in the doorway, looking across the crowded sitting room at her daughter. Abi was passing round spicy *gateaux piment*, cheese straws, curried chicken pastries and tuna tarts. She smiled inwardly at her daughter's scowling face. How she hated doing this. Hilary agreed with Abi's protest that Charlie should have to pass round canapés too, but Carl said it wasn't a boy's job. She'd known that if she'd spoken up for Abi, it would have made things worse, so she'd bitten her tongue.

Someone came up behind her. A soft hand brushed her arm. "My Goddaughter is growing into a beautiful woman," Douglas said softly.

"Isn't she, even when she's in such a foul mood."

"Not her favourite job?"

"Definitely not," Hilary said, "but Carl insisted."

"Aah." The one syllable spoke volumes. He changed the subject. "I should warn you that Tony is bringing his son with him."

Hilary drew in a sharp breath and tensed at the name.

"The boy is staying for a couple of weeks," Douglas went on, "while the Durban schools are on holiday."

She glanced up at him and then away. "Why on earth did Carl invite Tony?" she whispered.

"To test you."

"You think he knows?" There was panic in her voice.

"No, no," he reassured her. "But he's always expecting you to abscond with any handsome bloke that comes within a mile of you. As far as he's concerned, Tony's just another of those."

"I suppose. I just hope Carl behaves. I wouldn't want the boy upset."

"He's pretty self-possessed for a fifteen-year-old. I think he'll be okay."

They'd been so absorbed that neither of them had noticed Carl pushing his way through the crowds towards them.

He ignored Douglas and gripped his wife's arm. "For God's sake woman, circulate. You're the hostess. This do is your responsibility."

Hilary knew it would be pointless to remind him the party had been his idea and that most of the guests were his friends or acquaintances, people he wanted to impress or do business with. Carl glared over her shoulder at her cousin.

"Please don't keep her talking, Douglas. She's got a job to do."

Douglas held his hands up in mock submission. He didn't want to rock the boat as it would only make things worse for Hilary.

"Far be it from me to keep her from doing your work for you," he said, his eyes full of contempt. Carl's eyes slid away, but he didn't respond.

"Off you go, sweetheart," Douglas said, smiling warmly at her. "You look gorgeous, by the way, very elegant."

Hilary smoothed down the soft grey-blue of her dress, such a contrast to the bright satins and taffetas around her. She was grateful for his praise.

With a smile here, a few words there, she made her way through the crowded room, only half her mind on what she was doing. The other half was wondering when Tony would arrive. What would his son be like? Would he like her? She knew very little other than that Tony and his wife were divorced, and the boy lived with his mother in Durban, but Tony had always given the impression they were on good terms. It was so important the children should get on well. Her heart began beating harder at the thought of them meeting up.

About ten minutes later she was standing pretending to listen to a boring colleague of Carl's who was complaining about the problems of getting the machinery at the factory serviced to the standard he required.

"Trouble is these Mauritian engineers have no pride in their work. Just isn't the same since independence."

Hilary thought what a fool the man was, with his tight collar and sweating face, flushed as much by the numerous beers he'd consumed as by the heat. She glanced round, worried that his tactless booming would offend somebody, and it was as she did so that she caught sight of Tony coming into the room. Her heart gave a joyful leap at the sight of him, tall and broad shouldered, his dark hair swept back from his forehead. Beside him was a slim teenager, dark as his father and nearly as tall.

"Excuse me," she said to Carl's red-faced colleague, "I must go and greet a new arrival." She made her way across the room as quickly as she could. "Good evening," she said formally, but she knew her cheeks were flushed, and she could feel her hands trembling. "I'm so glad you could make it. And this must be your son?"

Tony showed no sign that the formality was unusual, but when he shook hands her body reacted immediately to the warmth of his hand.

"Hallo Hilary. Sorry we're a bit late. Yes, this is David." He put a hand on the boy's shoulder. "This is Mrs Kendall, I've told you all about her."

Hilary felt a lurch of apprehension. What had he said? But Tony gave her a reassuring smile, and David said, "Hallo," in a perfectly normal voice, but his blue eyes, so like his father's, studied her closely.

She gave him a hesitant smile. "Let me introduce you to my daughter. She's busy passing food round. I'm sure she'll be delighted to have an excuse to stop." She led them across to Abi. "Abi darling, this is David Chandler, he's on holiday with his father. Why don't the two of you go off and find Charlie?"

"Can I stop doing this then?" She jiggled the platter in her hand, nearly tipping the few remaining pastries on to the floor.

"Of course," Hilary said. "Off you go." And taking the dish from Abi, she watched the two children make their way through the crowds. So far, so good.

"Do you remember David Chandler?" Charlie asked Abi the following evening.

The name gave Abi a jolt. The phone, wedged between her hunched shoulder and her ear, nearly slipped out of her grasp. She stopped tapping away at her laptop and put her hand up to catch the handset.

"Yes, I do. Hard to forget him."

"Of course, you had a hell of a crush on him, didn't you?"

That wasn't exactly what Abi had meant.

"I did. At thirteen that sort of thing is rather intense. Why do you ask about him?"

"I came across his name last week, I read an article of his. He lectures at Wits University in Johannesburg and he was writing about some Bushmen flints they've found somewhere in the Cape, fascinating stuff."

"How do you know it's the same person?"

"There was a biographical blurb and it said something about his father, that he'd worked in Mauritius. It didn't say anything about Tony's death, though, which I thought was a bit odd."

"Maybe David didn't want that raked up."

"Perhaps," Charlie said.

Abi clicked on the website address she'd been searching for and a flight timetable came up with a selection of special offers. She continued to tap away, searching for the best deal she could get and wishing that Charlie would change the subject. What was the point of all this? A moment later she found out.

"If you do go to Johannesburg you could look him up," Charlie said.

"Oh no. I'll only be there for a couple of days, time to have a look at the site for the school in Soweto, then back home."

"Go on, Abi, we knew him pretty well, and it might help."

"What on earth do you mean?"

"Sort of like easing you into it. Meet up with him in Jo'burg, he's connected to Mauritius but not part of it now, and then you go on. A bit like a slow reintroduction of a food you used to be allergic to."

"You do have the most extraordinary ideas," Abi said, laughing in spite of herself.

"Come on Abi–"

"Charlie! Leave it, will you?"

To Abi's relief he changed the subject. "When are you actually going?"

"Not sure yet. Depends when I can get a reasonably priced flight. Anyway, I must get on, love," Abi said, not wanting to return to talk of the Chandlers, son or father.

"See you on Saturday."

"I can't wait," said Abi, wishing that she could skip work and go to Cambridge that evening, but no chance. As it was, she was going to be hard put to get everything done and avoid working at the weekend.

But when she put the phone down, she didn't go back to her laptop immediately. Instead she slid it on to the coffee table and sat back, her hands clasped behind her head. For quite some time she stayed like that, thinking about what Charlie had said. David Chandler. She could visualise him clearly, brown curly hair, thin and angular. She had adored him, and when he'd returned to Durban they'd kept in touch for a while, until her father had intercepted one of his letters. An instinctive urge to escape from the rest of that memory had her jumping up.

Abi had received several more e-mails and texts from Justin, and reluctantly she'd saved them all, as Sarah had instructed. With Maisie's co-operation she'd continued to leave for work through the back alley, but she hated having to disturb her neighbour, and she didn't think it'd be long before Justin worked out what she was doing.

The feeling of being hunted, and the fear of Justin turning up at the office and making a scene, was beginning to wear her down. She hadn't slept properly for ages and felt desperately tired. Then Lawrence had dropped into the office on Friday afternoon and suggested a way out. How about a visit to Soweto to talk to the charity in charge of the school project? He'd be back in the office on Monday, they could have a few days of catching up together, and then she could get going. The thought of being out of Justin's reach for a while was irresistible.

# CHAPTER 17

"I need to know more about him before I go back to the arts group," Raj said. It was late Thursday afternoon, and he was standing in the door to his office, leaning against the jamb as he watched Georgette check the computers before turning them off.

"For a start," he went on, ticking the points off on his fingers, "I need to know exactly who he's working for, how much influence he has over Antoine, and hopefully, something against him. Antoine isn't going to tell me, so I have to find out some other way."

"You could always ask Hari Persand," Georgette suggested.

"Why him particularly?"

"I know his wife, Deepti, and when I saw her a couple of days ago, she was boasting about his promotion to Chief Inspector. What's more, he's gone from immigration to fraud and both those departments might have something on Brandt."

"I've always found it difficult to think of Hari as a police officer. He was in my year at school, I remember him being terminally lazy."

"His father was in the police force," Georgette said drily.

Raj smiled. "That could explain it." Then he frowned. "But I'll have to be careful how I approach it. If I phone him out of the blue and ask a direct question he's bound to go on about confidentiality, privileged information, all that. He's so bloody pompous, and he's not yet forgiven me for winning that case against the Immigration Department last year."

"Isn't he a member of the Kestrel Country Club?"

"What's that got to do with it?"

"Well, you are too."

"I know, but I hardly ever go there. All I did was inherit Papa's membership."

"Still, you do use it occasionally for meeting clients. Can't you just go along and, sort of, bump into him? Deepti's always complaining he spends far too much time in their bar, goes in nearly every evening before going home for dinner."

Raj grinned. "Is there anything you don't know?"

"Not much," she said. "Go on, do it now. The club is on your way home."

Raj straightened, decision made. "I will. Thanks Georgette. Oh, and have you had the time to get those papers of Papa's out of the archive cupboard? I might have time to go through them this weekend."

"Sorry, Raj, I haven't. I'll try to get around to it tomorrow, but it's more likely to be Monday."

"No problem. It's not urgent." As soon as he'd said it he wondered if that was true, but he didn't want to nag her.

Half an hour later Raj stood in the doorway of the bar at the Kestrel searching round for the short, rounded figure of Hari Persand. Georgette had been right. There he was, a beer gripped in his fist as he held forth to two other members. As he came up to them the other two men took the opportunity to escape.

"Raj! *Qui manierre?*" He gave Raj a thump on the back.

"*Bien, bien.* I'm fine," Raj said, feeling a fraud, but needs must.

"Long time since I've seen you. Still fighting to let in all those undesirables?"

"I only fight for the ones with a legitimate claim," Raj said stiffly, then pulled himself up, now he was the one sounding pompous. "Congratulations on your promotion, and a new department, impressive."

Hari preened a little. "No peace for the wicked, or rather, the wicked give me no peace." His braying laugh echoed round the room. "So, what have you been up to since that case last year?"

"There's plenty of work around, mostly on the civil side. I see some of our old school mates occasionally, in and out of court."

"More out I hope." Hari's eyes were alight with curiosity.

Raj smiled. "Absolutely, for instance I met up with Antoine Beaumont a couple of days ago, seems to be doing well for himself."

"I heard his father had died. Not one of my favourite teachers, all that art and poetry. What's Antoine doing these days?"

This was just the direction he wanted the conversation to take. "He doesn't seem to be following in his father's footsteps. He's more into property and finance."

"I suppose he inherited the estate – Belle Etoile, is it? What's he going to do with it?"

Should he mention he was Douglas's executor? Maybe not.

"I'm not entirely sure." That was true enough. "His mother still lives there, and it's early days yet."

"It's not an idle question," Hari said and gave Raj a sharp, considering look. "Look, it's a bit of a coincidence, your mentioning Antoine Beaumont. We're keeping an eye on this South African chap, had him in for an informal chat a few days ago, and he mentioned Antoine as his local contact."

Raj could not believe his luck. He kept his face expressionless. "Can you tell me his name?"

"I shouldn't." For a moment he chewed at his lip, studying Raj's face out of the corner of his eye, then he grinned. "But we Royal Collegians must look after each other, eh?" He gave Raj another thump on the shoulder, then his voice dropped. "His name's Pieter Brandt, very smooth operator, part of a consortium called Leisure & Property International. They're very keen to set up locally. They seem legit, but we've found out they've got connections with a syndicate the European authorities are interested in. I've got a request for information out. It doesn't look good."

"Not the Chinese then?" Raj said.

Hari was dismissive. "This is nothing to do with them. The company seems to have a presence in Dubai. If you're any friend of Antoine's I'd tip him the wink, tell him not to have anything to do with them. Do you remember those two chaps who were beaten up at the Mango Night Club? One of them's still in a coma."

Raj nodded. He'd heard of the case, and he knew no one had been arrested yet.

"And the Triolet murder?"

"Wasn't that some local feud or other?"

"That's what we gave to the press, but no, both cases seem to have a connection, albeit loose, to this consortium Antoine's involved with. The trouble is it's all hearsay, we haven't been able to prove a thing." He gulped down the last of his beer. "I must say no more. Said too much already."

Damn, Raj thought.

"Just warn Antoine, okay?" Hari urged.

"I will, and I'll do it tactfully, without involving you."

"You'd better," Hari said firmly.

"No problem. Look, can you keep me posted? Nothing sensitive, but anything you feel you can pass on."

Hari gave him a considering look. "I don't remember you being that close to Antoine in the past."

"Family," Raj said, knowing this would carry weight. "His father and mine were like brothers, it's like he's a cousin."

"That explains it." Hari shook Raj's hand and gave him a considering look. "You owe me, my friend."

Raj nodded but said nothing.

"I really must be going, or the wife will be complaining again," Hari said. "*Salam.*" He lifted a hand in farewell and left.

Raj stayed on long enough to finish his drink. That had produced a good deal more than he'd hoped for. Knowing the name of Pieter Brandt's company was useful and he'd re-established contact with Hari, which could also prove useful, so long as he could avoid pay-back time. Well done, Georgette, she deserved a bonus!

* * *

Abi managed to relax a little over the weekend. She didn't mention Justin, and Charlie and Beth tactfully kept off the subject. On Saturday morning she and Beth went to the market, and on Sunday Abi and the boys went for a walk along the Cam. They stopped for a drink at a pub near the Mathematical Bridge and settled in seats overlooking the river. As Abi took a sip at her gin and tonic, she caught a moment of silent communication between the twins, a raised eyebrow from Matt, a nod from Pip.

"What are you two plotting?" she asked.

"Not plotting exactly," Matt said. He'd always been the more forthcoming of the two. "Just wondering about something."

"Anything I can help with?"

"Sort of," Pip said. "You ask her," he told his twin.

"No, you."

"Come on fellas," Abi wondered what on earth was coming. "Spit it out?"

"What with you and Dad talking about Mauritius lately…" Matt said.

"He told us about that Mauritian lawyer bloke," Pip added. "And the house and stuff."

"We were thinking, we know Mum's side of the family, what with Gogo and Gramps living in Bury St Edmunds. They've told us all about South Africa–"

"How they had to get out quick in the sixties–"

"And everything, but we don't know anything really about yours and Dad's parents."

"Dad doesn't really talk about them much–"

"And sort of changes the subject when we ask–"

"So, we thought we'd ask you," Pip finished in a rush.

They both gulped down some of their beer and waited, their almost identical faces watching Abi expectantly.

"Oh guys," Abi sighed, wondering what on earth to say. She wasn't any more keen to talk about their parents than Charlie was, but she felt she had to give the twins some kind of answer. "I'm a bit like your Dad, I don't really enjoy talking about our father. There's no getting away from it, he was a cold-hearted bully. I think he resented the fact I was a girl, wanted his eldest child to be a son, you know, the son and heir." Abi could hear the bitterness in her own voice and smiled to try and hide it. "Carl and I did not get on, and your Dad wasn't nearly macho enough for him."

"Dad usually calls him Carl too," Matt said. "Why is that?"

Abi looked at her two nephews and decided honesty was best. "Maybe," she said quietly, "because we'd rather he hadn't been our father."

"Jesus!" the twins said in unison.

"But Mummy," Abi went on, smiling a little, "she was very different: beautiful, kind, but not strong, very much under his control. The only thing he'd let her do without his supervision was what he called her dabbling in good works. I think she needed it to get her out of the house, because he wouldn't let her get a paid job. She used to be involved with a couple of schools, helping kids with their reading and things like that. Children always responded well to her. Maybe it's because of her I've always worked for NGOs and charities, trying to be more like her." Abi gazed out at the willows bending low over the water and the punters pushing up and down, but she saw none of it. "And then she died."

"How?" Pip asked.

"That's one of the things Dad doesn't want to talk about," Matt said.

Abi couldn't bring herself to talk of suicide. "It was an accident. She fell from a cliff. We stayed on in Mauritius for another year, but then Carl lost his job at the sugar mill and, after that, he decided to drag us all back to England."

Both boys, eyes wide, were drinking in all this information, but it was just a story to them. Abi glanced at her watch then drained her glass. She didn't want to think about the past anymore.

"Come on, lads," she said, pushing aside the memories. "Let's get going, or we'll be late for lunch."

As they left the pub, Pip put an arm round her. "I hope all our questions didn't upset you."

"Course not, sweetheart," she lied. "One of these days I'll tell you both the whole story." But not now, she thought.

* * *

As Abi got back to her flat late on Sunday, she could feel herself tensing up. How many of Justin's damn messages would there be on her answerphone? Thank goodness she no longer had to worry about her mobile, and she hadn't looked at her e-mails since early on Friday. Best do that now. She sighed in relief when she saw there was nothing from Justin, then smiled as she saw that there was one from Raj:

> *Hi Abi,*
> *I'm glad you liked the photos. Narinda tells me she has a few others you might be interested in. I'll try to get hold of them next time I see her.*
> *I had a meeting with Antoine and one of his associates on Monday. I can't say I took to the man so I'm doing some checking on his background. Antoine seems to be getting a bit desperate, keeps asking if you've made a decision yet. I don't want to push you, but I do need to be able to give him an answer, even if it's just a holding exercise. Can you get back to me as soon as possible?*
> *All the best,*
> *Raj.*

She was no longer smiling. She knew it was a perfectly reasonable request, but she still felt hounded.

On Monday morning the whole office was in a positive mood, ready to welcome Lawrence back, but by the end of the day Abi wasn't quite so pleased to see him.

"Oh no, Lawrie! I really don't want to do that!"

"Why not? Look Abi, it'd be much more economical to book flights to Mauritius from Johannesburg, rather than coming back to the UK and then having to go back again from London."

"Have you been talking to my brother?"

Lawrence frowned. Abi was sure there was a smile hidden behind it.

"This way you can wrap up both projects in one trip," he said.

"But I haven't agreed to going to Mauritius at all. Why don't you go? You're suggesting I should wrap it all up into a work and holiday package. You could do the same."

"I've just been off for three weeks."

"That was sick leave."

"Why do I feel this is such an up-hill struggle?"

Abi rubbed her hands over her eyes and then looked at her boss. He looked back with a quizzical lift of his brows above his half-moon glasses.

"You told me a bit about it when I was in the office the other day," Lawrence said, his voice gentle. "Don't you think it'd be a good idea to go back and lay the ghosts? Quite apart from that, what about your local knowledge?"

Abi opened her mouth to protest, but Lawrence held up a hand. "Hear me out. I know the island will have changed, but you speak the language, and that could be very useful. Deep down I don't think you'll have lost the feeling of a place, the dos and don'ts. Come on, Abi. At least think about it."

It was late in the afternoon after a busy day of catching up, and Abi was feeling bone tired. She really didn't want to have this conversation, but nor did she want him to feel she was being obstructive.

"Okay. I will."

"Great. I've read through the draft proposal that Amrakash sent. It looks good. This project is right up our street, and I don't say that because you have a personal involvement. To be honest, it made me pick it to pieces even more than I would normally do." Lawrence pushed himself up from his chair. "Sue will be here to fetch me soon. Poor love has been ferrying me back and forth without a word of complaint, but I'm sure it's getting her down."

Abi was relieved by the change of subject. She was about to apologise for being obstructive when there was the sound of raised voices in the outer office.

They heard Evelyn say, "I'm sorry but she's busy." Rangi's deep voice rumbled, "Like Evelyn said, you'll have to wait." And then there was a high-pitched squeal from Mina.

"What on earth is going on out there?" Lawrence said as the door crashed open.

Justin stood there, Evelyn, Rangi and Mina crowding up behind him. He was breathing hard, as if he'd been running. His face was flushed, and his shaven head gleamed with sweat. For a moment nobody said anything, then Justin turned and slammed the door shut.

"If the mountain won't come to Moham— Mohammed," he said, his words slurred. He was staring at Abi in an owlish way as if finding it hard to focus, "Then Mohammed—"

He got no further. "How dare you barge your way in here?" Abi's voice shook so much she could barely articulate the words. "Get out!"

"Oh no," Justin said. He walked over and sat down heavily in one of the chairs, pushed his hands into his pockets and leant back, his legs thrust out in front of him. "'lo Lawrence," he said. "Sorry to barge in, but Abi's being really shtubborn, so I decided to come and check on her. You don't mind, do you?" He grinned and hiccupped.

"I do actually," Lawrence's voice was icy. "And it's pretty obvious she doesn't want you here, so please go."

"Your leg's still not right yet, I see," Justin said, eyeing the walking stick that Lawrence was leaning on. "Shouldn't be back at work, should you? I don't think it'd be senshible for you to try to throw me out. No, no, no." He waggled a finger back and forth in front of his face like a metronome. "I'm going to talk to Abi whether you like it or not."

Abi's heart was beating so hard she thought it would suffocate her.

"If you don't go, I'm going to call the police. I have before, remember?"

"Do as she says, Justin." Lawrence was firm and quiet.

With shocking suddenness Justin sprung up and thrust the chair back.

"Don't you fucking order me around, you, stupid cripple," Justin shouted, swaying slightly. "Is she screwing you as well as her precious Mauritian? A slag, that's what she is, a fucking slag."

"Enough!" Lawrence roared. Abi was stunned. She had never heard him raise his voice to anyone before. He made his way swiftly to the door, in spite of his bad leg, and pulled it open. "Rangi, Darren," he said as he jerked his head at Justin, "do me a favour, get rid of this drunken prat."

Rangi and Darren stepped forward with obvious enthusiasm. Looking much less sure of himself, Justin began to back away. "Don't you dare touch me!"

"Come on." Rangi's deep voice was calm. "Let's not make this difficult."

"Get away from me! I'll sue if you touch me!"

"Okay, Darren," Rangi said, sounding resigned, "you take the left arm, I'll take the right."

Backed up against the wall, Justin hadn't a chance against the two men, one a rugby player, the other a judo enthusiast. It was soon over. They frog-marched him from the office, ignoring his cursing and shouting all the way. A moment later Abi heard the front door slam, then Rangi and Darren came back, both grinning.

"I don't think he'll be back in a hurry," Darren said, brushing his hands together.

Abi managed to thank them, but she couldn't return their smiles. She was trembling all over and her legs would no longer support her. Feeling sick with humiliation she sank into a chair, put her head in her hands and felt tears fill her eyes. Somewhere in the background she heard Lawrence ask Evelyn to bring some tea, then the door closed, and his limping footsteps came back across the room. His warm hand patted her on the shoulder.

"I'm sorry. I'm so sorry," Abi muttered.

"I don't know what you're apologising for." Lawrence subsided into his chair. "It's not your fault."

Abi rummaged in her bag for a tissue and blew her nose as Evelyn came back into the room carrying a tray with three mugs of tea on it. She put it down on the desk and handed them out.

"You tell her, Lawrie. The poor girl's been putting up with that jerk for months and it's only now she's told us about it."

"Evi, there's nothing you could have done," Abi protested.

"At least I could have supported you."

"You've always been there for me, love. I know that."

Abi wrapped her hands round the mug, sipped and found the tea comforting. Looking at her two friends, she gave them a wan smile. "What am I going to do?"

"First thing, I'd say, is to report this to your neighbour's granddaughter," Evi said. "She's a police officer, Lawrie. We'll all back you up. Have you got her phone number on you?"

"Oh no, Evi–"

"Why not, Abi," Lawrence asked. "I don't think you can let it go. If you don't tell her what's been happening, she can't help you. I suppose we should have kept him here until the police arrived, although I'm not sure how we could have done that, short of tying him up."

Abi gave a slightly hysterical giggle. "I'd like to have seen that."

"You see, I said the tea would do you good," Evelyn said. "If you press charges and we all agree to be witnesses, he'll be in serious trouble. It might just do the trick."

Sue arrived at that moment, so Abi was spared any further discussion. Lawrence gave his wife a brief account of what had happened, and she insisted they give Abi a lift back to her flat.

As they drew up, Lawrence turned in his seat. "You will phone the police, won't you?"

"Yes, I will," Abi promised. "But it doesn't mean he'll leave me alone. I've done some research on the net. Some people keep this kind of thing going for years, police or no police. What do I do then?" She hated the defeatist note in her voice but couldn't help herself.

Unexpectedly Lawrence grinned at her. "I think you're going to make that trip, first Soweto then Mauritius. He's not going to follow you there, is he? How about it?"

# CHAPTER 18

Abi sat curled up on her sofa and dialled her brother's number. "I'm going, Charlie," she said without preamble when he picked up.

"Going where?"

"To Jo'burg, then Mauritius."

There was silence for a moment, then he asked carefully, "How come you've changed your mind?"

Wearily, she told him what had happened at the office.

"Well, I'm glad you have decided to go." There was a pause and then Charlie said, "Abi, there's something I've been meaning to tell you. About Uncle Douglas and Nanny V. I think they did go on writing."

"What do you mean?"

"I would have talked to you about it ages ago, but what with your reluctance to talk about the past, and then the Justin business, it went right out of my mind."

"Charlie, you're worrying me. Get to the point."

Slowly he began to tell her about hiding in the larder at Cousin Rose's and the conversation he'd overheard.

"Carl told her to destroy anything from Mauritius. It would explain why the letters suddenly stopped."

Abi truly wanted to believe him, but she'd spent so many years telling herself they'd been deserted, by their mother then by Uncle Douglas and Nanny V, that it was difficult to imagine anything else.

"Look, I'm not making this up," Charlie insisted. "Think about it. It may help."

"Yes, love, but it makes no difference. At the moment I'm just shit scared," Abi said, her voice shaking a little. "God I'm such a wimp."

"You do talk a load of crap at times."

"Thank you, brother dear." She smiled, but the smile soon faded. "I can't really believe I'm going. Lawrie says to stay on for a bit of a holiday, but I don't think so. I'll just check things out and come back. I feel as if I'm running away because of Justin."

"Oh, for goodness sake, Abi," he said, then his voice softened. "I do understand, but what I think is that you're dealing with the situation in the best way possible and doing your job at the same time. I think it could really turn things around for you."

"I wish you were coming too."

"Perhaps we'll all go one of these days. How about it?"

"Sounds good," Abi said with very little enthusiasm. All she could think of was the churning apprehension in her stomach and a strong desire to behave like a small animal in winter, batten down the hatches and hibernate.

* * *

Abi had e-mailed Raj to let him know that she would be coming to Mauritius the week after, but hadn't given him a day or a flight number. Would that be Monday, Tuesday? Raj wondered. She'd ended with a casual "I'll see you then", and that was it. He'd sent one back asking for details, but there'd been no reply, and he hadn't got time now to send another e-mail. He had to be in court in a matter of minutes. He was halfway out of the office when Georgette called him back.

"Don't forget you've got that do at the Vythelingums's later on."

"Damn. I had forgotten. What time?"

"Six."

"I'll go straight from court."

Raj hated these gatherings, the small talk and gossip, the constant questions from sharp-eyed inquisitive people he hardly knew. What's more, Antoine would almost certainly be there. But the host and hostess were cousins of Parmita's, and clients as well, so he knew he couldn't duck out of it.

At ten past six he made his way through the Vythelingums's jungle-like hallway. He'd never seen so many pot plants in such a small space. He was greeted like a long lost relative by his host and questioned in detail by his hostess about his private life, criticised playfully for not having married again, and told not to worry, she would soon find him a nice wife. As he made his way through the crowded, noisy room, he smiled at a couple of people he knew, lifted a hand to another, but all the time he was keeping an eye out for Antoine, keen to avoid him.

After three quarters of an hour Raj thought it might be possible to leave without causing offence. The crush and the noise level had increased, and Raj couldn't wait for the quiet of his flat and some mindless television to watch. Having said as quick a goodbye as possible to his hostess, Raj was making his way to the front door when, in a room to his right, he heard someone mention his name. He froze, then made his way as quietly as he could to stand by the half open door.

"It's as well for you I had to be away for a few days." He recognised the South African accent. "Now I want some answers. What about that arrogant bastard, Amrakash?”

It takes one to know one, thought Raj grimly.

“I haven’t seen him.” This was Antoine, his tone tinged with fear. “He’s avoiding me. I’m going down to see my mother tomorrow evening. I’ll talk to her. Raj will probably listen to her more than me.”

“I thought you said the old bat was out of it.”

“It comes and goes. And don’t talk about my mother like that.”

“I’ll talk about your mother any way I like. Maybe I should come and have a word with her too.” Brandt sounded as if he was smiling.

“No!” Antoine protested, fear much nearer the surface now.

“Why not? I’m very good with the ladies, know just how to persuade them to do what I want.”

“Pieter, you must leave this to me.”

“And where the hell does that get me?” Brandt snapped. “My friends are getting seriously impatient and, believe me, you really don’t want that.”

“I’ll do what I can with my mother tomorrow.”

“But just to make sure, I’ll be there too. You needn’t worry, I’m not about to start beating up old ladies, not yet at any rate. What time are you going?”

“That’s none of your business.” It was a last bid for escape, a fish wriggling on the end of a hook of his own making.

“Listen to me, Antoine, if we don’t get some movement on this very soon, you’ll really have to start worrying, about yourself as well as your old mother.”

Raj stiffened. He should intervene. But he wanted to hear more. He desperately needed to know when Antoine was going to be at Belle Etoile.

“So, what time?”

“Half past six.” There was a world of defeat in Antoine’s voice.

Raj heard footsteps coming towards the door of the room. He ducked behind one of the enormous palms and flattened himself against the wall. All this cloak and dagger stuff felt ridiculous. Any minute now the dancing girls in multicoloured saris would appear from behind the foliage. But this was no Bollywood movie.

He had a glimpse of Antoine's back as he made his way quickly across the hall and out the front door. Raj waited, giving him time to drive off, but then he heard Brandt's voice again speaking into a mobile phone. Raj crept closer.

"… down there to suss out the mother tomorrow, but I want you to go ahead. He's on his way home now." Raj heard Brandt giving Antoine's address. "Just give him a fright. Okay?"

A moment later the South African followed Antoine out of the front door. Raj stood still, waiting and wondering. At least now he knew what he was going to do. He wished he could have heard the other side of that phone conversation.

* * *

The following day, as Raj drove slowly up Belle Etoile's winding drive, he saw there were two cars parked in front of the house, a sleek Porsche Boxster Raj hadn't seen before, and Antoine's showy Mercedes.

Instead of going through the house, where his footsteps on the wooden floor would advertise his presence, he went through the garden. On the lawn his feet made little sound as he walked past the windows of Douglas's studio. He came to a halt when he heard voices. Where he stood, he was hidden by the spreading branches of the frangipani shading the outside steps to the studio. He inhaled the heavy scent of the waxy flowers and smiled grimly to himself. He seemed to be doing a lot of eavesdropping behind foliage these days.

"Maman, you know it has to be done," Raj heard Antoine say. "You can't look after yourself."

"What do you mean?" Her voice wavered as she spoke. "How can I leave Belle Etoile? What about your father?"

"He is gone, Maman."

"No. For me he is still here, always here."

"Papa is dead. He has been for months now." Raj could hear the harsh exasperation in Antoine's voice. Clenching his teeth against the anger that rose in him, he waited.

"There's no need to be so cruel, Antoine," Monique said, her voice rising in pain. "I know he's dead. *Bon dieu*! Only God knows how much I grieve for him. I cannot leave this house that he loved so much. It's my duty to look after it for him. And I have all the help–"

"Help! From a bunch of geriatrics!"

"But they are my friends." She was beginning to sound even more distressed, but it occurred to Raj that there was no sign in her voice or words of the confusion he'd noticed the last time he saw her.

"Friends that are not going to last much longer."

"What do you mean? They would never leave me."

"But they're getting on, Maman. What if Zabette died?"

"Now you are wishing my friends to be dead too?" Monique's voice shook as she cried out. Raj could bear it no longer; he stepped out across the lawn to join them.

"*Bonsoir Tante* Monique," he said. She wasn't his aunt, but he'd called her that as a child and there was no harm in using the term to make a point.

Antoine leapt up. "What the hell are you doing here?"

Pieter Brandt was there too, in a chair a few feet away. His eyes narrowed in anger, but it was soon quenched, and he remained where he was, one arm draped casually over the back of his chair.

Raj ignored both men and bent to kiss Monique, taking her hand and giving it a comforting squeeze.

Her face lit up at sight of him. "My dear boy, it is so good to see you."

"Are you well?" he asked.

"*Comme ci, comme ça,*" she said, waggling her hand back and forth in a familiar gesture. There was deep weariness in her voice. "I miss Douglas so very much." In the circumstances the simple statement was heart wrenching.

Only now, with his anger under control, did Raj turn to acknowledge the men. Antoine scowled at him. Brandt's face was expressionless, but Raj could sense the tension in him.

Raj's voice was cold as he said, "*Bonsoir* Antoine," but he still shook him by the hand, Monique would have noticed if he hadn't. Antoine winced and gave a grunt of pain.

"What's up with you?" Raj asked.

"Just a heavy game of squash yesterday."

"Must have been," Raj said, then turned to nod curtly in Brandt's direction. "We meet again."

The man's eyes narrowed. "We do."

"Why are you here?" Antoine demanded, glaring up at Raj.

"I've come to see your mother," Raj told him, lifting a cool eyebrow. "Just as I presume you have. As for your friend I don't know." He glanced at Brandt and shrugged, then turned and pulled a chair up close to Monique.

At that moment Zabette came bustling out of the house, her bright flowered overall flapping as she moved. She told him in Creole that she'd heard his voice, asked why it had been so long since he visited, then dropped her voice just a little and remarked in ominous tones that at least it was good to see him, which was more than she could say about some people. Raj grinned and gave her a hug. She slapped his arm, grinned, told him to behave, and asked if he wanted beer, tea, lemonade? He chose beer and noticed the others had no drinks, wondered if they'd even been offered.

"You can bring us all a beer," Antoine snapped at her.

She looked at him and he might have been five years old. "What has happened to your manners? A please would be acceptable, my boy," she said and stomped off towards the house.

"Now do you see what I mean?" Antoine said, glaring at his mother. "You have to get rid of her."

Monique had lent her head back against the cushions and closed her eyes. Raj wondered if she'd dozed off, but he thought not as he watched her fingers tighten on the arms of her chair.

"Why on earth? I don't think that would be a good idea at all. Quite apart from anything else, if Zabette wasn't here, who would look after your mother?"

"Very soon that won't be a problem."

God Almighty! Raj would have loved to let rip and tell Antoine exactly what he thought of him. But that wouldn't help. He'd come here to try to find out what they were up to, and to protect Monique if he could, and losing his temper wouldn't help.

"What exactly does that mean?" he asked as coolly as he could manage.

"I'm making very comfortable arrangements for Maman, not that it's any of your business."

"Ah, but that's where you're wrong, Antoine. As your father's executor and your mother's lawyer, and close friend, it's very much my business." Raj looked from Antoine to Pieter Brandt as he spoke and was surprised to see the man smile.

"I'm sure Antoine understands that very well," he said. It was only the second time he'd spoken since Raj arrived.

"I'm glad to hear it. So, is this your first visit to Belle Etoile?"

"Not exactly, but last time was very brief. It's a beautiful place, so out of the way and isolated. A valuable piece of real estate as I pointed out when I was at your office."

"And an even more valuable piece of Mauritian history," Raj said. "You're probably ignorant of the fact that Antoine's father was one of the most important artists and poets in the southern hemisphere. Have you seen any of his paintings, read any of his poetry?"

"I can't say I have. I'm not really into that sort of thing."

"No, I don't suppose you are." Raj didn't bother to keep the contempt out of his voice but, as he'd noticed when they met before, the man was difficult to rattle. "A pity. Antoine should show you some of his father's paintings. The house is such a great venue for them."

"Not for much longer," Antoine muttered.

"How come? I wasn't aware anything had changed since we last met."

Antoine glanced quickly at his friend. "Maybe not, but it will soon, once we get Abigail Kendall sorted. I don't care what you say Raj, she's going to agree to the sale, we'll see to that." His eyes flicked to his associate once again. "I've given my word to Pieter and I'm not going back on it."

"I'm glad to hear it," Brandt said quietly.

"What about your duty to your mother, and to your father's memory?" Raj asked.

"Look, Raj." Antoine glanced at his mother. Her eyes were still closed. Although he dropped his voice, the urgency in it had increased. "Obviously I want the best for Maman, but she needs proper care. The only way is to sell up, and that would pay for her to go to a nursing home. Belle Etoile is falling apart, renovating it would cost millions. You've had some bad advice, I'm afraid. The only answer is to pull it down."

Before Raj could say anything, Monique's voice broke into their exchange. "What's that you're saying?" she demanded.

"Don't worry, Maman. Just business."

"Pull down Belle Etoile? No! No! That must never happen. Douglas would never agree. Antoine, never say that again. Do you hear? Raj, you must tell him."

"Calm down, Maman," Antoine said, putting his hand out to take a hold of her arm.

She shook him off, glaring at him.

"How can I when my only son says such terrible things?" Her voice had risen to a sobbing shout.

Zabette came rushing back out. "Now look what you've done, *mauvais garcon*! How dare you upset your mother so! Take your foreign friend and go. Monsieur Raj, make them go."

She knelt by Monique's chair and soothed her as if she was a child, holding her hands and crooning quietly.

Raj rose from his chair. In spite of the heat of the day, he felt cold with the anger consuming him. He needed time to think, and for Monique's sake he couldn't afford to put a foot wrong.

He put a gentle hand on Monique's shoulder, bent to speak to her. "Don't worry, *ma chère*. Leave it to me. Zabette, take her inside. I'll talk to them."

With strong arms supporting her mistress, Zabette guided her back into the house, glancing back anxiously a couple of times as they made their way across the grass. Raj watched them go, glad of the moment to collect his thoughts. Only when they'd disappeared into the cool of the house did he turn to the two men who were standing a little way off, deep in muttered conversation. Raj strode over to them. He elbowed Brandt out of the way and grabbed Antoine by the elbow, heard him grunt in pain again, but ignored it.

"Well done!" He didn't bother to hide his anger. "Was that what you came down here for? To add to your mother's grief?"

"Shut up, Raj!"

"Oh no. It's your turn to listen. Belle Etoile may need a few small repairs and a coat of paint, but the structure is fine. I have a survey to prove it in your father's papers at the office, so don't give me any of that crap about pulling it down. There's absolutely nothing you can do to push this sale, given Douglas's will, and I'm beginning to understand why he made it. I suggest you forget your grand schemes—"

"I'm afraid he can't do that." The quiet, threatening voice interrupted him, and Raj swung round. Brandt went on. "It's obvious Antoine hasn't made it clear to you that he's agreed to sell us Belle Etoile, signed on the dotted line, heads of agreement done and dusted."

"He may well have done so," Raj said, "but it makes no difference. Without Abigail Kendall's agreement they're null and void."

Pieter Brandt smiled at him. "I think we'll be able to persuade her."

Raj turned his back on the South African again and said to Antoine.

"What's more, the decision on heritage status is still pending, so you can't do anything on that count either. Next week, once Abi has seen all this—"

"What do you mean, next week?" Antoine asked quickly.

Raj could have kicked himself. But it was too late now.

"She arrives at the end of the week."

"Why didn't you tell me?" demanded Antoine.

"I only just found out."

"You were going to keep it to yourself, weren't you?"

"Of course, he was," said Pieter Brandt.

"Antoine." Raj continued to ignore Brandt. "You and I, and no one else, will meet up with Abigail and discuss the situation when she's here. I'd advise you to stay within the law on this because, if you don't, I'll come after you." He turned to Brandt. "And you. Understand?"

"All I understand," Pieter Brandt said quietly, "is that you're in my way and that's something I won't stand for. You have no idea who you're dealing with, Amrakash. Watch yourself. Come on, Antoine."

Before Raj had the chance to respond, Brandt turned and strode back across the lawn. With a look of panic in his eyes, Antoine hesitated, then hurried after his friend.

Raj let out his breath. That certainly could have been handled better, he thought. Angry with Antoine and angry with himself, he muttered a few choice Creole curses.

As he stood staring out across the garden, he suddenly remembered a conversation he'd had with Antoine a couple of months ago.

"My days of playing squash are over. Buggered my wrist. I'll have to think of some other sport." Had he started playing again? Perhaps his wrist was better. But, if not, why had he lied?

Raj made his way back into the house, his mind racing. He thought again of what Brandt had said, telling himself it was just a bully's bravado, but deep down he wasn't so sure. Halfway to Monique's salon, an idea occurred to him. He stopped and punched out a number on his mobile.

"Georgette?"

"'allo, Raj? What's up?"

"I need a favour."

She laughed. "More overtime?"

"No, not this time. You know that cousin of yours, the chap who's a night club bouncer?"

"Jacquo? What about him?"

"You said he was looking for a better job."

"Well, he works as a driver during the day, that's okay, but he got fed up with the nightclub work, he's already given it up."

"Good. I think I've got just the thing for him."

# PART II

# CHAPTER 19

The pilot had announced there were ten minutes before landing. The four-hour flight from Johannesburg had passed so quickly. They were nearly there. Abi craned to see as much as she could out of the window.

Immediately below was the sea, dark indigo, but a minute later they flew over a rim of white waves. Within the safety of this curling reef, the sea changed colour abruptly to a clear, sun-glittered turquoise, then there were scattered black rocks and creamy sand. She recognised the sway of sugar cane with the ever-present breeze crawling across it like an unseen hand, then a motorway full of cars, surely that was wider than it used to be. Either side of it were scattered groups of concrete houses, some with corrugated rooves, and an occasional bamboo pole holding a fluttering red flag to mark a Hindu shrine.

A moment later the wheels thumped down on Mauritian soil. She was back.

As they rumbled along the runway, a mountain range in the distance rose and fell, and ended in a crouched lion shape, *Le Montagne du Lion*. She felt a lump rise in her throat at sight of it. Uncle Douglas had painted that great mass of rock from so many different angles.

As she stepped out of the plane the heat enveloped her, carrying with it the overwhelming scents of her childhood, a mixture of so many different things – sugar cane, vanilla, spices and coconut, hot sun on red earth. The impact was physical. All this was overladen by the familiar fumes of a busy airport. In a daze of memory, she made her way down the steps and across the tarmac.

The airport buildings were unfamiliar. With the tourist industry so important now, and still growing, the building had been extended beyond recognition.

"They'll never manage to keep it going," she remembered her father saying scornfully about tourism. "Too much like hard work." He'd been proved so wrong. Well done, Mauritius. For a second, thoughts of her father took her back to the meeting with David Chandler. She pushed it away. She wasn't going to think about that now.

As she waited to go through immigration, she listened to the chatter of passengers and airport workers around her, some speaking Creole. How long would it take for this colourful language, the first she'd ever spoken, to come back to her? She'd thought of buying a phrase book, but something in her had resisted. Phrase books were for tourists. If she concentrated, she could understand most of what was said, but then she'd hear another snatch of conversation and be lost again. They spoke so fast. And then of course there were all the other languages. French was clear enough, although the Mauritian version differed a little in dialect. Then there was Hindi, Urdu, Mandarin, and others she couldn't identify, and there were also the many different languages of the tourists.

After half an hour of queuing it was her turn at the desk. She handed over her passport to the unsmiling young man. He leafed through it, studying the pages carefully, then looked up grinning, his face transformed.

"*Ou fin nez ici?*" he asked, then said in English, "You were born in Mauritius?"

"Yes," said Abi, returning the smile, surprised that it could give him such pleasure. "This is my first time back, though."

"You return for a visit to your family?"

"I'm afraid I have only one member of my family left here."

His face fell. "That is very sad. You are on business or holiday?"

Abi wasn't sure how on earth to answer this question. "A bit of both," she said.

"Welcome home." He handed back her passport with another broad smile. "I hope you enjoy your visit."

"Thank you," Abi said, blinking very hard.

She piled her cases onto a trolley, put her cabin luggage and handbag on top and made her way out into the bustle of the arrivals hall. The hotel was only a few miles from the airport and she planned to get a taxi over there and just chill out for the rest of the day. She'd decided not to ask Raj to meet her, but part of her regretted that now. She wasn't at all sure she wanted to be on her own with nothing to distract her from her thoughts. But she couldn't do anything about that now, and at least it would give her time to prepare for what was going to be a stressful week.

Raj had told her he'd be in court all day tomorrow, but he'd arranged meetings for Abi with two members of his committee. The Junior Minister, Devina Edouard, was away until the end of the week, so a meeting with her would have to wait. Abi didn't feel quite so phased by the prospect of meeting them. That was all about work, which was always easier to deal with. Then there'd be a meeting at Raj's office to go through the paperwork, and at some point she'd have to meet up with Antoine, which brought Abi back to that sinking feeling in her stomach. And there would be a visit to Belle Etoile to see Monique, but she pushed that to the back of her mind.

There were several young men and boys hovering around, bright eyes watching for an opportunity to make a rupee or two by offering their help as porters. Abi gave in, hooked her handbag over her shoulder, and let a smiling lad of about fifteen take over her clattering trolley. He'd hardly be able to run off with it, heavy as it was, and she was too tired to resist.

She said, "*Je veux une taxi.*" French would have to do. He nodded and replied, "*Sweev moi, sweev moi.*" She did as he asked and followed him as he chatted away, telling her that his cousin had a very good taxi.

It was as they came to the top of a ramp and into the bustle of buses and cars, that she heard someone call her name. Taken aback, wondering if she'd imagined it, she swung round.

"Welcome back to Mauritius, Abigail." The man who was approaching her was immaculately dressed in a crisply ironed shirt and beige chinos. His coffee-coloured skin, dark hair and pale eyes were vaguely familiar, but she couldn't place him.

"You don't recognise me?" he said and smiled, head on one side. "I'm disappointed. But then, I suppose I was only ten when we last met."

"I'm sorry, I—" then it dawned on her. "Antoine?"

"Correct. Well done."

Abi was even more taken aback when, still smiling, he leant forward and kissed her, first on the right cheek, then left, then right again. She took a step back.

"How on earth did you know I was coming to Mauritius?"

"You obviously don't believe in coincidence." His tone was teasing.

"No, I don't," she said firmly, but smiled to soften the words.

"Just a bit of detective work on the net. Google is so useful, don't you think? Then I phoned your office, and your assistant gave me all the information I needed."

Ah, Mina. She might have known. Although this wasn't the time she would have chosen, she supposed she would have been meeting up with Antoine soon enough. Abi remembered him as a rather round, sulky little boy, but he'd grown into a good-looking man.

"Why didn't you let me know when you were arriving?" he asked.

"I'm sorry, I–" Abi was saved from continuing by the sight of a tall familiar figure approaching them. Having decided not to tell Raj what flight she was on, she was surprised at how her heart leapt at the sight of him. Quite a reception committee! She had an insane desire to giggle. Tired and emotional, that's my problem, she thought.

"It's good to see you, Abi," said Raj, holding out his hand to shake hers. There was none of the elaborate kissing that Antoine had favoured, and his voice was cool. Abi felt as if she'd done something wrong and her pleasure at seeing him diminished.

Antoine was glowering as the two men shook hands and Abi noticed him wince.

"I see the squash injury is still troubling you," Raj said, his tone sardonic.

"What are you doing here?" Antoine snapped at Raj.

"Meeting Abigail as promised."

As promised? She opened her mouth to protest, but Raj didn't give her the chance. There was clearly a whole lot going on between these two that she knew nothing about. It was obvious they didn't like each other, and Antoine's expression reminded Abi of the way he'd looked in Narinda's photo.

Raj took hold of her trolley. The boy, who had been hovering, unwilling to let go of his prize, protested, then his eyes widened as Raj pressed a crisp note into his palm. A grin split his brown face and he tapped his forehead in thanks, then rushed off to find another customer.

"My car is this way," Raj said, turning towards the car park.

"Here. What do you think you're doing?" Antoine's voice rose.

"Taking Abi's luggage to my car."

"But I was going to drive her." Antoine's protests were ignored.

Abi could feel irritation mounting. This was ridiculous. She felt like a toy being argued over by two children and opened her mouth to say so, but Raj was already across the other side of the road. Just then a coach drew up and began to disgorge its passengers, preventing Abi and Antoine from following him.

"*Merde! Si arrogante!*" she heard him mutter under his breath. Abi could sympathise with the sentiments.

Antoine rushed on. "We need to talk, just you and me, Abigail. This business with the summer house and the *arpen bas* at Belle Etoile, it must be sorted. I don't think Raj understands how important it is. My father's will was somewhat eccentric. I'm sure you understand my concerns."

Abi thought she did, but no way was she going to discuss it now. "Of course," she said, trying to remain cool. "That's one of the reasons I'm here, but–"

"Let me take you to your hotel. We can talk on the way."

That was the last thing she wanted. She would have preferred a taxi to either of them, but retrieving her cases from Raj's grip would be too embarrassing.

"No," she said firmly to Antoine. "I arranged for Raj to pick me up," she lied. "I have to go now."

"But Abigail–"

"I'll see you soon, Antoine."

The bus was gone. Raj stood, scowling, as he looked back towards them. With a wave of her hand, Abi crossed over to join him, narrowly avoiding a taxi. She heard Antoine call out after her but ignored it.

They wove their way between the cars in silence, then Raj said. "You're staying at Hotel L'Aigrette near Blue Bay, aren't you?"

"How did you know that?" Abi asked, feeling hounded.

"You told me in your last e-mail."

"Oh, of course," said Abi. Now she felt stupid. "But I didn't tell you which flight I was on."

Raj had a slight smile on his face. He seemed to be enjoying her discomfiture. "No. Lawrence e-mailed me. He seemed to think you would need looking after."

What was it with all these bloody men? Abi could feel the heat rise up her neck into her face. "I can't think why."

"Nor can I." It wasn't the response she'd expected. "You seem very capable to me."

"Why did you tell Antoine we'd arranged it between us?"

"I thought it best. I had to get rid of him somehow."

"But I might have wanted him to give me a lift." Abi knew she sounded petulant but couldn't help it. "I might even have given him my flight number."

"You might have. But still, don't you think it would be best if you had a rest and recovered from the journey before tackling Antoine? He can be difficult, and this is a delicate situation, wouldn't you say?"

Abi felt irritated, mainly because she knew he was right. He was only echoing her own thoughts, but did he have to be so patronising? Antoine was right, he was arrogant. She bit her lip and said nothing, afraid she might say too much, and glanced sideways at him. His face gave nothing away. She found it hard to work him out.

When they'd first met again two weeks ago, she'd thought him disdainful and cold, but she couldn't escape the fact she'd behaved badly herself on that occasion. Then, when they'd had dinner together, she'd begun to enjoy his company. At the meeting in her office she'd seen yet another much softer side to him, and his gift of the book had been thoughtful as well. The phone call from Heathrow had surprised and pleased her, and in the e-mails they'd exchanged since, he'd been business-like but friendly, and she'd tried to respond in kind. Now here she was feeling like a gauche teenager again, and he was back to being arrogant and annoying. Perhaps it was the fact she was so exhausted after those few disturbing days in Johannesburg. Added to that, she'd been up since half past four in the morning, at least that's what it had been South African time. And it was all down to coming home, as the young immigration officer had called it.

"You are finding it hard, this first return to the land of your birth?" Raj asked, his tone suddenly very different.

Her irritation disappeared and she gave a shaky laugh. "I suppose I am."

"It's hardly surprising. I think the places where we grow up always leave the deepest imprint, don't you?"

Abi was saved from responding by their arrival at Raj's car, a dark green classic MGB. She was surprised. It wasn't the sort of car she'd have expected him to own.

It seemed he read her mind again.

"My one indulgence, this car," Raj said, sounding slightly embarrassed and, as a consequence, more human. "I really ought to get rid of her and buy something more practical, but I can't bring myself to do so."

Raj packed her luggage into what space there was and strapped a bungee over the half open boot. Abi sank down into the soft leather seat and leant back. She could feel his dark eyes on her as they waited to get out of the car park, but she said nothing. Her senses were so over-loaded, she didn't feel capable of conversation.

As they turned left at a roundabout just outside the slip road to the airport, Raj said, "Your hotel isn't far from where my sister, Narinda, lives. Did you ever go to Ile aux Aigrettes? That's the island the hotel is named after."

"Yes, Uncle Douglas took us there once," Abi said, glad of the neutral subject. "Charlie and I were talking about it the other day. It's got that sort of undercut, hasn't it? Like a giant mushroom."

He smiled, seeming impressed that she'd remembered that much detail. "Yes. It's home to some of the pink pigeons Gerald Durrell helped to save from extinction, and it has some of the few remaining ebony trees."

He kept up a steady stream of small talk and Abi responded to some of it, but with only part of her mind.

The rest was concentrating hard on keeping control of her erratic emotions. As they turned onto the coast road, with occasional glimpses of the ocean through the *filao* trees, or beyond the houses that hugged the beach, she could smell the sea. Unable to stop them, she felt warm tears begin to creep down her cheeks. She prayed he hadn't noticed, then realised he had when a hand came out holding an ironed and neatly folded handkerchief.

Taking it from him, Abi muttered. "Thank you, and sorry about this."

All he said was, "Not long now."

She was grateful for his tact and for the warning which gave her time to pull herself together before arriving at the hotel. Minutes later they turned in at a driveway with a single pole barrier across it. A uniformed security guard came out of a small concrete hut as Raj lowered his window.

"*Mam'zelle* Abigail Kendall," he said.

The man checked a list he had on a clipboard, nodded, then lifted the barrier to let them through, and the car crunched along a short sandy driveway into a car park surrounded by flowering shrubs.

Another uniformed man bustled up, all smiles.

"Welcome to Hotel L'Aigrette," he said, taking hold of her luggage.

They followed him into a large reception area with raked sand on the floor interspersed with slabs of stone. Everywhere was the scent of lemon verbena. The lighting came from spheres of smoked glass lit from within, some on the floor, some on low tables, and round these were cushioned seats. The atmosphere was calm and relaxed.

"So, shall I leave you to check in then?" Raj asked, sounding a little awkward.

"Yes, I'm sure you must need to get going. Thank you for meeting me, and for the handkerchief?"

"Don't worry. Keep it. It's just that—"

"Yes?" Abi said, suddenly reluctant to let him go.

"Well…" Now he seemed even more unsure of himself. "It's just that my sister, Narinda, wondered if you'd like to come and eat this evening. As I said, she lives not far from here. I could pick you up." He gave her an apologetic grin. "Narinda likes to get her own way but, if you just want to relax, please say so."

Abi was torn. She glanced at her watch. Hard to believe it was only half past one. Part of her wanted to be on her own to deal with her turbulent feelings, but the thought of being alone, trying to keep the ghosts at bay, scared her. Before she could stop herself, she had already replied.

"I'd be delighted. What time should I be ready?"

She couldn't tell if he was pleased or not at her response.

"I'll pick you up at seven thirty, is that okay? That would give you time to unpack and have a rest. *À tout à l'heure.*"

There was one of those awkward moments when the decision between a kiss and a handshake has to be negotiated, then he thrust out his hand, shook hers, and turned and left. Abi stood looking after him, not quite knowing what to think.

Her room, when she got to it, had a balcony overlooking a garden crowded with palm trees, bamboo and other familiar flowers and shrubs. She recognised the tissue paper flowers of bougainvillaea, some bright red hibiscus and pale mauve morning glory. Beyond was the white sanded beach and the sea. There was the sound of water splashing, children's voices, a man's laughter. Just below where she stood on the first floor, two gardeners were raking the sandy path and talking in low voices. She wondered what they were talking about, then she heard the words Manchester United. Of course, football.

Pulling the door closed, she turned back into the cool, air-conditioned room. Flipping off her sandals, she lay down on the enormous bed. Several large cushions in different ochre shades were piled against the headboard.

She pulled one over, curled up and hugged it to her body. Five minutes later she was asleep.

# CHAPTER 20

*September 1992*

Abi's father stood at the window of his study, his hand gripping the frame. He didn't look at her as he said, "You're a young woman now." He made it sound like an accusation. "It's about time you took some responsibility for the household. I don't think you realise you won't have servants waiting on you hand and foot when we get home."

"But why can't Charlie help with the packing? It's not fair."

"He's not old enough, and it's women's work. You've got Nanny to help you."

"I don't see—"

"Enough, Abigail." He turned and gave her that familiar cold glare. "Just do as you're told. Make a detailed inventory of everything as you pack. If anything disappears in transit, I want to be able to claim on the insurance. And make sure you take note of exactly what is packed where."

Abi could feel anger and resentment churning inside her, but there was no point in protesting. She bit the inside of her cheek to stop herself saying anything, then unclenched her teeth when she tasted blood.

The glare intensified. "And if you find anything which belonged to your mother, you are to hand it over to me immediately. Do you understand me?"

"Yes, Father," she said. Yes, she understood what he was saying. No, she wasn't agreeing to do as he said. This small rebellion was all the satisfaction she got out of the conversation.

Nanny V had chattered away as they wrapped, packed and listed, but behind the smiling face was a pain equal to her own.

They were very close to finishing the job when Abi found the small brown leather box wedged tight behind a drawer in her mother's dressing table. She'd found little else of her mother's, not the diary Abi knew she'd written secretly, nor the many letters she used to receive, or the mementoes she collected. Abi thought her father had probably destroyed them. Now, with her heart beating hard, she thrust the box deep into the pocket of her shorts. Nothing would persuade her to give it to him. Nothing.

It was their last day. All the crates, trunks and boxes had been carted away, stashed in the cavernous hold of a container ship for transportation. All the packed suitcases stood in a row on the verandah. In half an hour the car would arrive to take her, Charlie and their father to the airport, and that would be that.

Abi wandered round the garden, visiting old haunts. She wanted to scream aloud in agonised protest, but still the rigid calm persisted. She ran her hand down the trunk of the lychee tree, remembering how many times she and Charlie had climbed it, hiding from Nanny and eating all the fruit they could reach. Down at the bottom of the garden the flamboyants were in bloom, dropping a carpet of crimson on to the grass below. Her mother had loved those trees. Abi scuffed her shoes through the fallen petals then turned to walk back up the lawn. Avoiding the dip where the great banyan had stood, she went around to the back of the house. She was going to visit Nanny's room just one more time.

But at that moment she heard her father's voice calling, "Abigail? Come on girl. Time we were off."

For an insane moment she thought of hiding, but what was the use? That would only delay the inevitable and make him angry. Her stomach lurched and she could feel the pain of tears gathering in her throat. But she wouldn't cry. She wouldn't.

He and Charlie were standing by the verandah steps, her father with his hand on her brother's shoulder, making Charlie look small and vulnerable. Seeing his face, pinched with anxiety, she tried to give him a reassuring smile.

As the car made its way down the drive, she looked back. There was Nanny, waving frantically, tears pouring down her brown cheeks, and beside her stood Janisha, crying too. Abi watched until the car was through the gates and she could no longer see them. She felt Charlie's hand slide into hers and glanced at him. His eyes were wide with fear, but he wasn't crying either. She held fast to his hand, her lifeline.

It was when they were driving through the crowds of Quatre Bornes that the question insinuated itself into her mind. It had been lurking there for weeks. Now it came to the surface and she was desperate to ask it. "Father." The word came out louder than she intended.

"Yes?"

For a moment she couldn't go on.

He turned in the front seat to look at her. "Well, spit it out, girl."

Before she could change her mind, she blurted out, "When will we be coming back?"

Too scared to look at him, she stared out the window, waiting for his reply. Seconds ticked by. Maybe he hadn't heard.

She was about to ask the question again when he said, "I thought I'd explained the situation clearly enough. We will not be coming back. I start my new job in Malawi in two months' time. You and Charlie will live with Cousin Rose in order that you can continue your education."

"But why?"

"Abigail! What is all this?"

"I just—" But how could she explain that to leave the island felt like being torn from her mother yet again? How could she explain this was her home, not cold, far away England? He'd never understand, and it would make him angry.

For the rest of the journey to the airport she planned what she would say in her first letters to Nanny V, Uncle Douglas and Monique. Once on the plane she'd start a letter, describing each stage of the journey, every detail, then she'd post the letter as soon as they arrived in England. And once there, she'd write every day. The thought of getting their replies was the only bright spot in a bleak future.

*November 2018*

Abi's eyes snapped open. Where was she? The sun slanting through the windows and the smell of sand and sea reminded her. With a rush of mixed emotions, she rolled onto her back and covered her face with her hands. She lay like that, holding her breath, then let it out in a long sigh and glanced at her watch. She was relieved to find it was only a quarter past six.

Dusk was falling. Golden light filled the room, reflected from a beautiful sunset. She got up and opened the sliding door onto the balcony. Humid heat flowed in and she stood there for a moment, drinking in the scents and sounds, then her mobile phone beeped from the depths of her handbag. She rummaged for it. There were three messages; one from Lawrence asking her to e-mail a report on the Soweto project as soon as she'd rested, another from Charlie asking if she had arrived safely in Mauritius, and a third was from Evelyn saying more or less the same as Charlie.

Feeling a bit of a coward for not phoning any of them immediately, she tapped out quick replies. She could always send e-mails when she got back from Narinda's.

Now she must unpack. After doing so and having a quick shower, she wondered what on earth to wear. It would have to be whatever was the least creased. A dark red crinkle silk skirt seemed to have survived the journey best. She shook it out, that'd have to do. A sleeveless cream top, also silk, was unscathed, and she'd wear the amber earrings Beth and Charlie had given her for Christmas. At the last moment she pinned on the filigree brooch.

Once she was dressed, she began to wonder if the outfit was too formal. Or maybe it wasn't formal enough. She felt irritated with herself for worrying about trivialities, but at least it filled her mind and stopped her thinking about anything else. Giving herself a quick spray of perfume, she pushed her feet into sandals, dropped her mobile into her bag, and made her way down to reception to wait for Raj.

It was as she was sitting in the softly lit room watching the bustle of new arrivals that one of the receptionists approached her.

"Miss Kendall?" she said in English, her accent making the name sound more like candle.

"Yes?"

"There is a telephone call for you. If you would like I am able to put it through to that phone over there." She pointed to a low table in an alcove.

Abi thanked her. It would probably be Raj telling her he was going to be late. She remembered that time keeping had never been a strong point for Mauritians. But when she picked up the handset it was Antoine's voice she heard.

"I hope you like the hotel."

"It's delightful, thank you."

"I thought it would be a good idea to make contact and fix up a meeting, since Raj didn't give us the chance to do so earlier on."

Abi supposed this was reasonable, at least from his point of view. But she wanted to go through everything with Raj first. She needed his input before she tackled Antoine.

"I'm not sure of my itinerary at the moment."

"You sound very business-like."

"I usually am."

"Good, that's good." She didn't think he meant it. "Perhaps then you won't mind me being frank with you. I found my father's will very difficult to understand, even unfair. I'm sure you appreciate that?"

"Yes, of course."

"What persuaded him to leave part of the property to you?" he asked, his tone accusing.

"Antoine, I've no idea. I certainly had nothing to do with it."

"No, of course not."

He didn't sound convinced. Surely, he wasn't holding her responsible for what Uncle Douglas had done? At any other time, the irony of that would have made her laugh.

"Look," Abi said, "I'll be meeting up with Raj soon, and I've got a meeting with a couple of his associates tomorrow."

"What associates?"

Damn! Why had she said that? She needed to know what Antoine had been told. Raj should have primed her, for God's sake!

"Just a couple of people he thought I'd like to meet." She tried to make it sound as casual as possible.

"This is too bad of him. He ought to be keeping me informed." The words were mild, the tone wasn't. "I am wondering all the time what it is he has to hide."

Abi didn't respond and, at that moment, Raj came striding through the main door of the hotel. She felt a wave of relief at the sight of him and lifted a hand to attract his attention, then regretted doing so. She should have got rid of Antoine first.

"I have to go now," said Abi. "Give me your mobile number. I'll get back to you as soon as I know what my plans are."

He rattled off his number and she keyed it in. "But Abigail–"

"Bye," she said quickly and put the handset down.

"Who was that?"

The question was abrupt, and Abi replied, "Antoine," without thinking.

Raj's dark brows came together in a frown.

"What the hell did he want? Or did you phone him?"

Abi had recovered herself by now. She threw her hands up in protest. "Look, he phoned me, okay? And I'll decide what I do while I'm here. I hope that's understood."

All Raj did was glare at her.

"Anyway, Antoine's involved, isn't he? After all, he is Uncle Douglas's son."

"His adopted son."

Adopted? Abi hadn't known that, but she didn't say so.

"What difference does that make?" she asked. "It's still not surprising he's keen to sort things out."

"Maybe," said Raj, but added, "you must be careful of him. He's not to be trusted."

Abi said nothing. She was tired of confrontation and being ordered around. *The way I feel,* she thought, *I could so easily lose it and say a whole pile of stuff I'd regret.*

She was relieved when Raj said, "Shall we go?" and she followed him out to his car. An uncomfortable silence surrounded them as he drove out onto the sandy coast road.

* * *

Raj hadn't been entirely honest. Yes, Lawrence had e-mailed to tell him what flight Abi was on, so had Charlie, but only in response to e-mails from him asking for the details.

On the drive from the airport, he'd studied her profile. Her eyes had been shadowed, but there was no sign of the bruise that had been so obvious on her cheek the last time he'd seen her. He wondered what she'd said about this trip to the man who'd hit her. She said she'd thrown him out, but had she taken him back? It happened so often that way.

Now he was angry with himself for handling things so badly. Stupid to react like that to Antoine's phone call, and he'd felt equally wrong-footed when Antoine appeared at the airport, worried that Abi would be taken in. Abi was the one person who could guarantee the Belle Etoile project went ahead, and surely that was what mattered most. There was some English saying that described how careful he'd have to be. Treading on eggshells, that was it. So far all he'd managed to do was smash a few.

Abi was silent as they drove, and Raj concentrated on avoiding the clapped-out old trucks whose drivers thought keeping your hand on the horn would prevent accidents, and the ubiquitous Mauritian scooter riders and cyclists, sometimes two or three to a bike.

"I don't remember this much traffic before, except in Port Louis."

"Twenty-five years ago, there wasn't." He was happy to talk about something neutral. "It's so much busier now, especially in areas like this where every other building is a hotel or restaurant. Traffic accidents are a daily occurrence."

"And yet so much is just the same. The plants and flowers, the smells, and the way the heat wraps you up like a blanket."

Raj smiled. "I'd never thought of it like that," he said, then added, "here we are."

A pair of automatic gates opened to admit them and closed after the car. Narinda, slim and petite in a bright green sari, opened the front door. She welcomed Abi like a long lost relative, with a hand on each shoulder as she kissed her cheeks.

"It is so good to see you. Come in, come in," she said, ushering them into the house. "This is my husband Vijay."

Vijay took both Abi's hands as he looked up at her. Abi was half a head taller than both him and Narinda. He echoed the words of welcome, then turned to Raj.

"But why didn't you tell us how beautiful is this friend of yours? You want to keep her to yourself, *ein?*"

Abi gave an embarrassed laugh and Raj noticed her cheeks colour up. He gave her an apologetic grimace and wondered what she thought of all this Mauritian effusiveness, but her face gave little away.

As they crossed the sitting room, with its cool tiled floor covered by an occasional Afghan rug, Abi suddenly stopped in the middle of the room. Her face paled as she stood staring up at the double portrait.

"That's one of Uncle Douglas's, isn't it?" she asked.

Narinda stopped beside her. "Yes. I was twelve and Raji was five." She gave Abi a glance full of curiosity, then smiled over her shoulder at her brother. "I had such trouble making him sit still. Wriggle, wriggle, the whole time, that's all he did."

"As usual you exaggerate," Raj told her.

"I certainly do not," protested his sister.

But it was obvious Abi wasn't really listening to this exchange.

"Douglas did one of me and Charlie together. Charlie has it in his study in Cambridge. And he did another of me on my own, but I don't know where that is now."

"The one of you is at Belle Etoile, in Monique's *salon*," Raj said quietly. "I noticed it when I went down to see her recently."

Abi swung round to look at him. He found the expression on her face hard to interpret. Surprise was there, but pain too, and something else.

"It is?" she said.

"You can see it when you go there."

"I suppose I can," she said.

He couldn't tell if she liked the idea or not.

Raj was grateful to Narinda when she plunged into the awkward silence that followed.

"Let's go through to the verandah. Vijay, can you bring the drinks tray I put ready? It's on the table in the kitchen."

"*Allez* right," said her husband, and Raj got the impression he was pleased to escape from the undercurrents.

"Vijay is a dab hand at making cocktails. You must try one, Abi. And, of course, we have some locally made Phoenix beer."

"I had some when Raj took me to his friend's restaurant. It's very good."

"Was that Navin's?" asked Vijay as he came back, carrying a loaded tray.

"Such an old show-off, but a divine cook," Narinda said, smiling.

They settled in wicker chairs and Narinda and Vijay kept up a steady stream of questions about Abi's journey, her work, Charlie's family. Although Raj was extremely grateful for his sister and brother-in-law's easy hospitality, there was no doubt that the more Narinda showed an interest in Abi's life, the more Abi tensed up.

Once dinner was over, they began to talk about more general subjects and Abi relaxed a little. Narinda talked of a conference she was due to attend in Reunion, and Vijay made them all laugh with an account of a home visit he'd made to a patient whose chickens, goats and dogs wandered in and out of her bedroom the whole time he was there. He flung up his hands, opened his eyes wide.

"Am I a vet? I asked her this. She said the animals were fine, it was her that was ill, and when she needed a vet, she'd call one because he might do a better job than I was doing."

They went on to talk about the changes in the island, and about Abi's job, but this led on to the plans for Belle Etoile, to Monique, and to Douglas. Raj could see the wariness return to Abi's face. He searched for a change of subject.

"So what's this conference in Reunion about, Narinda?" he asked and was relieved when she picked up on his cue after a quick, questioning glance at him.

"It's the Society of African Psychotherapists. It could be interesting, but it's more likely to be boring, everyone trying to make out their theories and treatments are the best."

"Then why go?"

"Networking is always useful," Narinda said.

"And it means she gets to have a few days' holiday in a decent hotel all paid for by someone else," said her husband, teasing.

"How come?"

"I'm presenting a paper."

"Well done, you," said Raj, more interested now.

They spent most of the rest of the evening talking about Narinda's job, but Raj knew Douglas's will and all its repercussions were lurking just below the surface.


# CHAPTER 21


*March 1991*


The eerie quiet in the house was even more frightening than the cyclone had been. While the clatter of rain and the roar of the wind raged, it masked other sounds – her parents' raised voices, her mother screaming, and the shouting outside. Who had that been? Abi and Charlie hadn't been able to get out of her room. Their father had locked them in. They pressed their faces to the window, but all they could see were the trees in the back garden forced into a wild dance by the driving rain and frantic wind.

After what seemed like hours and hours Nanny came to let them out, comforted them, and urged them to be good. The crescendo of noise had been terrifying, but now the whispering tension, the murmur of adult voices that stopped as soon as they entered a room, the feeling that her father was only just under control, all this was much worse. And the blank look in her mother's eyes was the scariest thing of all.

Once the storm had passed there'd been lots of coming and going. Police tramping through the house, the clang of the ambulance bell, the men with saws cutting up the old tree, firemen with lifting gear. She'd not been allowed to go on watching them, but that hadn't stopped her imagination conjuring nightmarish visions, made worse by the glimpse she had later of the stretcher, its contents covered by a grey blanket. Then Uncle Douglas had arrived to take her, Charlie and Nanny V to Belle Etoile.

Standing in the middle of her bedroom as Nanny packed a bag, Abi had protested.

"Please, Nanny," she'd begged, "I don't think we should leave Mummy."

As Nanny V put her arm round her shoulders, Abi was certain she didn't want to go either.

"Your father says we must. It is best."

"No, no!" She pulled away and made a rush for the door.

"Abi–" Nanny got no further. The door had crashed open and her father stood there glaring at them.

"Why aren't you ready yet? You're keeping Douglas waiting."

"What about Mummy?" Abi had wailed.

"Abigail!" he barked. She flinched and her protests died in her throat. Nanny V put a protective arm round her shoulders and ushered her out to the car.

Curled up in the back, with Charlie pale and quiet beside her, Abi gazed blindly out of the window at the devastation left by the cyclone. Proud banyans, like the one that had fallen in their garden, had been torn from the ground, their plate-like root system now pointing to the sky, while palm trees stood tall, relieved from their bending to the wind, shredded leaves hanging forlorn. There were clothes from snapped washing lines wrapped tight round telephone wires, sheets of corrugated iron bent grotesquely round tree trunks, and houses collapsed into piles of splintered wood. Their progress was slow, with frequent stops while the road ahead was cleared, or Uncle Douglas negotiated scattered debris or impromptu lakes of muddy water. Charlie dozed off. There was no way Abi could sleep, but she did close her eyes.

After a while the murmur of voices from the front of the car began to filter through the turmoil in her mind. Uncle Douglas and Nanny spoke quietly, but if Abi concentrated hard, she could make out what they were saying.

"What possessed him to try to see her in the middle of the storm?" Uncle Douglas asked.

"I do not know," Nanny's voice was husky, as if she'd been crying. "The master, he has been in a terrible mood for days. She was very afraid. Perhaps she telephoned Monsieur Chandler before the cyclone came. Or maybe he tried to phone her and, when he could not get through, he decided to come to the house."

"Has she said anything?"

"No, nothing. She is too shocked."

"This is dreadful, dreadful, after all their plans. Tell me exactly what happened."

Abi held her breath. Now she would find out what the screaming and shouting had been about. She stayed as quiet as she could. She must hear more.

Then Charlie muttered in his sleep and Nanny turned in her seat. Abi held her breath. Keep still, keep still.

"I will tell you about it when we get to Belle Etoile, *Missié* Douglas. We must not wake the children," she said.

Abi wanted to shout, "No! Don't stop now!" but there was no point. She had no choice but to sit there, feigning sleep and trying to avoid the awful pictures in her mind.

*November 2018*

Although Abi had been longing to get back to her hotel room, once she was there a wave of loneliness hit her. When Raj dropped her off, she almost asked him to stay, have a drink with her in the bar – anything to stop him leaving. But common sense had prevailed.

On the one hand she'd enjoyed the evening, Narinda and her husband had been hospitable and kind, but their probing questions and inquisitive eyes meant she'd had to be on her guard. But other than them, and Raj, who else did she know on this island now? A sweet, gentle face hovered on the edge of her mind, but she pushed thoughts of Nanny V away. Of course, there was Monique, and Antoine too. Abi had to admit she was curious about Antoine. It was obvious he was no friend of Raj's. Perhaps he didn't like being ordered around by Raj, but she was sure there was more to it than that.

Outside in the garden discreet lights set into the ground shone up into the foliage of shrubs and palm trees, creating extraordinary shadows all around. She could hear the shushing sound of the waves on the shore, the counterpoint of the breeze whispering through the trees, and all around the high-pitched chatter of crickets. Occasionally there was a murmur of voices in the corridor outside her room, the sound of music farther off, probably coming from one of the bars.

A sudden wave of panic gripped at her stomach at the thought of the five thousand miles that separated her from Charlie and everyone else.

Pouring herself a whisky from the duty-free bottle she'd bought in Johannesburg, she sipped at it slowly. It steadied her. She settled cross-legged on the bed. What time would it be in Cambridge? Eleven fifteen here, seven fifteen there. Monday evening, Charlie should be at home. She picked up her mobile and sent her brother a text, asking if they could Skype. A response came through within minutes – *Great minds, I was just going to phone.*

She took up her iPad and tapped out the number and, to her relief, he picked up immediately. A lump rose in her throat at sight of his grinning face, the untidiness of his piled bookcases behind him.

"Beth will be cross she's missed you, she's out at choir. So, how's it going?"

"Oh Charlie, I wish you were here."

Tears squeezed out from under her lids. She rummaged in her handbag, found Raj's handkerchief and scrubbed it across her eyes. It smelt of his aftershave.

"So do I," Charlie said softly, then asked briskly, "What's the hotel like?"

"Great, right on the beach, let me show you."

She walked out on to the balcony and turned the iPad, moved it slowly round to take in the view of the gardens.

"Looks good," Charlie said. "I like the lighting."

"Lovely, isn't it, although I haven't been much beyond my room yet. I'm looking forward to a swim tomorrow." She sat back on the bed and balanced the iPad on her knees.

"Is the island still the same?" Charlie asked.

"Yes, and no. Lots more traffic and new roads, but the tarmac still crumbles into the ground at the edges. There are an awful lot of new buildings, concrete mostly, the old wooden ones seem to be few and far between now. But the people are just the same, talkative, friendly and incredibly inquisitive. I had dinner with Raj's sister, Narinda, and her husband this evening and I had quite a time fielding their desire to hear my life story since we left, in detail, with pictures and suitable soundtrack."

Charlie chuckled. "That rings a bell. Don't you remember Carl going on about it – these people don't know how to keep their distance, and all that crap."

Abi immediately felt guilty that she'd fended off Narinda's friendly probing.

"It's not that I didn't want to answer her questions. But mostly she was interested in me, us, and that was what I really didn't want to talk about." Abi got up from the bed and refilled her glass.

"At least you've got your whisky." Charlie grinned.

"Essential." She sat back down on the bed. "To be honest, I'd much rather have talked about work, much safer. You know what I mean?"

"Of course."

"I tell you someone else I met again today – Antoine."

"Good Lord. That soon? Had you let him know you were coming?"

"No. He found out where I work, and that bloody Mina gave him all the information."

"Oops. Still, you were going to have to see him at some point."

"I know. I think he'll be in on a meeting with Raj and his friends this weekend. I don't see any way of keeping him out of it. But he's been pushing for us to talk before then. I've got Raj ordering me not to trust Antoine, and Antoine saying the same about Raj. It's glaringly obvious they loathe each other, and it really pisses me off being pushed around by these bloody men."

"That's good to hear," Charlie said.

Abi knew he was thinking of Justin. She changed the subject.

"The project in Soweto looks good. It'll be a great use of our money."

"Did you manage to meet up with David Chandler?"

"Yes, I had lunch with him the day before I left Jo'burg."

"Why didn't you phone and tell me about it?"

"Don't you start ordering me around!"

"Sorry." Charlie grinned. "What's he like now? Do you still fancy him?"

"God no," Abi said.

"That sounds pretty definite," Charlie said.

It was Charlie's fault. He'd e-mailed and told David Chandler that Abi was going to be in Johannesburg and David had been very insistent they should meet up. In the end she'd given in, in spite of the memories it would bring to the surface. Those intense few weeks when she was thirteen and David fifteen had been hard to forget, but she'd managed to push it all to the back of her mind, like so much else.

At first, she hadn't noticed the tall, rather gaunt man approaching her table at Zoo Lake. His short cropped grey hair and beard made him almost unrecognisable, but then he took off his sunglasses and she noticed the scar just above his left eyebrow. At thirteen she'd thought it incredibly romantic, that scar.

"He's changed a lot," she told Charlie now. "I have to admit it wasn't the most enjoyable encounter."

"How come?"

"Well, at first we talked about my job, you and Beth, the twins. He remarked on the fact the two of you are in the same field, stuff like that. But it was very obvious there was something else on his mind." Abi paused, thinking back. "It was when he asked after Carl that I felt, somehow, we were getting to the real reason for our meeting. When I told him Carl was dead, he almost seemed disappointed."

"That's odd," Charlie said, frowning.

"I know. He said how beautiful he'd thought Mum was and that his father had thought so too, which I also thought was a bit strange, then he suddenly changed the subject and asked if I remembered the cyclone and did our parents ever talk about it. Even though I said no, he wouldn't leave it alone. And then he asked how much I knew about his father's death."

"Oh dear," Charlie said, "that must have been horrid for you, love."

"It was rather. And when I pointed out it was an accident, he said that that was the official version, but he thought there was more to it than that."

"What on earth did he mean by that?"

Abi sighed. "He has a Mauritian friend who did an MA at Wits University, where David works. This friend is a Mauritian CID inspector. David asked him to do some research into the forensic reports of his father's death, and apparently there were doubts expressed at the time. David didn't think the investigation had been thorough enough."

Charlie's frown deepened. "What on earth does he think you'd know about it? You were only thirteen, for goodness sake."

"I know. But I think he's a bit obsessed with it all and I felt rather sorry for him. But there was nothing I could tell him that he didn't know already."

"I suppose it's understandable." As always, Charlie was trying to be fair. "But I wish he hadn't bothered you with it, you've got enough on your plate."

"I know, but Charlie—" Abi had no idea how much Charlie actually knew. He'd been that much younger than her.

"Abi? What's the matter?"

Even over thousands of miles she couldn't pull the wool over Charlie's eyes. "He was so intense. And it did make me wonder."

"What about?"

"Well – was it really the tree that killed Tony?"

"Hard to tell in a cyclone," Charlie said sensibly. "He could have been hit by flying debris."

Abi felt an enormous wave of relief. Why hadn't she thought of that?

"Nothing can alter the fact that he died," Charlie went on. "Seems to me it's pointless raking it all up now."

"It seems to matter a hell of a lot to David. And now it's getting to me too."

"Look, Abi." She knew that stern expression and that tone of voice. "It's so long ago. Leave it alone. Have a bit of a holiday, concentrate on Uncle Douglas's legacy and Raj's project, and don't let all the rest of it haunt you."

"I'll try."

But when she ended the call, turned out the light and lay back under the cool, cotton sheet, she knew it would be impossible to take Charlie's advice.


# CHAPTER 22


*November 1991*


"Have you heard any more?" Prem Amrakash looked across at Douglas as he asked the question.

"No. The police are saying it was probably suicide. I suppose they could be right." But there was a world of doubt in Douglas's weary voice. "It's just that I find it impossible to believe Hilary would leave her children. There's no doubt that she had little other than them to live for, but she loved them so dearly."

"You mean little to live for since Tony died?"

"You knew about their relationship?"

"Yes, but don't worry," Prem said. "It's just that Marie guessed and let something slip. She and Hilary were very close. She's absolutely convinced it wasn't suicide."

Douglas sighed. "But to be left tied to Carl. What a life."

"But the cyclone, when he died, that was over eight months ago. She'd kept going this long."

"I know, but…" Douglas took a deep breath, as if to go on, but then was silent.

The two men sat on, thinking their own thoughts, shaded from the midday sun by the roof of the verandah. A few feet away, sitting cross-legged on the lawn under the shade of a large umbrella, sat a young girl, head bent, her face hidden by her curling golden hair. She appeared to be totally absorbed in the book balanced on her knees, but Douglas doubted she was actually reading it.

"How she suffers, that child," he said quietly to his companion.

"I'm afraid that's inevitable."

"I know, and there's little I can do to help her. Thank God for Vimala Mootian, without her I dread to think what would have happened to Abi and Charlie."

"They have you and Monique."

"But we're not there all the time. And Carl cares little about the children. So long as they behave and ask no questions, he goes on as though nothing has happened."

"He's never been one to show his emotions."

"Or feel any, for that matter," Douglas said contemptuously, "except anger. That he shows, as poor Hilary found out."

Prem looked at his friend, eyebrows raised. "He was violent towards her?"

"Yes, he kept her in a state of fear."

"*Bondiè!* Is there nothing he isn't capable of? What with your own experience and then that business at the sugar mill."

They were interrupted by Monique who came out through the French windows carrying a tray of glasses and a jug of lemonade, ice tinkling as she walked.

"Hallo, darling." Douglas smiled and pulled up a table for her to put the tray on.

"I thought we could do with something cool." She lifted her hand to shade her eyes, called out to Abi. "Do you want some lemonade, *chérie?*" There was no reaction.

"Leave her," Douglas said. "She'll come in when she's ready. Where's Charlie?"

"He's helping Antoine put the train set together." She sat down with them and poured out the lemonade. "Bless him, he's being very patient. He has a lot of his mother in him, Charlie."

"They both have, thank God." Douglas met his wife's eyes, smiled at her. The look spoke volumes.

"You're right," Monique said, looking out again to where Abi sat, apparently absorbed. "I wish I knew how to help her," she said, her eyes filling with tears.

"I know. But Prem and I were just saying, there is very little any of us can do."

"Has she spoken about it yet?"

"No. Not a word."

"Maybe I should–"

"*Ma chère,*" Douglas said, "I think we must just wait. She will talk to Vimala if she talks to anyone. And maybe I'll try to get through to her if this silence goes on for too long."

They sat for a while sipping their drinks, then Prem broke the silence.

"Would you mind telling me again exactly what happened?"

Although Douglas was reluctant to go over it all, he was willing to do as Prem asked. Perhaps his lawyer's mind would shed some light on the awful events of the previous week. Monique put her hand out to take her husband's, clasped it warmly in hers as he began to speak.

"Inspector Nundoo probably told me more than he should have, but he's an old friend and I pressed him somewhat," Douglas said. "Hilary and Carl were walking at Gris Gris. Carl says they wanted privacy to discuss some serious concerns, he didn't say exactly what, and they thought there wouldn't be many people around. According to him they had an argument and Hilary rushed on ahead of him. He didn't follow immediately, but when he saw she was near the cliff edge he called out to warn her. She took no notice, so he began to run towards her, but before he could get there she stumbled and either fell or jumped. Carl says he tried to climb down to where he could see her on the rocks below, but it was too dangerous, so he ran back to the car, drove to the nearest house and asked the owners to call the emergency services."

"And you think she didn't commit suicide?"

"I'm as sure as I can be. It could have been an accident." Douglas put a hand up to his mouth for a moment, then went on. "Carl insists he was too far away to tell exactly what happened, but he told the police that she was mentally ill, that he'd been urging her to see a doctor, but she'd refused."

"Was she mentally ill?" Prem asked.

Monique answered this question, her voice low and full of emotion.

"She was trapped in a marriage to a monster and grieving for the man she truly loved. Yes, I'd say that was enough to make her ill. But, like Douglas, I don't believe she committed suicide." Her hand tightened on Douglas's and her voice had risen a little. "And I don't believe it was an accident either. She knew the dangers of those cliffs. She wouldn't have gone so near the edge. I think that man—"

"Hush, my darling," Douglas said quietly. "The child."

"Well, you know what I think," she said, then rose abruptly and left them.

Prem watched her go. "I'm sorry," he said. "I didn't mean to upset her."

"My problem is," Douglas was almost whispering now, "I think she may be right."

"What?" Prem was shocked. Equally quietly he asked, "You think he pushed her?"

"I believe he'd be capable of it. The trouble is Vimala heard them talking about going out to talk things over, at least, she heard Carl saying they must do so, so that bears out his account. And there were no witnesses. Hilary and Carl were entirely alone. As Inspector Nundoo said, there's nothing to indicate what Carl said isn't true."

"What a terrible thing for those children to have to live with." Prem looked out to where Abi still sat over her book.

"I know," Douglas said, looking in the same direction. "They don't know the details, but Abi is bound to speculate. She knew perfectly well things were far from right between her parents. And there's another thing," Douglas added, "Carl gave Nundoo a half-written letter, in Hilary's handwriting. The inspector thought I should know about it because it was addressed to me. It was only a couple of short sentences, but it said something about not being able to go on, that she felt it would be better if she was no longer around. Carl insists that it's proof she was planning to kill herself."

"On the other hand, it could have been a cry for help."

"Absolutely. Or it could be a letter she'd started before Tony died, about their plans to go to Durban. It's just that, well, it's horribly convenient, isn't it?"

"Anyway, I have to fetch Raj from football." He smiled as he spoke. "He's got into the school team. He's so proud of himself."

"Bless him. And Narinda?"

"Doing well, studying hard, she has her mother's single-mindedness, that child."

"Give them both my love."

After Prem left, Douglas remained seated, watching Abi and waiting. He was sure she knew Prem had gone. Although she would not have been able to hear their conversation, she'd glanced up when Prem called goodbye. At last she closed her book and made her way up to where he sat. Her face was pale and she was painfully thin. His heart was wrenched at the sight of her, so closed in, so unnaturally controlled.

"*Comment ça va, ma mi?*" he asked softly as she came up the steps.

"I'm okay."

Eyes wide and dark, she stood looking at him, but he didn't think she was seeing him. He waited, then put out a hand to take hers, drew her down to sit in the seat Prem had left half an hour before.

"Do you want to talk, sweetheart?" he asked.

"No, thank you."

Douglas's heart contracted. Her flat, dull tone was almost more than he could bear.

*November 2018*

Abi had not slept well. She woke just after dawn, the sunshine filtering through the cream linen curtains. Maybe a swim before breakfast would revive her. She had plenty of time before the hire car arrived at ten, and her first meeting, with Philippe Siew Yen, wasn't until eleven.

Once changed, she made her way down through the gardens and along a gravel path to the beach. *Filao* trees had scattered their marble-sized cones on the ground and Abi was glad she'd thought to put on a pair of sandals, she remembered well how those needle-sharp cones could cut into your feet. Slipping her sandals off, she felt the sand gritty between her toes. It was beginning to warm up, later in the day it'd be too hot to walk on.

Abi waded out into the clear water and, as she sank down into it, began to feel more relaxed. At first she struck out, swimming fast up and down as she did at the leisure pool at home, then she slowed and began to notice tiny silvery shoals of fish glinting past her, and small pink and grey crabs scuttling on the sand below. By the time she returned to her room and showered, it was eight o'clock and she was hungry and feeling much better. Time for breakfast.

In the thatch-roofed dining room, open to the beach, several tame sparrows visited the tables, looking for scraps. Abi had to chase them away as they tried to steal from her plate of fruit, then gave in and scattered some crumbs from the sweet coconut pastries she'd chosen. The room was half full of people in bright holiday clothes, most of them tanned, some red from sunburn. She heard German and French spoken, and nearby was an English family, their accent making their Yorkshire origins clear. She envied them the day of sun, sea and relaxation they were probably looking forward to.

Another sparrow, bolder than the rest, landed next to her hand and made her jump. "Bugger off," Abi said, shooing him away, but all he did was hop to the other side of the table and stare at her.

"Persistent, aren't they?"

Abi looked up. The man who'd spoken had a tinge of a New Zealand accent. He was sitting at the next table, his eyes smiling in his tanned face.

She returned his smile. "They just won't take no for an answer."

"Are you here on holiday?"

"Partly, and you?"

"Oh yes. Lovely place isn't it?"

"Yes." Abi wondered if he was on his own.

"I'm Paul Harper, by the way," he said, putting out a hand and stretching over to shake hers. His hand was warm and well-manicured.

"Abi Kendall."

"Is this your first visit to the island?"

"No, I lived here as a child, but I haven't been back for years."

"What an idyllic place to grow up."

"I suppose," Abi said. She didn't want him asking about her childhood, so she changed tack. "Do you have your family with you?"

He laughed. "No, no. All on my own. It's easy to pop over from Cape Town where I'm based." His smile was warm and slightly flirtatious. "I'm very glad I did so."

"I've just come from Johannesburg."

"Do you live there?"

"Oh no. I was there on business."

"And here?"

"Just returning to my roots, I suppose. I haven't been back for nearly thirty years. It's changed quite a lot, but the people are still just the same. Is it your first visit?" she asked.

"It is. I think I'd enjoy it even more if I had some company." He paused, seeming uncertain for a moment, but then went on. "I hope you don't think me pushy, but would you like to have lunch later, or dinner? Being on my own isn't as much fun as I thought it would be. Do take pity on me."

Abi was amused by the way he put it, and a bit of company would be welcome.

"I'm not exactly sure what my plans are," she said. "Can I get back to you?"

"No problem. I'll wait to hear from you, I'm sure reception will pass on a message."

Abi watched as he made his way between the tables then lifted a hand to wave before disappearing into the reception area. It might be fun to meet up with him, she thought. Maybe tomorrow.

* * *

Just before ten, having filled in all the paperwork for the car, Abi set up the sat nav, thank goodness it had one, and, with a deep breath to calm her nerves, drove out onto the coast road. She turned in the direction of the A10 and the motorway, which would take her on to Vacoas where Philippe Siew Yen had one of his galleries.

The gallery was an airy, glass fronted building, full of bright, colourful paintings, and the occasional thoughtfully placed modern sculpture. Philippe soon put her at ease. He was a charming Chinese Mauritian with laughter lines round his small, dark eyes and a ready smile. They went through his ideas for Belle Etoile in some detail, and Abi was surprised to feel a growing enthusiasm for the project.

After a light lunch, Abi was back in the car. Rashad Kurmah had asked to meet her at his home, so her next stop was Quatre Bornes, where Abi and her parents had lived until they left the island. There was no fear of seeing her old home. David Chandler had told her it had been pulled down, but she was anxious to avoid the surrounding streets as well. Unfortunately, there was no way of avoiding some familiar landmarks, such as the old market building with the date of its completion, A.D. 1941, above the main door. She remembered going there with Nanny V to buy fruit and vegetables. Crowds of people of all nationalities were swarming in and out, tourists and locals alike, and she noticed familiar street vendors of snacks and fruit, as if they'd never moved.

She found Rashad's house easily enough. He was a small, neat man in his late forties with a bald head so hairless it shone in the sunlight. He welcomed her, served tea as they sat in his shaded garden, and they spent some time discussing the literary side, talking about Douglas's poetry, and about the young writers Rashad wished to involve in projects at Belle Etoile.

As Abi climbed back into the car, she took a deep breath. What a day! She'd managed to keep her emotions and memories in check. Now she was exhausted. All she wanted was to get back to the hotel as fast as possible and relax for what was left of the day. But, distracted by the sights and sounds around her, and by the chaos of hooting cars and weaving bicycles, she took a wrong turning and got lost in the pattern of streets behind the market square. It wasn't until she had to stop behind a large lorry that she suddenly realised where she was.

In spite of the heat, a chill shiver ran through her. David had been wrong. There by the wall a street sign said Rue St André, and behind it was the house which had been her home for her first fourteen years.

The lorry moved on. She could ignore the house and drive away, but she didn't. Instead, she parked on the grass verge and slowly got out of the car.

Some of the garden had been sold off and two small bungalows had been built, but the original wooden structure was still standing. When they'd lived there it had been brightly painted with white walls, bottle green shutters, and every detail of the French colonial architecture had been intact. Now it was desperately shabby and obviously deserted. Paint was peeling and some of the shutters hung at crazy angles. Several roof tiles had fallen off, and there were gaps like missing teeth in the verandah railings. The garden was wildly overgrown and there was nothing to show where the enormous banyan had once stood.

Hands clasped around the bars of the rusting, wrought iron gate, Abi stood gazing at her old home.

*October 1989*

Abi was hiding in one of her favourite places. Here she could curl up between two of the spreading roots of the banyan, two feet high either side of her. Unless whoever was looking for her came right round the tree, they wouldn't know she was there. She was engrossed in a book called *Tales of Heroic Animals* that Uncle Douglas had given her, and she didn't hear the voices until there was no escaping. The sound of her father's voice pinned her down, unable to move from where she was.

"What would it matter to you anyway, Hilary? You have all you need, don't you? The children, servants, your devoted cousin dancing attendance." Abi could imagine the scorn on her father's face. "And quite apart from anything else, you should know better than to listen to gossip."

"But is it true?"

Abi could hear the tremble in her mother's voice. She heard her father laugh.

"You'd really like me to tell you it is, wouldn't you? That way you could go all self-righteous on me. And even if it is, what are you going to do about it? You're so bloody boring in bed, and half the time you're not particularly willing. I can hardly be blamed for going elsewhere."

"But the girl is only fifteen." There was outrage in her mother's voice.

Abi didn't want to hear any more. She put up her hands to cover her ears, but it made no difference. They must have been standing close to the other side of the tree. She thought of humming to cut out the sound, but that was no good, she might be heard. All she could do was sit tight. Please, please God make them go away.

"These Creole girls mature early, that's what I like about them. And it wouldn't be the first time. You know that, don't you? So does your bloody cousin! This girl makes the best of herself, unlike you." She could hear that he was smiling. "I don't think I'll tell you if it's true or not, I'd rather leave you guessing. That way, whenever we meet her parents, you just won't know what to say. I'll enjoy watching you squirm."

"Please, Carl, don't go on with it. She's barely older than Abi. It's so wrong."

He laughed. "According to whom? You're such a bloody prude, Hilary. Anyway, your moralising has never stopped me before and it's not going to now, so you might as well shut up."

"So, it is true?"

"Did I say so?"

"No but–" There was total silence for a moment then her mother went on speaking, her words tumbling over each other, as if she wanted to get them out before she ran out of courage. "I shall tell Douglas. I'll ask him to speak to her parents. Then you'll have to leave her alone. You wouldn't want to lose–"

There was the sound of a stinging slap. Abi heard her mother cry out. Oh God, she must do something. But all she did was press her hands even harder over her ears.

"You'll do nothing of the sort, you bitch." His voice was different now. Quiet and much more frightening. "Remember what I said about the children? That wasn't an empty threat. You'll keep quiet or I'll take them away from you, understand?"

The only response was a whimper, no words.

"I think this conversation is over. I'm out this evening, don't bother to wait up."

Heavy footsteps retreated. Abi could hear the sound change as her father went from the lawn to the gravel path, then quickly up the steps to the verandah. There were no more sounds from her mother until the door into the house slammed. Then Abi heard her begin to cry, muffled sobs, as if she had a hand to her mouth. The sound slowly retreated as she heard her mother's footsteps going back over grass, gravel, steps, then there was silence.

Abi felt sick, with guilt, with anger, and with fear. She should have gone to her mother, comforted her, told her it was all okay, like Nanny did when she or Charlie was hurt. But she couldn't move. She sat there for a long time in the shelter of the banyan roots, arms wrapped tight round her knees, her book forgotten.

# CHAPTER 23



*November 2018*

The weather had changed suddenly, as it often did in Mauritius, and Abi sat in the dining room, drinking her after-dinner coffee, waiting for the short downpour to stop before going back across the garden to her room. She was exhausted and drained, but reluctant to go to bed for fear of the dreams that might come. Seeing the house this afternoon had shaken her to the core, brought back so many memories, echoing voices and conversations she understood so much better now than she had as a child.

She saw Paul Harper weaving his way between the tables towards her. Thank God for that, the distraction of someone to talk to would be very welcome.

"Hi," he said as he arrived at her table. "It certainly knows how to rain here, doesn't it?"

"It does indeed, but it won't last long. Would you like to join me," Abi asked.

"I'd be delighted." He lifted a hand to a passing waiter, asked for coffee. "So, have you had a busy day?"

"Somewhat, meetings and stuff."

"What kind of work do you do?"

"I work for a charity."

"With a presence on the island?"

"Not yet, but we could be taking on some work here."

"What kind of work's that?"

"Educational," Abi said, making it vague. "And what do you do?"

He smiled as the waiter brought his coffee, gave the man a tip. "I'm in the wine trade, I'm sure you've heard of Cape wines."

"Of course."

"I'm originally from New Zealand, another place for great wines," he said, "but Cape Town suits me best. The wine is fantastic. I've been trying to persuade the manager here to take some of ours."

Abi laughed. "I thought you said you were on holiday?"

"I am, but I thought I'd just mention them to him."

"And did you have any success?"

"I think so," he said. "I've given him a couple of bottles to sample. I'll just have to wait and see if he takes the bait."

"Do you always go on holiday with samples of your wine?"

"Very often." He grinned. "But I actually bought these at a supermarket in Port Louis. Please don't tell him!"

Abi smiled. Her coffee was finished. She was feeling very tired, and yet she was enjoying the company. She was just about to suggest they had a liqueur in the bar, when his mobile rang.

"Excuse me," he said, with an apologetic grimace. "I'd better take this. Maybe the manager's made up his mind."

He leant to one side in his chair and glanced at the screen, frowned then held the phone to his ear.

"Yes? And that's definite? How many of them? Right, go ahead as planned." With the mobile held to his ear, he glanced up at Abi, gave her a quick smile. "Why not? Okay. I'll sort it out now."

He switched the mobile off, lifted his hands in a gesture of regret.

"I'm afraid I'm going to have to desert you. Holiday? What holiday? I have to send a couple of e-mails, confirming an order for a Jo'burg restaurant chain. Can't risk losing that, can I?"

They both rose.

"Perhaps we can meet up again tomorrow?" he said.

"I'd like that. At breakfast maybe? I'm going for a swim first thing."

"It's a date." He gave her arm a squeeze, then turned and walked away.

Loneliness rushed back at Abi. What to do now? She glanced at her watch. It was half past nine. She could phone Charlie and tell him about seeing the old house, but she really didn't want to talk about it. Or maybe Evelyn, she hadn't spoken to her yet, but Evelyn would want to know more than Abi was willing to tell. She could phone Raj and ask him about the meeting on Thursday, but she didn't want him to think she couldn't manage without constant contact.

In the end she resigned herself to going back to her room. As she passed the bar she saw Paul in deep conversation with another man, a Mauritian in smart dark trousers and open neck white shirt. She smiled. He was obviously doing well on the wine front.

As she opened the door of her room the phone by her bed was ringing. She picked it up, wondering who it could be, and was delighted when she recognised Raj's voice.

"How did things go today with Philippe and Rashad?" he asked.

Abi lay back on the bed, cradling the receiver.

"Pretty well, I think." She brought him up to date on what had been discussed. "I liked them both. They said they're looking forward to our meeting at the weekend. Is that still on?"

"Yes. Sunday afternoon, at the gallery in Vacoas."

"Shouldn't we invite Antoine to that?"

"I don't think so. Best to get things straight between us before we involve him."

"He was pushing to be included."

"I thought he might be. From the CAF point of view, Abi, it's up to you. You made it clear yesterday you were going to make your own decisions."

Abi smiled. "I did, didn't I."

"Decisively." His tone was teasing.

"Sorry about that."

"You had reason. Let's talk about it on Thursday." He changed the subject. "So, what have you got planned for tomorrow?"

"I hadn't really thought." Abi wasn't looking forward to a whole day to fill with nothing but her own company. "I've got the car. Maybe I should do some sight-seeing, pretend I'm on holiday."

"It's annoying that I've got to be in court all day, and I've got a really boring meeting in the evening, but there's no way I can get out of it." There was a little silence, then he said, "I feel I'm neglecting you."

She was surprised when she felt quite pleased by this.

"Don't be silly. I'll think of something. Maybe I'll visit that museum in Mahebourg, the naval one, there's a leaflet about it by my bed."

"You should do that. It's interesting. I love museums."

"So do I. And what about art galleries?" She asked, thinking of the one she'd been to that morning.

"Absolutely. I went to the Tate Modern while I was in London, that fantastic space on the ground floor is stunning."

With the receiver tucked between shoulder and ear, Abi poured herself a whisky, added iced water, and listened to Raj talking about his favourite paintings in the Tate. She could hear music in the background, asked him what it was, he said Peter Gabriel, she said he was one of her favourites, and this took them on to discussing music. For more than an hour they talked, going from music to books, then films, then food. By the time they ended the conversation it was nearly eleven.

It wasn't until Abi was sitting on the edge of her bed, a lingering smile on her face as she rubbed at her numb, flattened ear, that she realised only the first few minutes of their conversation had been about Belle Etoile or her reasons for being in Mauritius.

* * *

"Is she here yet?" Raj asked as Georgette brought the post in to him late on Thursday morning.

"Raj, I would have told you if she was. She's only a quarter of an hour late."

"I know, it's just that these English, they're obsessed with being on time."

"Come on, that's a bit of a generalisation, isn't it." Halfway to the door she turned back. "By the way, Jacquo moved in at Belle Etoile over the weekend. He was welcomed with open arms and a great deal of food by Zabette and Tushti. He says he's using Zabette's old room, the one above the garage next to Tushti's, as it gives a clear view of the driveway."

"Good idea. Now we wait and see what Antoine's reaction is."

He didn't have to wait long, at least that's what he thought when Georgette popped her head round the door ten minutes later.

"Patti says she's got Antoine on the line," she said. "Do you want her to put him through?"

"Okay. I might as well get it over."

But Raj was surprised when Antoine made no mention of the new member of the Belle Etoile household. He wanted to know, yet again, how things were going with Abi, said he'd tried to get hold of her at the hotel, but she'd been out all day yesterday, and had Raj seen her. He sounded subdued and rather nervy. Raj got the distinct impression there was something Antoine wanted to tell him but couldn't quite bring himself to do so. This, much more than his pushiness, worried Raj and made him inclined to give a little.

"Look, Antoine, I'll set up a meeting between the three of us when I speak to her. When are you free?"

He was even more surprised by Antoine's reply.

"I'm not sure. I'll get back to you."

"But I thought you wanted to meet up as soon as possible."

"I do, but– look, Raj, it's a bit difficult at the moment."

"Because of your friend Pieter?"

"What the hell do you mean?" Antoine snapped.

"What's up, Antoine?"

"Nothing. I'll get back to you."

"You haven't been down nagging your mother, have you?"

"Christ Almighty, Raj, what do you take me for? I haven't been down to Belle Etoile for days, too busy."

So that explained why he hadn't mentioned Jacquo.

"Look, I've got to go. Just keep me posted." And the call was abruptly cut off.

Raj sat for a moment staring at the phone as if it could answer the questions in his mind. Then he glanced at his watch. Where on earth was Abi? She was half an hour late. He tried her mobile but got no response. He phoned the hotel but was told she was out. There was a muttered conversation in the background then the receptionist told him she'd ordered a taxi and left the hotel hours ago. Raj wondered what had happened to the hire car.

By midday he'd gone past being annoyed and had started to worry. He told himself to forget it. Maybe she'd just changed her mind. As he turned to his computer, determined to concentrate on a long list of e-mails, the phone on his desk rang and he snatched it up.

"Is she here?"

"No," said Georgette. "It's a Doctor Castelain wanting to speak to you, from the Clinique Hennessy."

Raj had heard of it. It was a classy private hospital not far from his office. "Did he say what it was about?"

"I asked, but he insisted on speaking to you."

"Okay. Put him through. He's probably being sued or something," Raj said irritably.

"Monsieur Amrakash?" a pleasant voice asked.

"Speaking."

"I have a Miss Kendall in my clinic. She gave me your number. She has had an accident but—"

"What kind of accident? Is she all right?" Stupid question, Raj thought. She wouldn't be there if she was.

"She will be fine. I will give her the phone. She will tell you about it."

A minute later Abi came on the line.

"Raj? Look I'm so sorry about this. I told the taxi chap I was fine, but he insisted on bringing me here."

"Hold on. Go back to the beginning. What taxi?"

"I had to get one this morning. The hire car wouldn't start."

He heard her take a deep breath and when she spoke again her voice shook just a little. Maybe she was more seriously injured than she'd made out.

"I was on my way to your office. We were driving along the main road in Curepipe, just past the school where Uncle Douglas used to teach. It all happened rather quickly. I think it was the bus trying to pass us that caused it, or the cyclist, I don't know."

"You should have phoned me, is your mobile not working?"

Raj heard her give a shaky laugh and wondered if she was getting hysterical.

"You can be a bit bossy, can't you? I put it on charge before I came out and then forgot it. Where was I? Oh yes. The driver had to brake hard and I suppose I must have jarred my wrist. Anyway, the taxi was fine, just a bit of a bump on the wing, but when the driver realised I'd hurt my wrist, he insisted on bringing me straight here to be checked over."

"I'm very glad he did."

"Yes, well, there you have it. And this lovely Doctor Castelain has strapped it up. He says it's just a sprain, but I told the driver to get going because he had another job to go to, so I'm stuck, rather, unless I get another taxi. I was going to, but Doctor Castelain insisted I phone you."

"I'll come and fetch you now," Raj said. "I know the place. It'll only take me five minutes to get there."

"Thank you, Raj. I'm really sorry to give you all this trouble."

"Don't worry. It's not your fault. I'm on my way."

# CHAPTER 24

Abi had really enjoyed her day out. She'd wandered round the Naval Museum, bought several presents to take home from the shops in Mahebourg, found one shop that sold saris and bought two before she could stop herself, and found some garish T-shirts for Mattie and Pip which she had a suspicion they would never wear. She enjoyed trying out her Creole and had several friendly conversations. "You speak like a *Morisyen*" she was told. She ended up with two invitations for dinner, one for tea, and a smiling proposal of marriage from an elderly man selling soft drinks from a cool box attached to his bike.

Back in her room she'd phoned Charlie and brought him up to date on what she'd been doing and spoken to Beth to tell her about the T-shirts. After that she had a brief chat with Evelyn, fielded several probing questions about Raj, then spent some time sending off a few e-mails. By the time she went to bed, she'd felt more relaxed than she had in ages.

But now all that had changed. She was angry with herself. Angry that she felt so shaken and out of control, and angry that she'd gabbled away at Raj like a child. She so wanted to convince him she was business-like and in charge, ready to tackle anything thrown at her, but that was hardly the impression she was giving him.

The nurse showed her out to the gleaming reception area where she suggested Abi sit down while she brought her a glass of iced water.

"You are sure you will be okay? Your friend is coming?"

"Yes, I'm fine. And thank you so much."

"It is nothing. Now you must enjoy the rest of your holiday."

"I'll try," Abi said wishing that was all it was.

She sat there fuming. Even if they brought her another hire car, she wouldn't be able to drive it. She let her head rest back on the soft leather and closed her eyes, only to snap them open again when she heard approaching footsteps.

"You seem to be having an eventful morning." Raj was standing before her, his smile teasing.

Abi was completely taken aback by how delighted she was to see him and tried to cover it by saying, "God Raj, you made me jump! Look, I'm really sorry about this."

"Stop apologising. Didn't I tell you yesterday, road accidents are a Mauritian institution?" He put out a hand to help her up.

"It's only this." She waved her bandaged arm at him, then winced.

"I'd keep it still if I were you." He put an arm round her as if she was an invalid. Abi didn't protest. He smelt rather nice, that same lemony scented aftershave she'd noticed on the handkerchief he'd lent her.

"Does it hurt?" Raj asked.

"Not much, and the doctor gave me some pain killers. But I expect my front will be a bit bruised from the seat belt."

He gave her a sideways glance. "Blue boobs."

"Raj!"

"Sorry. I shouldn't have said that." He was grinning but there was a slight flush under his dark skin. "It must be something to do with having lived abroad for a while, I've picked up nasty foreign ways."

Their relationship seemed to have changed. Maybe it was because of that long phone conversation the night before last. Strange how well you could get to know someone over the phone.

"I suggest we pop into my office and pick up the papers we need and have lunch at the restaurant next door," Raj was saying. "It's run by a friend of mine."

"Do all your friends run restaurants?"

Raj smiled. "Only two."

They didn't talk as Raj drove through the narrow streets to the main road then wove skilfully through the traffic. Abi closed her eyes against the chaos, but a moment later things quietened down, and she opened them to see that they'd turned into a street just past a church. Raj parked outside a modern office block.

"Stay here," said Raj. "I'll go and get the papers."

"But I want to see your office."

"Why?"

"I just do. You've seen mine."

He shrugged, gave her a half smile. "Okay. If we go in the back way it'll be quicker," Raj said.

They went in through a small door at the side and took the lift to the third floor. At the end of a glassed-in balcony overlooking the busy street below, was a door with a highly polished brass plaque on it that bore the legend *'Amrakash Chambers, Attorneys at Law, Notaires Publique'*.

Two women looked round as they came in, avid curiosity in their eyes. A young receptionist, not unlike Mina in looks, sat behind a curved desk to one side. Behind her another woman sat at another desk, her curling hair, more African features and flecked hazel eyes, evidence of her mixed Creole ancestry.

"We've just come in to collect the paperwork, Georgette," Raj said to the hazel eyed woman.

She came forward, smiling, and shook Abi's hand.

"Miss Kendall, I'm Georgette Pillay, Raj's clerk and office manager."

"Yes, sorry, I should have introduced you," Raj said.

"And this is our receptionist, Patti Blackburn," Raj said and Patti smiled at her shyly.

"Such bad luck," Georgette said. "It is our terrible drivers. Totally insane. Was the doctor able to tell you what damage has been done?"

"Only a bit of bruising, I think. It's just a nuisance, really, as it means I can't drive for a couple of days. The hire company are delivering another car to the hotel this afternoon. I'd better contact them and tell them not to do so."

"Don't worry," Georgette said. "Give me the details and I can do that for you."

"Are you sure?"

"Certainly. No problem."

"It means another taxi to get back," she said ruefully.

"I can take you back after lunch," Raj told her.

But Georgette intervened. "You haven't forgotten you've got the Leong case conference starting at half past three, have you, Raj?"

"Oh damn. Yes, I had."

"I can take Abigail back. My grandmother lives in Mahebourg, near the hotel. I usually visit after work on Thursdays."

"That would be so kind. I'm sorry to be such a nuisance."

"No trouble at all." She picked up a file from her desk. "Here are the papers, Raj."

They left the office to smiles and goodbyes and walked back the way they'd come.

"I noticed at the hospital the doctor and nurses spoke English to each other, and all your colleagues do too. I know it used to be like that, but I'm surprised it still is."

"They'd think it rude to speak anything but English if you're involved in the conversation. They've no way of knowing if you speak French or Creole, or Hindi for that matter."

"What do you speak as a general rule?"

"It depends. A mixture I suppose, English and French in court, then Creole or Hindi with friends and family, and English of course."

It was only a couple of minutes' walk to the restaurant which had tables in a small courtyard. Raj chose one in the shade of a large fig tree. Once settled and served with plates of smoked marlin, Abi realised cutting up her food wasn't going to be easy, not with the injury to her wrist. Raj looked up, saw her problem, and grinned.

"Here, let me do that. I can't bear to watch you struggle."

"I feel such an idiot," Abi said, watching him.

"You don't like asking people for help, do you?"

She met his eyes across the table, her smile rueful.

"No, I don't. But thank you anyway."

"*Mo plaizir*," he said, and the fact that he spoke in Creole seemed to make the situation more intimate. She was relieved when Raj opened the file and they got down to business. .

Raj produced a floor plan of the house at Belle Etoile, pointed out which rooms could be used for the different purposes.

"Even with Monique still living there," he said, "as long as we staff it properly and protect her privacy, we could start by converting some of the east wing for functions, say the library, Douglas's studio, the sitting room. And we could extend into the attics, there's plenty of potential to develop them, maybe as an art gallery."

Abi looked at the plan and tried to fit her memories of the house into this two-dimensional image. The studio, the wide back verandah, where she and Charlie had learnt to play table tennis on an ancient chipboard table, the library next door to Douglas's studio, wood panelled and lined with bookcases on three sides. She'd loved that room, spent hours in there pouring over books, old and new. And the guest room, at the other end of the front verandah, that was where she and Charlie had slept when they stayed at Belle Etoile.

She realised she hadn't been listening to what Raj was saying and dragged herself back to the present.

They went through the costings Raj and his friends had put together, and the sketches, by Philippe Siew Yen, of what the rooms would look like once the project was up and running.

"It was good to meet Philippe and Rashad," Abi said. "They're both so enthusiastic. Is the Arts Minister as keen?"

"Devina? Yes, I think so, although, being a politician, she's not made any cast iron promises yet."

"I'm looking forward to our meeting on Sunday."

"I hope Devina makes it. She's notoriously difficult to pin down, but since you're here for such a short time she'll probably make an extra effort. By the way, how long are you staying?"

"I'm booked to go back on the nineteenth."

"Right, which gives us a few days yet." He glanced at her, but she couldn't read his expression. "I hadn't expected you to be here so long."

"Lawrie said to have a bit of a holiday as well."

"Good idea. Get away from things."

Abi was grateful when he didn't elaborate.

"I'm not working on Saturday," Raj said, glancing at her across the table.

"Do you usually?"

"Quite often, in the mornings at any rate. I wonder," he said sounding diffident, "maybe I could take you to have a look round Port Louis, or go to the botanical gardens at Pamplemousses?"

"I'd like that," she said.

"And of course, we must go down to Belle Etoile as soon as possible. Apart from anything else, Monique wants to see you."

Abi took a deep breath. "Yes, I suppose that must be done. I mean, seeing Belle Etoile. It's not that I don't want to see Monique, it's just going to the house."

But if the truth were known, visiting the house, meeting up with Monique again, all of it filled her with a sense of panic.

# CHAPTER 25

*September 1991*

Hilary didn't have much time, but still she lingered. This was her life saver, her one link with Tony. Each time she'd come down to Belle Etoile, she'd brought a little more to hide away, here where Carl couldn't get at it.

Carl had been taunting her about going back to the UK for weeks now. How was she going to take all these precious possessions with her? Should she leave them with Douglas? Or maybe parcel everything up and send it to Rose? No, Rose was terrified of Carl, she'd blurt it all out. And there were still a few things missing, like the filigree brooch. She'd searched everywhere in her bedroom but still couldn't find it. The thought that Carl might have taken it made her feel sick, but it was impossible to ask him. Douglas had assured him that it was his gift, but if

Carl realised how much she cared about it he'd never let her have it back.

Crouched on the floor, she rocked back and forth, arms clasped round her thin body, unable to fight the tears. She sobbed until she was drained and exhausted and her throat was raw. At last, she managed to regain control. Douglas might come to find her. She mustn't let him see her like this, he would worry so. Think, think. What could she do? It wasn't fair to involve Douglas. He'd already done so much for them. Now she knew what Carl was capable of, there was no way she could risk Douglas or Monique being harmed.

Once more she opened the tin box, lifted out a man's handkerchief with TC embroidered in one corner. She stroked the letters with the tip of a finger, remembered putting in every stitch. Lifting it to her face, she cradled it against her cheek. Was there the barest ghost of the smell of him? She tried to convince herself there was. Then she picked up a photo. His face looked back at her, the smile that went up on one side more than the other, the eyes crinkled with laughter lines, his hair curling slightly over his ears. The longing in her body was a pain she could hardly bare.

She thought of his last letter. She knew it by heart now.

> *My darling Hilly,*
> *I've told David you'll be coming to live with us. He can't wait, although he did ask if that meant he and Abi would be brother and sister. He seemed quite anxious about it. I assured him it didn't.*
> *I'll be booking flights tomorrow and will send you the tickets via Douglas...*

Carefully she put the photo and the letter back, laying the handkerchief next to it. A moment later she heard a voice calling her name. A few seconds of icy fear crawled through her, but surely it had been a woman's voice, not

Carl's. He was still away. Yet knowing that didn't quite banish the fear that he might appear without warning. He'd lied to her before about the time he'd return from a trip, he could do it again.

It seemed to take an age to replace everything in the steel box, but finally it was done. Last of all was a cream envelope. She hesitated, but no, it would have to stay there for a while longer. Quickly she placed the box safe in its hiding place, then put her sunglasses on, adjusted them carefully, and stumbled up from the floor. As she got to the door, someone was coming up the steps.

"Hilary? Hallo, my dear," said Marie Pillay, her smile kind and tinged with curiosity. "How are you?"

Relief flooded through her. "I'm fine," she said. The words were meaningless, but what else could she say?

From under their heavy lids Marie's kind eyes scanned her face, but all she said was, "Monique asked me to find you. She's made tea. Come and join us."

*November 2018*

Georgette and Abi left Curepipe behind and drove along a steeply cambered road. Abi watched the heat haze as it rose from the tarmac, remembering how her mother used to describe the shimmering blur as fairy air. She looked out of the window at the sugar cane fields stretching either side of the road and, in the distance, the mountains. This landscape was so much part of her that she wondered how she'd managed without it for so long. She was glad when Georgette's voice broke into her thoughts.

"I hope you don't mind, but I phoned my grandmother and told her you were here," Georgette said. "I wonder, would you mind if we popped in for a few minutes on the way back to the hotel? She tells me she knew your mother well, and she would very much like to see you."

Abi felt a lurch of apprehension.

"I'd love to," she said. To refuse would seem rude after Georgette had been so kind.

"I was wondering if you remember my grandmother," Georgette said.

"I'm not sure. Perhaps when I see her–"

"She certainly remembers you, and Charlie."

Abi wasn't sure how to respond to this and was glad when, a moment later, Georgette said, "Here we are."

They pulled up in an overgrown lane and parked next to the grass verge. Abi got out of the car and followed her companion to a gateway masked by lush vines and other greenery spilling over the tall fence, making the gate difficult to push open. Once inside she was delighted to find a beautifully tended garden, very different from the sad neglect she'd seen at her parents' old house. This was full of pink, red and green leafed caladium, bright canna lilies and half a dozen other flowering plants. A path wound its way to the house itself, a clapboard bungalow painted a pale sky blue. At one side the spreading leaves of an enormous avocado tree shaded the red corrugated iron roof of a glassed-in verandah.

"What a gorgeous place," Abi exclaimed.

"It is, isn't it. Raj's father bought it for *Grandmère* when she retired."

"Sounds like a good boss."

"He was, and a good friend. Raj is very like him."

Abi glanced at her. Was their relationship a closer one than employer and employee? That's not how they'd come across but, she told herself, it was none of her business.

Georgette pushed open a mesh screen door onto the verandah.

"*'allo, Grandmère? Mo èna en visitaire pou toi.*"

"A visitor for me? Come in, come in."

The elderly woman who greeted them was small and a little stooped, with hooded eyes and a wide smile. A look of recognition came over her face at sight of Abi.

"*Bondiè!* Abigail!" she exclaimed. "I would have known you anywhere. You look so like your dear mother."

Abi, who had never thought she looked anything like her mother, was taken aback and deeply moved.

"Oh yes indeed, you have her smile, and the same golden hair. You are just as beautiful."

Marie Pillay clasped her shoulders, reached up to kiss her cheeks, and Abi laughed, embarrassed, unable to think of how to respond to the compliment.

"But what has happened to you?" she asked, looking at her strapped-up wrist.

"Nothing to worry about," Abi assured her. "A silly accident, that's all, but I'm afraid I can't drive for a few days, so Georgette kindly offered to give me a lift back to my hotel."

The old woman bustled around, plumped cushions on several plastic garden chairs, pulled three into a group, and urged them to sit down.

"I will bring tea, and I've just made some *gateaux patates*, do you remember them? Your mother used to love them, and some *gateaux gingeli*, that's what Georgette always asks for. This is good Mauritian food to put a few pounds on you. You modern girls, you're too thin, you need some curves, that's what the men like."

"*Grandmère!*" Georgette protested. "Stop fussing. I'll get the tea. Stay here and talk to Abi."

They sat opposite each other and Marie folded her hands in her lap and stared at Abi, head on one side like a bird.

"I am very pleased to see you," she said, smiling.

"Thank you," said Abi.

"Do you find the island changed?"

"In some ways. It's much more built up than it was, and there's more traffic."

"*Ayo!* This is very true. Cars, buses, lorries, there are far too many, and our roads are full of holes. Was this accident you had in a car?"

"Yes. The taxi I was in had an argument with a bus."

"An argument?" She looked puzzled, then light dawned, and Marie laughed. "That is a good way to put it. Yes, yes, an argument." And she laughed a little more.

Abi couldn't help smiling. "One thing that hasn't changed is the people, everyone is so friendly and relaxed."

"Too relaxed sometimes. Perhaps if they weren't, more would get done."

"Perhaps, but I rather like it the way it is."

"Georgette tells me this is the first time you have come home in all these years." She was suddenly serious, reached over and patted Abi's hand. "But I think I can understand why. I still think of your mother often. She was a very good person."

It was as if she was contradicting a suggestion that it might have been otherwise.

Abi couldn't think what to say and was relieved when Georgette arrived back with a loaded tray. She placed it on a low table and handed out brightly coloured little napkins, delicately painted bone china plates and poured the tea into matching cups, then handed round the cakes. Abi bit into a small half-moon shaped *gateau patate* and memories flooded back as she tasted the sweet potato and coconut filling.

"You like them?" Marie asked.

"Delicious. Our Nanny used to make them."

"Was that Vimala Mootian? Will you be seeing her while you're here?" Marie asked.

"I– er... I don't know. We, my brother and I, haven't heard from her for a very long time, since the early nineties."

"But how can that have happened?" exclaimed Marie.

"I'm not sure," Abi said hesitantly.

"*Grandmère*," Georgette said, picking up on Abi's discomfort. "You ask too many questions."

"But that is so sad," Marie insisted. "Is she still alive?"

"I don't know," Abi said, wishing she could think of a way of changing the subject.

"It would be very easy to find out," the old lady said brightly. "I have a friend who might know, I will ask."

"Oh, please don't trouble."

"It will be no trouble at all. So, tell me, how is your hotel?"

Abi was relieved, this was much safer ground. She plunged into an enthusiastic description of the hotel, then they went on to talk about the accident and Marie seemed delighted that Raj had come to her rescue when she needed picking up.

"Bless him, such a lovely boy. You must get him to show you around while you're here," Marie said decisively, then asked, with a gleam in her eyes, "So, there is no good-looking young man in your life?"

"No," Abi said, but Justin came into her mind and she realised with a jolt how little she'd thought about him in the last few days. "I'm not sure a young man is what I need, I'm getting on a bit myself."

"*Po, po, po*," the expression was full of kindly scorn. "You are all youngsters to me, and you're beautiful, successful, what man wouldn't be delighted to have you for his wife? We will have to find you a nice Mauritian husband, although these Mauritian men, they need a firm hand. Ask my Georgette. Her boyfriend has a responsible job in a bank, earns good money, but he doesn't seem too keen to getting married."

So, Georgette did have a boyfriend.

"You are a terrible old lady," Georgette said, reddening, and Abi got the impression this was a subject often discussed. "We'll get married in our own good time. And anyway, how would Raj cope without me?"

Marie surprised Abi by dismissing this objection. "You could go on working."

"But what if I had children?"

"I could look after your children."

Georgette laughed. "You see what I have to put up with?" she said to Abi. "She has spent all her life organising everyone around her and she's not about to give up now. *Tonton* Prem, Raj's father, used to say there was no problem on this island that *Grandmère* couldn't sort out, and nothing she didn't know that was worth knowing."

"And he was right," her grandmother said, grinning. "When I knew your mother, I was still working for Prem, in his office in Port Louis, and whenever she came into town, we used to have lunch. Was it 1991 that you left Mauritius?"

"1992," Abi said, hoping this wouldn't lead back to more talk of her mother, but it did.

"Ah yes, a year after your poor mother passed away. I saw her at Belle Etoile just before she died."

"*Grandmère*, perhaps–" Georgette tried to intervene, but her grandmother didn't seem to hear her.

"I just couldn't believe the news when I heard it a few days later. Such a terrible accident."

"Accident? But Carl– my father told us she committed suicide." The words were out before Abi could stop them.

"Oh, my dear, no, no, not Hilary." Marie sounded absolutely sure of herself.

Abi had the sensation of falling with no parachute. All her life she'd believed her mother had chosen to die. That's what Carl had told them. She had spent all this time believing that her mother hadn't loved her enough to stay alive. And now this small, forceful old lady was telling her that wasn't so.

"But what makes you so sure?" Abi was amazed that her voice sounded so normal.

"She would never have killed herself. She loved you and your brother far too much. No, it was an accident." There was absolute certainty in her voice. "Of course, there was talk–" She stopped suddenly, her lips tightening over the words she might have said. Then she leant forward and pressed Abi's hand. "I have upset you. I'm a stupid old woman. Let us talk about happier things. Tell me, how is your brother? He was such a sweet boy, Charlie. Is he married? Does he have a family?"

Abi could hear her voice as if she was listening to someone else, telling Marie about Charlie, Beth and the boys. She said nothing about her work and Belle Etoile. That might lead to more talk of the past.

At long last Georgette suggested they get going. Their conversation had filled her mind with so many questions, she really didn't think she could have kept up the social facade much longer. They said their goodbyes, Marie urged her to come back again before she left the island. Abi said she would try but felt torn. Part of her wanted to hear more about her mother and Marie's memories, but part of her couldn't bear the thought of what she might find out.

On the short drive to the hotel, Abi noticed Georgette give her an occasional anxious glance, but the last thing she wanted was to be asked if she was all right, or anything else for that matter. As they drew up in front of the hotel, Georgette gave her another worried look, put her hand out and touched Abi's arm.

"Abi, I hope *Grandmère* didn't upset you."

"Of course not. I so enjoyed seeing her again, she's a wonderful woman," she said quickly as she opened the car door. "And I'm sure I'll see you again soon. Thank you so much for giving me a lift. Bye." And she walked away across the gravel as fast as she could.

As soon as she got back to the privacy of her room she punched out Charlie's mobile number, but there was no reply. She tried the direct line to his office. Nothing. She'd tried to speak to him last night, longing to tell him about coming upon the house so unexpectedly, but there'd been no reply. Had they gone away? What difference did that make? He'd have his mobile with him. Maybe if she tried Beth. She did so, still no luck. Lying down on the bed, Abi flung an arm up over her closed eyes. All the unanswered questions, the long-remembered pain, and the loneliness of having no one to share them with, rose up inside her, a force she could no longer control.

* * *

The case conference had taken far longer than Raj had expected. It wasn't until six that he left his client's office, so he decided to go straight home rather than back to work. As he walked to his car, he turned his mobile back on. It buzzed immediately. There were several texts, one from Antoine saying, yet again, that he needed to talk urgently. Raj's thumb hovered over the keys, then he decided it could wait. Another from Narinda asking how it was going with Abi. He'd phone his sister later. And the third was from Georgette asking him to phone her as soon as possible. He replied to this one.

"Georgette. You wanted me?"

"Where have you been?"

"Old Mr Leong went on and on, you know how much he loves the sound of his own voice. I've only just got out of there. Why? What's up?"

"I dropped Abi off at the hotel after having tea with *Grandmère*."

"Thanks. How's your grandmother?"

"Fine, fine, but Raj, you know how *Grandmère* is."

"What do you mean?"

"So inquisitive, wanting to know everyone's business."

He grinned. "Yes," he said, but then his smile faded. "Was she giving Abi the third degree?"

"She was rather. Raj, she talked about Abi's mother."

Raj's heart sank. "What did she say?"

"It seems Abi thought her mother had committed suicide."

"I know, that's what she told me."

"Well, *Grandmère* says no, she was very definite about it. I'm sure she said it for the best of reasons, you know, to reassure Abi, and I think she might have said more, but *Grandmère* could see it was upsetting her."

"I see," Raj said, frowning.

"Anyway, it struck me Abi was far more upset than she was letting on. I was going to ask her if she'd like to come and have a meal this evening, but she rushed off when we got back to the hotel and I didn't have the chance. The thing is, I'm a bit worried."

"Okay, but Georgette, what do you think I can do about it?"

"I don't know really." But he was pretty sure she had something in mind.

"I'll give her a ring. That's what you want, isn't it?"

"Not exactly. I think she'll just say she's fine if you do that."

"Well, what else?"

"You could drop in at the hotel, have a drink with her or something," Georgette said, her voice deliberately casual.

Raj wasn't taken in. He liked the idea, but he wasn't going to admit that to Georgette. He thought back to lunch time. Abi had seemed distracted at times and he knew he'd been insensitive. He'd been so taken up with going through the future of Belle Etoile, he hadn't thought about the effect it would have on her. What was that quote his father had been fond of? An Irish poet called Yeats, he thought it was, '*Tread softly because you tread on my dreams*'.

"You said you had nothing on this evening," Georgette was adding. "You could let her think you're on your way home, after visiting your sister or something."

This made him smile again. "You know something, you get more like your grandmother every day."

Georgette chose to ignore this. "Look, I'm not exaggerating. I am worried about her. She looked as if she'd seen a ghost, and she's all on her own in that hotel at a time that must be pretty traumatic for her."

"I do understand," Raj assured her. "Don't worry, leave it with me."

"Thanks Raj." She sounded relieved. "I'll see you tomorrow."

# CHAPTER 26

Abi stood in the shower and let the water pour over her body. It would be lovely, she thought, if I could let the water wash through my mind and get rid of everything I don't want to think about. She was desperate for distraction. She'd forced herself to concentrate on making notes about yesterday's meetings and about her meeting with Raj, then noted down a few points she needed to take up with him. She wanted to phone him, but no, she mustn't, he'd done enough for her today.

The bruising from the taxi's seat belt hadn't been nearly as bad as she'd expected, and her wrist was more comfortable now. Two positives, she told herself firmly. As she let the dryer blow her hair anywhere it wanted, she watched the television. There was a news item about a new clothing factory, a government official saying how good it would be for employment, then something about Chinese funding of a housing development. Abi found she was beginning to understand the Creole much better now.

When her hair was dry, she glanced at her watch, but it was still only seven o'clock. The evening stretched ahead with nothing to take her mind off the Pandora's box Marie Pillay had opened up. Unable to bear being alone in her room any longer, she grabbed her key and made her way down to the dining room. She'd have something to eat, then go and sit in a bar she'd noticed earlier on. It was on some decking at the top of the beach next to a small granite swimming pool, quieter than the main bar.

Half an hour later she'd settled herself on a high stool. All along the bar were flickering candles in round glass containers and, in the decking around them, lights were set into the wood under circles of glass. It made for an intimate atmosphere, perfect to be shared. From where Abi sat, she could see the last red and orange wisps of sunset disappearing beyond the horizon. The waves whispered up and down the sand, and from the dining room and around the main pool came the sound of people enjoying themselves. She ordered a champagne cocktail – what the hell, she could pretend she was on holiday. Too late she remembered champagne had been her mother's favourite drink. Shit. There was just no escape. Abi took a deep breath, closed her eyes and pressed her fingers against them for a moment.

"Are you all right, madam?" the barman asked. "You have injured yourself?"

"Just a silly accident. I'm fine." She watched as he mixed her cocktail then placed the tall, frosted glass in front of her.

"Thank you," she said, and took a sip. As she placed the glass back on the bar, she looked up and saw Paul Harper making his way towards her along one of the lighted paths through the garden. He was smiling as he raised a hand in greeting, then suddenly turned and made his way off down another path and disappeared behind some palms. Puzzled, she glanced behind her, wondering if he'd been waving at someone else, but there was no one in sight.

Feeling disappointed, she turned back and leant on the bar. Ah well, at least he knew she was here. She took another sip from her glass, then nearly fell off her bar stool as a voice right next to her said, "*Bon soir*, Abi."

* * *

Raj had been telling himself he simply wanted to do as Georgette had asked and check up on how Abi was, but he knew there was more to it than that. He found her mixture of confidence and vulnerability, business-like efficiency and barely controlled emotion, fascinating. And extremely attractive, if the truth were known, but he'd never admit that to Narinda. He wanted to know more, particularly about her childhood, but was reluctant to probe too much.

He asked for her at reception, but when they checked her room she wasn't there. At this time, a quarter to eight, she was probably having dinner. Raj wandered through the softly lit area and across the garden to the dining room. It was crowded with holiday makers, but Abi wasn't amongst them, neither was she sitting in the main bar. As he made his way back to reception, he noticed a signpost to the Palm Bar, turned in the direction of its pointing arm, and finally tracked her down sitting alone, head bent, slowly twirling a champagne glass between long fingers. He greeted her and she swung round sharply.

"God, Raj, you made me jump!"

"Sorry, I seem to be making a habit of that today." He slipped onto the stool next to her. "You were miles away."

"What on earth are you doing here?" she asked, but the smile she gave him was welcoming.

He didn't answer her question directly, just asked, "What's that you're drinking?"

"A champagne cocktail. I decided to try and behave as if I'm on holiday even if I'm not. Would you like one?"

"Sounds good, yes."

He held a hand up to attract the barman's attention.

"You still haven't told me what you're doing here."

"I've just been to see Narinda, thought I'd come in and say hallo on my way home, check that you're okay."

"Checking up on me? I'm not sure I like the sound of that."

"That's not what I meant," he said quickly. "How's the wrist and the… er… bruising?"

Abi laughed. "Both much better than I expected. I feel a bit of a fraud, all that fuss over nothing."

"Hardly nothing. So, did you enjoy your visit to *Tante Marie*?"

Elbows on the bar, Abi gave him a quizzical look. Maybe he'd tried too hard to keep his tone casual.

"Have you really been to see your sister?" she asked.

He chewed at his lower lip, embarrassed. "Well, I did pop in, but not for long. I wanted to come and see you as well, but Narinda has antennae." He waggled his fingers either side of his head and made a clicking sound. "They tell her immediately if I drive past without going in to say hallo, which means I had to, didn't I?"

"You're an idiot, you know that?"

"Many have told me so," he said, grinning amiably.

This was a side to Raj she'd not seen before, and she liked it.

"What does your checking entail?" she said.

As he looked at her, her expression became bleak, and the pain in her eyes showed suddenly clear.

"What's wrong?" he asked.

"I just thought of my father, he was always checking up on the rest of us, Mum, me, Charlie."

"I'm sorry." He decided to be honest with her. "It's just that Georgette phoned me and said you were a bit upset, so I promised – I didn't mean to intrude."

"It was kind of her to think of it, and you're not intruding. I'm delighted to have some company." She drained her glass before going on. "I suppose coming back has forced me to realise I can no longer shut off the past. There are so many unanswered questions, and every person I meet presents me with another question."

Before she could finish the sentence a rowdy group of tourists swarmed in from the direction of the dining room. Their loud voices and even louder laughter destroying the peaceful atmosphere. Raj raised an eyebrow at Abi and picked up their now empty glasses.

"Shall we get a couple more of these and go and sit on the beach," he suggested.

"Good idea," Abi said.

With an understanding grin, the barman mixed two more cocktails and they made their way down some steps from the decking and into the half-light. Slowly they walked along the sand, leaving the noise of the holidaymakers behind. They didn't speak until they came to a couple of loungers where they sat down and lay back, looking up at the sky. It was the colour of dark navy ink and covered in pin pricks of light, as if some giant had thrown up a handful of bright sand and it had stayed there, suspended.

"I'd forgotten about all the stars," Abi said, pointing up to their left. "Isn't that the Southern Cross?"

"It is."

"When we first went back to England, I couldn't understand why there was no Southern Cross in the sky. It was one of Uncle Douglas's favourite things, star gazing. He taught me all their names, but that's the only one I can remember now."

"I can't remember any of the others either. The only reason I remember that one is because it's part of the Mauritian coat of arms and we learnt about it in history at school. Which school were you at?"

"Queen Elizabeth College, for the last three years."

"Do you remember Narinda there?"

"No, I don't, but then she was probably one of those scary prefects. They were more important than God," she said, then continued on a more serious note. "I loved that school. It was a haven, an escape from home, like Belle Etoile was." For a moment there was silence. "It's strange, it seems so much easier to talk about the past in the dark. Why do you think that is?"

"Maybe the dark's protective. In this light it's only voices that count, body language and all the rest of the package isn't giving you away."

"You're very perceptive."

"In my business I'd be in trouble if I wasn't. When did you last hit your wife, Monsieur Patel? How dare you? I never did such a thing! But his hands clench, he won't meet your eyes, and his wife's mouth drops open in amazement. I ask the question again. I've seen the bruises, Mr Patel, when did you last... and so it goes." Then Raj felt a rush of guilt and embarrassment. Every time he opened his mouth, he seemed to say the wrong thing. He sat up and swung round to face her. "Not that I've picked on that particular scenario on purpose."

"Don't worry. These things stick in the mind."

"They do," he said grimly, "and I'd certainly like ten minutes with that ex of yours. Was that the first time, when I saw you in your office?"

"First time that he'd hit me? Yes. We had this enormous row, because of your letter actually."

"My letter? Why on earth?"

"He was always pathologically jealous, hated anything to do with my past before he came on the scene. Ironic really, since I was busy trying to deny I ever had a past. Anyway, he accused me of having an affair."

"With me?"

"Oh, don't worry, if the milkman had been knocking seventy and looked like a box of bolts, Justin would still have thought I was about to jump into bed with him."

Raj laughed out loud. "That certainly puts me in my place!"

She grinned at him. "I'm sorry. But if he'd actually met you, my life would have been absolute hell."

"Now I think that might be a compliment."

Her laughter was tinged with embarrassment, but she didn't contradict him. "It was almost entirely because of his behaviour that I ended up deciding to come. He kept sending shitty texts, bouquets of flowers and notes, and hanging around outside my flat. A police officer friend of mine warned him off, but it didn't seem to have any effect.

Then he came to the office and was completely out of control, so Lawrence got the boys to chuck him out. That was the last straw, so I agreed to do this trip to get away from him."

Raj was surprised at how angry he felt with this unknown man. "What's his name, this *couyonnaire*?"

"That sounds nasty."

"Sorry. Still, it's appropriate."

"His name's Justin. I was thinking earlier on that since I left home, he's retreated in my mind. I'm even finding it hard to remember what he looks like. That has to be good, doesn't it?"

She sounded so anxious, it was all Raj could do not to reach out and touch her, but he held back.

"I'd say so," he said firmly. He picked up his glass from where he'd pressed it down into the sand, took a sip to give himself time to think. "What you said just now about unanswered questions, do you think I might be able to answer any of them?"

She turned to look at him, eyes glittering in the dark, and for a long moment she didn't respond. Raj was just about to apologise and tell her to forget he'd asked, when she got up and walked down to the water's edge, her footsteps crunching in the sand, then turned to look at him.

"How well did you know Douglas?" she asked.

"Very well indeed, particularly towards the end of his life. He and Monique were close friends of my parents, and they were always around when we were kids." He watched as she paced up and down. "I suppose that's a bit like it was for you. But it was when I took over as his advocate that I really got to know him, as a friend I mean. He was an extraordinary man. Quite apart from his talent, he was one of the kindest and most selfless people I've ever known."

"Up until I was fourteen," Abi said, "he was much more of a father to me than Carl ever was, and then it all stopped, just like that." She made a slicing movement with her hand. There was deep pain in her voice as she spoke, but he noticed there was no bitterness now. "That second page of his will, I can't get those words out of my mind – *'her absence and my loss of contact with her has been a great grief to me'.* It just doesn't fit in with the fact he stopped writing. But Nanny Vimala's weekly letters stopped at exactly the same time. All these years I've thought they just deserted us, but what if they went on writing and we just never got the letters? That's what Charlie thinks."

"How come?"

Abi sat down beside him. He was acutely aware of her closeness in the dark, her warm shoulder touching his.

"Charlie thinks Carl told Cousin Rose to destroy any letters that arrived. We talked about it just before I came away, but my mind was so full of Justin and his shitty behaviour that I didn't think much more about it at the time."

"Hadn't you talked to your brother about it before?"

"No. Like I said, I'd always avoided talking about the past, but now I feel the opposite." She sounded surprised by what she'd just said. "Now I really want to find out more."

"Just about the letters," he asked gently, "or about everything that happened back then?"

"What do you mean?"

"Your mother's death?"

"Did Georgette tell you what her grandmother said?"

"Yes, she did."

He heard her let out her breath in a long sigh. "That too," she said.

* * *

But Abi wasn't only thinking about her mother's death. She was thinking of David's father too. Ever since they'd met in Johannesburg she'd known, in the end, she'd have to return to the questions he'd asked and the doors he'd opened. In the dark she felt Raj take her hand, bringing her back from that awful meeting in Johannesburg.

"Do you really mean that?" he asked.

For a moment, distracted by his touch, she couldn't work out what he was asking, then it came back to her.

"Yes, I think I do. When I left Rashad's house yesterday, I got lost in that maze of streets round Quatre Bornes Market. I'd been so determined to avoid the area we lived in. I'd been given to understand, by David Chandler, that it had been pulled down, but I didn't even want to go near where it used to be. Then, there it was. Maybe my subconscious led me there. It's derelict now, and the banyan tree is gone, but it was definitely the same house."

Raj said nothing. Gently his fingers played with hers as he listened intently to what she said.

"It's very strange," she went on, "and disturbing, but in the space of a few short weeks I've gone from this cell I've lived in all these years, closing the door on my childhood, to wanting to know all of it."

"I've been intending to have a look through my father's papers," Raj told her. "They're stashed away somewhere in our archive cupboard at the office. I'm sure there are boxes marked Beaumont and Belle Etoile. You never know, there might be something in there."

"Would you do that? Oh Raj, that'd be such a help. It's like having had a phobia for years and then, faced with your fear, suddenly it's no longer there."

She felt his fingers tighten. His body was warm against hers as she smiled up at him, and she saw his teeth glint in his dark face as he smiled back. Abi had no idea what would have happened next if the clamour of a mobile phone hadn't intruded.

Raj swore, Creole words whose meaning Abi could only guess at. He let go of her hand and rummaged in his pocket.

"'*allo? Oui.*" Suddenly his tone changed, no longer impatient but sharply anxious. "*Comment? To fin telephoner la police?*" He glanced at his watch and she understood when he said he'd be there in twenty minutes.

He switched off the phone and jumped up. Abi did too.

"Who was it? You said something about phoning the police. What's wrong?" she asked, grasping his arm.

"I'm sorry, Abi, I've got to go." He clasped her hand briefly, gave her a swift hard kiss on the mouth, then began to walk back towards the hotel.

Abi grabbed her bag from the sand and followed. "Raj! What is it?"

"That was Jacquo Pillay, Georgette's cousin. He's moved into Belle Etoile to keep an eye on things."

"And?" Abi wondered why, but she could find that out later.

"He says someone has tried to set fire to the house."

"What?" Abi's exclamation even silenced the tourists who were still crowded round the bar. They watched, curious, as Raj and Abi rushed past them.

"I'll let you know what happens."

"Oh no!" Abi wasn't having that. "I'm coming too."

This stopped him in his tracks. By then they'd reached the reception area. Several members of staff stopped to watch them, curiosity shining in their eyes.

"Are you sure?"

"I'm coming, Raj," Abi said, striding off towards the car park. "Come on, we're wasting time."

* * *

As Raj started the car Abi asked, "What about Antoine?"

"Jacquo didn't say if he'd phoned him. I'll try him when we get there."

From then on neither of them spoke. Once they were off the motorway the roads were almost deserted. The car's headlights lit up the trees on either side, blinding the occasional fat moth into colliding with the windscreen, scaring small creatures who scuttled for the edge of the road and disappeared in the undergrowth. Raj, driving fast, hands tight round the steering wheel, obviously knew every inch of the way. At last he slowed and spoke for the first time since they'd left the hotel.

"We're nearly there. I'm worried about you."

"Raj, let's just concentrate on what's happened, think about the rest later, okay?"

He smiled across at her in the dark and she smiled back, feeling more alive than she had in years.

"Bless you," he said. He lifted his hand from the wheel, and she felt his fingers brush her cheek.

They were near the coast now and, moments later, they turned left through a gateway. The wrought iron gates had been pushed back and, as they drove up the driveway the familiarity of the place hit Abi like a blow to the stomach. This was not how she'd imagined returning to Belle Etoile after all this time.

# CHAPTER 27

*August 1992*

When Douglas came into the library Abi was sitting on the window seat gazing out at the garden, her arms wrapped round her bunched-up legs, her chin on her knees. He came to sit beside her.

"That was your father on the phone. He'll be here to fetch you in half an hour."

When she looked up at him, her dark-lashed eyes were so full of pain he almost cried out, but he didn't dare speak in case his feelings showed too much in his voice.

"Why do we have to go, Uncle Douglas?" She'd spoken so quietly that he only just caught the words.

"Because your father says so," he told her gently. "The factory won't give him his job back, and he has to find work to support you and Charlie."

"What happened at the factory?"

"I'm afraid there was an incident. Your father got into an argument with one of the workers."

"Was it Monsieur Rougier?"

"Yes. How did you know that?"

"I heard Zabette and Nanny V talking. They said Monsieur Rougier's daughter got pregnant and he thinks it's Father's fault."

Douglas sighed. He took her hand and held it in both of his. How to respond? What would Hilary want him to say? This late in the day, honesty was probably the only option.

"I'm afraid so. Whether it's true or not, I'm afraid your father hit Monsieur Rougier and, after that, they really had no choice. They had to sack him."

Abi turned back to look out of the window again.

"I think it's happened before."

Douglas frowned, not quite understanding. "What has?"

"Father and girls. I once heard him and Mummy talking, it was about a girl who was only my age."

"Yes, well my darling, some men are like that." What else could he say to the man's fourteen-year-old daughter?

"But why can't we stay here with you?" It was a desperate plea. He could feel her thin fingers gripping his. "That's what Mummy would have wanted, isn't it? We can stay with you and *Tante* Monique, and I can finish school at Queen Elizabeth's, and Charlie can go to your school, and Nanny V can look after us."

"Darling, it's just not possible. You know that. The arrangements have been made, the flights are booked, half the packing's done. And I can't take you away from your father," he said, as firmly as he could, wishing with all his heart that it wasn't so.

"It… Is… So unfair!" There was an agonised gasp between each word. "I hate him, hate him, hate him!" And then she burst into tears, sobs that shuddered through her as if her body would break apart with the force of them.

"Don't say that, sweetheart," he begged, holding her hard and close. He felt such a hypocrite, knowing he felt just as she did. "I'll write every week, and Monique will too, and Nanny Vimala will write as well. Soon you'll have finished school, then you'll go to university or college, and then you'll be able to come back home and get a job. What do you think you'll study once you leave school?"

But she wasn't willing to be distracted. "I don't care," she muttered into his shoulder. "Nothing matters anymore."

"You're wrong. Abi, listen to me, my darling. Once you're independent and earning your own money, you can make your own decisions. Always remember that. You must study hard and never forget we're your family, you know that, don't you?"

She lifted a tear-stained face to look at him. He could see her thinking this through. "So, then I can come and live with you?"

"Of course. I promise. I'll be waiting for you."

"But what about Charlie?"

"He can come too. You wouldn't leave him behind, would you?" He forced himself to give her a reassuring smile, put as much conviction into his voice as he possibly could, but deep down he knew that, unless something happened to Carl, it was a promise he might never be able to keep.

The lights at Belle Etoile were blazing, but there was no sign of flames or smoke. Raj felt a wave of dizzying relief. Both he and Abi were out of the car seconds after it came to a halt. Raj glanced at her as she stood for a moment, her gaze sweeping across the facade of the house and into the shadows of the garden. He took her hand. She must be finding this so difficult. But her expression was hard to read in the gloom, although she did manage to give him a brief smile.

"Stop worrying," she said.

There was a police car parked on the gravel and four men standing in a group, three of them in uniform, the other in jeans and a T-shirt. They all turned as Raj and Abi approached and the tall, muscular young man in the T-shirt came to meet them.

"Jacquo, *mon brave*, well done," Raj said, clasping the man's hand in both of his. "This is Abigail Kendall, Douglas and Monique's niece." He glanced at Abi as he said this, saw her eyes widen. He got the impression the description pleased her.

Jacquo gave her a brief smile and handshake, then turned back to Raj, speaking rapidly in Creole. Raj wondered if Abi was keeping up. If not, he'd explain it all later.

"There was only one car, I didn't catch how many were in it. I didn't hear it until it was right up there," Jacquo said, pointing to the other side of the fountain. "They must have been going slow and without lights as they came up the drive. It was bloody lucky I was out here. I'd left my iPad in the kitchen, went to fetch it and was on my way back to the annexe, that's when the car appeared. Its heads came on, and it speeded up and swung fast round the fountain then back off down the drive. I started to run after them, but it was pointless, and then I realised they'd thrown something out of the car window because all hell broke loose."

One of the policemen strode up and broke into Jacquo's story.

"Inspector Beejadhur, Mahebourg Police," he said. "And you are?" He didn't seem very pleased to see them.

Raj introduced himself and Abi. "I'm Madame Beaumont's advocate. My friend here" – Raj put a hand on Jacquo's shoulder – "phoned me and, since I was nearby, I thought I'd check up on things. Perhaps you'd be kind enough to tell me what you think."

The inspector seemed to accept Raj's explanation.

"I think it was some kind of home-made firebomb, but an insignificant one, maybe a bottle with a bit of petrol in it, and some wadding pushed into the top. Light the material and the petrol catches fire when the bottle breaks. Crude but efficient."

The steps were blackened, as were patches of the gravel below, but the only other sign of the fire was the acrid smell that lingered in the night air, and pools of water where the fire had been doused.

"How come it didn't set fire to the whole verandah?" Raj asked. He felt chilled at the thought of what might have happened.

"It seems your young friend here," the policeman said, "is a very quick thinker. Tell *Missié* Amrakash, my boy."

Jacquo shrugged. He pointed to a coil of green hose lying beside the bougainvillaea clambering over the verandah.

"I'd been doing some watering for *Tonton* Gabriel and forgot to put the hose away, just left it there. Lucky I did. When I saw the flames, I just grabbed it, turned the tap on and prayed! Zabette came out, but I shouted to her to get back inside and phone the police and the fire brigade." He threw up his hands. "*Bondiè!* I couldn't believe my luck when the fire died down. It took a couple of minutes, but it seemed like ages. Once I was sure it was out, I phoned you."

"The fire service will be here any minute," said Beejadhur. "Just to check things over, and they'll do a full inspection once it's light. I'll leave a couple of men here for the rest of the night to keep an eye on things. I've reassured Madame Beaumont that all is safe now. So as not to worry her too much, I told her it was probably a kid's prank."

Raj could hear the doubt in the man's voice. "But you don't think that's so?"

"No, I don't. There's a malice in this that worries me. Why do this to an isolated house with a couple of elderly ladies living in it? If you want that kind of fun, there are much more interesting targets than this."

"I think I might be able to help you there. It's all speculation, but I think you'd find it interesting," Raj said.

It was only then that he realised he still had hold of Abi's hand because, when he said this, he felt her fingers tighten on his. He glanced at her. Even in the half-light he saw the alarm and questioning in her eyes. He turned back to the policeman.

"I'll go and talk to Madame Beaumont. Could I come to the station and speak to you first thing tomorrow?"

"By all means." He didn't sound that enthusiastic, but added, "Eight o'clock?"

"Fine. I'll be there."

There was the sound of sirens. A moment later a red van followed by a fire engine appeared on the twisting drive between the palm trees.

"I'll have a word with these chaps," the policeman said, "and I'll try to find someone to take over from my men in the morning."

"And if those *fes cassé* come back," Jacquo said, "I'll enjoy smashing their faces in."

"I'll pretend I didn't hear that," Beejadhur said, "but I don't think they'll be back, not tonight at any rate."

He lifted a hand in salute and strode off to join the firemen who were swarming out of the two vehicles.

Raj turned to Jacquo. "You deserve a bonus for this, my friend."

The young man grinned. "It was quite exciting really." He looked a little self-conscious about this. "Not that I'd want a thing like that to happen, of course. Anyway, I'll go and sort out who's doing what with those chaps over there." He indicated the three police officers who were waiting by their car.

Raj turned to Abi who'd been waiting quietly by his side. Through all the excitement she hadn't said a word.

"Are you okay?" he asked anxiously, putting an arm round her shoulders.

"Yes, I'm fine, but Raj, you don't think–"

"We'll talk about it later. Let's go inside."

* * *

Abi followed Raj up the steps, across the verandah and into the sitting room. All the furniture was just as she remembered, from the faded rugs covering the polished wood floor to the ceiling fans, not moving now in the cool of the night.

"Zabette? Monique?" Raj called out.

Immediately a small, elderly woman in a flowered print dress came from the bedroom at the back.

"*Missié* Raj!" she exclaimed, then stopped in her tracks, a look of wonder on her face. "*Bondiè!*" she murmured and clutched at her neck, "*Mam'zelle* Abi? *Bondiè, bondiè!* What a night! How are you here?"

Abi went to her and took her hands then bent and hugged her hard.

"I came with Raj," she said in Creole, surprising herself at how naturally she now slipped into the language of her childhood. "We'll explain all that in a minute. Is *Tante* Monique alright?"

"Yes, yes. Oh dear. Come. Madame is in her *salon*." She turned to make her way back to the room she'd come from, but Raj stopped her.

"Have you contacted Antoine?"

Zabette's lips tightened. "I tried, there's no answer. He's probably out with his rich friends. He cares more about them than he does about his mother, that one."

Raj glanced at Abi then turned back to Zabette. "Leave it with me. I'll try later."

She ushered them through the door with no further comment. Over by the window Monique was sitting in an armchair, her head resting against the high back, her eyes closed. She looked almost as Abi remembered her, except for some grey in the short cropped curly hair, and she'd lost some of her round, cuddly curves.

"Madame," Zabette said as they made their way across the room, "it's *Missié* Raj and you're not going to believe who's with him."

Monique's eyes opened slowly. She looked infinitely tired as she gazed at them then, very slowly, like a warm light turned on in a cold room, she smiled and held out both her hands.

"*Mo ti fille*, oh my little girl, you've come home. Does Douglas know? He would be overjoyed."

Abi felt her throat constrict and her eyes fill with tears. She swallowed hard. She mustn't cry, she might not be able to stop. Unable to speak, she took Monique's hands and bent to kiss her.

"And Raj," Monique said, "have you heard about those stupid boys? But Jacquo says there's no harm done. Is that why you're here?"

"Yes. Jacquo phoned me. I was at the hotel where Abi is staying, and we came straight round. It must have been very upsetting. Are you all right?"

"We're fine. The policeman says he'll leave some men to watch over the house."

"*Zotte ti cretin*!" Zabette muttered. "If I could get my hands on them."

"Jacquo was saying much the same thing," Raj said, smiling.

"Have you come home for good, Abi?" Monique asked. "We've waited so, so long to see you again."

"I know. I'm sorry. I've only got ten days, but I'll come and see you properly while I'm here."

She glanced at Raj, wishing she could ask him what she should and shouldn't say. She wanted to tell Monique how grieved she was at Douglas's death and how much it meant to her that he'd remembered her in his will. But she couldn't say any of this if Monique thought Douglas was still alive.

Suddenly Monique looked infinitely sad.

"If only Douglas was here to welcome you."

Abi wondered if she thought he was out, or in his studio or some other part of the house, but when Monique went on, she realised this wasn't so.

"He never forgot you and Charlie. To the day he died he spoke of you nearly every day. Does your brother know you're here?"

"Of course. He would so have liked to come too."

"Oh no. He doesn't come very often."

Abi frowned then realised that Monique was becoming confused again.

"Is Charlie with you?" Monique asked.

"No, *Tante* Monique," Abi said. She could hardly get the words past the lump in her throat. "Like I said, just me – this time."

Raj smiled at her and she thought he understood what a big step forward this was.

They stayed for another hour, soothing Monique, talking about the past and, when they rose to leave, Monique took Abi's hands.

"Come back tomorrow, *mo ti fille*. Come and sit with me and we'll talk."

"I'll try. If not tomorrow, then soon," Abi said as she bent once again to kiss the soft cheeks.

On their way out, Raj went through the security precautions with Jacquo, then they started the journey back to the hotel, down the driveway between the dark palms. At first neither of them spoke, but after a while Abi turned to look at Raj. There was something she needed to ask.

"You agree with that inspector, don't you?"

"Did you manage to understand all that?"

"More than I expected. Raj, do you think Antoine had something to do with it?"

"Not exactly, no."

"Then who?"

"Antoine's got some dubious friends. I have this feeling it might be something to do with them, but I've got no proof at all. I'll have to do a bit more digging."

"But what a completely stupid thing to do. It was so—so incompetent, and didn't the policeman say that it was only a small device."

"He did, but if Jacquo hadn't been on his way from the house to the annexe, things might have been very different. What if it had got as far as the verandah? Those old houses go up like kindling. It doesn't bear thinking of."

Abi felt sick. "I know."

There was silence in the car for a while, both deep in their own thoughts. It wasn't long before they were on the coast road a couple of minutes from the hotel. The security guard at the gate lifted the bar to let them through and Raj parked and switched off the engine. Abi turned and gave him a hesitant smile.

"What an evening. I feel as if it's ages since we were sitting on the beach. What time is it?"

"Nearly midnight."

"Didn't you say you'd meet up with Inspector Beejadhur at eight tomorrow morning? But Raj, you've got to drive all the way home now and then back again first thing."

"Don't worry." He put out a hand and tucked a curl back behind Abi's ear. "I'll survive. If it hadn't been so late, I'd have gone to Narinda's, but they've both got an early start tomorrow. I'd better not get them up at this time of night."

"I'd ask you up for a drink," Abi found herself saying. "I've got a bottle of rather good whisky."

"That sounds tempting. But you must be exhausted."

"You'd have thought so, but I feel wide awake. Would you like to come up?"

He lifted his hands in mock defeat.

"What can I say? It'd be rude to refuse."

They made their way through the hotel, quiet now, except for laughter coming from the main bar. As Raj followed her into her room, she felt a need to fill the silence.

"There are some glasses on top of the fridge over there. Do you want water? There should be some ice too. I'll get the whisky." She stooped and got the bottle from her bedside cupboard, then pulled back the sliding doors. "Shall we sit on the balcony? The chairs are quite comfortable."

"Yes, fine," Raj said. As he dropped ice into two glasses, Abi noticed his expression.

"What are you grinning at?"

He laughed. "You."

"Why?" She was unable to stop herself smiling too.

"All of a sudden you're behaving like the perfect hostess. After the evening we've spent together, and I'm not just talking about going to Belle Etoile." He sat down in one of the comfortable chairs. "It just made me laugh." But the next moment he was serious again. "I'm sorry," he said. "How are you feeling?"

She leant on the railings and looked out at the gardens with their discreet lights under the palm trees.

"I don't know really," she said quietly. "That certainly wasn't the way I thought I'd be returning to Belle Etoile for the first time, but perhaps it was a good thing, like being pushed into the sea and having to swim. And now I just can't wait to go back there and explore the whole place, and I'm so looking forward to talking to Monique."

"Go round tomorrow as she suggested."

"I'd love to, but remember," Abi said as she lifted her bandaged wrist, "I can't drive, and I'm not too keen on taxis after today."

"I'll take you on Saturday then."

"That'd be great. Thank you."

Abi sat down, picked up her glass and took a sip. Raj said nothing more, just watched her. She gave him an uncertain smile, wondered what he was thinking.

"Earlier on, just before Jacquo phoned, you mentioned someone called David Chandler. Who was that?"

"It's a long story. His father, Tony, was a friend of my parents, well, of my mother's. Looking back on it, and I've only really thought about it recently, I think they were probably lovers. Strange. It was Carl that used to have the affairs, not Mummy. And she had far more reason." She sighed. "Tony was killed," she said, "during the cyclone in '91. He was crushed by a tree."

"How awful."

"But it was a bit more complicated than a simple accident. At least, that's what David seems to think."

"You've seen him recently?"

"While I was in Jo'burg." Abi thought back to the intense, bearded man, and shivered. "It was all rather horrid. He's sort of obsessed."

Raj leant forward in his chair, elbows on his knees, hands clasped. "In what way?"

"He'd been back to Mauritius recently and, with the help of a police officer here, he was delving into the records of the investigation after his father's death. The officer he spoke to had pointed out some inconsistencies in the forensics, David said. He told me the investigating officer had doubts at the time, but nobody followed up on it. He asked if I knew whether his father was dead before the tree fell and if I saw anything."

"You were there?" Raj said, horrified.

"Yes, you see, the tree that killed him was in the garden of our house, the one I saw on Tuesday."

"How awful for you. I didn't know that."

"Why would you?"

"Well, I suppose my father was around at the time."

"I hadn't thought of that. The thing is, it's made me wonder." She turned to look at him, her voice pleading for understanding. "I was only a kid, Raj, and nobody told us anything. I wanted to stay with Mummy, but Carl wouldn't let us, and then Charlie and I were scooped up by Uncle Douglas and taken to Belle Etoile. If I'd stayed, been there to look after her after Tony died, maybe she wouldn't have committed suicide."

"But, Abi, Marie is convinced she didn't kill herself. It was an accident."

"I suppose, and maybe she's right, but after all these years, it's hard to change your mindset."

"Look, let's not talk about this anymore now." Raj got up. "You've had enough today. I'll leave you in peace and you can get some sleep."

Without any warning a wave of panic swept through her. She took a step towards him. "Raj, I can't!"

"What is it?"

"I can't – I just don't want to be on my own." She looked up at him, silently begging him not to go, feeling a weak fool for doing so.

For a long moment he didn't say anything, just studied her face. She was about to tell him she was being silly, not to listen to her, when he bent and kissed her lips, then said, with an arm lightly round her.

"I'll stay on one condition." He grinned at her. "Can I have some more of that whisky of yours."

Abi gave a shaky laugh, put her head on his shoulder for a moment in gratitude. "You can have the rest of the bottle if you like."

"Tempting, but not a good idea, I've got that meeting with Beejadhur. At least staying here saves me driving all the way home and back. Come, let's get some more ice."

Having asked Raj to stay, Abi had another moment of panic, would he think she was asking him to make love to her? But he seemed so relaxed, chatting away about his work and his family as they finished their drinks. It was as if he'd deliberately stepped back from their earlier closeness. By the time Raj came out of the bathroom, Abi was curled up under the sheet. She glanced up at him, feeling ridiculously shy as she watched him drape his trousers and shirt over a chair. She turned her back, not wanting him to think she was staring, and felt him get into the bed beside her.

"Goodnight," he said, touched her gently on the shoulder, turned the light off on the bedside table and said no more.

Abi was convinced she would not be able to sleep a wink. She was wrong.


# CHAPTER 28


The beach, the woman, the wind, they were all the same, but this time there was a difference. Abi's toes still gripped the rock as she tried to balance. She still screamed, "Mummy! Mummy!" to the woman on the shore. But a shadowy figure was slowly getting closer to her mother, his outstretched hands ready to push her towards the crashing waves. Abi strained to see who it was. Any moment she'd be able to. Yes… no… NO…

"Abi? Abi!"

Her eyes flew open. At first, she couldn't understand who was calling her name with such urgency.

"Abi, what is it?" At last she recognised Raj's voice.

"Oh God, oh God."

She was shivering violently. He gathered her into his arms, and she clung to him in the dark. After a moment, he lifted himself on to one arm and stroked her tangled hair back from her face with a gentle hand.

"You were calling out. Is it your arm?"

"No. A nightmare." She was still shivering. "It keeps coming back."

"Shh, shh," he soothed. "Don't worry. I'm here."

His fingers went from her forehead and slowly down her cheek, her neck, continued softly down. She could feel her body react and heard his breathing deepen, saw his velvety dark eyes gazing down at her in the half light. Abi put up a hand and touched his mouth, feeling the softness of it. The dream receded, faded and was gone. She slid her hand into his hair and slowly they began to kiss, gentle at first, but with increasing urgency. Raj pushed the pillows onto the floor. Hampered by her bandaged wrist, Abi tried to struggle out of her nightdress. Raj helped her. It joined the pillows. His tongue explored her mouth and his fingers explored her body, setting up sensations she'd rarely felt before.

But suddenly he was still, pulling back.

"Don't stop," Abi begged.

"What about your arm?"

"It doesn't matter."

"I don't want to hurt you."

"You won't, you won't."

"Abi – I haven't got any–"

"It's okay."

"Are you sure?"

"Yes, yes," she said as she slid a hand down the smooth skin of his back to the curve of his hips.

"I think," he whispered, tracing a finger round her lips, "that I've wanted this since you walked out on me in London."

"I think I have too," she murmured against his mouth.

From then on neither of them said anything coherent for quite some time.

* * *

Abi woke to the sound of the shower. Raj's side of the bed was empty. The sun, only just up, made the light in the room warm with the glow of dawn. She curled up, closed her eyes tight and let her mind think back to what had happened.

Making love with Raj had been a revelation. Nothing in her past had prepared her for it. She'd never experienced such gentle, deep exploration of her body, nor felt such freedom to respond. They'd slept a little, wrapped in each other's arms, then woken to make love again. It had been glorious, shattering, and frightening, because – what would happen now? For her this had been no one-night stand.

The sound of the shower stopped. A moment later she heard Raj's bare feet on the tiles of the floor coming around the bed to her side. She held her breath, didn't move, felt his weight as he sat down beside her.

"Abi," he whispered, "I have to go."

Slowly she opened her eyes. He was looking at her anxiously. Again, he seemed unsure of himself. In a strange way this gave her confidence. She reached up and ran her fingers through his dark hair, still wet from the shower.

"Hallo," she said, smiling sleepily up at him.

His smile was full of relief as he bent to kiss her. Her lips were sore, but she didn't care as she felt her body react, wound her arms round his neck. He responded, but too soon he pulled away.

"It's past seven. I've got to go and meet Inspector Beejadhur."

"Oh bugger," said Abi.

Raj laughed, then was serious. "You don't regret last night?"

"Not one bit," she said and was surprised how much she meant it.

"I hope I– it's been a long time."

"For you?"

"Yes. No one since Parmita died."

Abi wasn't quite sure how to respond to this. Was he asking for reassurance? He was such a strange mixture of confidence and insecurity. She sat up, clasped his face in her hands.

"Raj, I've never known anything like it. It was glorious."

He grinned. "I'm glad. For me too. I was worried you'd feel I'd taken advantage."

"Raj! Don't be silly. I think last night was a combined effort."

"And what a delightful one."

He kissed the end of her nose, then reached for his clothes. Abi watched as he got dressed. He really did have the most beautiful body. But soon the fire and its repercussions intruded on the conversation.

"We still haven't contacted Antoine," Abi said.

"I know. I tried him again just now, still no response."

"Do you think Zabette might have spoken to him?"

"I doubt it. You must have noticed last night how she feels. Zabette thinks he's a *mauvais fils*."

"Yes, well it seems he hasn't been the best of sons to Monique. Will you come back when you've seen the inspector?"

"I can't. I'll have to go straight from there to the office. I've got a meeting at half ten, then another at lunch time, which is probably going to go on for ages. I'll phone you. We'll have dinner tonight – we'll talk."

"And?"

He came back, pulled her towards him and kissed her hard. "You are an amazing woman," he said.

"You're not so bad yourself."

He grinned and quickly left the room.

Abi lay back and stretched. Her arm ached, which was hardly surprising, but she couldn't have cared less. As far as she could work out, they'd had less than three hours sleep. That didn't seem to matter much either. A luxurious weariness came over her and she closed her eyes, allowing the night to replay in her mind. It wasn't long before she was asleep again.

* * *

There were dark shadows round Beejadhur's deep set eyes as he welcomed Raj into his office.

"You look as if you've been up all night," Raj said as he took a seat opposite the inspector's desk.

"I have," the man said, his voice gravelly with lack of sleep. He leant his arms on his desk, put up a hand and rubbed at his eyes. "It's been one hell of a night. Quite apart from the usual workload you'd expect anyway, we've had four more arson attacks, the last one at five this morning. I'm stretched to the limit, my boss is away, and we have an international conference going on in the Blue Palm Hotel, you know the new one just outside town, which has quite a few of my men tied up on security. Some *couyonnaire* is playing games with us, but I can't work out what's behind it."

"Were the others the same as the attack at Belle Etoile?"

"The devices used were similar. I know I said last night I didn't think it was a random attack but given these other incidents I'm beginning to wonder. The fire department's still investigating, they'll come back to me once they've got more information, but I'm afraid I haven't any further news for you yet."

"Not to worry," Raj said, trying to hide his frustration.

"I can't understand what's behind it," Beejadhur went on. "I'm far too old a hand to believe in coincidence, but what's their motive? That's what I want to know." He narrowed his eyes as he looked across at Raj. "Is there anything you can tell me that'll point me in the right direction?"

Raj didn't reply immediately. He had his own theories, based on rumour and scraps of information, from Vijay, Hari Persand, and his own observations, but no concrete evidence at all. And he was wary of referring directly to Antoine. On the other hand, would it do any harm to suggest he should be questioned? Maybe not – it was his property that had been attacked, after all.

"Have you managed to contact Antoine Beaumont yet?" Raj asked.

"No. We've only got his office number and we've left messages, but he's not got back to us."

"Same here. I can give you his mobile, I should have done so last night." Raj got his phone out and read out the number. Beejadhur jotted it down.

"Thanks for that," he said. "I'll get the office to chase him up. Do you think this could have something to do with him?"

"It is his family home."

"I realise that." Beejadhur sounded irritated. "What I mean is, could this attack be personal not just random?"

"I think he might well have a few enemies," Raj said carefully.

Beejadhur gave him a sharp look. "I was wondering why young Pillay phoned you and not *Missié* Beaumont last night," he said.

"I'm the one that asked him to move into Belle Etoile."

"I see." The policeman waited for him to go on.

"I'm Douglas Beaumont's executor. He was a close friend of my father's and I've known the family all my life. I was rather worried about Madame Beaumont and her old housekeeper living there alone. It is rather isolated." I'm beginning to sound like Antoine, Raj thought.

"And is her son not worried as well?"

"I'm not sure. Perhaps not in quite the same way."

"It seems strange to me that you're the one who is looking after Madame Beaumont's interests. There's more to this situation than you're telling me, isn't there?"

If Beejadhur was worth his salt, he'd probably be doing some background checks anyway. If that took him to Hari Persand, he'd find out all about Antoine's dubious friends, but Raj wasn't going to be the one to drop Antoine in it, not yet.

"There are a few problems over the future of the estate," he said carefully. "The two legatees, that's Antoine Beaumont and Douglas's niece, Abigail Kendall, you met her last night, haven't yet come to an agreement about where to go from here."

Beejadhur sat staring unblinkingly at Raj. The silence stretched out. Raj could tell that, in spite of his exhaustion, the inspector wasn't the sort to miss anything.

"I have this strong feeling you're not telling me everything you know," the inspector said at last. "I'll give you a little rope, but please don't end up hanging yourself."

"I'll do my best not to," Raj said with a grin. He leaned forward in his chair. "Look, it's known the place might go on the market and there are some aggressive property developers around who could jump the gun. I didn't want the old ladies bothered by anyone snooping around trying to work out how much it's worth."

"Why would you think that might happen?"

"Antoine's been in discussion with some developers who can be a bit pushy. I thought they might take things into their own hands and go down there to try to persuade Madame Beaumont to move out."

"And do you think that's what her son wants, for her to move out?"

"Possibly."

Beejadhur sat forward in his chair. "And you think they might use an arson attack to frighten her into doing so?"

"I'm not sure. These other incidents make it unlikely, wouldn't you say?"

"I'm still thinking about that. They don't appear to be copy-cat attacks, they all happened too close together for that."

The inspector put up a hand to hide a cavernous yawn. Raj took pity on him.

"Shouldn't you be going off duty?"

"I should have gone home hours ago. You're right, I'd better get my head down for a couple of hours or I'll be no use to anyone."

"I'll let you know if I hear from Antoine."

"Thank you." As they shook hands, Beejadhur frowned. "Keeping things from the police is never a good idea, *Missié* Amrakash," he said.

"I'm an advocate, Inspector," Raj said, giving him a cool smile. "I'm fully aware of that."

The inspector nodded, but he didn't seem entirely reassured.

"Do you still have men at Belle Etoile?" Raj asked as they made their way out into the early heat of the day.

"No. I hope to have one of my patrol cars do a random check or two through the day, but that'll depend on manpower. Like I said, we're stretched to the limit. Is your young chap there today?"

"Jacquo Pillay? Not all the time. He has a chauffeuring job, but the hours are erratic. He'll certainly be back tonight though."

"Good. I think they'll be fine during the day. I doubt that those idiots will try again any time soon."

Raj hoped he was right.

As he got into his car and started the drive back to Curepipe, his thoughts returned to Abi and last night. He still found it hard to believe what had happened. It was four short weeks since they'd met up again. Had he really been thinking about making love to her since that morning in the hotel in London? Yes, but it hadn't been a conscious thought. Not until the last two days had he acknowledged his feelings. He wanted so much to believe Abi felt the same. Nothing would make him regret what had happened, but what now? In a few short days Abi would be leaving Mauritius. Would she just step out of his life? Would she return to that Justin creature? Thinking about it made him feel sick. He turned the radio on loud and put his foot down. The sooner he had to concentrate on work, the better.

He'd only been in his office a matter of moments when Georgette came in.

"How did it go with Abi last night?" she asked.

Raj swung round, wondering how on earth – but of course, she wanted to know because she'd asked him to check on Abi after the visit to Marie. Georgette obviously noticed his reaction, gave him a sharp look.

"You did go and see her, didn't you?"

"Oh yes." Raj nearly laughed. "We talked for quite a while, and then we were interrupted by a call from your cousin, some idiots tried to set fire to Belle Etoile."

That distracted her. "They what? You should have texted me."

"I haven't had time. First thing this morning I had to go and talk to the officer who's in charge of the investigation."

"But tell me what happened!"

He did so and Georgette homed in on what was most important to her. "Abi went with you to Belle Etoile?"

"Yes, she refused to be left behind. Anyway, we were wondering if Antoine had anything to do with it."

"Oh, Raj, surely not! Even he wouldn't go that far."

"It's not a comfortable thought, is it? They should have more information later today." Raj ran a hand through his hair. "This inspector isn't stupid. He's going to be talking to Antoine, might even do some research into his dubious friends. He could put two and two together."

"So, what is Abi doing today?" She grinned at him. "Are you two going to meet up?"

"We're going to have dinner, but I don't know what else she's planned. When I left her, she hadn't decided."

He turned to his computer, switched it on. He should be more careful. Georgette knew him too well and she was as sharp as a knife, but the memory of last night wasn't for sharing with anyone.

Raj sat back in his chair, oblivious to the computer screen coming to life in front of him. A slow smile grew on his face. He was still sitting there, daydreaming about Abi when Georgette came back in.

"Oh Raj, you know those boxes you wanted me to find in the archive room? I've got them for you. Beaumont, 1985-1988 and Beaumont, 1989-1991. There's another one that goes up as far as 1996, but I couldn't find anything beyond that."

"Great. If it can be avoided, I'd like to take no calls for a bit."

"Fine." But Georgette didn't leave immediately. "Raj, what are you looking for?"

"I'm not sure, but I have a feeling I'll know when I find it."

* * *

Raj took the lid from the first box. Inside, were several files crammed with documents. Some were labelled, some weren't. Raj looked at the label on the first file. It said, '1974 - Sugar Bonds'. He flicked through the contents — nothing there to grab his attention. He looked through the next, and the next, nothing but investments and the maintenance of the Belle Etoile estate.

It wasn't until he came to 1985 that something made him sit up and take notice. It was different to the rest.

Neatly printed on the label were the words, 'Antoine (Adoption)'.

Raj had never thought much about Douglas adopting Antoine. Was Monique his birth mother or his adopted mother? He had no idea. She had always been devoted to her son, but there was something more to it. It was as if she was watchful, waiting for him to behave in some way she'd find hard to control. This too Raj had never thought much about, but now he wanted to know more.

He lifted out the papers, placed them on the table and began to leaf through. Antoine's birth certificate was amongst them. It confirmed that Monique was his birth mother, but the father was not named. Then there were the adoption papers, drawn up in July 1985, when Antoine was two and a half. There was no mention of Antoine's natural father. Raj was about to put the papers back in the sleeve when he discovered something else. A piece of pale grey, faintly lined paper attached to the back with a rusting paperclip. He recognised his father's handwriting immediately, and what he read made him sit down heavily in the chair behind him.

Unbelieving, he read it again. Good God! It explained so much, but how much difference did it make? And what the hell was he going to do about it?


# CHAPTER 29


The sun was high in the sky the next time Abi woke. She squinted at her watch. It was half past ten and the phone by her bed was ringing. For a second her heart lifted, then she remembered Raj had a meeting. She picked up the receiver.

"Hallo?"

"*Mam'zelle* Kendall? This is reception. There is a visitor—"

Abi could hear an agitated voice in the background, then someone else came on the line.

"Abi? It's Antoine. I need to see you."

Her heart sank. He must have found out about the fire.

"Can I come up?" he asked.

"No, don't do that. I'll have a quick shower and be down in ten minutes."

"Well, all right." He didn't sound pleased.

"Go to the bar, get yourself a coffee. I'll meet you there."

Abi replaced the phone and threw back the sheet. After her shower, she put on a soft linen summer dress and muttered to herself as the bandage on her wrist caught in the material when she slipped it over her head. She couldn't wait to take the damn thing off, especially if Raj was going to stay again. No. She must concentrate on Antoine. Just before she left her room, she pinned on the filigree brooch.

Antoine was sitting slumped at the bar, a cup of coffee in front of him with a glass of brandy next to it. Abi didn't comment on the brandy.

"*Bonzour*," she said as she came up behind him.

He swung round and she noticed how drawn he looked.

"There you are," he said. You'd have thought she'd taken hours rather than minutes to join him. He made an effort to smile, but it didn't reach his eyes. "You're an elusive woman."

"I've only been here since Monday, Antoine." Even as she said it, she found it hard to believe.

"What have you done to your wrist?" he asked.

"I was in a taxi yesterday, it bumped into a bus. It's nothing serious."

He didn't enquire further. It was obvious he wasn't really interested. Abi hitched herself up onto a stool and ordered coffee and croissants.

"Have you been to see your mother this morning?" she asked him.

"Why do you ask that?" he said, frowning, as he picked at some dry skin on his thumb.

"Did Raj get hold of you?" Abi asked.

"No. I haven't spoken to him for days."

Oh shit, Abi thought, he doesn't know. It wasn't really for her to tell him about last night, but someone had to.

"Antoine, there was a fire last night, at Belle Etoile."

"What the hell are you talking about?" His exclamation attracted the attention of the barman who turned and gave them a curious glance.

Abi did not want to be having this conversation in the first place, but certainly not with an audience.

"Let's find somewhere to sit."

She didn't wait for his agreement. The barman assured her he'd bring her croissants and coffee, and both men followed her over to a group of armchairs by windows which looked out on to the beach. People were lying on loungers in the sun, children running in and out of the sea. It all looked so normal and relaxed and Abi wished she was out there and not stuck inside with this unpredictable man.

Antoine threw himself down in a chair. She noticed he'd brought the glass of brandy but not his coffee. He leant forward, glaring at her. "Now, what's all this about?"

Quickly she told him what had happened. "It was probably a bunch of louts. And there was very little damage, thank God."

"But how come Raj found out?"

"Jacquo phoned him."

"Who's he?"

"Georgette Pillay's cousin," Abi said, wondering how to explain. "He moved in to keep an eye on things."

"I didn't know anything about that. Who arranged it?" He spat the question out.

Abi felt completely out of her depth. She broke off a piece of croissant, noticed her hand was shaking and tried to steady it as she dipped the croissant in her coffee.

"It was Raj's idea," she told Antoine, then wished she hadn't.

"Why the hell does he have to interfere all the time? I wish he'd keep his damn nose out of my business."

"I'm sure he's not meaning to interfere," Abi protested, but she knew it wasn't true. Raj was interfering because he felt he had to, and Abi understood much better now.

Antoine gave a derisive snort. "What would you know about it?" Then he looked directly at her, noticed her raised eyebrows, and pulled himself together. "Sorry. It's not your fault. The trouble is he thinks being Papa's executor gives him rights he doesn't have."

"He would have spoken to you last night if he could have. He tried to contact you several times."

"Raj was here with you?"

"I told you, he was having a drink with me when Jacquo phoned, that's when Raj tried you, but he couldn't get through. Zabette tried as well. Where were you?"

He looked at her, then his eyes slid away.

"I was busy," he said. "And my mobile's been playing up. This Jacquo, do you think he had anything to do with the arson attack?"

"Of course not," Abi protested. "It was Jacquo who put the fire out. If it hadn't been for him, the whole house might have gone up."

They sat in silence for a few minutes. Abi made herself finish the croissants, although she'd lost all appetite for them, and drank the rest of her coffee. The silence stretched out.

"I must go and see for myself."

"Of course, you must." Part of her couldn't wait to get rid of him, but she found herself offering to go with him.

He frowned. "I don't think that's a good idea."

This made Abi determined to go. "I promised your mother I'd come round this morning," she said, "but I can't drive, because of my wrist. I won't get in your way."

The frown deepened. "Okay, if you must."

Not waiting for him to change his mind, Abi grabbed her bag and followed him from the bar. As they made their way through the garden, she thought she saw her wine merchant friend. She lifted a hand to wave, but when she looked again, he was gone. As she handed her key to the smiling woman on reception, she left a message that she'd be at Belle Etoile to be passed on should Raj phone.

"I hope you understand I'd like some time with my mother on my own," Antoine said as they got into the car.

"Of course." What else could she say? "I haven't been down to the summer house yet. I'll go and have a look at it while you're talking to Monique."

He glanced at her, seemed about to say something, but changed his mind. Antoine drove fast, impatient with anyone or anything that got in his way. It wasn't long before they were screeching to a halt by the fountain.

Without a word Antoine got out of the car and ran up the steps so fast that Abi had no time to point out the blackened stones where the fire had been. She hurried after him through the house as he called out, "Maman? Maman?" They found Monique sitting on the back verandah, reading.

Her face lit up as she saw them.

"Antoine! Zabette has been phoning you, where have you been? Abi my dear, I am so glad to see the two of you together."

Antoine bent to kiss her cheeks then sat down beside her. Abi sat too and pushed her handbag under her chair, determined not to leave them together quite yet.

"I heard what happened last night," Antoine said, and Abi was glad that he kept his voice calm. "This is the sort of thing I was afraid of, Maman. Now do you see why I don't want you here on your own?"

"Don't be silly," Monique said. "It was just some stupid boys. They won't come back."

"How do you know?"

"Raj said so, and Jacquo will be here. You really don't need to worry."

Antoine's jaw clenched then he took a deep breath. "Maman, you must understand, I want the best for you and I really don't think the best is for you to stay at Belle Etoile, particularly after last night."

He glanced at Abi as he spoke. There was resentment in that look. Aware of the promise she'd made, she had no choice but to leave them. She gave Monique a reassuring smile.

"I'll go for a walk. I won't be long," she added, hoping Antoine would get the message.

Slowly, glancing back a couple of times as she did so, she made her way down the steps and across the lawn towards the tall bamboos. Although out of sight from here, she knew that in amongst that crowd of tall rods and sharp leaves was the tunnel that shaded the flight of shallow steps, and then the acre of land that was now hers. Her heart began to beat faster. Soon she'd see the familiar octagonal building that had been such a feature of her childhood.

Emerging into the sunlight at the bottom of the steps, she could see how weather beaten it was, though nothing else had changed. The railings were intact, the shutters were in place. She walked slowly round it, reluctant to go inside. First, she would walk down to the cliff edge. In the past there'd been a low wooden fence, but it had rotted away, and she could find only the occasional stump in the ground to show her where the posts had been. The land fell away to the sea and the rocks below. The tide was high, and waves were crashing up close. As she stood there, she could feel a fine spray born on the wind as it whipped at her hair.

Abi had no idea how long she stood there, but at last she turned and made her way up the gentle slope, mounted the steps to the circling verandah, and saw the key in the lock. She hoped it would turn easily, remembering how difficult it had been if the lock hadn't been oiled. She smiled in relief as the key moved easily. It was just as she was pushing the door open that she heard a shout behind her.

"Abigail!"

Turning, she saw Antoine running towards her. Leaving the door ajar, she hurried back down the steps, a sense of dread rising up inside her.

He came to a halt in front of her, arms wrapped round his ribs, breathing hard. His pale blue eyes studied her face as if he'd never seen it before and his mouth worked.

Abi was frightened but determined not to show it. "What's the matter?" she asked.

"You knew, didn't you?" he hissed at her.

"Knew what?"

"About your father." He gave a hysterical crack of laughter, then pointed with a shaking finger back and forth between them. "Our father."

Abi shook her head. "I don't understand." But she did. Slowly everything slid into place. The pale eyes so like her father's, the way he lifted his head to avoid your gaze, the pick, picking at his thumb, just like Charlie. Oh yes. Now she understood.

*February 1985*

"*Missié* Carl is here to fetch Abi. I've put him in the library."

Douglas could hear the contempt in Zabette's voice as she stood in the doorway of his studio. The twist of her lips was almost comic. Had things been different he might have smiled, but there was nothing to smile about in this situation.

"Where are Madame and the children?" he asked, frowning.

"Antoine has gone shopping with Tushti. Abi is in the garden with Madame. I haven't told her he's here."

"Bon, bon. Tell him I'll be with him in a minute."

She sniffed expressively and stomped off, outrage in every line of her body.

He put down his brushes, slowly wiped his hands on a piece of rag, but there was no point in keeping Carl waiting. He took off his paint spattered overall and hung it from the hook on the back of the door.

Carl was standing looking out of the window, his hands clasped behind his back, fingers fidgeting with the dry skin on his thumb. When Douglas came in, he swung round, scowling.

"There you are. What's all this about? I've got to get the children back and then return to the mill."

"Sit down."

"I'm quite happy standing." But something in Douglas's face must have got through Carl's thick skin. He threw himself into an armchair and sat back in a parody of relaxation.

"So, what's all this about?" Carl demanded again.

"It's about Antoine."

Carl's eyes slid away.

"Monique has told me who the father is," Douglas said.

"I don't see what that's got to do with me?"

"Please don't take me for a fool, Carl," Douglas's voice was icy. "I'm planning to adopt Antoine as my own. Since the father is unnamed on the birth certificate and my wife has no wish that he should have any involvement with the boy's upbringing, it will be a simple process. However, I wish to make it clear that, should there be any trouble, I am more than willing to make the facts known. I have Monique's permission to do so. Do you understand me?"

He waited, but Carl said nothing.

"And, as a small insurance, having got you the job at the sugar mill, entirely for Hilary's sake and for no other reason whatever, I am willing to arrange for you to be sacked if you should cause trouble in the future? Am I making myself clear?"

"You may know what you're gabbling on about, I don't." But it was an empty protest.

"I've always known you were an arrogant, selfish bastard," Douglas said quietly, "but I didn't realise you were a fool as well. Believe me, nothing would please me more than to see you ruined, but I won't do it while my cousin is part of your life. Watch your step, Carl."

Carl glanced at him, then quickly away again, but not before Douglas had seen the hatred in his eyes.

"I think we understand each other." Douglas pushed himself wearily from his chair. When they were halfway across the room Abi suddenly ran in from the garden, then stopped dead as she saw her father.

"Come on, girl," he said, grabbing her wrist. "I haven't got all day."

Douglas stood on the verandah and watched the car disappear down the drive. Empty words, he thought. How could he possibly allow the man to lose his job, when if he did, Hilary would suffer just as much as her husband? They may even be forced to leave the island. He felt a chill run through him at the thought.

*November 2018*

"My mother tells me you are my half-sister. We have the same father. Did you know? Did you?" Antoine snapped, glaring at her.

Unconsciously copying Antoine, she wrapped her arms around herself in a futile attempt to keep her emotions under control. For a moment she stood stock still, then lifted her hands as if to ward him off.

"No, I didn't, Antoine, not until this moment." She was amazed that her voice sounded so normal.

"I don't believe you."

"Why would I lie?" Now she was shouting too.

He turned away from her and walked up the steps to the summer house verandah, began to pace up and down. Abi followed him, her mind racing. How old was Antoine? A couple of years younger than Charlie. Abi did a quick calculation. Monique would have been fifteen. Douglas and Monique had married when she, Abi, was three. Had Monique been pregnant then? Maybe that was why they married when she was so young. But he'd been devoted to Monique, and she to him.

Antoine had come back to stand beside her. "She says she loved Carl."

Abi felt a wave of relief. "I'm glad."

"Why?"

"Wouldn't you rather it was that way?"

He stared at her wild eyed for a moment, then turned his back. "I suppose. I always knew Papa adopted me, but my mother never told me who my real father was, until now."

"Didn't you ever ask?"

"Yes, but she said it didn't matter, that Papa loved me, and I wasn't to ask again." He sounded calmer now. "I thought I didn't mind. When I was a kid, I used to pretend my father was some hero who died tragically, saving people from a shipwreck or something. I haven't really thought about it for years."

"Did she say anything else?"

"That your father," he spat the word out, "ditched her when he found she was pregnant. She was living here, helping Zabette, and when she told Papa she was expecting, he suggested they marry, give it out that I was his son. Selfless of him, don't you think?" he added bitterly.

"No! The age gap didn't matter. Monique loved him so much, and he adored her."

"Did he?" he asked scornfully.

"Oh yes." Abi was completely sure of it. "However their marriage came about, I know that for certain. And Douglas loved you as well."

"How can you say that? Particularly now he's screwed things up for me with that bloody will of his."

Abi had no answer to this.

"And your father didn't care about me either, so why should I care about you or this bloody albatross of an estate." He suddenly turned and yelled at her. "I wish to God you'd go back where you came from and get the hell out of my way." He swung round and leant his elbows on the railings, clasped his head in his hands.

They had both been so engrossed in each other that they hadn't heard the approaching footsteps coming up the steps behind them. It wasn't until a hand came out and gripped Abi's shoulder that she had any idea they weren't alone.

"Am I interrupting a family quarrel?"

Abi turned, then frowned. "Paul? What on earth are you doing here?" And then she realised the accent was different.

Antoine swung round, the look on his face a mixture of horror and fear. "Pieter! Where the hell did you come from?"

"I followed you from the hotel," the man said, a cold smile on his lips. There was no sign of the charming New Zealander. His look of cold contempt flicked from Abi to Antoine, who was staring at him like a trapped rabbit.

"What is going on here? Who are you?" she asked, fighting to keep her voice steady.

"Not a wine merchant, unfortunately. I quite liked that idea. The name I use most often is Pieter Brandt, and I'm an associate of Antoine's." He gave a short laugh. "I must say I found your conversation quite fascinating. Sister and brother. Well, well. I suppose it complicates matters a little, but never mind. We can resolve it, can't we, Antoine?"

Antoine said nothing. Abi could almost smell the fear in him.

"I suppose we owe her an explanation, don't we?" Turning to Abi, he went on. "You're an intelligent woman. I've realised that since I moved into the hotel to keep an eye on you. This is the way it goes."

But Abi didn't want to hear any more. All she wanted was to get away, from this awful man, from Antoine, from the whole situation. She gave Antoine a quick glance, almost of apology, then turned towards the steps. But Brandt was too quick for her. He grabbed her by the wrist, her bandaged wrist, and yanked her back towards him. She screamed in pain.

"Let her go, you bastard!" Antoine shouted.

"No way." Brandt laughed. "For Chrissake, you fool! Don't you realise she's standing in the way of everything you want?"

The grip on Abi's wrist hurt like hell. She kicked out at her captor, but he dodged, yanked at her wrist again and, as she cried out, laughed as if he was enjoying himself.

"Look. We could be friends." His gaze slid slowly down her body and he smiled. "I bet you're great in bed. We could have some fun, you and I."

Anger flowed up through Abi's body, consuming the fear.

"In your dreams, you disgusting toad," she hissed at him.

He swung his free hand up, but she managed to duck, and the blow didn't connect. A second later Antoine seemed to lose it completely. He leapt at Brandt, who dropped Abi's wrist and swung a punch which caught Antoine in the ribs. Antoine doubled up, gasping in pain.

Abi could hear herself screaming for him to stop but Brandt took no notice.

"Haven't you learnt your lesson?" he said, standing over Antoine's crouched body. "I've had you beaten up once. I'll enjoy doing it myself this time."

He hit out again, his fist connecting with Antoine's chin. Antoine staggered back, teetered on the edge of the steps, arms flailing, then somersaulted backwards. A second later he was lying still at the bottom of the steps.

She knew she should run down and help, but she couldn't move. Pieter Brandt grabbed her wrist and dragged her to the door of the summer house. With a violent push he sent her sprawling inside. Her head hit something hard and light exploded. Blackness engulfed her.


# CHAPTER 30


Raj had looked through the rest of the box but found no more revelations. His mind was still racing, trying to work out what was best to do. As he sat there, he read again the one short paragraph on the piece of grey lined paper, then took his mobile from his pocket. For a moment his thumb hovered over the keypad, but no, he wanted to be with Abi, ready to pick up the pieces, when he gave her this news.

"Raj, it's twenty to twelve." He hadn't noticed Patti pop her head round the door. "You're due at your next meeting at midday, and you've got to get across town yet."

"Okay, I'm on my way." He was about to put the papers back in the box but changed his mind and pushed them into his briefcase. In the end he sent Abi a text as he went down to his car:

*Thinking about u, thinking about last night,*

By the time Raj managed to escape from the meeting it was after three o'clock. He was barely out the door when he turned on his mobile and keyed in Abi's number. It rang and rang, but she didn't pick up. Back at the office, he had plenty of messages and e-mails to deal with, but he tried Abi's mobile several times more. No response.

* * *

Abi could hear groaning. She tried to open her eyes, but her eyelids were weighted down. When she moved her head, hammer blows of pain throbbed through it. She realised the person groaning was her. When at last she forced her eyes open, she saw thin shafts of light criss-crossing the room she was in, dust dancing in them. There was a familiar smell of salty air, mouldy canvas and wood. The summerhouse.

It took her a few moments to pluck up the courage to move again, but she knew she must. There was something she had to do. It was urgent. Fighting down nausea and a swimming head, she pushed herself up to lean on one arm, gasped as the pain in her head pounded in time to her heartbeat. But her mind was clearing. Bit by bit it came back to her. Antoine, her half-brother? And Paul – no, Pieter. She opened her mouth to call out but shut it again. What if he was still out there?

The minutes ticked by as she sat propped on her good arm, waiting for the dizziness to subside. How long had she been in here? It was still daylight outside, but in the gloom, she couldn't see her watch.

By hanging on to a sturdy table in the middle of the room she managed to drag herself upright. They used to play games on that table. The wooden games box with the brass hook and eye was still there. So many memories.

She stumbled across the room to one of the shuttered windows, subsided on to the window seat and held her watch to a shaft of light shining through a crack. Ten past twelve. When had he pushed her in here? It can't have been long ago.

Feeling her way round to the door, she tried the handle. It was locked. Finding a slightly larger crack in the shutter, she squinted through it. There were the steps, but Antoine was gone.

Of course. Her mobile. Relief flowed through her. Where was her bag? But then she remembered putting it out of the way, under the chair on the verandah. Tears sprang to her eyes. Stupid woman, no bloody point in crying. Do something. Check the windows. There may be a loose shutter. In a minute, when she felt stronger, she'd check them all.

* * *

At half past four Raj phoned the hotel but was told Abi's key was at the desk and there was no reply from her room. No, she'd left no message. Frustrated and worried, he sat back, chewing at his bottom lip.

Georgette came in, took one look at him and asked, "What's the matter?"

"Nothing. It's just – I've been trying to get hold of Abi all afternoon. She's not answering her mobile."

"Have you tried the hotel?"

"Yes. No luck there either."

"She's probably on the beach."

"Perhaps, but why hasn't she got her mobile with her?"

"Perhaps she's gone for a swim. She can't take it in the water." He didn't respond to this and she frowned. "Raj, what's up?"

He didn't look her in the eye. "It's not important. It's just that we were going to meet for dinner, I wanted to find out what time."

"I can tell there's more to it than that." There was a dawning smile on her face. "Have you two–"

"Leave it, Georgette."

His tone must have got through, but she still smiled.

"If you've arranged to have dinner together, why don't you go to the hotel after work anyway."

Now it was Raj's turn to smile. "Good idea. Thanks, Georgette."

"Any time. Two nights running, *ein?*"

Raj glared at her. "Haven't you got any work to do?"

"Okay, boss," she said and winked at him as she left the room.

* * *

Abi had waited half an hour – it felt like much longer – then she'd shouted till her throat was sore, but no one came. She gave up. The shouting made her headache worse. She'd checked all the windows, but there was no escape, the shutters were barred on the outside. Exhausted, she'd curled up on the window seat cushions. They smelt mouldy, but she didn't care. Perhaps, if she rested for a while, her head would stop hurting so much. After a while she slept.

When she came to, she straightened up and her hand touched her beloved brooch. Had it been damaged? No, it was safely in place. Her heart rate calmed and when she lifted her head, the aching wasn't as bad.

The angle of light had changed. She pushed herself up and went to the crack of light to check her watch. Five o'clock. Oh God! She'd slept for ages. It would be dark in less than two hours. The panic threatened to return, but she refused to let it take hold. If she was going to get out of here, she had to think clearly. When Raj got to the hotel and she wasn't there, surely he'd get her message and come looking for her. For a moment she felt much better at the thought of this tenuous lifeline, but the feeling didn't last. What if Brandt came back? She must be prepared. Looking round, she found a croquet mallet leaning against the wall; she picked it up, felt the comforting weight of it.

She wondered if she could push the mallet handle through the shutters at the top and break the glass? Then anyone passing would be more likely to hear her shouting. But she couldn't reach. If she pulled the table over and stood on it, that might help. She picked up the games box, gritting her teeth against the pain in her bandaged wrist, then stumbled and dropped it. Crashing to the floor, it burst open and dominoes, mahjong tiles and marbles flew everywhere.

"Shit, shit, shit!" Abi muttered, and crouched down to gather up the mess. The last thing she wanted to do was step on the marbles and go flying. There was a gap in the floorboards and one, then two, then more fell through. She heard them land with a metallic clang. Abi frowned, wondering what was down there. Crawling across the floor, she looked at the boards. There were several gaps. She pushed a finger down but couldn't get a hold. This was getting nowhere. She'd just sit on the floor for a moment, then try to drag the table out of the way.

* * *

"I'm sorry, sir," the young man at reception told Raj. "Miss Kendall's key is still here, and there are no messages. We've checked her room and the rest of the hotel. Perhaps she went on a tour?"

Raj tried not to be annoyed. The man was doing his best. He checked the time again. It was half past five. He could go to Narinda's and come back later. No, his sister could read him like a book, she was bound to ask too many questions.

The receptionist was still standing there, waiting for him to say something when another member of staff came from the office behind him. She gave Raj an enquiring look.

"Can I help?" she asked.

"This gentleman is enquiring for Miss Kendall, but we have no–"

A flush rose in her brown cheeks as she looked at Raj. "There was a message."

"From Miss Kendall?" Raj snapped. "What time was this?"

"This morning, about eleven o'clock. I'm so sorry, sir. Miss Kendall left it with me and I'm afraid I didn't pass it on to my colleague, we were very busy." She was searching behind the counter as she spoke and brought out a piece of paper. "Are you *Missié* Amrakash?"

"Yes."

"I really am sorry."

"Fine, fine. What was this message?"

"She said to tell you she was going to Belle Etoile and would phone you later. She went with the gentleman who came to see her."

"What did he look like?" Raj demanded.

"He – um…" She was obviously disturbed by the urgency in Raj's voice. "He was about your height, Mauritian, black hair but he had blue eyes, I noticed particularly."

Antoine, he was sure of it.

"And then there was the other man. One of our guests, Mr Harper."

"What about him?"

"Well," she hesitated, then said in a rush, "I think he was following them. He went through reception, *tres doucement*, waited behind the door until the other man's car had gone, then he too left."

Her colleague interrupted. "The South African? With the Porsche?"

She turned to him. "Yes, that's the one."

When they turned back, Raj was leaping down the steps to the car park.

* * *

Raj could tell Monique was upset. As he came in, she looked up, a sudden flash of hope in her eyes, but it was soon replaced by a worried frown.

"Oh Raj, thank goodness."

He sat down beside her. "What's wrong?" he asked.

"Antoine and Abi. I've waited all afternoon, but they haven't come back. *Tonton* Gabriel checked the *arpen bas*, but they aren't there and it's all my fault."

At that moment Zabette bustled in. "*Missié* Raj, Madame is worried, you must help."

"I intend to." Raj turned back to Monique. "Tell me," he said.

"I told him, but I shouldn't have, not like that. Ah *Bondié*!" Leaning her head back against her chair, she closed her eyes.

Raj wanted to fire questions at her, but that would do no good. He took her hands, clasped them warmly in his.

"Monique. I can't help if you don't tell me what's happened. Begin at the beginning, tell me."

She opened her eyes and looked at him. She seemed to focus and become calmer.

"They came to see me this morning. I was so pleased to see them together. It's been my wish for so long. But Antoine wanted to speak to me on his own, so Abi went for a walk. I asked him why did he not want her here? She is your sister, I told him, and then I realised what I'd said. He made me tell him the whole story."

"That Carl Kendall was his father."

"Yes! How did you know?"

"My father left a note with Antoine's adoption papers saying who the father was in case Antoine ever needed to know. I only found it today."

There was silence for a moment. Zabette sat down and Raj glanced at her. He didn't think she was surprised. After a while Monique began to speak again, gazing out over the garden as she did so.

"I thought he loved me. But when I got pregnant, he said if I told anyone about us, he would take my baby from me." Then she smiled. "But Douglas came to the rescue, and soon I realised it was him I loved, not that—" She stopped suddenly and turned to look at Raj. "You mustn't think badly of me. I was so young."

"Of course I don't think badly of you." Raj desperately wanted to ask more about what had happened earlier, but he didn't want to pressure her. He hoped to God she'd tell him soon.

"I suppose, in a way," she went on, "Hilary and I had a bond. He was cruel to me, and he was cruel to her, and yet at one time we'd both loved him."

"Monique." He couldn't wait any longer. "Was Abi here when you told Antoine about his father?"

"No. She went to look at the summerhouse. When I told him, he dashed off after her. Not long after that, Zabette heard Antoine's car start up. By the time she got out to the driveway, they'd gone."

Unable to stay still any longer, Raj paced to the window and back again. The two women watched anxiously.

"And you've tried Antoine's mobile?" he asked.

"Yes," said Zabette, "several times."

He paced back to the window. "I've tried Abi too, but I'll try again now." He stood by the open window. Dusk was falling but the heat was still oppressive. He keyed in Abi's number, listened. He could hear a mobile ringing and turned to Zabette.

"Is that yours?"

She shook her head. At the same moment they realised the sound was coming from outside.

Raj jumped over the low windowsill onto the verandah. It didn't take him long to discover the source of the ringtone. Under a chair was a multicoloured handbag he recognised. Inside, Abi's phone was ringing. He looked at the screen. There were six missed calls. A cold sense of dread crept over him as he stood there with her mobile in his hand.

# CHAPTER 31

Raj's mind was racing. Every time he'd seen Abi she'd had this distinctive bag with her. Monique had told him Abi and Antoine had arrived about half past eleven. That was over six hours ago. And they'd left again without saying goodbye. He could quite easily believe that of Antoine, but not of Abi. She'd have come back for this bag and to say goodbye.

When he stepped back into the room, he did his best to sound calm.

"She must have forgotten it," he said. "Now we know why she hasn't been answering my calls."

"But why didn't she come back for it, Raj?" Monique asked anxiously.

"I don't know, Monique, but I'm sure there's a rational explanation. You mustn't worry." He wished he could take his own advice.

They all heard a door open then close at the front of the house, closely followed by footsteps. All three of them swung round expectantly. It was Jacquo.

"*Bonsoir* Madame, Zabette. Raj, *qui manierre?*" He stopped halfway across the room and frowned. "Is something wrong?"

"No, not really," Raj assured him. But the feeling of disappointment was like a physical blow.

"Monique." He took her hand, forced himself to smile. "I certainly won't leave without saying goodbye. I must have a quick word with Jacquo. I'll be back in a minute."

Still gripping Abi's bag, he gave a nod towards the door and made his way out of the room, relieved when Jacquo followed him without question.

"Madame asked me to check the *arpen bas*," Jacquo told him, "but there was no sign of them, and his car was gone from the drive. Do you think something bad has happened?"

"I don't know," Raj said, "but I'm worried. Maybe it's the fire last night that's rattled me, but I've got a bad feeling about this. Abi and I were due to have dinner together this evening. It's nearly seven, getting dark. Where the hell is she?"

"Do you want me to have a look around?"

"For what? There's no point," Raj said. "I'll go into Mahebourg and have a word with Inspector Beejadhur. He'll probably tell me not to waste his time, but it's worth a try."

"Hadn't you better check he's there first?"

Raj ran a hand through his hair. "You're right. I'm not thinking straight." He took out his mobile, scrolled down to the station number. When he got through, he was told Beejadhur was out. Raj asked if they could get a message to him, the officer said he'd do his best.

"Maybe we could wander down to the *arpen bas* and take a look."

They were halfway round the outside of the house when Raj's mobile rang. He grabbed it from his pocket. "'allo?"

"*Missié* Amrakash? Beejadhur here."

"Thanks for phoning back."

"Phoning back? You've been trying to contact me?"

"I left a message with one of your officers. You might think I'm worrying unnecessarily, but after last night I—"

"Hang on *Missié* Amrakash, I've had no message. Where are you?"

"At Belle Etoile."

"That's good. I'm on my way there now."

"What's going on?"

There was a slight pause before Beejadhur answered.

"A body has been found, on the rocks at the bottom of the cliff at Belle Etoile."

Cold dread gripped Raj's stomach. He opened his mouth to speak, but no words came.

When the inspector said, "A man's body," the relief was inexpressible, but then he added, "We think it might be Antoine Beaumont."

"Antoine?" asked Raj, the fear returning.

"I'll explain when I get there."

Beejadhur ended the call. There was nothing to do but wait.

Raj told Jacquo what had been said.

"Go in and take Zabette aside. Just tell her the police are on their way, say it's something to do with the fire last night. She's sharp as a pin, she probably won't believe you, but you'll just have to persuade her to stay with Madame and keep her inside."

"Leave it with me," he said and turned to go back into the house.

Raj looked down at the bag, still in his hand. He lifted it to his face. It smelt of Abi's perfume. He took her mobile out of the bag and put it into his pocket, then walked round to the driveway and put the bag into his car. Putting his hands deep in his pockets, one clasped tight round Abi's mobile, like a talisman, he went to sit on the steps to wait for the police.

* * *

In the dusk, with no distractions, he could no longer keep the dread at bay. While he'd been able to think she might be with Antoine, it hadn't seemed so bad. He thought back to last night, Abi waking, and the aftermath, but no, he mustn't go there. Head in his hands, he made a futile effort to control his imagination.

Moments later Raj heard the sirens. There were two police cars, a Land Rover marked 'Police Rescue', and an ambulance. Uniformed officers poured out of the cars and the van. Beejadhur strode up to Raj.

"A bad business," he said.

"Tell me what's happened."

"A local lad who was fishing from the rocks found the body about four this afternoon. He dialled the emergency services. There's no way to get a boat in there, what with the undertow, so two of my men climbed down at Pointe aux Hirondelles, as access is easier from there. One of them recognised Antoine Beaumont. We've had a look at the maps, and we can confirm that the point where he was found is immediately below the southern corner of the Belle Etoile estate."

"Below the lower terrace?" Raj asked.

"Yes. I'm sorry but would you be willing to identify the body? Much better than his poor mother having to do it."

"Of course," Raj said, his stomach churning at the thought.

Jacquo came out of the house towards them. He made the suggestion they take the Land Rover across the lawns and down to the point at which the stand of bamboos ended.

"There's a space between the bamboos and the cliff, you'll be able to take the Land Rover down and get access, although I don't think the ambulance could make it."

"We'll have to stretcher him up," Beejadhur said. "Can you show my men the way?"

"Sure."

"Ok, I'll go in and have a quick word with Madame Beaumont," Raj said. "And Inspector, there's something I should tell you. *Mam'zelle* Kendall was with Antoine this morning here at Belle Etoile. As far as we know they left in his car. She hasn't been seen since."

"*Ayo!*" The man's exclamation spoke volumes. He gave Raj a sympathetic look. "I'll inform the office. They can start working on *Mam'zelle* Kendall's whereabouts. Now, let's get this body up."

* * *

Raj found Monique and Zabette where he'd left them. He tried to smile, but when Monique looked up, he knew he'd not succeeded in hiding his feelings.

"Raj, what's going on?"

"There's a body been discovered down at the bottom of the cliff. The police have to bring it up, and the only way is to take a rescue vehicle down there."

"It must have been swept in by the sea," said Zabette, giving Raj a straight look. "It happens sometimes. Nothing for you to worry about, Madame."

"How I wish Douglas was here," Monique said.

Zabette got up and said, "I'll make some tea." She went to the door and beckoned to Raj to followed her out.

"Now. Tell me what's going on," she demanded once they were in the kitchen.

Raj told her as much as he knew himself. She put a hand up to her mouth as if to stifle a cry, then let it drop.

"*Pauvre* Madame," she said. "I will sit with her. You must go down there, wait for them to bring that poor boy home."

He put his arm round her thin shoulders and gave her a quick hug, then went out into the garden in time to see the lights of the Land Rover in the distance as it made its way down. As he hurried after it, he took out his mobile and pressed in a number.

"Raji, I was just thinking about you."

Relief flowed through him as he heard his sister's voice, but he had no time for preliminaries. "Listen, Narinda. I'm at Belle Etoile. I need your help."

He heard her gasp as he told her what had happened. "Could you come. You might be needed when we tell Monique. Is Vijay at home?"

"Yes. He'll come too. Is Abi with you?"

283

"No. Narinda, she was with Antoine earlier on. I've found her bag here, but there's no sign of her. Oh God, Nari!"

"Raji darling, we'll be there as fast as we can."

Raj thrust the mobile back in his pocket, ran to the tunnel of steps and hurried down.

* * *

Abi sat curled up on the cushions. Her body ached. Her mind felt strangely empty. The shafts of light had turned rosy and gradually faded. While the light lasted, she'd tried hard to find a way out, but it was no good. For the last hour she'd sat on the cushions, staring into the darkness and rocking a little back and forth, not entirely aware of her surroundings anymore.

But suddenly she was wide awake again. The shafts of light were back, not rosy now but bright, making erratic patterns across the room. She could hear vehicles, then voices. Abi jumped up, ignoring her swimming head as she stumbled to the door, nearly tripping over the discarded mallet as she went. She picked it up and began a ragged rhythm of swinging the mallet back and forth, banging on the wooden panels of shutters.

At first her voice didn't want to work properly, but she finally managed to call out.

"Help! Please help!"

Nothing.

There were people out there and she needed to get their attention. She forced herself to try again.

"Can anybody hear me! Please help! Please!"

A moment later she heard someone running up the steps to the verandah.

"I'm in here!" she shouted. "Help me!"

"Abi? Abi is that you?"

"Raj! Please, let me out. Please Raj!"

"The key's gone. Hang on."

"Raj!" she screamed, terrified that he'd been a figment of her imagination. "Don't leave me."

"I won't. I'll be back in a second."

She stood slumped, arms lifted against the door, listening with her whole body for his return. She heard voices and then rapid footsteps.

"Abi, we'll have to prise the door open. Stand back."

She leant against the table listening to the beautiful noise of a crowbar working its way into the gap. Wood creaked and splintered. At last, the door gave way. There was barely enough space when Raj pushed his way through and was across the floor and gathering her into his arms.

* * *

"I've re-bandaged her wrist," Vijay said to Raj. "She'll be fine now."

"I've told Beejadhur what she said about Brandt. He's going to put out a general alert." Raj's voice shook. "What I wouldn't give to get my hands on that bastard."

"I'm with you there," said his brother-in-law.

"They'll be looking out for him at the harbour, airport, marinas, all of it."

"Good," Vijay said with satisfaction. "I've told the inspector I don't want Abi disturbed for questioning until morning." He glanced at Raj. "Stop worrying. She'll be fine, a mild concussion, nothing more."

"Thanks. I don't know what I'd have done without you and Nari here to help. Is she still with Monique?"

"Yes. Tell me, did you know Abi and Antoine were half brother and sister?"

"Not until this morning when I was looking through the papers Douglas left with Papa."

"Dreadful to find that out and then" – he threw up his hands – "the man is dead the next minute. Poor girl."

"She's had a lot to cope with in her life. Her father has one hell of a lot to answer for. I hope now she can begin to move on."

Vijay smiled at him. "With you?"

Raj couldn't stop himself returning the smile.

"Yes – well, it's early days. I know how I feel, but I'm not sure about Abi."

"From what I saw earlier, Raj, I don't think you have anything to worry about."

"Nah," Raj said. "She was just glad to be let out of the summerhouse."

Vijay grinned, but was soon serious again. "Are you going back out now?"

"I have to. Beejadhur wants me to identify the body."

"I'll come with you."

When they got back down to the cliff edge, the *arpen bas* was a hive of activity.

Spotlights lit up the scene. Raj and Vijay stood with Jacquo as two men abseiled down, taking a stretcher with them, then inch by inch it was brought back up and laid carefully on the ground. Steeling himself, Raj went to where the Beejadhur was shining a powerful torch down on the body. Raj looked down at the grazed and bruised face.

"Yes," he said quietly. "That's Antoine Beaumont."

The inspector leant over and covered Antoine's face. Two of his men took hold of the stretcher and slowly began to trudge back up to the ambulance.

"I must get back to the station," he told Raj. "I'll keep you posted. Unless Brandt took a flight out this afternoon, he can't get far. It would give me great pleasure to slap him inside and throw away the key."

"You're not the only one," Raj said.

After a great deal of hand shaking, the police were finally gone and Raj, Jacquo and Vijay made their way back to the house. Raj went to check on Abi in the guest room, the room where she and Charlie had slept all those years ago. She was fast asleep, her good hand tucked under her cheek on the pillow, her golden hair spread across it. He crept out and went to look for his sister and brother-in-law.

Vijay came out of Monique's bedroom. "That poor woman," he said. "When Nari told her about Antoine she didn't really seem surprised. All she said was, poor boy, I knew he'd lost his way."

"I think I understand what she meant," Raj said.


# CHAPTER 32


Bright sun shone round the edges of the curtains at the head of the bed. Above her were the white painted planks of the ceiling and a brass fan swinging lazily round. On the wall by the door was a familiar watercolour of the beach at Flic-en-Flac. Abi closed her eyes again, then slowly opened them. Yes, it was all still there. She was in her bedroom at Belle Etoile. Slowly she turned her head on the pillow. The movement set up a dull throb. She groaned.

On the sofa in the corner of the room, Raj threw back a cotton spread, stumbled up and came across the room. He put out a tentative hand and touched her cheek.

"How are you feeling?"

"My head's aching a bit." The words were difficult to get out. "And my mouth's so dry."

Raj picked up a glass of water from the bedside table and helped Abi to sit up and take a drink. It was the best drink she'd ever had.

Snatches of the day before began to return to her. "Vijay was here, wasn't he?" she asked.

"Yes. He checked you over last night."

"What day is it?"

Raj smiled. "Saturday."

"What time?"

"Half past eight in the morning."

They sat for a moment, his arm around her, her head on his shoulder. She could feel his soft breath on her forehead. Abi noticed that she was wearing her own nightdress.

She plucked at it. "How come I've got this on?"

"I fetched your things from the hotel."

Abi thought back to the last time she'd worn it, remembered it following the pillows on to the floor. She wondered what was going through Raj's mind. Was he regretting their night together?

"Raj, the other night, you don't have to feel–"

"I don't have to feel what?"

"I asked you to stay. It was very kind–"

"Kind!" He held her away from him and grinned.

"Is that what you think I was being? In my book that's a lot of kindness we went in for."

But a moment later he was serious. "Abi, when I found your handbag on the verandah I was so scared, and when Monique told me Antoine had gone to find you, and she hadn't seen you since." He looked suddenly stricken. "Oh Abi. I thought I'd lost you."

It felt so good to rest her head back on his shoulder and put her good arm round his body.

"But you haven't, and I'm all right."

They stayed like that for some time.

"I'd love a bath."

"There's a bathroom just next door."

"Oh? That's new."

Raj helped her into the bath. Between them they washed her hair, taking care to avoid the sore lump behind her left ear. It was a slow process and very intimate. They talked about what had happened and Raj told her about finding his father's note attached to Antoine's adoption papers.

Tears came to her eyes. "A brother I never knew we had, and now he's dead." She wiped the tears away with the corner of a towel. "I've just remembered, Raj, he tried to protect me from Brandt."

"You must tell Monique."

"I will."

By the time she was dressed, most of the gaps in her memory had been filled. Abi sat down at the dressing table and took up her hairbrush. Someone had arranged it neatly with her moisturiser, perfume bottle and sun lotion, and next to them her brooch.

"Did you put all this on here?" she asked Raj.

"Yes," he said, looking slightly embarrassed. "I just brought what I thought you'd need this morning."

"And my brooch?"

"You were wearing it when I found you."

"Thank you," she said, and kissed him.

"Are you hungry?" Raj asked her.

"I think I am," she said. "You know what I'd like, some paw paw, and good Mauritian bread, *ti dipain*."

Raj grinned. "You can get the girl out of Mauritius, but you can't get Mauritius out of the girl. I'll go and find Zabette."

As Abi carefully brushed her hair, she thought how unfair it was that she should feel so incredibly happy when Antoine was dead.

* * *

Zabette looked up at Raj came into the kitchen. "*Mam'zelle* is awake?" she asked.

"Yes, she's feeling much better."

"*Merci Bondiè*," she said, and crossed herself. "I'll make breakfast."

Raj glanced out of the kitchen window. He could see the police van parked on the lawn down by the gap in the bamboos.

"Those police are still crawling all over the place, wearing strange suits, searching, searching. They'd better not disturb Madame," she said fiercely. She lifted the tray, now stacked with Abi's breakfast. "But at least *Mam'zelle* Abi is back now. You must make her stay."

"I'll do my best," Raj said, smiling down at her.

"I've poured you some tea. Oh, and that inspector phoned ten minutes ago, said you weren't answering your mobile. He said for you to phone back as soon as you could."

Raj sipped his tea as he scrolled down to Beejadhur's number. He answered straight away.

"We have more information about the arson attacks," Beejadhur told him. "It seems the grapevine has already spread the news of Antoine Beaumont's death. Normally I'd be annoyed, but this time it's loosened some tongues."

"How do you mean?"

"Four of our local young layabouts were on the doorstep first thing this morning, herded in by the mother of one of them. They owned up to the attacks but were very anxious to deny all knowledge of Beaumont being killed. The younger three are chattering like a flock of *cateaux verts*. Apparently, they were paid well, but insist they have no idea why they were asked to do it."

"Did they say why several fires were started?"

"To keep us busy apparently, which they certainly did. I think the Belle Etoile attack was the important one, the rest were just for distraction."

"If Brandt was behind it, I suppose that makes sense. Who paid them?"

"Now that's the interesting bit. The ringleader, who's older than the others, tried to stop them telling us, so we separated them and after that it didn't take long to get some more information out of the younger three. They said they were paid by the older chap, but two of them saw him taking money from a foreigner. The description fits Brandt."

"I'm amazed he wasn't more careful."

"There are those whose arrogance makes them foolish, which is always useful to us. I'm waiting for a photo of him to come through from Inspector Persand at Immigration – thanks for that tip, by the way. We'll show it to the boys, see if they recognise him."

Raj thought back to the meeting he'd had with Brandt and Antoine in his office. What was it he'd called Mauritius? A small, rather backward community. Hopefully he was about to find out how wrong he'd been.

"And talking of risks," Beejadhur went on, his voice more serious now, "I'd like to put a guard on *Mam'zelle* Kendall, just until we've caught that *fézer*. She witnessed the attack on Beaumont, that puts her in danger."

Raj felt a chill of fear. "It'd be foolish beyond belief for him to come anywhere near Belle Etoile," he protested.

"Yes, but I'd rather be safe than sorry. I'm sending one of my female officers along. And I'll be round this afternoon to ask her a few more questions. I hope I'll have more news for you then."

* * *

Charlie had not slept well. He was too worried. He'd tried to get through to Abi several times over the last couple of days, but there'd been no response.

"Surely no news is good news," Beth said. "Don't nag her, love. Maybe she's actually having a good time."

He'd wanted to believe this was true, but still he worried. Ever since they were small, they'd had this sixth sense when one of them was in trouble, and he couldn't shift a feeling of dread.

On Saturday morning, immediately after Beth had gone out, he tried again. It was half past eight, that'd be twelve thirty with Abi. He listened to her mobile ring, once, twice, then it was answered.

"Abi, where the hell have you been? I've been trying to get hold of you for days."

A man's voice answered. "I'm afraid it's not Abi."

"Who's that?"

"Raj Amrakash."

291

"Raj! It's Charlie, Abi's brother. Is she okay?"

There was a moment's pause.

"Ah, Charlie," Raj said. "Yes, she's fine now. I'll put her on."

"Hallo love." Abi sounded tired. "I've been so longing to speak to you."

"Then why didn't you pick up yesterday?"

"I'm sorry. Things got complicated. I didn't have my phone. It was only this morning Raj remembered where he'd put it. Oh, Charlie, I'm so, so pleased to hear your voice."

"Abi, what is going on?"

Hesitantly at first, Abi began to tell him. It took a while, with many an interruption from Charlie, and an occasional interjection in the background from Raj, but at last it was done.

"God! Carl really was an absolute shit, wasn't he?" Charlie said bitterly.

"I think we knew that already."

"Poor Antoine, he didn't really have a chance."

"Monique and Douglas loved him."

"I suppose. What now then?"

"I'm going to stay here with Monique for the rest of the time. Raj is looking after me. He fetched my things from the hotel and helped me bath."

"He helped you what? You two seem to be getting on rather well now?"

There was a gurgle of laughter. "You could say that." Before he could pursue it, she changed the subject.

"The inside of the summerhouse had piles of stuff I remembered in it. I think that's what kept me going, familiar things around, even down to the box of games on the table."

There was a sudden silence and he wondered if they'd been cut off.

"Are you still there?" he said.

"I've just remembered something. You know the base of the summerhouse?"

"Yes. There's a space under the floorboards," Charlie said, "and a trap door you can pull up."

"How did you know that? I always thought it was solid, until yesterday."

"No, no. Antoine and I explored it once. We got told off by Monique and she told Mum who said we must never go in there again. She was very angry, for Mum."

"When I was trapped in the summerhouse the games box fell off the table. Stuff went everywhere, and marbles were rolling about and falling between the floorboards. Charlie, the marbles that fell through made a metallic clang when they landed. I wonder what could be in that cellar that's metal?"

"I've no idea. I don't remember anything except spiders and cockroaches. There's not enough room to store much. It could have been a bucket, one of the ones we used to take to the beach."

"That could explain it. Raj says he'll have a look later, but the police are still down there at the moment."

"Look, Abi, you must get some rest," Charlie said. "We can skype later. Put me on to Raj. I want to thank him for looking after my big sister."

"Okay. Love you lots."

Beth got back at half past eleven, the same time the twins lumbered downstairs in search of food. While she put the shopping away, and the twins ate mountains of toast, Charlie brought them up to date.

"She let slip that Raj helped her bath, and she was calling him darling."

Beth was grinning from ear to ear. "Oh, that's great!"

"You think?" Charlie wasn't so sure. "Long distance relationships aren't easy."

"Granted, but let's just wait and see."

"When are we going then?" Pip asked.

"To Mauritius," Mattie added.

"Have to be soon," Pip said.

"Sooner the better."

"Before we start Uni."

"I'm not sure what the logic of that is," their father said repressively. "It's bloody expensive and I'm not made of money."

"But it would be nice," said Beth, still grinning.

* * *

It wasn't until the following morning that the police finished on the *arpen bas*.

"Jacquo and I will go and check under the summerhouse floor," Raj told Abi. "You don't have to come with us. I don't want you upset again."

"You worry too much," she told him. "I'm coming with you, Raj. If I don't do it now, I might never do it. I've spent too much of my life running away from things I don't want to face."

Abi stood on the lawn, her arms clasped round her body, and watched while the two men removed the shutters. Once they'd done so, Raj turned to look at her, then came down and took her hand. They walked up the steps together.

The inside was bright with sunlight and looked very different to the room that had been her prison for eight long hours. Abi breathed a sigh of relief. This was how she remembered it from her childhood.

Jacquo and Raj moved the table and some chairs and revealed the hinged floorboards Charlie had described. The hinges were rusty and crusted with dust.

"I brought this with me," Jacquo said, taking a tin of oil out of his pocket. Abi and Raj stood and watched while he squeezed oil on to the hinges, worked it in with a piece of bamboo, then heaved at the boards. With a shriek of protest the trap door lifted revealing a dark cavity below.

They all peered down and in the light from the torch they could see a hole, half a metre deep and festooned with cobwebs. At the bottom, pushed to one side, was a tin box.

"So that's what the marbles fell on," Abi said. "Look, two of them are lodged in the handle on the lid."

"How're we going to get it out?" asked Raj.

"I think I can reach the handle if I lie flat on the floor," Jacquo said.

A moment later he placed the box, sludgy green with a rusting padlock, on the floor at Abi's feet.

"You inherited the summer house and its contents," Raj said, smiling at Abi and putting an arm round her, "so, this belongs to you. Shall we have a look at what's inside?"

But before they could do so they heard someone calling them. "*Missié* Amrakash! *Mam'zelle* Kendall!"

They both went to the door and saw the young police officer who'd been sent to look after Abi, running across the lawn towards them.

"Inspector Beejadhur is here," she said. "He wishes to speak to you urgently."

"We'd better go," Raj said.

"Don't worry," Jacquo told them. "I'll bring this up to the house."

* * *

Beejadhur was pacing up and down in the library. As they came in, his face broke into a broad smile.

"We got him," he said.

Abi sat down rather suddenly. Raj gave her a quick glance and came to sit on the arm of her chair.

"Where? How?" he asked.

"I had my suspicions about the ringleader. I was sure he hadn't told us all he knew, so I had him followed. It paid off. Earlier today he went around the coast to that inlet at Roche Noire, you know where the road bridge is?"

Raj nodded.

"He turned in from the coast and we followed him through the mangroves. Someone had taken a small cruiser as far as it could go without running aground. This lad left his motorbike and waded through the water, then pulled himself up on deck, and guess who comes out to see him – our arrogant South African. We've got them both locked up and I've spent most of the afternoon questioning Brandt. At first he denied any knowledge of *Missié* Beaumont's death–"

"Bastard," Abi exclaimed. "I was there. I saw it."

"I know, *Mam'zelle* Kendall."

"Has he admitted anything yet?" asked Raj.

"Let me tell you what happened. After we'd been questioning him for a couple of hours, the officers we'd sent to search Beaumont's office returned. They found evidence of his dealings with Brandt's outfit, Leisure & Property International. Beaumont was in debt to them to the tune of about three million rupees, and he'd signed undertakings to let them have a major holding in Belle Etoile in lieu of the payment of that debt. When we challenged Brandt with this, he insisted it was all perfectly legal, so I tried a different tack." Beejadhur gave Abi a slightly apologetic look. "I reminded him that you were a witness to the fight."

Raj protested but the inspector held his hands up.

"It paid off, particularly as the lad we followed has been telling us quite a lot about *Missié* Brandt – it's not the first time they've had dealings with each other. Apparently, Brandt paid him and a *copain* of his to beat up Beaumont a week ago."

"That doesn't surprise me at all," Raj exclaimed. "I knew Antoine had been in some kind of dust up."

"The post-mortem confirms it. The pathologist says he had two cracked ribs which happened days ago and weren't caused by the fight or the fall from the cliffs."

"Does he think I saw everything?" Abi's stomach churned at the thought.

"You were a witness to the fight. He can't deny that. I didn't tell him whether or not you saw anything else."

"I have an absolutely clear picture in my mind of Antoine lying on the grass with his feet resting on the bottom of the steps. He was so still."

Abi looked up and intercepted a glance between Raj and the Inspector. She thought Beejadhur gave a little nod.

"What? There's something you're not telling me."

Beejadhur spoke gently. "*Missié* Beaumont's neck was broken. We believe he was already dead before he was pushed over the cliff."

Abi pressed close to Raj and he put his arm around her. "Is that all, Inspector? I think *Mam'zelle* Kendall has had enough."

"Yes. I'm sorry. But there is more evidence that could help put Brandt away."

"Please. I want to know what it is," Abi said.

The inspector gave her a considering look.

"Very well. It's obvious from some parallel markings on the grass that *Missié* Beaumont was dragged from the summer house to the cliff. Someone tried to scuff the marks up, but they were still there, and we've found a couple of clear footprints. We're checking Brandt's shoes."

"When I looked through the crack in the shutters," Abi told him, "Antoine was gone."

"Can you remember what time that was?"

Abi frowned and chewed at her lip. "I'm sure I looked at my watch, but I can't remember exactly."

"Never mind. Perhaps it will come back to you."

"One thing I've been wondering," Raj said. "What happened to Antoine's car?"

"Ah yes, that's something else we got out of the lad who led us to the boat. He was paid to move Brandt's car, apparently it was hidden in that copse opposite the gate. Brandt must have taken *Missié* Beaumont's, but we haven't found it yet. We will though. With all this, I think we've got him. He's now asked for a lawyer. I don't think it'll be very long before he's trying to make a deal, much good may it do him. I'm pretty sure he won't get bail, too much of a risk that he'll abscond."

* * *

Some hours later Raj and Abi sat close together on the back verandah. Only the nearest trees and shrubs were visible in the lights from the house, and the stars blinked in and out from behind clouds blown by a warm wind. Earlier they'd gone to the hotel to pick up the rest of her belongings and she was now settled in her old room at Belle Etoile. It seemed so right, and so did having Raj there with her.

"Do you want to have a look at what's in that box?"

Abi took a deep breath. "Yes, I think I do."

"You don't sound too sure."

"It's just that I'm a little afraid of what I might find."

"We can leave it if you like."

"No, I'm being a coward."

"Not a word I'd use to describe you."

She smiled up at him and he bent to kiss her, but she drew back. There was something she needed to know.

"What will happen now?" she asked. "To Belle Etoile. Will Monique inherit it?"

Abi couldn't interpret the expression on Raj's face. He seemed surprised she'd asked the question.

"Abi, Douglas made his wishes clear."

"I know. Monique has life enjoyment. But now Antoine's gone–"

"Did you not read the last paragraph of Douglas's will?"

She thought back to that day a month ago, sitting on the sofa in her flat. She remembered those words in Uncle Douglas's scrawl '... *her absence and my loss of contact with her has been a great grief to me.*' That short phrase had meant so much. She remembered closing her eyes tight to stop the tears. Then when she'd opened them the familiar signature had drawn her eyes down. She realised now there had been something she'd missed.

"Well, I might have missed the very last bit."

Raj let out a bark of laughter.

"You are amazing. I don't think I've ever met anyone less – less self-interested. I think you must be very like your mother." He turned and took her by the shoulders. "Abi," he said, speaking slowly so that there was no doubt she'd understand, "the last couple of lines of Douglas's will say that should one of you die, you or Antoine, the other inherits the whole estate. Belle Etoile, my darling, is now yours."

# CHAPTER 33

"Beth!" Charlie called. "We're back."

Beth came rushing into the kitchen with the twins close behind. She flung her arms round her sister-in-law. "Abi love! It's so good to see you."

After a glass of champagne and once the twins had gone off to the pub to meet friends, Charlie turned to Abi with a look of apprehension.

"I didn't want to get it all out until the boys had gone, but now, can we–?"

Abi took a deep, steadying breath. "Let's do it. Where's my hand baggage?"

"Here." Charlie lifted the small suitcase onto the table.

As she unzipped it Abi told them, "I put everything we found in the tin box in here. I didn't want to be parted from it. It didn't give me much room, but Raj, bless him, managed to talk the people at the airport into letting me have two bags in the cabin."

The case was full.

First, she brought out several packets of letters tied together with pieces of blue or yellow ribbon.

"These are Mum's letters to Tony," she said, indicating those with yellow ribbon, "and these are his to her. In one of her diaries, she says Douglas got Raj's father to retrieve them after Tony died – he knew the policeman in charge of the investigation."

She took several leather-bound notebooks out of the case and put them down by the letters.

"These are her diaries. They go from the mid-sixties to 1991."

Charlie picked one up, started to leaf through it, his face expressionless. Beth pulled her chair closer to his, put her arm round him.

"There are several keepsakes, such as this handkerchief with his initials embroidered in the corner. Do you remember how she was always doing embroidery, Charlie? I'm sure she must have done this. And in this bag, there are things like bills from restaurants, tickets for concerts, some dried flowers, stuff like that."

Abi paused, then took out a South African Airways folder.

"These are airline tickets to Durban for Mum, me, you and Nanny V." She tried to keep her voice steady. "They're dated for a month after Tony died. But the worst thing of all is this."

She handed him a cream envelope. On the outside was written 'Douglas Beaumont' in their mother's handwriting.

"It was still stuck down when I found it. He obviously never got it."

"And you opened it, when? A few days ago?"

"Yes. I don't think I'd have had the courage to read it if Raj hadn't been with me. It's dated the week after the cyclone."

Charlie pulled several sheets of paper from the envelope and flattened them out on the table. The top sheet was dated the thirteenth of March. With Abi and Beth leaning over his shoulders, he began to read.


*Dearest Douglas,*

*I pray that one day, for the sake of my children, I'll have the courage to send you this, when I feel they'll be safe from him. I must write down what happened and what I saw. If I don't, I think I'll go mad.*

*It's my fault Tony is dead. Four days ago, when the first cyclone warning went out, he phoned to check we were alright. I told him I was afraid Carl knew about us. He said he'd come, but I begged him not to.*

*I didn't expect Carl home until after the third warning, so took a risk and phoned Tony again. I desperately needed to hear his voice. I should never, never have done it because Carl caught me. He came in so quietly, and the wind and rain were so noisy I just didn't realise he was there until he grabbed the phone. He recognised Tony's voice and said such dreadful things to him. Then the line went dead, which made Carl even more angry. He seemed to think it was Tony's fault.*

*The children were in Abi's room and he locked the door and sent Nanny V to her room, so she couldn't help me. He forced me to sit down and listen to what he was going to do. He said he'd kill us both. I tried to reason with him, but it was useless. Nanny came back, then the banging on the front door started. I could hear Tony shouting and I tried to get to the door, and so did Nanny, but Carl threatened us with that awful African club of his. He locked me and Nanny in my room, but I watched through the window. Carl still had the club and I could see them in the garden, but I couldn't hear anything because of the storm.*

*I saw him hit Tony with the club, and when Tony fell by the banyan, Carl hit him again, I don't remember how many times. I screamed to him to stop, but it made no difference. Then I heard this cracking and groaning louder than the storm. Carl was running back to the house, and behind him the banyan fell, right over Tony, but I think he was dead already. Carl killed him. I saw it. I couldn't move. I just stood there until he came in.*

*He told me there'd been an accident and he'd get the ambulance when the wind died down. He insisted that was what it was. He kept repeating it, over and over. I was to tell them we didn't open the door and Tony was leaving when the tree fell. I was to stick to that story because, if I didn't, he'd kill me, and I should have no doubt that he could get away with it. I believed him, so that's another reason for writing this, in case something happens to me.*

*He said it was all my fault, that I must always remember that. And he's right. It is my fault Tony is dead. And I know Carl will do what he says if I tell anyone what I saw. But I had to tell someone, and this is the only way I can think of.*

*I have the children. They are my reason for living and I'll never, ever let him take them from me. I love them so much. I'll do anything, even do as Carl says, if it means I can go on living for them.*

*Your loving cousin,*

*Hilary*


There was absolute silence in the kitchen for some time after Charlie stopped reading.

Abi took a deep breath.

"You okay?" asked Charlie.

"Yes," she said, but she didn't sound it. "You?"

"It's strange," Charlie said. "I could almost hear her voice as I read it."

"I know what you mean. Do you think Uncle Douglas knew that Mum kept her treasures in the summer house?"

"He couldn't have. He would have got the box out, wouldn't he, and found the letter? I think the only person who knew was Mum. It explains such a lot."

"I know, and it's so, so sad."

Abi sat back, rubbing at her eyes with the back of her hand. Charlie took out a tissue and blew his nose hard.

"Do you remember that night?" he asked.

"In snatches," Abi said. "I remember the noise of wind and rain, the shouting and screaming, and I remember being locked in. Another thing I remember is Mum being all strange in the morning. Then Uncle Douglas came and picked us up."

Slowly Charlie folded the pages of tight packed writing, slid them carefully back into the envelope.

"At least now we can answer David's questions."

"Do you think we should tell him?" Abi asked.

"I suppose it depends on why he wants to know."

"I got the impression knowing the truth would mean a lot to him. It would give him some kind of closure."

"What did Raj think, being a lawyer?"

Abi shrugged. "He said it was up to us."

While Beth got lunch ready, Abi and Charlie sat looking through their mother's possessions, talking about the past in a way they'd never done before.

"I've learnt so much from Monique," Abi told him. "I spent the whole of one day – Tuesday, I think it was – talking to her while Raj was at work. I asked her why the letters stopped. She says she and Douglas went on writing for a year afterwards, but then Carl wrote and told them we'd moved to another address and we didn't want anything more to do with them. She says Douglas wouldn't let her read the letter, just told her about it, and she thinks he didn't tell her everything that was in it. We'll never know exactly what he said, but at least that explains why they gave up trying. And there's another thing."

"What?" Charlie asked, giving her a sharp look.

"I– I asked her if she thought Mum's death was an accident."

"And what did she say?" Charlie sat very still as he waited for Abi's response and Beth, who was at the fridge, turned with her hand on the open door and waited, eyes darting from brother to sister.

"She thinks it was. Like Marie Pillay, she's convinced Mum never would have committed suicide, but she doesn't think Carl would have killed her either. She wasn't very clear why, but I have a feeling she thinks he would have wanted Mum around so that he could gloat over the fact she was alive, and Tony wasn't."

"That's terrible," Beth burst out.

"But it fits," said Charlie quietly.

"And another thing. She says Mum used to talk of how Carl was when they first met, that he was loving and such fun to be with, but not long after they married, he was in a car accident. Apparently, he hit his head and after that his personality changed. I asked Vijay about it and he said it's possible, something to do with the frontal lobe."

Closing the fridge door with a snap, Beth came back to the table, bringing a bowl of salad and a salmon mousse. She placed them on the table, brought cheese and French bread, then sat down.

"Let's talk of happier things," she said. "Come on, Charlie, open the wine. Now, Abi, what are your plans. You're going back, aren't you?"

Abi smiled. "There's nothing firm yet, but Raj and I do want to be together, and it's easier for me to move than him. Our plan is that, once I've wrapped everything up at the Foundation, I'll go back, and we'll move into Belle Etoile to look after Monique and start converting parts of it into the arts centre. If it gets off the ground, and I think it will, I'll be in charge of it. It's right up my street and I'd love to do it, for a start it'd be like being in contact with Uncle Douglas again." She looked from Charlie to Beth. "The only disadvantage is being so far from you lot, but

I'll be coming to the UK regularly, or maybe you could get a job at the university in Mauritius, Charlie!"

Later that afternoon as Abi sat at Charlie's desk, the phone cradled on her shoulder, talking to Raj, she felt strangely at peace about her mother and Douglas. So much had been explained. She tried to tell Raj how she felt, stumbling over what she said, thinking the distance between them would make it difficult for him to understand. It didn't, and that, as much as anything, convinced her the decision she'd made was the right one.


# EPILOGUE


It was six weeks since Abi and Raj had seen each other. They'd had two weeks together in London and Cambridge over Christmas and Raj had had a business trip to Paris just before Easter where Abi had joined him for a few days before he flew home. Now the wait was nearly over. In a few hours' time she'd be seeing him again.

Abi looked across the aisle of the plane at Charlie. He was fast asleep. Next to him Beth was too, her head on her husband's shoulder. In the two seats beside Abi, the twins were engrossed in watching a film. She smiled, closed her eyes, and let her mind explore what life would be like from this moment on.

"Raj!" As soon as she saw him, Abi waved frantically, thrust her trolley at Mattie, and rushed through the crowds, dodging arriving passengers and the people meeting them as she went. She'd imagined the feel and the smell of him for all those weeks apart. As she stood amongst the crowds, wrapped in his arms, the reality was as good as she remembered.

The family joined them and there were hugs and handshakes all round, then the twins pushed the clattering trolleys up the slope. For a moment Abi's mind went back to the day Antoine had come to meet her all those months ago, and she felt a stab of regret that she'd not been kinder to him.

Jacquo was waiting for them, grinning from ear to ear. He'd brought the car he used in his chauffeuring job and they piled their luggage into the boot.

Raj turned to Charlie. "Before we take you, Beth and the boys to Narinda's," he said, "shall we make that detour? I've let them know we're coming." He turned to Abi. "You've brought it with you?"

"Yes," she said, feeling a lurch of apprehension in her stomach. She glanced at her brother, gave him an uncertain smile and he gave her arm a quick squeeze.

"Let's go for it."

"Riviere des Anguilles," Raj told Jacquo. "*To capave suive moi.*"

"Is that Creole?" Mattie asked.

"What did it mean?" Pip added.

"Just that Jacquo's going to follow me," Raj told them.

"Cool."

"We'll have to learn some."

"You can teach us, can't you?"

"That'd be great."

Raj laughed. "I see what you mean about the double act, Abi."

Charlie and his family climbed into Jacquo's car, Abi and Raj led the way in his MGB. It wasn't a long drive and they said very little. She got the feeling he was leaving her to prepare herself for what was to come. Soon they drew up in front of a bungalow behind a high wall.

Raj took Abi's hand, glanced at her anxiously but said nothing. Jacquo stayed tactfully in his car, but the others followed them to a metal gate. Raj rang the bell beside it. Almost immediately they heard quick footsteps approaching. The gate was pulled open by a woman of Abi's age wearing jeans and a bright cotton blouse, her long dark hair loose down her back.

"Janisha?" Abi said, in an uncertain tone.

"You recognise me? I'm glad. Come in, come in. It is so good to see you," she said, smiling, kissing Abi, Charlie, Beth and, to their surprise and embarrassment, the twins as well. "Maman is waiting."

Raj and Beth held back a little, letting Abi and Charlie go first.

The front door opened straight into a brightly furnished sitting room. In the corner, sitting in an armchair, was a woman of about eighty years old. She was small and plump, her long grey hair in a plait that hung over one shoulder. Beside the chair was a walking frame. Tears in her eyes, she struggled to get up, but Abi rushed forward, knelt by her chair, followed closely by Charlie who sat down next to it.

"We're back, Nanny V," Abi said, blinking hard.

"My little ones," she said as she put her hands up, one to Abi's cheek, one to Charlie's.

"We've got something for you," Charlie said.

Abi took the small brown leather box from her handbag. She pressed the button on the side and the top flew open, the spring was just as good as ever. Inside, the delicate gold filigree hibiscus, studded with seed pearls, lay on its satin bed.

"Charlie and I want you to have this, Nanny," she said.

# CHARACTER LIST

Abigail (Abi) Kendall – Assistant Director of the Commonwealth Arts Foundation.

Vimala (Nanny V) Mootien – Abi and Charlie's Mauritian nanny in the 1980s/1990s.

Douglas Beaumont – Anglo-Mauritian poet and artist, Abigail's godfather and her mother's cousin.

Rajen (Raj) Amrakash – friend of Douglas's and his lawyer.

Justin Bennett – Abi's ex-partner.

Charlie Kendall – Abi's younger brother, Professor of Archaeology at Cambridge.

Elizabeth (Beth) Kendall – Charlie's South African wife.

Mattie & Pip Kendall – Charlie & Beth's twin sons.

Lawrence March – Abi's boss at the CAF.

Mina Patel – works at the Commonwealth Arts Foundation.

Rangi Karaka – works at the Commonwealth Arts Foundation.

Evelyn Albani – works at the Commonwealth Arts Foundation.

Benson Rudd – works at the Commonwealth Arts Foundation.

Darren Shuttleworth – works at the Commonwealth Arts Foundation.

Monique Beaumont – Douglas's wife.

Antoine Beaumont – Monique's son, adopted by Douglas.

Zabette Laventure – Monique's cook and carer.

Philippe Siew Yan – one of Raj's Mauritian associates on the Belle Etoile project.

Rashad Kurmah – one of Raj's Mauritian associates on the Belle Etoile project.

Devina Edouard – one of Raj's Mauritian associates on the Belle Etoile project.

Maisie Broderick – Abigail's neighbour.

Sergeant Sarah Broderick – Maisie's granddaughter.

Navin Naidoo – Friend of Raj's who owns a restaurant in Islington.

Janisha Mootien – Nanny V's daughter.

Hilary Kendall – Abi and Charlie's mother.

Carl Kendall – Abi and Charlie's father.

Rose Andrews – Carl Kendall's cousin with whom Abi and Charlie lived in the 1990s.

Tony Chandler – Hilary's lover in the 1980s/1990s.

David Chandler – Tony's son.

Narinda Vencatasamy – Raj's elder sister.

Vijay Vencatasamy – Narinda's husband.

Prem Amrakash – Raj's father, Douglas's lawyer in the 1980s and 1990s.

Marie Pillay – Prem's secretary in the 1980s and 1990s.

Georgette Pillay – Raj's PA and Marie's granddaughter.

Jacquo Pillay – Georgette's cousin.

Pieter Brandt – Business associate of Antoine Beaumont.

DCI Hari Persand – Inspector with Fraud Squad of Mauritian Police.

DI Nalen Beejadhur of the Mauritian police.

If you enjoyed this book, please let others know by leaving a quick review on Amazon. Also, if you spot anything untoward in the paperback, get in touch. We strive for the best quality and appreciate reader feedback.

editor@thebookfolks.com


www.thebookfolks.com

*A standalone romantic thriller*

Having become stranded in the English Channel after commandeering her cheating boyfriend's boat, Caro is rescued by a handsome stranger. But when the boat is impounded on suspicion of smuggling, she once again finds herself in deep water.

*The first book to feature Fabia Havard and Matt Lambert*

Having left the police following a corruption investigation, ex-superintendent Fabia Havard is struggling with civilian life. When a girl is murdered in her town, she can't help trying to find the killer. Will her former colleague Matt

Lambert stop her, or realize the value of his former boss to the floundering inquiry?

When an overbearing patriarch and much begrudged ex-army officer is found dead in his home, there is no shortage of suspects. DCI Matt Lambert investigates, but struggles with a lack of evidence. He'll have to rely on his former boss, ex-detective Fabia Havard, to help him. But will their fractious relationship get in the way of solving the case?

Almost ten years after he went missing, a student's body is found. Forensics show that he was murdered and a cold case is reopened. But when detectives begin to investigate his background, many people he knew are found to be keeping a secret of sorts. Faced with subterfuge and deceit, rooting out the true killer will take all their detective skills.

Hopes for a town pantomime are dashed when a participant is found murdered. The victim was the town gossip and there is no shortage of people who had a grudge to bear against him. Detective Matt Lambert leads the investigation but draws on the help of his girlfriend, ex-police officer Fabia Havard. Can they solve the crime together?

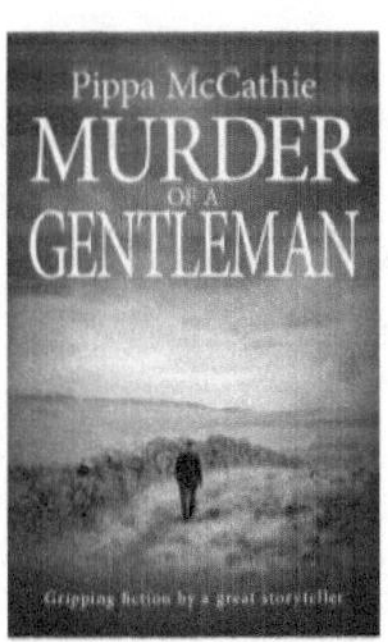

When an important film director returns to his native Wales for retirement it arouses the interest of the locals, not least Fabia Havard who discovers a family connection to him. So when he is later found dead, defenestrated, she'll stop at nothing to find his killer. With too many suspects, she and Matt Lambert will have to suss out the motive.

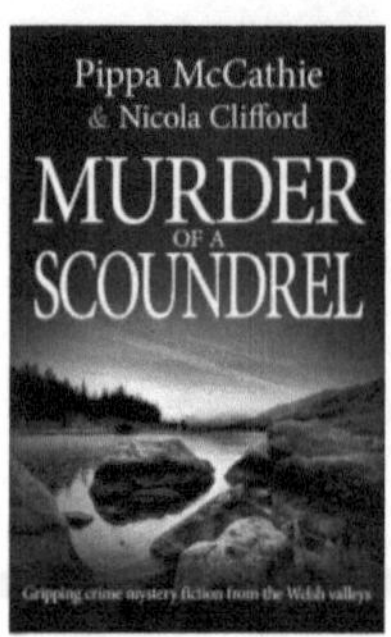

DCI Matt Lambert was hoping for some home-time with Fabia and their newborn baby when a man is found dead in a disused railway tunnel. And more sleepless nights are heading his way when another body is found in nearby wasteland. Clearly foul play, the rural community is up in arms. Can he root out the killer without Fabia, whose mind is on other things?

www.thebookfolks.com

www.ingramcontent.com/pod-product-compliance
Lightning Source LLC
Chambersburg PA
CBHW031936210726
48290CB00006BA/1632